Also by Sol Yurick
from Rocket 88:
The Bag

This edition published in the United Kingdom in 2013
by Rocket 88, an imprint of Essential Works Limited
29 Clerkenwell Green, London EC1R 0DU

First published in the United States in 1966 by Trident Press;
first published in the United Kingdom in 1966 by W. H. Allen & Company

Cover artwork: Jonas Lara

ISBN (hardback) 9781906615628
ISBN (paperback) 9781906615635
ISBN (ePub) 9781906615642
ISBN (Kindle) 9781906615659

rocket88books.com

FERTIG

SOL YURICK

Chapter 1

Fertig was furious when he came home. His car had broken down, he had to walk a long way, and his back hurt. Now he was calm. The furnace was finally fixed; he had a good time playing with Stevie before he went to bed: that balanced things. Now his personal account books were spread in front of him on the table. His sleeves were rolled up. His collar was open at the throat. A straight stream of cigarette smoke, beside the glass of beer, rose through the bright lamplight and into the darkness.

Sara said, "Harry, you work at it all day. How can you keep on doing it at home?" But she said it admiringly.

Fertig told her, "But, after all, these are *our* books."

Sara was watching television. Fertig could see her face and the screen at the same time. "Come sit by me," she told him.

"The books..."

"... can wait."

Fertig sighed. He looked at Sara half-lying on the couch. She was serene. He saw that her bosom had got fuller. Her eyes were luminous and loving. Her hair, which was long now, shone. The television light flickered over her soft, white throat. She didn't look forty-one at all, he thought. He looked at the picture of her: turtle-necked sweater, centre-parted hair plastered tight against her skull, sucked-in cheeks – she had looked older when he first met her. Even though he hated the picture, he could finally accept it. The past three years had brought her a long way; all the harshness of her striving to maintain what she thought she had been before they were married, thirteen years ago, had almost gone from her face; in a few years it would be perfect. Having Stevie did that, he thought. And if this had happened to her, what had happened to him, he wondered? Nothing, Fertig thought; but he felt warm and relaxed and all the little tense aches he used to have were gone. "You're watching television," Fertig told her; it was an old joke.

"There's a good show tonight, Harry."

"*Television*, Sara," Fertig smiled.

"Jimmy Stewart and Carole Lombard. An *old* film, Harry."

"A real art-film," Fertig laughed.

"The man repaired the furnace, Harry. Notice? No hum."

She said it so tranquilly, "furnace" and "hum" sounded seductive. Her lips were fuller too, he thought; was it possible? The light from the television failed to pale her lips. The heroine in the film was kissing Jimmy Stewart; the hero nuzzled Carole Lombard's soft, blonde hair. He vaguely remembered having seen that film a long time ago, when he was young. He felt an old, romantic warmth; had he, he wondered, once fallen in love with Carole Lombard? Sara patted her hair. Fertig noticed it was fluffed out; separate strands shone as if lights were caught there and he was surprised to feel himself getting excited. Forty-three-year-old men don't feel like that in the middle of the week, he thought, not unless they could afford exotic mistresses – like his boss, Mr. Grenoble; he felt ridiculously proud. But they wouldn't do anything about it; after all, it was the middle of the week. He had to go to work the next day. But he switched off the table light, got up, and went to sit near her.

If anything, the oil burner was working a little too well. Soft heat suffused the room. He felt a little sleepy, able to enjoy the picture, happy he didn't have to feel guilty about it either. He unbuttoned another shirt button. Stevie's toys were scattered all over the floor; "I'm losing the battle," he said.

She turned her face to him and smiled, but her eyes remained on a loving embrace on the screen. "What battle?"

"I don't care about the toys."

"It'll pass, Harry; it's a rebellious phase. Dr. Spock says –"

"... they all go through it. I didn't."

She looked at him. She pursed her lips. She kissed him. "You did. You forgot. You did. There he goes," she said and put her hand on his hand.

Stevie began to cry. Stevie was three; they still hadn't won their battle with him. The baby books had told them what should be right or wrong every step along the way, but... perhaps it was having Stevie so late, so long after they had stopped expecting it, hoping, caring. Knowing what they had now and remembering what they were before ... *that* was what made Stevie so precious. His thin wail drifted down from his bedroom, floated down the hall, down the stairs, through the blackness of the foyer, and into the living room. He sounded so lost. Sara's warning took away some of the shock Fertig always felt when he heard Stevie crying like that, but he couldn't help jumping. Some trick of acoustics, some fault in planning, never corrected by construction, made Stevie's voice come too clearly, loud as if beside them. His cry could cut through any reverie or any television show.

Nervous and tense. Fertig wondered how to interpret the cry. Stevie continued to cry. Sara became a little restless. Did the cry mean Stevie was merely being cranky, attention-getting, or was he really sick? Were there dream horrors coursing through his dark room? Then he must be told, Fertig thought, that the horrors were only a television set's sound distorted by distance; a car roaring by down a quiet street; neighbours' voices carrying far and clear in the autumn quiet. He looked at his watch and began timing. "He should learn to be alone." Then he stood up.

"Don't go," Sara told him. "Give him fifteen minutes."

"I'll be hard tomorrow. Tomorrow I'll practise discipline. It's only this time," Fertig said.

"It's always 'only this time'," she said, smiling.

"Was he all right today? He looked a little feverish."

"He was fine," she said, turning back and trying to look at the television set. "Fifteen minutes."

He stared at her face; it appeared calm, abiding in the television light in which the heroine held her baby in her arms, smiling down at it, happy, while the father jittered nervously, not understanding. In the films, fathers never understood, he thought. Fertig wondered how Sara had managed to change from a pale, anxious woman to this calm, lovely creature. "But it might be serious. He's screaming."

"He's screamed before, Harry. We're spoiling him."

The screams became louder as though the annoyance, the frustration, the indignation – because they were taking so long to come – were adding up to an expression of genuine pain. They waited a long time. Fertig sat there, seeing nothing, letting his eyes drift. The soft glow went slowly out of Sara's face; that old nervous greyness came slowly back; her mouth tightened, thinned. On the screen, an aeroplane was buffeted in a storm. The face of the pilot, tense, determined, was wet from storm water shooting into his face. Fertig stood up. "I'll see what he needs. After all, it's time we were going to bed anyway." She stood up with him, grateful he had weakened. They walked up to Stevie calling, "It's all right, Stevie. Don't cry, sweetie. All right. We're coming. Stop crying."

But Stevie had a fever. His face was red, darker than his reddish-blond hair. Where Fertig's body began to panic, the mind he had trained to patience held him back. They had grown wiser together, a little less apt to get hysterical. Sara took Stevie's temperature. Stevie said, looking tragically at them, that his throat hurt so badly, but he felt better now they had come. Stevie's temperature was high. Fertig went downstairs and phoned the pediatrician and told him what was wrong.

"You people," the doctor said. "You people."

"But he has a high fever."

"Children always run high fevers."

"His throat hurts badly."

"How do you know?"

"He said so, doctor."

"Pick him up; he won't hurt so much."

"Maybe you should come, doctor."

"Give him aspirin and let me know in the morning."

"But…"

"Fertig, give him an aspirin. Look, I'm not cold hearted, but I told

7

you a thousand times; that child is strong as an ox. You're spoiling the kid."

Fertig was somehow happy to hear the harsh, unconcerned voice, as though the casualness of it, the roughness of it was reassuring. They gave Stevie aspirin, and after a long time, Stevie became calm. The fever seemed to recede; his throat hurt less; he finally slept.

They went back to the living room. They turned on the television set again, but it was all meaningless. The picture was coming to a climax, but they saw it was another filial. They kept watching, restless, but they couldn't concentrate.

As they went to bed, Fertig looked in on Stevie; he was sleeping quietly. Fertig got into his bed and looked at the pale silver swirl a passing car's headlights made as they flashed across the ceiling. He turned to Sara as she came in from the bathroom. "He's better. He's all right," he told her. She came towards him. Her mouth was half-open, almost laughing. They grabbed. They held on. He could barely slip off his pyjamas. He was like a snake shedding skin, seeming to do it so softly. Watching in the half-light coming in from a street lamp outside their window, he saw Sara softly slither out of her nightdress; the rustle-sound of her slipping cloth tingled his skin. The last button of his pyjamas stuck and was ripped off. He felt for it a second on the bed, but her arms were around him again, pulling him, and he forgot the button.

What was in him that had always been a little self-conscious, an auditor always examining – less and less present these past three years – was shouldered aside now by some surprising rough beast emerging, tearing, shouting. And there was something so urgent about it, so frightening ... so new. And, before he went ... under, he remembered thinking again – it almost made him laugh – that they should never have sex in the middle of the week: he would be too tired tomorrow and, after all, he was a middle-aged man – almost.

They made love. They cried out. They shrieked. They were in pain. They were one sweet animal crying, weeping, clawing. The room burst, for one second, into a terrible light and he thought "I'm going blind" and what was happening to him had never happened before and his throat growled something like "I love you" but it couldn't have been that, but something shameful, more bestial. The blood beat and rushed in his ears; she was screaming and he was proud to make her scream this sweet scream. He twisted his head away from her mouth. His faced ached with grinning. The muscles in his side cramped painfully. And he began to control again, coming back to watching, to the room, but that new, strange voice of hers kept screaming in ecstasy and he thought, before he understood, How many times could they both take something like *that*? But drained, wet, he was glad he had gone through it. There was a thick mist in the air, humid and alien, like the stench of someone else's sweat pouring up from the basement through the hot-air vent.

She pulled away. She sat up. Her eyes were glazed. She was still screaming. It was *Stevie* who was screaming. Harry's face was bleeding. "I told you to cut your nails," he told her, getting up and reaching for his bathrobe.

This time they went to Stevie right away. Stevie was burning. The fire inside him came out of his glittering eyes. Fertig looked at Stevie, trying to recognize his son. Stevie was something convulsed, throwing himself from side to side, crippled; and Fertig thought, "That's not my son; that's someone else's child." Then Stevie moved and something inside Fertig fluttered. He wanted to run away but he forced himself to go downstairs, back into the living room, pick up the phone, and carefully, as though he were doing something difficult, working out an intricate problem that required the intensest concentration, dial the doctor's number without making any mistakes. The line was busy. He wondered who would be calling the doctor at this time. He dialled again; the line was still busy. He went back to look at Stevie. Sara was leaning over him, watching him, taking care, doing what she could to comfort him with her presence. She had given him more aspirin. The convulsions abated; after a long while they stopped. Stevie's fever seemed to go down slowly reluctantly; he was quieter, but he told them his throat hurt him terribly.

Fertig phoned again. He got the doctor's answering service. Fertig told the girl about it. He was talking loudly.

"I'll try to get him. He must be out," she said.

"Please try. It's serious." He raised his voice again, as if the doctor were in the same room, listening... as if the doctor had to be convinced by the urgency of his voice.

"Have you tried aspirin?"

"Are you a doctor?"

"No, but –"

"Then you know nothing about it," he said. It was silly, he thought; after all, the answering service wasn't at the doctor's house.

"All I can recommend, if it's really serious, is that you take your child to a hospital..."

"Hospital? But the doctor's supposed –" He stopped himself and hung up.

He called the nearest hospital for an ambulance. He explained carefully what was happening. A low voice – for a second he wasn't sure if it was a woman's or a man's – kept interrupting. The voice spoke to him as if he were some sort of crank. They couldn't, it said, go sending ambulances for everyone who thinks they're sick. Not without a doctor's say-so. Not without the police. Not without verification, the hard voice told Fertig. "Have you called the police?"

"The doctor isn't –"

"Do you have his OK?"

"No … What do the *police* have to do with –"

"You see?" It crowed triumphantly and hung up on Fertig.

"… I'm trying to tell you he's not in …"

When Fertig went back upstairs, Stevie looked a little better, but they didn't dare wait any longer. They dressed quickly. Fertig tried to knot his tie, but his fingers wouldn't work; he threw it down on the bed. They bundled Stevie in a blanket and went out. They had to walk three blocks to get to a street with traffic. Taxis passed them by. Fertig waved. Fertig shouted. "Do they think I'm some sort of criminal?" his voice screamed. Nobody stopped. The air was chill and damp; it was about to rain. Fertig was angry. "Don't they see we have a baby?" he yelled at Sara. "Harry, please," she said. Stevie lay quietly in her arms, seeming to understand that they were trying to help him. His eyes glittered up at them from the bottom of a cylinder of shielding blanket. They stood under a street lamp for ten minutes till, finally, a taxi stopped.

The taxi rushed through the quiet Brooklyn streets. The driver understood; he was kind. "I know what it's like. I got three of my own and, believe me, there is not a sickness they haven't had, not one. Mumps, measles, scarlet, virus every other week, you name it, not a sickness." He comforted them and drove swiftly. "They all give you the same kind of trouble, but they make it. It'll be all right. So will you, you'll see," and he laughed. Sara and Fertig laughed automatically, almost hysterically; the laughing made them feel better and they almost believed the driver as if he had been a doctor. They kept talking to the driver, asking about his troubles with his children, listening eagerly, finding hope in how, bad as it looked then, the driver's children miraculously recovered. They kept watching Stevie's face, touching his forehead … was it hotter? … Was the fever going down? Sara's hands adjusted and readjusted minute blanket folds. Fertig felt sure a draught was coming in through some small opening in the wrapping. He groped for Stevie's foot through the blanket: it was cold. He held it, squeezing gently, warming it, feeling its shape. Stevie began to come out of the grip of whatever held him; he was beginning to look as if he would suddenly say something normal, something irrelevant, something cute. They got to the hospital and asked the driver to wait. They went into the emergency room.

There were two rows of white, paint-flaked benches. Old, tired men, bedraggled women sat, outlined clearly in the deadening fluorescent light, waiting patiently. Along the outer aisles, against the walls, yellowed by the dead lights, figures lay on stretchers, blanketed, bundled, unmoving, their faces invisible under rules, notices, a Red Cross poster showing a mothering nurse reaching out to protect, a five-language warning that v.d. was on the rise again.

One man sat, his head dropped, hands folded; a slow trickle of blood leaked down the side of his face; he didn't seem to care. A woman lolled, her legs far apart, her stockings torn; dirt-smeared raddles of white flesh ballooned through rents; her head hung on the bench back, the eyes open but unseeing; she drooled. Fertig could feel himself recoiling from them, disgusted.

Between the rows of benches there was an aisle leading to a desk. Sara sat down with Stevie as far away from the others as she could get. Fertig walked to the desk, where a clerk was bent over small piles of forms and a huge ledger, seeming to write, but Fertig saw she was only sitting in a position of work; he always recognized a faker. "Did I talk to you over the phone?" he asked her.

"Who are you?" she asked, looking up.

She had garish, yellow hair. When he leaned over, he saw she was wearing a bright, dyed wig that splayed out like a yellow mane. She wore heavy, horn-rimmed glasses, and the thick earpieces moved up and down as she chewed gum steadily. Her face was old and red; her eyes bulged; her cheeks had cracked into thick, permanent folds, rimmed over with thick powder. "Who are you?" she growled. Fertig began to explain. She motioned him to sit down and wait to be called. He sat down in the front row.

Behind the clerk, Fertig could see a door that led to the examination room. There was a young doctor there. Fertig could see him leaning against a stretcher table, smiling, smoking, chatting with someone who was just out of sight: he had a sharp, wolfish look. He didn't seem to know, or care, Fertig thought, that anyone was sitting on the bench, bleeding, waiting in pain. A Negro woman rocked steadily, half-moaning half-singing, next to him.

Fertig couldn't wait. He got up again and went to the clerk and told her they had to see the doctor right away. She told Fertig that there were others waiting. He started to tell her what was wrong. She didn't care. She pretended not to notice him. The smell of the place was terrible; gangrenous fumes rose from the floor; perfume and powder and dust stench seemed to rise from her; it all mingled with ineffective antiseptic odours and the sour smell of wet mops used too many times. The wet paint was flaking leprously. Coming from behind him, he could smell, he was sure, the faint effluvium given off by those dirty, sick people, ... a tang of faeces and urine. A pipe, punctured by a rusty sore, dripped. He wrinkled his nose. She saw the expression on his face; she saw the controlled recoil of his body, the obvious disgust. When she spoke to Fertig she was nastier; her voice growled again, surprisingly bass for a woman, outraged that he should dare to be disgusted, as though disgust were only permitted her.

She insisted that he sit and wait his turn. Fertig wouldn't. Maybe they didn't understand. "No. No. Look," he said patiently, "you don't understand. It's not me. It's the baby. My son…"

"I heard you the first time."

"But –"

"I'm not deaf, you know."

"But look… the child … he – look, it's a child…"

She leaned to the side and looked past him. "He looks all right to me," Fertig turned around; Stevie *did* look a little better; he felt foolish. He turned back and saw the clerk's expression of hate and wondered why; after all, he had never seen her before. Her voice became harsher, strident. "You'll have to just wait like everyone else." She looked at Fertig with contempt and he couldn't understand why; he had done nothing to her. Was it because Sara and he had put on their clothes so hastily, so sloppily? He needed a shave. He touched the just-dried scratch on the side of his face. Suddenly, sharp and overwhelming, he smelled his and Sara's sex smell; he jerked his hand away. Did the clerk … ? But didn't the clerk understand he wasn't like the others: the idea revolted him. "Look," Fertig told her, leaning close over the desk, "if it's a question of money …" Sara came up behind him; she was frightened and didn't say anything. "We have to see a doctor," he said. Sara held Stevie; she plucked at Fertig's jacket, trying to calm him.

He stopped himself. He took a deep breath. He tried to smile, to ingratiate himself, took another deep breath and smelled it all again, he couldn't stop himself from becoming a little hysterical. In a few seconds he was shouting at the clerk, who roared back at him. While he was yelling at her, the doctor came to the door and was staring at him, unexcited and uncaring. Fertig started to go to the doctor, but a man in a guard's uniform came up and blocked his way. Fertig tried to tell the guard that he had to see the doctor. The guard told him to calm down and walked Fertig back with his stomach till he was at the desk again. Sara plucked at his sleeve and Fertig turned on her, exasperated. From her arms Stevie looked up at Fertig with big, frightened eyes: Fertig calmed down.

The clerk turned to a fresh page in her ledger and began to ask questions. "But the baby is sick; we shouldn't waste time," Fertig told her.

"No one is going to tell me how to run my job," she said and began to ask for pertinent information, putting each item down in the ledger and on to various forms. She repeated slowly and insolently what he told her as she inked each entry in carefully. She asked about his religion. He told her it didn't matter. She insisted on knowing. A nurse had come up and was looking over the doctor's shoulder at Fertig. The doctor was grinning and whispering something in the nurse's ear.

Fertig could feel himself blush a little. "I have no religion," he told the clerk.

"I might have known," the clerk said and bent to write something. The nurse whispered something back into the doctor's ear: did her lips touch his ear?

"Would you please hurry. While we're going through this nonsense the baby could die."

She put down her pen deliberately, leaned back, and looked at Fertig. "Nothing can be done unless you stop interrupting," she told him. "You people" – it seemed to Fertig that she stressed "you people" and lingered insultingly over the words – "come in here and expect us to drop everything."

"The baby is sick. Nothing else matters, can't you understand? It's a matter of life and death," Fertig shouted.

"I'm doing my best. There's a reason for everything and you just have to co-operate. If you won't understand that, we can't get anything done. There's a reason for everything. It's *your* attitude that's causing the delay."

"But –"

"Nothing will get finished."

The guard waited lazily. "After all," the clerk said, "I can't just drop everything every time some baby is brought in here with the sniffles, you know." She went on and on. Fertig tried to protest, but she wouldn't give him a chance. She had her say, giving him a detailed account, item by item, of what the world had come to: manners were gone; the world was populated by hooligans and degenerates. She spoke, it seemed to Fertig, with agonizing slowness, throwing out paragraphs, sentences, phrases, finally outraged single words as her voice rose to high-pitched little screams directed no longer only at Fertig, but at the others who waited quietly. They didn't seem to care. They even seemed to take it for granted. They knew her. They were too sunk in pain to care. The doctor, the nurse, the guard were grinning, appreciating it all. Fertig couldn't understand it. He wondered what he had done to provoke this outburst. Her face became redder. She was choking with indignation. The pen trembled in her hand and the tip made random lines marring the neat writing. "Look what you made me do," she screamed and, for a second, tears stood in her eyes and she sobbed. And then her eyes shrunk to little black points swimming in an immensity of red-veined eyeball stretched tightly by blood and rage. Veins snaking down from underneath her wig stiffened and pulsed hard. Her tongue, swollen and gross, seemed almost black between her shifting teeth. The fluorescent lights cast a red glow. Fertig turned around and looked at Sara and shrugged his shoulders. Sara made soothing gestures at him and it angered him. But the look of fear and misery on Stevie's face made Fertig wait. And he stood still till the clerk had finished.

And when she had finished, they went back to the bench and sat. Fertig knew they were making a point to him, the three of them. The taxi driver came in to see how they were. They asked him to wait and assured him, because he seemed to worry, that they could pay him. The driver went out and came back with coffee and a newspaper and sat down to read the racing results.

More people kept coming in and sitting down. Three Negro boys brought in a friend whose arm was bent at a strange angle. They sat him down on a bench, and he sat, restlessly, shaking his head and shaking his foot and breathing fast. Suddenly the boys left him. Fertig found himself again and again, *having* to look at the arm, which seemed to have another joint under the sweater sleeve.

Two men kept talking to one another in low voices. Two woman, stupefied with drink sat, slowly, swaying together, in time to a slowed-down music. Fertig wondered how long they had all been waiting. No one seemed to care. The bleeding man made whimpering sounds. Another man sat there; he had thick, greasy hair and didn't notice that vermin were crawling along the margin of his collar; he kept grunting and coughing, muttering, rumbling, and pain had turned him incontinent.

Fertig heard the institutional seconds ticked out by the wall clock. Sterilizer steam condensed and dripped in the other room. Sara crooned and rocked Stevie, who dozed a little. Fertig heard the faint clinking of surgical instruments and it seemed as if they were denied to Stevie. He heard the spiteful breathing of the clerk, the scratch of her pen, and the purring laugh of the nurse as she talked to the doctor. A little dizzily, he told himself that the more patiently he suffered for his outbreak – he didn't know how long they would punish him – the sooner they would take care of Stevie. Hours seemed to pass, but it was much shorter than that: he no longer noticed the smells.

Finally the nurse called them into the examination room. She took Stevie from Sara and put him on the examination table. He was much better; the fever had gone down to normal. The nurse was friendly to Stevie, baby-talking to him, but looked at the Fertigs with contempt. She was sleek and catlike in her movements. The doctor examined Stevie and asked the Fertigs what had happened. Fertig knew that the doctor had heard it all out there but that, for some exasperating reason, chose to ask again. Fertig talked; the doctor looked, probed, lifted Stevie's eyelid casually, listened with his stethoscope, pressed down Stevie's white tongue, swabbed roughly at Stevie's throat, hardly listening to what Fertig said. The examination seemed cursory. Fertig wondered if he should suggest a few things for the doctor to look at, but he controlled himself.

Finally the doctor nodded wisely and told the Fertigs that there was nothing wrong with their child. Patiently he explained that Stevie had a sore throat. Children were subject to high fevers. Children always had more alarming symptoms than were warranted by the facts. The doctor said that their excitement had been for nothing; "Go home, you're being over-anxious." Fertig tried to tell the doctor about the convulsions again, but the doctor didn't pay any attention, he was washing and the noise the stream of tap water made rushing over his hands drowned Fertig's words. Fertig told the doctor that his son should be admitted to the hospital for a fuller examination. The doctor wouldn't do it; he became exasperated and told them he had no grounds for keeping the child there. "There's nothing wrong with the kid. Go home." There was no emergency: the hospital was overcrowded. Fertig told the doctor that they had the money to pay.

"That's not the point," the doctor said. "If you want to get your son admitted, you have to do it through your own doctor. I won't take the kid any other way. It's pointless to argue about it. There's nothing wrong with that kid. Go home."

The Fertigs took their child and rushed out to go to another hospital. As they left the strident voice of the clerk called after them; she hadn't finished taking all the information. Fertig didn't pay any attention. The taxi driver dropped his empty coffee container on the floor and crushed it as they left.

It was dark in the taxi. It had been raining outside and the lights kept flashing by, looking for their immersion in drops and pools of water, brighter, hotter. They were driving along Eastern Parkway to another hospital, driving down the long, tree-lined street with the great memorial arch at the end of it. The November wind shook the shining branches and waved them in and out of cones of light as the cab passed. The air coming in through the open taxi window was fresh, clear, smelling of rain, earth, wet bark. The face of the driver was illuminated in his identifying photographs. Fertig smelled damp leather. He heard the sounds of the tyres hurrying over the wet asphalt, rustling swiftly over wet leaves, sounding more clearly than the motor.

Stevie began to choke; he turned red; his face twisted while his wide-open mouth rattled. His body stiffened as if he were reaching, stretching, shaking in that reach, but unable to recoil, unable to unstretch at all. Fertig grabbed Stevie away from Sara. Stevie's body shook. And Fertig wouldn't have thought a three-year-old could have that kind of strength. Fertig held him tightly but he couldn't unstiffen that body turning into stone. Stevie died.

Chapter 2

A year later, two deaths were reported simultaneously to the police, even though they had taken place about fifteen miles apart and, as was later discovered, probably happened about one to two hours apart. The heavy morning overcast started to thin out about this time and a brisk little wind began to blow the fume-smelling smog slowly out to sea. It was not noticed that both reports went into different police precincts coincidentally until later when a reporter looking for colour found this odd angle.

Dr. Cartwright, the eminent cancer specialist, was shot at 10.55 a.m. The patient – it later turned out he had given a false name and address – came in for a ten-thirty appointment. He was received at a quarter to eleven, and was finished in ten minutes. The shortness of the examination was not unusual, the nurse explained later. This patient, who was under Dr. Cartwright's care for six months, was a cancer-fixated hypochondriac who needed periodic reassurance.

At eleven, not hearing the summoning buzzer, the nurse went into Dr. Cartwright's office and discovered him slumped over his desk. Thinking he might have had a heart attack – he was a hard worker – she approached, nudged him, got no answer. She lifted him and saw that he had been shot. There was a small, hardly bleeding hole in his chest. She screamed and rushed through the waiting room and out into the street. Perhaps she panicked; perhaps she even thought she would catch the murderer – she said later – she had not really been thinking. The man was nowhere to be seen. No shot was heard by the other patients or the nurse.

The police came. Apparently the bullet hit the doctor, slammed him back against his spring-joint swivel chair. The recoil action of the chair catapulted his upper body back again and on to his desk.

About ten-thirty an important administrative problem came up at the Mercy Memorial Hospital. The administrator, Mr. Blumenthal, was the only man who could hand down a decision. But he had not reported to the office at nine-thirty. This was not in itself unusual, because Mr. Blumenthal, the most efficient administrator (and the first non-doctor) the Mercy Memorial ever had, frequently went on surprise tours of inspection before he checked in. They knew Mr. Blumenthal was in because his secretary, from the office window, could see his car in its reserved spot in the hospital parking lot. Mr. Blumenthal was paged: the voice on the intercom sounded, as always, calm, electronically polite. After twenty minutes someone was sent out to the car. There, the body of Mercy Memorial's administrator was found. The police were called, and they got to the hospital in about ten minutes.

Mr. Blumenthal had been shot through the heart. He had fallen between two cars in such a way that he was not likely to be seen unless one happened to be looking up the narrow file between cars. The story leaked out; newsmen came in. The body was cordoned; plain-clothes men circulated through Mercy; a list of personnel was procured.

Some early-afternoon papers came out with the under-headline bulletins about the deaths. Fuller reports were in the later-afternoon editions. Radio programmes issued short reports.

Meanwhile, at about one o'clock, it was noticed that one of the residents, Dr. Volpe, had not been seen for hours. He was supposed to have been on duty from about ten o'clock, more or less about the time Mr. Blumenthal's murder may have been taking place. Ordinarily, Dr. Volpe's disappearing was not surprising; it was even expected: he was known to be fond of his sleep. He was paged – this time the voice was insistent through the intercom static – but didn't show up. Dr. Volpe's tour-colleagues were angry and complained; another resident was asked to look in Dr. Volpe's room. A detective who overheard the disturbance thought Dr. Volpe's disappearance might be significant; so he accompanied the resident to the room.

Dr. Volpe was lying on his back. He had been shot, probably while sleeping. The police theorised that the man who shot the administrator also killed the resident – though there was no necessary connection yet. It was reasonable to assume that Dr. Volpe had been murdered before 10 a.m., when he was supposed to report for duty, but, on the other hand, considering his habits – he had never been more than one-and-a-half hours late – he could have been killed any time up to, probably, 11.30 a.m. It seemed certain that the administrator and the doctor were shot fairly close together in time, though the order was only a guess.

The Mercy was always crowded and it was realized that the killer had passed among them and must have been seen by at least a hundred people, probably more. The police went into action; reinforcements were called for; throwing a cordon around all Mercy was considered, so they could question everyone. The word ran through Mercy Memorial. More police came up. Phone calls to relatives were made. Dr. Volpe had parents in the Bronx. Mr. Blumenthal left a wife and four children in Forest Hills Gardens. Everything was still confused. The newspapermen were circulating fast; they questioned everyone they could. More newsmen were arriving. The police began an extensive search throughout the hospital. Somehow a rumour got started that the killer was still around. People began to get panicky; some tried to leave. There weren't enough police to keep everyone in. Patients who had been waiting since eight o'clock in the morning in the clinic started to leave.

The third death was discovered in time for the later-afternoon papers to make it a bulletin along with the first full reports of the killings of Dr. Cartwright and Mr. Blumenthal. Early-evening papers would carry fuller reports. Reporters were being sent to the families of the slain. A portable television unit was already on the scene taping interviews and scene-of-the-crime shots. The police refused to issue more than standard bulletins, but there were some don't-quote-me-but conferences.

At 3.05 the overcast had broken up into clouds. The wind was stronger, fresher. From the west, the coming clouds became smaller and smaller and it seemed as if vast areas of blue space were being borne eastward: patches of sunlight and shadow flowed across Central Park, Fifth Avenue, and dappled the buildings. A policeman was strolling up Fifth Avenue on his beat when he passed Temple Caiaphas. There is a huge, inlaid mosaic in front of the temple. It is made up of bits of coloured tile specially imported from Italy and designed to look like an optical illusion – pyramids and pyramidal pits which, if looked at for a while, can be made to switch from pit to peak at will but which, once started, cannot be controlled from switching in spite of the viewer's will. The policeman noticed someone was lying face-down, close to the great twenty-foot, solid bronze, relieved gate. He wondered if a bum had got drunk and passed out there; it sometimes happened.

The policeman walked over and nudged the ribs with his toe. The man didn't move. The policeman bent down a little and dug his club into the hip, but the man didn't move. The policeman tapped his club against the soles. The man wouldn't move. "Ail right, Mac," the policeman said, "let's move it buddy," and banged the leather insteps. Though he didn't seem to move, the man slid the slightest bit on the highly polished mosaic. The policeman bent down, grasped the shoulder, and pulled. As the body flopped over, one hand flung loose and free; the body seemed to lie there as if impaled on the pyramid points, buoyed up like a fakir. There was a little pool of blood underneath him and blood on the clothes; the shot had entered the ribcage.

People who had been gathering to watch both the policeman and the body came closer. A fashionably dressed woman with her purpled grey hair held under a white, sheer net, seeing who it was, shrieked: she recognized Rabbi Gordon of Temple Caiaphas. At this point, patrol-car police spotted the crowd and pulled up and radioed for help. The woman who identified the rabbi was having hysterics talking about what a saint Rabbi Gordon had been and that "they" had assassinated him and who was safe if such a saint was killed, and asking where were the police when you needed them, giving parking-tickets? And crying that the city was becoming a blood bath. People came rushing out of the temple. A positive identification was made by the rabbi's secretary, a tall, blond young man, who then fainted and was caught by the policeman as he began to fall on top of the rabbi's body.

When the evening papers came out they already carried fuller stories about Doctors Cartwright and Volpe and Mr. Blumenthal; and while they didn't have time to print more than a routine, prepared obituary for the rabbi, they did spread a banner headline for him; he was well known and a leader of New York Jewry. The Bishop of the New York Diocese expressed his horror at this evil act. A relationship among the victims was noted on the five o'clock News broadcast and for the first time was made public: all four had been involved with the Mercy Memorial Hospital, a fact that the radio, most mobile in its coverage, now exploited. Owing to the police method of crime reportage, the police hadn't made these connections yet: reports always first went into separate precincts and then were teletyped to headquarters and reteletyped to all the precincts. It remained to observant police personnel in the precincts, or at headquarters, to make the connections. But now The Department acted as if it had known these facts for a long time and had been acting accordingly.

But at four-thirty that same afternoon, the police were informed that Dr. Curtius, a world-renowned surgeon, the man who invented the Curtius forceps, the Curtius retractor, and the Curtius suture stitch, who had advanced the art of surgery, who was living now in invalided semi-retirement in the Riverdale section of the Bronx, had just been shot – sometime between four and four-thirty. Dr. Curtius had been wheeled out on the porch of his house and was sitting there, enjoying the brilliant sunset across the Hudson River, if it could be said that a man who was so old and paralysed and blind and deaf could enjoy anything... perhaps only the feel of the sun on his skin. His housekeeper had blanketed Dr. Curtius and had put him out at three o'clock, as she did every clear, warm afternoon day. The day had become so perfect that she was sure Dr. Curtius was responding to the sun's heat on his face and the tang of the now incredible November air. She looked out at three-thirty and again at four and at four-thirty: she watched him carefully to see if he needed to urinate or defecate.

At four-thirty she saw that Dr. Curtius had been shot in the face. The force of the bullet almost entirely shattered the frail head, splattering parts of blood, bone, and integument all over the porch. She swore she heard nothing at all. The bullet must have been fired face-on. The police deduced that, since the house was set on a steep hill, the murderer, to have shot the doctor this way, must have come up the hill, swung himself on to the porch, and probably approached quite close. As in the other killings, a silencer must have been used. There was some consolation in that the doctor couldn't have known what was happening.

The radio stations broadcasted the bulletins as they came in. The news of the newest killing was broadcast at five-fifteen. A frenetic disc-jockey interrupted "I want to hold your ha-a-and ..." to give details, announcing it slowly, almost in wonder, stunned enough to keep talking jive-talk. Five minutes later he interrupted a run of spot commercials to state that Dr. Curtius had been a member of the Board of Directors of the Mercy Memorial Hospital. Later, the police would be criticised for not providing protection for Dr. Curtius since it was obvious that members of Mercy's board were obviously targets.

The first television programmes were now showing tapes of the scenes of the first three crimes; meanwhile, two mobile TV camera units from rival networks were racing one another to Dr. Curtius's house via the West Side Drive, where they were being pursued by a patrol car because commercial trucking was forbidden on the Drive.

The Mercy Memorial was having trouble now. Since Mercy was obviously the target of the killer, much of the four-to-twelve shift – mostly the non-professional staff: nurses' aides, porters, cleaning women, elevator operators – were not showing up. The rumour persisted that the killer was still around. People living in the hospital area were coming and standing around in little clumps, watching, talking. Some of them tried to sneak into the hospital. Issuing an appeal for more professional staff from other hospitals was considered, but no one now had the authority to do so. Many patients went unattended.

At five-thirty, Betty-Lou Widmer came home from work. She shared a six-room apartment in the West Nineties with three other girls. Usually she was the first one home. She kicked off her shoes in the foyer and left them there. She went into the kitchen, as she always did, and made up a pitcher of stiff, eight-to-one Martinis for herself and her room-mates. She sipped and ate a few Cheezits, munched Fritos, and nibbled some Provolone so that she wouldn't get too smashed drinking on an empty stomach. Sipping and chewing, she went out of the kitchen and into her room. There, she took off her dress, stockings, and underwear and finished her Martini. She went back to the kitchen, refilled her glass, and went to the bathroom to shower. While she was showering, she kept reaching out and sipping the Martini, which she had perched on the washstand. She dried herself, put on a freshly laundered cotton housecoat, and started back to her bedroom, glass in hand, when she noticed there was an arm on the floor, sticking out from Jenine Carounnbois's room. Going closer, she saw that Miss Carounnbois was stretched out and wearing only a half-slip. She had been shot several times.

That Betty-Lou did not panic – it never even occurred to her that the murderer might still be around – and start screaming she later attributed to the fact that she was half-smashed: as a mater of fact, she said, at first she thought it was some kind of game.

Later, smudges of blood were discovered in the kitchen and in the hallway leading to Miss Carounnbois's room. She had been shot three times before she died. Apparently the killer had followed her, shooting from the kitchen (which had a service exit) to the hallway, and killed her, finally, in the doorway of her room. The first shot had skimmed her, creasing the lower margin of her left breast and burning along a side angle of her ribcage. The second shot hit her off the puff of flesh at the side of the thigh where her buttock and her leg joined, going in from behind. The third shot had hit her directly in the back, shattering her spine and deflecting off and through one lung.

Neighbours, those who were at home, swore they heard nothing at all. Miss Carounnbois had been a nurse at Mercy Memorial. She could have been killed any time between eight-thirty in the morning and five. She had a father in Quebec.

By six-fifteen, all the victims had been reported. Later editions not only carried biographies of the slain, but some papers already carried the first statements by police, by the shocked close relatives, by stunned hospital personnel. Speculation had begun as to who could have done it, and for what mad reason. Obviously, as more and more of the facts came in, a pattern established itself and *The New York Times*, coming out at about ten that night, tentatively hypothesised that the murderer killed in this order: Dr. Volpe and Mr. Blumenthal, between nine-thirty and ten (not Miss Carounnbois, for it was doubtful that he could have made it to the hospital in time for Dr. Volpe and the administrator) since the time required by either car or underground to get to the 10.45 appointment with Dr. Cartwright had to be considered. (It was well known in hospital circles that Dr. Cartwright never operated on Wednesday mornings.) Since Dr. Cartwright had been killed between quarter to eleven and eleven, and Rabbi Gordon probably at three, the killer had most likely shot Miss Carounnbois some time between eleven and three. Because there was no direct connection from Fifth Avenue via rapid transit to Riverdale, the killer probably travelled by car to get there by approximately four. The reporter assumed that the killer worked according to a time-table.

The possibility that there was more than one murderer was considered, but it seemed doubtful; the police were fairly sure, pending a ballistics report, that the same weapon was used in each case.

Radio reported each new development as it happened. Television was presenting more and more taped on-the-spot interviews. Commentators were beginning to speculate more. Preparation for the televising of memorial services, especially for Rabbi Gordon and Dr. Curtius, was going on.

Mercy was now in a state of panic: who knew where the killer would strike next? It was obvious to anyone now that the hospital personnel were his insane target. The police set up a patrol; a command post was established in the now-deserted clinic with radio connections direct to headquarters. Extra patrol cars roamed the streets around Mercy. Some tentative arrests were being made. Mercy, short on staff seemed almost deserted now; in fact, quite a few ambulatory patients checked themselves out and a few patients some seriously ill, were taken home by alarmed relatives ignoring the advice of their doctors. The surrounding streets were crowded now; people waited and speculated and watched in the fine night air; some of them were interviewed by radio and television reporters.

The next day the newspapers exploded, each, with the exception of the *Times*, vying in the wildness of their reportage. The *Times*, curiously, did come up with a sort of scoop: it secured the medical record of the man who, under a false name, was treated for some months by Dr. Cartwright. The nurse's description wasn't helpful; it didn't differentiate the appearance of the killer from thousands of other men in a certain socio-economic stratum, one which could afford Dr. Cartwright's fees. What *was* interesting was that a fairly minute physiological portrait *did* exist, though it was, so to speak, an *inner* picture: X-rays, blood pressure, heartbeat rate. This was the profile printed by the *Times*. But who could, passing the killer on the street, point him out and say this was the man? So perhaps the portrait painted by an *Afternoon Staff* writer was more realistic: "There is a killer among us, stalking the streets, striking terror into our hearts. He is a madman, diabolical, pitiless, a cold-blooded lunatic who carries, locked in his heart, an insane secret. He skulks, perhaps passing right by us: me, you, any of us…"

Two days later, aside from the fact that police, plain-clothes and uniformed, were all over Mercy Memorial, routine had been re-established and the non-professional staff were almost all back. Clinics were running to capacity again. It was noticed that for the second night in a row, the emergency-room clerk, Miss Malabar, was not in. Of course, being an old maid with all sorts of crotchets and fears, it was understandable that the excitement was too much for her. Allowances were always made for Miss Malabar – she had been with Mercy for eighteen years. Her apartment was phoned. There was no answer. Repeated phone calls were made. The police were notified. A patrol car was sent.

The door to Miss Malabar's apartment was not locked. When they went in they found that a terrific struggle had taken place in the bathroom. Miss Malabar had been clubbed to death or, possibly, her head had been smashed against the bathtub. That a variety of instruments were used seemed to indicate that Miss Malabar was a long time in dying. She was in the bathtub, partly covered with torn-down shower curtains; only her naked legs were sticking up. Towels were on the floor. Almost all the contents of her two medicine chests had been dumped or thrown on top of her. Bottles of all sorts, alcohol, perfume, medicine, nose drops, were hurled down at her, not only damaging her face and upper body but, piling up, had shattered against one another. Some fixtures had been wrenched from their connections and thrown at her. The tap water was running lightly, pouring over her, and draining steadily. At first rape was suspected.

To begin with, it was assumed that Miss Malabar was the victim of another kind of killer, even though she, too, was from Mercy, and that her death at this time was just a grisly coincidence: the *modus operandi* was so different, and the senseless savagery of the act contrasted with the cool and diabolical rationality of the other acts. But a questioning of neighbours the next day revealed that some grade-school children on the way to school saw a man whose description fitted the one given by Dr. Cartwright's nurse.

The killer was seen entering on that grey, overcast morning when the windless humidity held still the smell of the acrid industrial gases and petroleum fumes that drifted over from New Jersey. He went up and got in, somehow, to talk to Miss Malabar in her heavily draped, cluttered apartment. He lured her into the bathroom. The neighbours heard nothing, but then, it was an old-fashioned and solidly built apartment house.

Chapter 3

It took the police six weeks to catch Fertig. Not that he ran away: he waited.

Ultimately, the hysterical screaming of the newspapers, the enormous shock of the crime, indignant demands in the name of the public that something be done, the wild speculations – who? why? – began to die. But the police, carefully checking an enormous list of people who could possibly have held grudges against Mercy – patients, personnel, relatives – eliminating wherever they could and hoping they hadn't eliminated the murderer, moved through the steps of their system at an inexorable pedestrian pace and came, even though he was nowhere near the beginning of the end of their list, to Fertig.

After That Day, Fertig was drained. He could only wait and rest. Some days he slept almost twenty hours. He told Sara he was sick ... a low-level virus was debilitating him. He read the newspapers, watched the news on television, and slept a lot – slept more sweetly, more at peace than he had for the past year. It was as if he was making up for all the lost sleep of that year … of his life. Tranquil, he waited for the momentary knock … the police. He was impatient. What was taking so long. Lying around in his stupor, Fertig began to have a daydream. He would be in a room, a chamber, a hall, really… misty, fuzzy, one with many people in it.

He followed the developments with a growing detachment … as if it were all about someone else. In the second week, when they still hadn't come, he began to get restless; he had slept enough; he shook off the lethargy and paid more attention to what they were saying about The Murderer. How could anyone want to kill Dr. Curtius, a venerable man who had spent his life serving mankind and who was almost dead anyway? Or brutally kill Miss Malabar, a harmless old maid, a wonderful character, really? Or want to assassinate Rabbi Gordon, whose good deeds were beyond counting? Everyone speculated – news commentators, psychiatrists, police officials. What wild hypotheses they had, how far from the mark, how perversely wrong! He was annoyed, petulant. How silly could they get? And when they got close to understanding it, he would get oddly excited – yes! that was almost it – yet… exposed. Questions added and permutated into mad guesses.

He had a better relationship with Sara again, a permanent truce, really. He accepted it. It could never be what it was again: would it be when she found out? He would sit beside her every night as she watched the television set, abandoned to it. Or they talked about The Crime. It annoyed him that she didn't even know who the victims were. Hadn't they published the pictures? Didn't she remember the name of the place where they had killed Stevie? "What kind of monster could have done it?" she asked. "Only a madman." And she was understanding and compassionate about the poor killer: it angered him. She had gone back to her Dr. Anslinger; Fertig might have expected a psychoanalytic point of view from her. What if – he asked her – what if, just suppose, for the sake of argument, the victims had committed some sort of crime?

"What kind of horrible crime could they have committed," she would ask, "to merit killing?" And if there had been "a crime" – where did he get such an idea? – then wasn't it up to the *police* to … And he would begin to discuss it carefully with her, but never prevailing against her dogged and exasperating pity. If she knew what they had done, would she be so pitying? And, smiling, superior, he would invent a new, possible crime that the seven might have done. Sara, rejecting the hypothetical, was interested only in actualities. And, the excitement growing in him, he would break off, turn away to keep her from sensing, watching her to see if his hints reached her, burying himself in his book, feeling for the slightest apprehension. But she, tired, bored, relieved that the discussion had ended, watched the television set gladly when they weren't talking; she was insensitive to it.

When they didn't come for him at the end of the second week he wondered if he should go and give himself up. He read all the newspapers carefully: they were on the trail, they were no closer, they had new clues, they were closing in, they hadn't an inkling.

The Fertigs began to go out again with old friends, resuming old relationships. Everyone said what a wonderful recovery Fertig made after coming so close to... "I was worried for you," his friend Sam told him. "You don't brood for ever."

"No," Fertig said. "You don't."

"It's time you and Sara did something about it. After all, it's not too late." And wherever they went they heard talk about The Crime; they talked about it themselves. At first he kept himself from joining in. He kept thinking: if they only knew! It made the simple, friendly, comfortable contacts exciting, and, late one night, sitting in a coffee-house, sipping at a sweet mint-chocolate drink, he daydreamed, incorporating his friends into his dreams, planting them in the audience. But on rousing himself, he began to say that they'd better hurry home because the babysitter... when suddenly, he stopped himself in time, and then leaned back to daydream again.

Sometimes he even bought out-of-town papers. He was exasperated; no one seemed to really understand the nature of his act, exactly what it was about. No one had found out why it happened. He smiled at the contradictions, sometimes within the same articles: "madman", they say; "cunning, malevolent killer", "master planner", "berserker", "skulking monster", they reported. They sullied his deed: he would correct them. Yet, perversely, when they talked about The Crime, not only of the century, but of all time, he could view it with pride. It was a horrible thought, but it was a job well done.

The daydream grew. He would be standing in an auditorium. He could see himself talking: at his side, a judge, a man stern, yet benevolent, sat. He was telling them why he had to do it, talking about the evil in the world, the evil that had killed his son. He would talk about his feelings, the need, that ache to balance things,... the pain, that awful pain he suffered as he came – *grew* – to The Decision. Friends would be in the audience, strangers he overheard discussing The Crime, people he had never seen... the world... even the murdered, somehow resurrected, would be there. They filled an arena, and sat in balcony tiers that rose and receded till they disappeared into darkness. Each time he daydreamed it, it became clearer; his thoughts were more wonderfully organized. Of course he was no orator so he would have to speak softly, calmly, letting *truth* generate power, as it had invested him before with the strength to act. He made his account to the world.

In the third week he became restless: weren't they ever coming? He considered going out and getting a job. After all, he thought, he might as well gather as much money as possible for Sara; he felt guilty that he had depleted their joint bank account. He knew that if he wanted to, he could go back to work for Mr. Grenoble. Grenoble, after making sure that Fertig would sweat a little for their argument ("You'll be back, Fertig, on your hands and knees, begging me.") about Fertig's quitting on him like that ("But Fertig, can I trust you?"), would take him back. Perhaps Grenoble would even take away Fertig's title of comptroller; certainly he would reduce Fertig's salary. No, he decided, he wouldn't go back there; evidently, Grenoble hadn't discovered what he'd done to the books before he left. He wondered what his desire to work again meant. Why not just give himself up? Was he weakening? No: his plan was only to wait and do nothing.

As the third week ended with a crescendo of newspaper blasts and complaints of outraged citizens' committees, the police seemed to have achieved nothing. The police body bent forward and plodded on. They released communiqués that they were on the verge of catching the killer, or killers. Ballistics reports confirmed that one silenced gun had killed six of the victims; the brutality of Miss Malabar's death remained an anomaly. Perhaps the same person had *not* killed her after all. Every day there were crank callers threatening the deaths of more doctors, admitting to having killed the seven, tipping off the cops that bombs were planted in all municipal, voluntary, and private hospitals. And these reports had to be checked too.

As the fourth week began, Fertig began to hope. He knew it was wrong to hope; it was not what he wanted, but something inside of him had rebelled. It *was* a perfect crime and one of the most enormous crimes in history at that. He lay awake at night and hoped and damned himself for hoping; he wondered how his stock of courage had depreciated since that day ... that glorious day. He tried to anger himself with memories of Stevie, but Stevie was long gone, long faded, hardly evocable, not even real. When had he begun to forget? If he wasn't caught or if he didn't surrender, then his son's death would be written off. But he was depleted of anger now. One day he went upstairs into Stevie's room and opened the drawers with his clothes: and he could almost feel old feelings: the smell of his son, that almost-shape of Stevie's body, and his own body, stiffening itself to receive the impact of his son's charge. What had he done with his son, how had he played with him, how had he yelled at him, how did he twine his fingers into his son's long, golden hair? It was vague and far away ... but he could get angry that he could no longer even feel his son. He dreamed again of the Speech, the hall, the audience: he talked of his lost son. And he almost wept. And he began to have a second daydream – a fantasy, really – that the listening people were *understanding*, moved to tears, to love! But he suppressed it; it was an unrealistic vision, a wild indulgence. But it gave him the strength to wait again.

One day he made himself go as far as the local precinct steps, but he defaulted; they would catch him, Fertig promised himself, and he prepared for his moment.

In the fifth week the newspapers had almost dropped it entirely. A gossip columnist surmised that, according to a secret Cosa Nostra source, the murders were the first round in a terroristic extortion-war against the hospitals. He insisted on discussing this new, ridiculous theory with Sara and with Sam and Bea when they dropped over for coffee and cake one night. They were bored with the case; they had been talking about the murders for weeks now.

He listened to them talking – Sam, Bea, Sara. How their droning voices, their complacent, accepting, smug attitudes irritated him! He watched a crumb cling, stuck, to Bea's lipstick. How they clouded over That Day with their talk. And he began to argue with them, argue with their versions of the madman killer, taunting them with visions of a heroic killer. They, not catching his special agitation, responded only to the excitement of the argument and, their faces contorted, they shouted back at him good-naturedly, fighting him. "It could be anyone," he yelled. "You, me."

"Oh, how you go on, Harry," Bea laughed at him. "I'd just like to see Sam ..."

"I admit I couldn't do it. Even for you, my love," Sam said. "Kill me, but I couldn't do it."

"... because such a power is in any one of us – given the proper causes ..."

"What *cause* can justify such a horrible act?" Sara asked.

"Hate ... love," Fertig told them.

"How you talk, Harry. Have you lost your sense of proportion? Only a madman..." Sara's challenge was shrill.

"Well, it may interest you to know –" The crumb, loosened from Bea's moving lips, dropped. And he stopped himself. He had almost told them. They would know. They would see. He felt ... powerful. He stood up and pulled up his pants and squared his shoulders. They didn't notice him; they kept on discussing it. *They* would be in the audience; they would see; just a little while longer ... and he would see their faces as he talked.

At the end of the fifth week someone came forth and confessed and now Fertig hoped openly. But the police released the admitted killer; they said that they had ways of knowing the killer. What ways? he wondered; it frightened him. And why should it frighten him? He was supposed to be caught. Why didn't they hurry? He stopped reading police reports for a few days because he might find out they were getting too close and he'd feel like absconding. He couldn't prevent himself from fearing fully now, and he tried to allay the fears by forcing himself to daydream about his Great Confession. The newspapers dropped the case almost entirely and it began to look like it might be an unsolved crime; he began to become complacent.

But they came for him in the sixth week. It was all a matter of time, of eliminating possibilities, of riding miles and walking miles, of ringing doorbells, of checking records, of asking questions, and of walking some more, of climbing in and out of cars, of crossing names one by one off the long hospital lists, of climbing stairs or taking lifts, and of walking more. They came when the newspapers seemed to have forgotten; the world was interested in some newer crime. The bell rang early one evening. Sara answered the door. Two men stood, blocking out the light from the street lamps.

"Does a Mr. Fertig live here?" one of them asked politely.

She told them he did. She asked them who they were. They told her they were from the police and wished to talk to Mr. Fertig. Not understanding, she let them in. Her face was blank, dulled with not caring, not feeling; she struggled with it, not quite comprehending it. The possibility of evening contacts with the police was completely out of the range of her experience. They looked down at her; her grey-lined hair was centre-parted, flat against her head; her face was thin, severe, the lips a little slack, pale. The bewilderment seemed genuine. Fertig saw two huge men being led in. They were polite; they took off their hats. He stood up to meet them: he understood, immediately, who they were and why they were here. He felt relieved; good; at last. He expected them to announce dramatically that he was under arrest. He wanted to start babbling; he almost turned to Sara and said "You see!" but he controlled himself.

"Mr. Fertig, I'm Detective Donnell." Donnell was the senior partner. He was very wide. He wore a crumpled brown suit and no coat in spite of the early winter chill. His jacket was bunched and strained under his arms and along his sides, so the sleeves looked short; his wrists were thick; he was hard to fit. "I don't know how to explain this, but there's been some sort of mix-up." His wide, puffy face looked stupid; his small eyes puzzled. "We're from the police," he said helplessly. His partner, Martin, wondered who Donnell thought he was fooling with that act; he had seen it ten times that day.

The other policeman wore a neat blue suit. He was still young but was hardening fast; his face was becoming glazed into a permanent pink; his eyes already had that blank stare that neither accused nor acquitted but expressed a brutal, pitiless *knowledge*. "Someone has been telling us stories about you," Martin said and laughed a quick, insincere laugh, which sounded phoney to his own ears, "but it's something that bears investigation. A mere formality. You understand."

Sara stood in the middle of the room. She kept looking from one to the other, waiting for them to explain it. Since Fertig didn't look worried, she didn't either. Her attention wandered and she glanced at the television set. Fertig smiled and looked at her to see how she took it, if she understood *now* who he was – and was afraid, as if she would howl ... the way she had the night Stevie was killed. "I don't understand." Fertig told them.

While they stood for three or four seconds, arrested and embarrassed, the detectives committed everything to memory; if asked, they could describe the Fertigs and their house minutely. Fertig looked at them, his eyes going calmly from one to the other, waiting. He nodded, as if encouraging them.

Donnell, as soon as he saw Fertig, *knew*. He decided to take a chance instead of going through the whole rigmarole: Where were you on –? When did you have contact with –? It would be easier away from Fertig's home ground. Detective Donnell said, "We have to take you down to headquarters for questioning," which signalled Martin that Donnell knew he had his man. Martin didn't know how Donnell did it; he had contempt for the older man, but he had to admit that as far as some things went, Donnell always *knew* – by animal instinct. Martin's heart began to beat a little faster and he unbuttoned his coat.

Fertig nodded, expectant; they didn't miss that. Why didn't he protest, argue, and ask? They always did. "Someone has reported to us that you have been involved in an armed robbery." Donnell tried to say it lightly enough, almost as though what he was saying couldn't be true and that he wasn't even too interested, but he could never be light about anything. Martin thought the technique was simple-minded, and was surprised whenever it gave results. He watched Fertig look a little shocked as Fertig watched Donnell. Martin saw Fertig take a deep breath, shake his head, straighten his shoulders, and smile; they might have trouble.

Fertig understood the technique; it was such a shallow method, he thought. He nodded. He didn't have the strength to act outraged. He would play it for a while. He told himself he was glad they had come. "Of course it's ridiculous," he said, "but if you want me to come along, I will. Who told you this?"

"We have our sources," Donnell said. "We can't divulge them."

Fertig saw that Donnell was serious; so was Martin, but his gravity was not so brutal.

"What is he trying to say?" Sara asked.

"Now don't worry about it, Sara."

Sara looked at them, still struggling to come out of her lethargy. "I don't understand." Her flat voice sounded querulous, angry, like a child wakened unwillingly. "This is ridiculous."

"It's just that someone has reported that a man looking like your husband has participated in an armed robbery," Martin said. "We have to question, Mrs. Fertig."

"But that's impossible; you've been sick."

"But they say I've robbed." Fertig smiled: how ridiculous that smile made everything seem.

"Only someone who *looks* like you, Mr. Fertig," Martin laughed.

Donnell was absolutely sure now that Fertig was their man. If questioned, he couldn't have said why; if pressed, the reasons might have come out, one by one, dumped out of their neatly filed slots. He *knew*. His certainties were erected of an eyelash flicker, a smell of someone's fear-soured breath, a too-steady look, a fast pulse beating in the neck, a depressed eyelid; his senses were perfect. Fifteen years on the force had sharpened everything: his eyes, his ears, his nose, his mouth, even his skin; and those senses were supplemented by directives and informationals on methods of detection. He *knew*. He was less inclined to be polite now. Martin was beginning to get the same sense and felt the excitement mounting. He remembered the reward. They wouldn't get it all – but still…

"It's procedure, only procedure. Routine," Martin said to Fertig. After all, this was a man, appearance notwithstanding, who was a killer. He began to look at Fertig respectfully, warily.

"I'll put on my suit and get my coat," Fertig said and started to walk past them. Donnell turned to follow. Fertig stopped. His glasses gleamed as they caught light from the television set. His eyes widened for the barest second. The detectives caught the little motion; Martin moved his jacket aside, as if he was hot, ready to reach for his pistol. Here was a danger area; don't antagonize him; watch. Fertig, quick as they, caught the subtle little signs; it made him feel sure, stronger, that they had no real proof or they would have arrested him outright. "Procedure?" he asked, smiling. Donnell felt an old anger, the anger he felt whenever he had a wise guy. Martin just smiled politely and nodded.

Fertig went upstairs. Donnell followed. In the bedroom, Fertig started to close the door, but Donnell came in to watch him undressing and dressing. The stare made Fertig nervous; he didn't like to be seen without his clothes. He should have changed his underwear, and would have even preferred to take a quick shower, but couldn't – not while he was being watched. "And will anything I say be held against me? Just like in the detective novels?" Fertig asked, annoyed.

"You know it, buddy," Donnell said and swung his huge hands. Fertig knotted his tie slowly, carefully, looked at himself in the mirror, adjusted the knot, untied it and reknotted it, balancing it carefully between the wings of his collar.

Before they left, Fertig told Sara, "Now don't worry about this. Watch television. Don't worry. Sometimes these things take forever."

"But what if you don't come back?"

"Sara..."

"Listen, Harry, I've read about these things – false arrest, wrong identifications – I saw a film once.."

He was smiling. "You're getting hysterical."

Martin wondered if Donnell could be wrong. If he was, they might be in trouble. Fertig managed to grin and felt stronger for grinning. "Sara, come on. A robber, Me? Sara...

She nodded at him and then barely seemed to care.

"And don't call your mother. If I'm late, don't worry. Who knows, I may decide to sleep over at the police station," he told her and laughed.

"I'm sure Mr. Fertig will be back in a few hours," Martin said.

She still didn't seem to understand; his voice was a little shrill. She nodded and, suddenly, her face relaxed for a second: her eyes closed; the light shining on her slightly pursed lips made them soft, sensual, smiling. Fertig didn't understand the smile. Why should she smile? There was something spiteful about it. He wanted to ask her why she was smiling. Should he tell her? Did she *know*? Was she *happy* that he was being arrested? She looked so ... sated – that was it! – and he was shocked. He had to ask her, but Donnell pulled him gently and said, "Later, Mr. Fertig." And her face was cold again, severe between the cold dead slabs of pulled-back hair. Perhaps, Fertig thought, it had only been a facial reflex, a fear movement.

They walked out the front door. Martin led, Donnell followed; Fertig was small between them. He was wearing a grey suit and a dark-grey topcoat. He wore his dark-grey, almost black, hat. He took deliberate strides as if he had become unaccustomed to his own walk.

The three of them sat in the back of an unmarked car. A uniformed policeman drove. Martin chatted pleasantly to him, talking, at first, of the weather, the possibility of rain that could spoil the weekend's football game. Donnell was silent. He didn't care about football; his whole mind was working, grinding out a strategy; he began to sweat and his heavy smell filled the car. Fertig edged away from Donnell. He nodded politely and answered Martin. He decided to enjoy the situation as much as possible.

They drove down the Brooklyn side streets, on to the Gowanus Parkway, down the long ramp from which Fertig could see Manhattan shining ahead in the darkness, and into the brightly lit Brooklyn-Manhattan tunnel. He asked why they weren't taking him to the local precinct. Martin told him now that not only had there been an armed robbery, but a policeman had been killed. When Martin said that, Donnell growled. Fertig began, for the first time, to be a little afraid. He knew, certainly from what he read in the papers, in detective novels, from what he saw in the films, that the police would be quick to beat and torture, but slowly, to find out the truth when it came to one of their own. Had they made a mistake? The possibility was too fantastic, too ridiculous, he reassured himself: they *had* to be playing a game. But, he realized, game or not, that he was in their hands. He might reason with a Martin, he thought, but how would he reason with a Donnell?

"That's quite serious," Fertig said.

"It certainly is, Fertig, it certainly is," Donnell growled, and Martin's face seemed to have changed too; as if the seriousness of such a thing just occurred to him. Martin's face became cold, efficient, unsympathetic; all the friendliness was gone now. But, Fertig reminded himself, he had nothing to worry about. He *hadn't* killed a policeman. Martin continued talking. "Seems improbable, doesn't it? Look at you; family man, college education, good job, responsibility, money in the bank, good house, fine furniture, mild face, dress neatly, very neatly. Improbable? Average height, maybe a little shorter. Good manners. No previous arrests. Impossible!"

"Nothing to rob for," said Donnell.

"No. Not even built well, no offence. Not worried. Can't be," Martin said.

"Looks against it," said Donnell.

"But appearances, like they say, are deceiving," Martin said. "Look at a Willie Sutton. No one milder looking."

"Worst killer I knew was a fag," growled Donnell. "Killed his father. Six hold-ups. Fourteen muggings. Stood off half the force. Little sucker. Never know. Got his. Looked like you. Younger, but like you."

"My partner is a little frightening, isn't he?" Martin laughed. They were emerging from the tunnel. The heavy vapour lights were banked high over their heads. The car drove down the dark, deserted streets, through the Financial district, stopping frequently for traffic lights. "Still, it's a serious thing when one of ours is killed. We operate on a principle and that principle is respect for the law – all right, we'll admit it: fear. But what's respect, if not fear, right Mr. Fertig?"

"If a policeman is shot, not only does it mean that a friend, a co-worker has been killed, but more, the principle that protects us has been violated. Any hood is quick to learn. That's why …" He stopped. "But it's silly to talk that way, isn't it?"

Fertig felt there was something wrong with their approach. He understood they were trying to get at him from a direction other than the one he expected. If they would only ask, he would admit it. Presumably they would continue till, reluctantly, it would appear he was not the one they wanted. Then, when he was about to be freed, hoping for it, counting on it, they would spring their surprise: *You are the man*. And he, keyed to freedom, expended of defensive energy, would confess. Of course, he thought, they were working on the assumption that he didn't want to be caught... But they were investing too much effort in this peculiar dance. He would play their childish game just a little longer and when it looked like they couldn't get anywhere, he would announce – maybe even – if only Martin and Donnell didn't take themselves too seriously. He had not expected this: the intensity, the killed policeman. And yet, Fertig wondered, why not?

Martin stared ahead, but was watching Fertig carefully, wondering – how well Fertig acted – if he was testing his area of freedom, enlarging it, trying his strength in all sorts of directions, waiting for the weak place, ready to burst out. The thing was, Martin thought, to *really* convince Fertig they wanted him for that other crime, that he was the bastard who shot Bill Finnerty in that robbery. They said it again and again: show him you're not serious and the whole operation means beans. They had to wear him out.

Donnell had never thought about the process much. He accepted it the way he accepted the footwork; the way he had accepted wearing a uniform once; the way his body accepted and never noticed discomfort. What counted was that he *knew* Fertig was The One. The thing was to apply the crusher and let the little bastard scream.

"Of course," Martin said, "we've done a little investigation. Lost your job about six months ago."

"Who told you that?"

"Your old boss, Mr. Grenoble."

"I resigned."

"Where've you been working for the past six months?"

"I've been taking a holiday. After all, after fourteen years – no, it's more like fifteen ... Let's see, I began to work ..." He laughed. "It doesn't matter. I thought I was entitled to a long holiday."

"But what did you do these six months."

"I've been under an emotional strain. My baby died a year ago.

"Not working, no money coming in, how did you make do?"

"I have money in the bank. I've always been well paid. And my wife has been working. She's a teacher," Fertig told them.

The car pulled up in front of headquarters. Martin got out. Donnell, reaching over efficiently, put one great hand on Fertig's wrist before Fertig understood what was happening. Fertig got out, restrained, having to move slowly while Donnell shifted his great bulk after him in little car-rocking heaves. Fertig saw the green light-globes on the ornate cast-iron pillars, of which the solidness and the massivity of the stone were almost comforting, reasonable, as if the games had to stop here. They led him up the stairs and into the dark building.

"We'll take him down," Donnell said.

"Not to –?" "Not yet. Confirm first. I mean why play their errand boy. You lose out. Understand?"

Martin nodded. He remembered the reward.

"This way … this way we don't miss the parade. Wait till you're around a while, see?"

Martin was not sure he approved, but he went along with Donnell.

They could hear the cranking of the lift starting a long way off and coming slowly. The floor, except for where dirt and pieces of gum had been polished into the composition shone. They went into the lift and it started. For a second Fertig wasn't sure if it was going up or down and it alarmed him; down, he decided. They stood there, Donnell always a little behind him, holding Fertig's wrist with his wrist, watching him carefully. Martin stood to Fertig's side, appearing relaxed but watching. The policeman who had driven them didn't come along.

When the lift stopped, they all got out and walked down dismal corridors lit by bare bulbs till they came to a room. The room was surprisingly comfortable. There was a leather easy chair, a couch, a few hard office chairs; the yellow walls had seven or eight old group pictures, all buffed by age, of police in stiff poses. There was a green metal filing cabinet with a telephone on top of it against the wall. Everything quivered under the fluorescent lighting. Fertig had expected the hard chair to have been placed under a bank of intense lights, and surrounded by other chairs circling in the darkness, from where all the detectives would ask their questions. Martin unlocked the handcuffs. The policeman who had driven them came in bringing a folder of papers; he stationed himself behind the easy chair. Martin motioned Fertig to the soft chair. Fertig smiled and said he would rather sit on one of the hard chairs. Donnell looked impatient while Martin smiled wearily, sat himself down on the arm of the easy chair, and told Fertig to suit himself. Donnell looked through the papers quickly. Standing at the cabinet, he made a few notes, then put the folder in the cabinet and locked it.

"Comfortable?" Martin asked.

"Stop wasting time," said Donnell. "Word will get around."

Fertig wondered what that meant.

"All right, Fertig, before you bother to start denying or screaming for a lawyer, or shouting 'false arrest', it will be easier for us all if you confirm," Donnell said.

"I don't understand."

"We have a positive identification that six months ago you and two others held up the Farmingdale National Bank. While trying to make your escape, you killed an officer who tried to stop you. We know this."

Fertig started to speak, but Martin continued. "We've gone through it; on the face of it, ridiculous, considering you, your position, bla bla bla ... But is it?

They looked serious about it. Fertig felt his fear recede a little. Certainly, he thought, he could forestall them by asking *them* the right questions. He would lead them as long as he could. It was a game – he had to remember that – and it should – must – end with his confession: he had to remember that. And since he knew and had always known how it would all end, he had less to fear, didn't he? "Who identified me? How was I identified?" he asked.

"I told you, we can't give you the information. But we have someone willing to testify in court," Martin said.

Fertig smiled.

"This is no laughing matter," Martin said. His young face turned harder. He felt angry at Fertig for playing the game this way. He kept remembering Bill Finnerty. "One of our men is killed."

"Stop wasting time," said Donnell. He moved nearer.

Fertig began to worry a little. "I can't say anything other than that your charges are not true."

"But what were you doing all that time you weren't working?" Martin asked.

"I'd be glad to show you my bankbook. I've been taking money out all along."

"Damn your bankbook," said Donnell. "There's a dead cop." He was getting impatient. His impatience lent anger to the routine's words; he sounded outraged that such things could be. Hit Fertig two or three times and he'd come apart, he thought. He was standing near Fertig, his clenched first close to Fertig's shoulder.

Fertig began to be afraid. All the protests Fertig could have made, all the indignant objections, were stilled by the remembrance: he *had* killed. They were right in essence if not in substance. But could they, he wondered, really have been mistaken about it all? The newspapers had calmed down; his crime receded further and further into the back pages, along with police assurances that they were on the verge of uncovering the greatest criminal of the twentieth century. But what if it was not a game? What if there *was* some confusion? He read about such things all the time. What if there were *really* witnesses? Mistaken identity – false arrest – trial – conviction – prison – torment – intercession of his faithful wife and loyal friends – release – freedom at last, after years of imprisonment, and the vindication of innocence – the suit against the city – he giggled and stopped. A long ash had formed on Fertig's unpuffed cigarette and the flame was almost to his fingers. He cleared his throat. He moved to stand. He started to confess...

"We're not asking you about your bankbook," Martin said. "We're asking you how you spent your time." He was angry at Fertig's giggle.

"Nothing much. I wandered around. I went to a lot of films. I hung around the house. My son's death, you see..."

"That doesn't make sense, Mr. Fertig. A hard-working type like yourself to suddenly..."

What, Fertig wondered, was unreasonable about a man mourning the death of his son? Fertig could hear Martin's reasonable voice going on and on, denying the logic of his statement, wanting an account of his time. He had another funny thought: supposing he were to admit the robbery? "Supposing," he asked, interrupting Martin, "I admit I held up the bank?" His hand held up the cigarette and he looked around for an ashtray.

"On the floor," Martin said.

"Listen you," growled Donnell. His patience had reached its limit. He was ready to start hitting. Fertig dropped the ash into his cupped hand. Martin was annoyed; that oaf, Donnell, didn't have the patience to go along with his own game. Fertig saw it was the wrong thing to say. He was outraged at their attitude. He had to urinate. The cigarette coal was almost to his fingers.

Fertig smiled. "I shouldn't have said that. I was only joking."

"You don't understand how serious this is, Fertig," Martin said. He remembered Bill Finnerty. He was through playing games too. The uniformed policeman moved nearer. And while Fertig was not under the bank of hot lights he had imagined, he *was* on the hard chair, surrounded by hard, uncompromising police, and afraid of Donnell's boiling anger. His hand held the ash, cupped, held out as if begging something. The pressure became urgent. "Could I go to the bathroom?"

Martin pointed to a door. "Leave the door open."

As he rose, Donnell asked him, "What did you do for six months? Just mope? What were you doing during the days and nights?"

"At nights I was home with my wife. She was terribly depressed and when she wasn't occupied with work, she had to be ... well, watched." Fertig could feel the heat from the cigarette; he would drop it into the toilet.

"And in the days?"

"I told you; nothing." The pressure in his bladder was acute. He started towards the bathroom.

"It's hard to believe," Martin said.

"But my bankbook would show you I don't need money. I have other assets too: investments."

"Is it only money, Fertig? A man who wants, never has enough. There are girls, for instance," Martin said. Fertig edged towards the bathroom door. "Am I right? Fertig?" Martin asked.

Fertig had to drop the cigarette butt on the floor. "Do I look like the kind of man who could hold up a bank in broad daylight? And kill a policeman?" Fertig asked and stepped on the butt carefully.

"Who said it was in the day?" said Donnell.

Fertig's kidneys began to hurt; the need to urinate was excruciating. "I assumed ..." Fertig said and opened the bathroom door. He started to close it behind him. The place smelled heavily of urine.

"No," Donnell told him. "Leave the door open."

Fertig unzipped his trousers and stood there, his back towards them. He felt the eyes of the two detectives looking at his back.

"Who said day?" asked Donnell. He was very close again.

"I thought... banks are open during the day."

"Don't piss on the floor, Fertig," said Donnell.

"But why say day? Were you there? Fertig?" Martin's voice was at his other shoulder, almost at his ear.

Suddenly Fertig felt as though he didn't have to go. The pain and urgency stopped. He sighed and zipped up his trousers and turned around. "False alarm," he told them apologetically. They were staring at him, contemptuously. The anger beat in Donnell's chest. Martin was beginning to catch Donnell's impatience. The politeness was completely gone from their faces. Something, while Fertig was turned away from them, made them harder, colder. He blushed ... and the need to urinate returned.

He stepped back into the room. "I suppose it's all about the killings, isn't it? Isn't it really that?"

"What killings?" asked Donnell cautiously.

"The ones connected with the hospital. The ones the newspapers have been shrieking about."

"What about them?"

"All right. I admit it. I killed them." How easy it was, easy but disturbing because he didn't mean to confess this way. And he turned and went into the bathroom and closed the door. He dropped the ash into the water and urinated for a long time; it was pleasurable. He could hear Donnell's hoarse breathing right behind the flimsy door. He didn't care. When he came back he sat down in the easy chair. The springs were broken and he sagged far down so that he could keep his knees straight; it was very comfortable.

"Who did you kill?"

'Them ... the seven of them."

"What seven?"

Fertig sighed: they would settle for nothing less than a complete inventory. "Dr. Curtius, Rabbi Gordon, Dr. Cartwright, Mr. Blumenthal, the nurse Carounnbois, Volpe the resident, and the clerk."

"Why did you kill them?" Martin asked.

"They were responsible for the death of my son, Stevie."

"*All* of them?"

"Yes. You see, I came to it this way..."

"You are confessing to the killings?" asked Donnell.

"Yes."

"And you will sign a confession?"

"Yes. You see, after he died, I began to wonder why it happened, who was responsible –"

"It is my duty to warn you that you don't have to confess," Martin intoned the words; Donnell glared at him.

"Yes, I know. But then, one day –"

"I have to tell you that you can talk to your lawyer before you confess...."

"... someone – I think it was the day after the funeral – someone said 'Why don't you sue?' Well..."

"How did you kill them?"

"With a gun... a pistol."

Donnell and Martin looked at one another.

"It was quite easy... once I had made up my mind to do it; once I had practised – besides, I didn't care if they caught me."

"Sure," Donnell said. He didn't believe Fertig.

"In fact, the idea was to be caught so I could explain everything, how I came to do it, the reasons... why..."

"But why them?"

Fertig explained what had happened at the clinic the night his son died.

"All right, maybe the doctor, maybe the nurse, maybe even the clerk, but the *others* – the administrator, the directors – what did they have to do with the death of your son?" Martin asked.

"I thought it out a long time... or, rather... things added up, and six months or so ago I knew what I must do – since *they* ran the Mercy Memorial, they were responsible. You see, killing balanced it out, and my being caught closes the account. That's why I had to be caught."

"Jesus. You got even with interest," Martin said.

"No. It was an almost-perfect equity. So I got a gun. I followed them. I got to know their movements. You make an estimate and try to fit into a tighter and tighter schedule. You think of months, then weeks, then seven days, revising the schedule constantly, keeping an audit of run-through times, making entries in your book – and then I finally figured I would have to do it one day."

"Why?"

"Because once I got to know them I knew I mustn't have time to think about it, to worry. You have to close the books in one day and it merely became a matter of revising estimates and making adjustments and new apportionments of time and then more entries and trial runs – to say nothing of target practice – because you have to do it like you would audit some complex figures of a firm. So you operate – to be able to do it all – as if the people were unimportant. It's the only way."

"Just like that?" Martin asked

"Well, it wasn't easy. But I kept remembering my son, Stevie, and what they did to him … or didn't do for him – it's all the same – and what happened to my marriage, my life after that night … And, well, of course, *you* people know where to get guns. So do criminals. But I'm not a criminal."

"Jesus."

"I mean I wasn't. I tried the mail-order houses. I tried Abercrombie and Fitch. I tried pawnbrokers. After all, you need a licence." Fertig smiled. "But you know that."

"Yeah, we know," Donnell said.

"A rifle is too clumsy, too easily seen. And I'm not the kind of man who can use a knife … You have to be a certain kind of person to use – well, some kinds of violence – you have to be … a physical type." Fertig spoke pedantically. "You see," Fertig spread his hands, "I'm not."

"I see. Yeah," Donnell growled.

"And so you shot them all?" Martin said.

Fertig saw them glance at one another and said, "Except, of course, for the clerk."

"Miss Malabar?"

"Her. Yes."

"How did you kill her?"

Fertig was silent.

"Why didn't you shoot her too?"

"Look, do we have to go through this? I'll sign whatever you want me to sign."

They stood and waited for him. Martin said, softly, "We have to know, Mr. Fertig. You see, a lot of people make false confessions – publicity hungry – psychos – what they call misplaced guilt. It's quite common…. We have to know."

"I was going to shoot her – she was the first in the day's schedule, you see, but she surprised me. You see, the scheme was to ring her bell at eight-fifteen. Trailing her, I had observed that the fewest people were around at that hour. At eight-nineteen – I deduced from certain experiments that she was a heavy sleeper and it would take that long for her to wake, to put on a robe, to come to the door, to answer, to look at me through the peephole, to ascertain, to her complete assurance, that I was safe. You see, I pretended to be an agent from the corporation that rented her building. I pretended I was inspecting all the apartments with a view to raising the rents. I presumed that she'd be more than willing to talk to me.

"I rang. We talked. She let me in. She was more suspicious than I thought she would be, so I was already a half-minute late. I figured for a ten-minute margin of error. We went through all the rooms. She had so many things to complain about, it was taking a long time. She was eating up my safety factor.

"I had intended to shoot her in the bedroom but... she was showing me the cracked pipe in her bathroom. She was looking the other way. I started to pull my gun and then –" Fertig stopped.

"And then?" Martin said.

"I couldn't do it," Fertig said.

They waited.

"Well, you saw the way she was, didn't you?"

"How was she, Fertig?" Donnell asked softly; he was angry at Fertig, angry at the coldness of his recital, angry that the man could show no remorse, no shame.

"In the bathroom; in the bath."

"Shot in the bath?" Martin said.

"Why are we playing this game?" Fertig asked.

"You did it, but you mean you can't talk about it?" Donnell asked: the old lady's death had angered him. Martin tried to calm Donnell with a gesture.

Fertig pulled himself forward, slid on the leather and sat on the edge of the chair, his legs pressed together. His hands held his thighs right above his knees. "I couldn't do it. I started to put the gun away. She turned and saw the gun. She grabbed me. I didn't think a woman as old as that could move as fast. I hadn't prepared for a situation like this... She started to plead while she was wrestling with me and forcing me back – she's very strong for an old woman – and I was trying to tell her I'd changed my mind," he told Donnell, "but her voice got louder and louder and I was afraid someone would come and I wrenched my hand free," he said to Martin, "and hit her with the gun two or three times and she fell," he said to the uniformed policeman, "into the bath and I heard her head –

"It's a very strange sound. So final. But she looked up at me and I was sure she was trying to rise and I began to throw things – anything – down at her.

"I was eleven minutes late when I left, but fortunately I made up time on the next two killings."

Donnell reached for a picture in the folder. He held it in front of Fertig. "Is this it?"

Fertig turned away, closing his eyes. "No. My God... How..."

"And this one..."

"Please, stop this."

"Look at the picture."

Fertig looked. "Yes," he said, staring. "I believe that's the way it was."

Donnell said, "Alone? You did it all alone?"

"Of course. It wasn't so hard once I came to the understanding of who was responsible. Organization..."

"I don't believe it."

"No, really; I was alone."

"But you threw the gun away," Martin said.

"No, I –"

"While taking a ferry ride," said Donnell.

"No, no, it's –"

Martin said, "In New York Harbour while passing the Statue of Liberty."

"It's at home." Fertig almost shouted.

"Where?"

Fertig told them. Donnell nodded at the uniformed policeman, who started to leave. "And send down a stenographer on your way out."

"My wife doesn't know yet. Please be careful how you tell her," Fertig called. Donnell looked down at him contemptuously.

They all relaxed again and Martin gave Fertig a cigarette and lit it for him and then lit two for himself and Donnell. "You're very co-operative, Mr. Fertig," Martin said.

Fertig inhaled and puffed out smoke. "You see, that was the point of it... I didn't conceal anything... I expected, once I closed the books, that I would be caught right away."

"Yeah," said Donnell.

Martin was polite and solicitous again; he was barely able to contain his joy at what they had captured; he stuttered once or twice, Donnell's face relaxed; he almost felt languorous; he telephoned for coffee and cake. The police stenographer came.

They had Fertig go through it, point for point. Again, he wanted to explain everything from the beginning, but they told him he would have his chance later. They stuck to the essentials. Fertig was so busy retelling it that he didn't have time to eat his cake; he just had a few swallows of coffee. They made him go over it again and again. Martin was astonished at the painstaking planning, the perfection of it, the superb execution of detail. He kept shaking his head. Donnell was not moved so much. He knew how easy it was to kill and after all, he thought, Fertig said he didn't care if he was caught. That made it easier. Donnell sent out for more coffee while the confessions were being typed.

The stenographer finished typing up the confessions, came back, and gave copies to Fertig to read and sign. Fertig asked for a pen. "Aren't you going to read them?" Martin wanted to know.

Fertig smiled. He was very tired. "You would hardly exaggerate, would you? How did you find me?"

"You better read it," Donnell said.

Fertig reached for the pen.

"Remember," Martin said, "you have the right to be silent."

But Fertig took the pen and began to sign each copy of the confession. When he finished, Donnell took them. They smiled. Fertig relaxed completely now; more and more his feet stretched out and he slumped lower and lower. Donnell picked up the telephone on the cabinet and dialled. He listened. "Was it there?" he asked. "Knows nothing about it?" he asked. "Hang on there and we'll send some people down. Keep everyone out." He hung up. "It's there. Same kind of gun," he told Martin. "Silencer too."

"Of course," Fertig said.

"Where'd you get it?" Martin asked.

"You've got me, what else is necessary?"

"Where?" asked Donnell.

"No one else had anything to do with it, no one at all," Fertig said, trying to sit up straight and sliding a little on the slick leather.

"Not at Abercrombie and Fitch; not that kind of gun," Donnell said. "I got it."

"You know," Donnell told Martin. "I'll bet his wife's in on this ..."

"Must have known," said Martin.

"An accessory. No man could do it alone."

"I got it in a bar," Fertig said.

"He got it in a bar," Donnell said.

"Pick any bar. Fertig goes in blind and says, 'Bartender, I need a gun'."

"Yes, Bartender, where can I contact the underworld?"

"And the bartender he says, 'Anywhere. Don't you read the papers?'" said Martin.

"Yessirreee, you've come to the right place," Donnell chimed in.

"Or maybe he sent his wife."

"I don't want to get anyone in trouble."

Martin looked down at Fertig and said, "Jesus."

Fertig started to try and get up, but Donnell leaned over Fertig, his hands on the arm rests, close. "Come across, Fertig. Where?"

Martin tapped Donnell on the shoulder and Donnell straightened up and let the young man take over. "Look, Mr. Fertig, you won't get anyone in trouble. We have to establish where the gun came from and, for that matter, that no one, including your wife, no one else, helped you. You said you wanted to confess. You did. You have nothing to hide? No? Well, this will clinch it."

"But I told you, I did it myself. I told you how. I told you why. Look, if I told you how I came to understand what must be done, you'd surely see that no one else could have done it …"

"That's not the point. Co-operate with us – just a little more – and if no one helped you do it –"

"No one!"

"… no one will be involved, Harry."

Fertig thought about it. "I got the gun in a bar, in a place called Little Mike's Paradise."

"Where's that?"

"Two blocks from Mercy Memorial Hospital."

"I know the place," Donnell said. "Jesus, how'd you get down there?"

"I found it one night when –"

"I mean *down*" Donnell told Martin. "End of the line. Floozies, hoods, bums, you name it. How'd a guy like you ever…"

"Well, one night –"

"Who gave you the gun?"

"I don't really know …"

"Fertig-g-g."

"I mean, a girl I know there got someone to get it for me, but she didn't give it to me, not directly."

"The gun in the towels bit?"

"Yes."

"What's her name?" Donnell asked.

"Does it matter?"

"What's her name?" asked Martin.

"I won't tell you."

"All right." Then Donnell said to Martin that they would find out from the bartender. Donnell gave Martin another cigarette. Two more policemen came in. The word had got out. Fertig sat, sunk in the leather chair. He munched on the dried cheese Danish and waited. He sipped the sour coffee, made flat by too much evaporated milk, feeling the fuzzy edge of the container against his lips. The door was opening and closing now as policemen went by, stuck their heads in, looked at him, shook their heads as if they couldn't believe it, and went on. There were five uniformed policemen in the room now. The room was heavy and thick with cigarette and cigar smoke.

Someone took the pen out of Fertig's hand. There was a sense of celebration in the air. "All right, take that upstairs," Donnell said while giving a copy to a policeman, and then he let his body completely relax and he had an urge to laugh. Everyone was smiling and friendly now. "Hurry with that coffee, Fertig," said Martin.

Donnell went out of the room saying he'd be right back. He went out, upstairs, and out of the building to a public phone box a block away. He telephoned Roy Bleakie, the criminal lawyer. "Counsellor, we got him."

"Great! Who?"

"Fertig."

"He's who?"

"The big case, Counsellor. Madman slays seven. Biggest manhunt in city's history. Isn't that worth fifty?"

"Forty. Tell."

"Nothing to tell. A complete confession. He wanted revenge for the death of his son – called it criminal neglect – saying the victims were responsible."

"Looney."

"I suppose so. It makes sense in a crazy way."

"Open and shut. A bore, Donnell. Bin in a month."

"It's the way you make the rep, Counsellor."

"I *have* a reputation, Donnell. Thanks anyway."

"Uh ... Counsellor... I tried. You're the first to know ..."

"Thanks. Cheque coming. Keep it up."

"Listen, Counsellor ... he really looks sane. He don't *feel* crazy."

"Thank you, Sigmund Donnell. Thirty. A day after tomorrow's mail. Night."

Damn you, Bleakie bastard, Donnell thought and hung up. He went back.

"How did you find me?" Fertig was asking again.

Martin started to explain, but there was a hum of noise outside the door and it opened. Seven or eight more policemen came in – sergeants, lieutenants, captains, other uniformed men – all older men.

"Why didn't you let me know about this sooner, Donnell?" one of the men snarled.

Donnell shrugged his shoulders. "But we couldn't be sure, Captain. Not until we questioned him and checked things out."

"You're sure? Nothing they can throw out of court?"

"Everything tallies," Donnell said, waving a copy of the confession. "We even have the gun."

"Wise guy," a lieutenant said to him. "All right, get him upstairs and in a hurry. The commissioner's coming down and the D.A. is on the way."

They were pulling Fertig to his feet and handcuffing him to Donnell again and starting out of the door before Fertig knew what was happening. He let the container of coffee splash on the floor somewhere behind him as they all spilled through the door. The corridor outside the interrogating room was full of people. Fertig, shorter than most of them, was a little sunken eddy, towed along while everyone kept talking and standing on their toes, craning, trying to get a look at him. They took him up in the lift; it was crowded with police; everyone else used the stairs.

When they came up, they all piled out of the lift. The corridors were broader here, neater. Men were coming at a run from both ends of the corridor, their feet making drumming sounds, damning up outside the commissioner's office. When they took Fertig in, the commissioner was there, smiling. He looked at Fertig for a second and then shook the hand of a police captain. "I want to congratulate you on your job in catching this man," he said. "This is one of the finest pieces of detection the Police Department has ever done." Everyone was shaking hands and laughing and talking at the same time. Fertig wondered why no one shook Donnell and Martin's hands. "There will be a promotion for everyone involved," the commissioner said. People kept walking over to Fertig and looking into his face. "That's him," someone said. "He doesn't look like much," someone else said. "*That's* the great murderer?" someone asked the head of Donnell and Martin's unit. "Don't kid yourself. Looks are deceiving. He put up quite a little fight, but he gave in when he saw we had him." "Take him and book him and bring him to court," someone said. The mob swirled aimlessly around Fertig for a second, and then reversed its direction and started to break up. The police, with Fertig in tow, were pouring down the corridors again, down in the lift and the stairs, and out through the back way. They bundled him into a police van.

Fertig felt the cold air hit his face as they shoved him into the van. Three other men and their guards were sitting there. The door shut behind and the van started moving. The three criminals gaped at Fertig, unable to take their eyes off him.

There were a few reporters in the lobby of the precinct station-house. They were in the hallway, waiting for Fertig. A photographer took a few pictures. Fertig, surprised, grimaced at the flashes. Martin and Donnell, holding him by the arm and wrist, led by two policemen, followed by two others, pushed their way to the railing of the desk. A sign read "Stand Five Feet behind the Railing." But they all came close. The reporters, not paying attention, crowded around the railing; the photographer came up beside the desk sergeant so that he could get pictures of Fertig standing there. The room reeked of tobacco. Martin and Donnell stood, impassive. Police shoved the reporters away and came and fenced off Martin, Donnell, and Fertig. The sergeant tried to question Fertig; the reporters kept shouting their own questions till the sergeant yelled, "*Be quiet* or I'll shut you out in the cold," and they were quiet again for a while before they started in once more.

"*That* him?" the desk sergeant asked.

Donnell nodded.

"Confession?"

Donnell nodded.

"Name?" the desk sergeant asked Fertig.

Fertig didn't answer, waiting for the detectives to answer for him. Donnell nudged him sharply in the ribs. Behind him he could hear the pounding of feet on the rickety floor as new people kept joining the little crowd. The sergeant recorded it all in the arrest book. As the sergeant wrote, Fertig felt that the recording of it made it irrevocable. He was committed. He was surprised he could be so detached about it, almost watching himself. Someone's voice rang clearly through the noise, sarcastically. "Wild looking, ain't he?"

"Oh, it's them quiet ones every time."

They hustled him away to another part of the building. They fingerprinted him, photographed him, and took him out again. There was even a bigger crowd in the street and a mobile television truck. They followed Fertig with floodlights through the crowd that surged after him. The police tried to move through, pushing, saying again and again, "Come on boys, give us a break, come on. Please, let us through, make way, get out of the way. Watch it. Do you want him to get away? Watch it, watch it, for Christ's sake ..." And a long-armed reporter thrust two photos past Martin's face, pushing them in front of Fertig – pictures of Jenine Carounnbois' bereaved father and of Rabbi Gordon's ancient mother (who knew only that her son was away on a tour of the West) – and a high voice asked, "Don't you feel sorry for them?" Fertig, who had seen the pictures in the papers many times, jerked back. The flashbulbs exploded: Fertig, confused, blinked and grimaced and recoiled, was held and pushed forward, his face twisted, into the pulsating blaze of lights. He started to say, "Yes, I am," and there was a big murmur, almost a roar.

"Do you feel sorry for the deceased?"

"It isn't a matter of feeling sorry –"

"How did you feel when you confronted –"

But Donnell and Martin, their bodies in front of him, pulling him, cleared the way. They put him into the police van again. He was cold and tired and hungry now; he leaned back against the wall between Martin and Donnell, who looked as fresh as when they had come for him. Fertig almost fell asleep.

They nudged him a few minutes later. The van was pulled up in a courtyard. They led Fertig out to the back. Grey light was filtering down along a grey wall, but it was still dark. He didn't know how long it had all been going on.

They signed him over to the Correction Department. Correction guards led him down tiled corridors, past celled doors. They locked him up. He lay down and went to sleep ...

Chapter 4

When Mr. Grenoble came in to work at seven-thirty that morning, he was unaware that anything was wrong. He bought his newspaper as usual and, as always, because of his high blood-pressure condition and his weight problem, debated whether he should have sugar with his coffee, and, as always, picked up a Danish pastry and a container of coffee, light. He looked at the headlines and the front-page photos in the lift. The headline told him that the killer was finally caught. The bastard, he thought – because one of his dearest friends and most cherished associates, Rabbi Gordon, had been assassinated by that butcher. The picture of the killer, an AP torso-shot, showed the man trying to pull loose and attack the photographer. The face was distorted with hate … the mouth open in a terrible snarl, a grimace, a grin, even, of defiance. For a son of a bitch like that killing was too good. Grenoble folded the paper and put it under his arm and went out of the lift and into his office.

Even though he was a rich man, many times over, Mr. Grenoble came in early every day. "I couldn't sleep late if I wanted to," he often said; "I'm just not constituted that way." He walked through his deserted office and into his own private office. He put the bag with the coffee and the Danish pastry and the paper on the blotting pad, took off his coat and jacket together and hung them on the coat-rack in the corner. He never wore a jacket when he worked. He walked over to the window and looked out. The view was towards the west; he could see, between the pylons of bigger and blocking windows, still-shadowed fragments of the Hudson and the place where the Palisades began their rise northward: they were catching morning sunlight and all the reflecting surfaces; window, cars moving, chrome bits twinkled. Beautiful, he sighed, and went back to his desk and sat down and looked at the paper. Killer caught. He reached for the bag.

He was about to turn to the stock-market section. What kind of a bastard could shoot a man like that down, a saint? The kind of man whose mouth was curled back in a snarl; the kind of man who you could see didn't care for anything or anyone in the world: the mouth was open – a crazy grin … sparkle of light on the teeth – it jeered, All right, what are you going to do about it? Killer brought to bay,' a lead said; killer doesn't repent. Burn him; it was the only way, Grenoble thought; hang him. End of Long Manhunt: hate on the face of the killer, body lunging forward as if to assault the world, trying to break loose from the grip of detectives.

"Harry Fertig, a Brooklyn accountant, was tracked down at last in the greatest manhunt in the annals of New York City …"

Grenoble's body reacted. His heart began to beat fast. He became a little dizzy … as if he was passing out – a diabetic coma – like he was going to have a heart attack. Be calm, he told himself; be calm. He sat there trembling and looking at the picture, hand to his heart, as if the fingers, clawing in past the shirt-lip and digging into the under-shirt, pinching the plump flesh, could hold the beat of his heart down to steadiness. And he could feel the blood beginning to pound in his head like it always did when he got furious. Impossible! He looked at the picture. Another man. A physical impossibility. He got up and went to the window and looked out. The Hudson flowing. The lights reflected … sun from New Jersey. No clouds. A beautiful day. Impossible. He opened the catch on the window and pushed the lou-vred pane up. He felt a little dizzy and breathed in deeply. Better. He went back to the desk and looked down at the photograph. Couldn't be.

But when he looked again, calmer, when he read a little, though he still really couldn't recognize the picture, he saw it was Fertig. Same address. Wife, Sara, at the D.A.'s for questioning … denies knowl-edge … an accountant. He had to leave. He looked at the face. But that hardened-criminal's face – that crazy sneer – and he couldn't stop trembling. Why was he trembling? Did he expect Fertig, also once an early bird, to come in, per usual, and say, "Good morning, Mr. Grenoble, here are the figures for …" as he had for more than twelve years? Nonsense. He hadn't seen Fertig in six, seven months.

He tried to read it. Little phrases came through to him; words, sen-tences, somehow all familiar, yet not making sense – too frightening, much too frightening, his whole world going up, exposed … He put the paper down, flat, smoothed it, put on his desk-light, and looked again. The picture. Criminal defies police. Mass murderer says, "I'd do it again. They deserved to be killed," and doesn't feel sorry for vic-tims or their relatives. His friend, *his* friend, Rabbi Oscar Gordon, *he deserved* to be killed? Fertig killed Gordon? Planned it for a year, He trembled; he was frightened. Why was he frightened? Was it because Fertig must have been in the office while he was planning? They had disagreed. *He had* actually *argued back* with that madman! And you never knew what a man like that could say … But who could know? Who could know? Who could know that while he argued that the man was planning … ? He looked at the picture: the glasses, the little mous-tache, the narrow face – but yet, so different; of course, leaning into the photograph it made him look so much bigger, menacing.

Fertig had been picked up last night: he would be arraigned at ten or eleven that morning, as soon as Court opened. That meant they would be coming to see *him* – police, reporters, the rest of them. And *that* was what that call made yesterday had meant – not another employer, but the police checking on Fertig. Sure, Grenoble thought, he was crazy, nutty, but who could know? Did Harry Fertig give even one little sign? No. Never. Who would know? What should he do then? And what had Fertig done while he had been here? What if a man like that carried a grudge for some crazy reason? What mischief could he do? And to think how close to death he might have been God-knows-how-many times?

Grenoble looked quickly through the paper. They re-ran biographies of the slain. Fertig was quoted as saying that he had no feeling of remorse for his act – after all, they were total strangers to him. His blown-up picture was shown next to theirs with the caption. "They had a rendezvous with a killer." An aerial map of New York with an overlay of printed dots was entitled "Operation Fertig". Marvin Morgan had this to say in his column: "Sensible people are being asked to go against their common sense and believe that it was possible for a man who had no previous criminal record, no record of even *handling* firearms, to become a highly trained killer. There is more to this case than meets the eye. A source close to the FBI has informed Your Reporter that the confession is a blind. There may be – hold on to your hats, kids – COMMIE INVOLVEMENTS." Grenoble slammed the paper on the desk: What next? Were they all going mad? Fertig? A killer? A Communist?

What was he waiting for? How long could he sit there shaking like an old man? He took his address book out of his drawer, looked through it, found the number, and called up his close friend, a friend with connections – all kinds – knowhow, a political *macher*. "I know it's early, Irving, but you know I wouldn't bother you if it wasn't an emergency … No, I'm not in trouble. Listen, that lawyer, the famous one, the criminal one, your friend, what's his name? Roy Bleakie? No, I can't wait! Yes, even at home … Can I use your name? No, I'm not in trouble. Laugh, go ahead, enjoy. What are you saying? Bite your tongue! I can't say yet, but you'll know about it very soon, believe me. Very funny, Irving the joker. But if I'm an embezzler, then what are you? Fine, you're a pal. Listen, I told you, you'll learn before the day is out. No, Herby is not in trouble – how can you say a thing like that? I'll talk to you. Be good. I *am* good, you crazy cocker. Regards to your lovely missus. Together? Sure. Soon."

The reaction had been quick enough. He was functioning. His heart was a little calmer now, thank God. If you survived the first excitement you were all right. He opened the container of coffee and took a sip; it was almost cold now. He dialled. His voice was calm now, composed, deep, almost seductive. "Listen, I'm sorry to call you so early in the morning, but this is an emergency."

A grunt. Quiet. He heard breathing.

"Irving Hockstaff said I could count on you. I'm Jack Grenoble. Maybe you've heard of me?"

He listened and heard his own asthmatic breathing. He heard his bookkeeper, Mrs. Futterman, come in and wished for once she wasn't so diligent; diligence he didn't need today. "Hello? Hello? This is Roy Bleakie?" His voice was a little higher, a little more urgent.

"Roy Bleakie has an office. Hours."

"I know, I know, and I wouldn't for the world bother you if it wasn't important, Mr. Bleakie, not for the world."

"Give."

"I presume you've seen the papers, Mr. Bleakie?"

"*This* hour?"

"Well, let me fill you in. They've arrested the man who killed those seven people – a terrible thing – and one of them was a close friend and spiritual adviser, Rabbi Gordon, you know of him? A wonderful man, a saint. And ..." He was getting excited. Calm yourself, he thought, and lowered his voice.

"I know."

"Well, the criminal is a man called Fertig. Harry Fertig."

"So?"

"Well, this man worked for me for many years. In fact he was with me until only about six, seven months ago. It's hard to believe, but it says here in the paper that he confessed –"

"Beat it out of him."

"How do you know that, Mr. Bleakie?"

"Way of talking. So?"

"Well, not only did he work for me, but – well, this man was my chief accountant for many years; in fact the corporation made him comptroller last year, before he left."

"And?"

"I would like you to undertake his defence, Mr. Bleakie."

"It'll cost."

"I understand. Of course. Anything ... within reason. I understand you're a highly important man – a busy man ... I'm not a rich man, Mr. Bleakie, but I understand the value of an hour –"

"Don't con. Isn't a poor case. Roy Bleakie is not the poor man's lawyer."

"I understand. I understand, but how can you desert a man who was your best accountant for many years?" He looked down at the picture; he moved the paper around. It was a little more recognizable looking. They always loused-up newspaper photographs. "More than an employee, a personal friend ..."

"A retainer of three thousand

"That's a lot of money, Mr. Bleakie."

"... to begin with. Hard case."

"Of course the poor man lost his mind. His baby died, you see, and he wanted revenge; just lost his mind."

"Sure. You defend him, you know so much."

"I'm sorry. But, well, they were very attached to that child, too much if you ask me, but then it was their only one – and so late in life and I've seen such things before." He was excited again. "At least I have three."

"Yes?"

And he was calm; his voice was smooth. He would keep it that way. If any panic could be detected in his voice – well, Bleakie didn't know him and under the circumstances, who would help being excited? You work with a man, practically live with him, he, even, my God, does your personal income tax, is like a son to you, and knows, in certain cases, more about you than your own wife does ... He was definitely calmer. Could that demented face, straining defiantly, murderously forward be ... When had he ever seen Fertig like that? A little excited maybe, like the time he argued with Fertig. No. It was always Harry with the shy smile, at best, Harry with the worried look; on the other hand – no, *that* was Fertig; a little smile, a worried look, practically a *nebbish*.

But when he was going off his chump, how had Fertig looked at Grenoble? And when had that begun? Fertig walking through the office, glancing at him... Harry bending over the books, looking up at him, a sly look (?)... Harry arguing with him:

"Fertig, I was hoping not to have to say anything about it; I was hoping you'd snap out of it; but, Fertig, listen, your work is getting sloppier, weaker. You're behind. You're making mistakes. I find cigarette ashes in the books. Fertig, this thing is upsetting you – rightly so; the loss of a son is a terrible thing, but you got to get hold of yourself. How long do you mourn? Fertig, we can't make mistakes; you know what I mean."

"I don't make mistakes, Mr. Grenoble," Harry snapped back just like that.

Defiance from a man who never defied – cool words. Murderer's words. Madman's words. He had actually *fought* with this man! But who could know? The memory, the echo of those words, chilled him.

"Well, you know, Mr. Bleakie, that Fertig was in his forties; his wife, too. They had their kid late in life. It meant everything to them. You should have seen the change in him. You can understand what a terrible blow losing their child was...

"Sure." "A tragedy. Something snapped."

"Don't know. Not easy. Prove insanity...

"My God, isn't it obvious. I knew that boy like a son. We had him up to the house. I felt, actually, he was a fourth child. But you could see it coming."

"Proof. Legal proof. Witnesses. Outraging crime. Doctors. Famous rabbi. Innocents. Public indignation. Grounds for keeping the death penalty. Burn him. Cool, unrepentant killer. Malice aforethought, know what I mean? Have to disprove. Lot of legwork. Dig back, dig back. Witnesses. Not 'I saw' or 'I didn't see' witnesses. Also professional opinions. Cost a lot, not only in paying, you understand, but in time spent away from my other cases…"

"I'd be glad to – no one understands the value of time more than I do – I mean feel free – I'll be more than happy to testify myself. After all, he was my indispensable – you could see it coming – he could make the figures sing – a once in a lifetime genius…"

"Then why'd you let him go?"

"That's what I mean, the actions of a crazy man… arguments… At first, when he came back to work – only a week after the funeral, maybe he should have stayed home? – I thought he had made a remarkable adjustment. We all bent over backwards, you know. We were sympathetic – a terrible thing – we watched over him. Sure, we're a corporation, but we're also a family."

"He adjusted?"

"That's what I'm trying to tell you. He came to me and said, 'You've been kind, Mr. Grenoble, but you don't have to worry. I *want* to work! I *need* to work'." Grenoble remembered the thin pale face thinner, the glittering eyes, like he had a fever… "I told him, 'That's it, Harry, bury yourself in your work and, after all, you have to accept – God takes, God gives – you take your beating and cut your losses'."

"What did Fertig reply when you said that? How did he look?"

"I told him, 'After all, you're not an old man. Life goes on. You can have another child'."

"But he didn't," Bleakie said.

"I suppose they tried, but that's the way life is."

"And."

"He threw himself into his work. He went over the old records; I can't begin to tell you what he did: a complete and total re-auditing. I made him comptroller, Mr. Bleakie, not that he didn't deserve it, not out of charity. But then, gradually, something began to happen. He began to change. We argued now and then. He would be daydreaming, like a zombie. How long can you mourn? I said, 'Fertig, snap out; accept'. You could see it coming." If you knew, Grenoble thought.

"Hardly evidence, Mr. Grenoble."

"But there were other things. Why should he pick fights with me? I was good to him."

"See?" Bleakie said. "Statements like that are not enough. Lots and lots of statements like that, circumstantial – maybe it adds to proof. Time. Footwork. Digging. Money, Mr. Grenoble, money."

"Oh, I could tell you things, now that I think about it… Listen. You could see it coming *from the day of the funeral*!"

"Come on. You know better."

"No. No. I just reminded myself. Listen: I drove around to offer my condolences; you understand. I remember it particularly because I had to drive around the block three times; you see, I have this Cadillac and they're not easy to park. Finally I said the hell with it and double-parked. I went in. I shook everyone's hand. It was a terrible moment. The wife's mother was weeping. They were all so sad. You know, I offered condolences. We had a drink. It was a terrible time. 'Can I tell you how sorry I am, Harry,' I said. 'You know what we all think of you; the whole office feels with you, Harry.' And it cost me so much pain, that moment, I thought I was going to have an attack. I told him to drink up and forget. I told him, 'Listen, Harry, take as much time as you need'. It was terrible. And his wife, she was sitting, a zombie. And some loud-mouth, I hear him say, 'Couldn't they sue?' No consideration. It wasn't the time and it wasn't the place. People, they have no sense. Anyway, you can't sue doctors or hospitals, because I don't have to tell you it's impossible to win that kind of negligence. Where's the negligence? I told him, Harry, if the Good Lord sees fit ... What can we do, Harry, what can we do? And then the loudmouth says, 'Believe me, I'm sure they'd pay plenty to keep a thing like this out of the papers – a scandal.' Well, then Harry said something that showed me he was taking it hard, too hard – I should have sensed ..."

"What?"

"He said, 'There is no way of amortizing the life of a child, is there, Mr. Grenoble?' I said, 'I don't understand, Harry'. And he said something like, you can't declare that he cost so much and then divide that amount by his legal existence or by his estimated useful life, and at the end say, there he is, he's dead but accounted for, written off; you can't because you should figure on that ultimate loss, shouldn't you? I remember it clearly. The reason I remember such a thing is that I never heard him talk like that, never. And he had this funny look in his eyes. What kind of talk was that? I'll tell you the kind of talk it was, it was crazy man's talk."

"Not in court, Mr. Grenoble."

"I told him, 'Don't take it so, Harry; time heals', and then I hear some other loudmouth saying, 'Well, the house is nice, but it's too big for only two, but what with the *schwartzes* and the spics moving up the Slope, I don't think he could get rid of it so easily.' Terrible. Now I know: he didn't weep, he kept it in, and that's why it led to this terrible thing. Now me, I happen to be a very emotional man, I'm not ashamed –"

"Ready to testify?"

"What a question! He was like a son to me. A terrible thing. Listen, I have to tell you something else."

"What?"

"You know I actually *insisted* that Fertig go to see Oscar, Rabbi Gordon, for spiritual comfort. I could kick myself. But how could I have known?" Yes, he thought, this was the recognizable Fertig now – in the photo flash making his glasses look blank, that snarl on his face. So who was the man who had moved through his office? Who was the man who had said, coldly furious for the first time in their career together, "I don't make mistakes." What revenge had that stranger taken on him? He felt it; he knew it. "And listen, Mr. Bleakie…"

"Yes?"

"I should like that my name be kept entirely out of this." Had he said it calmly enough? Was he detached-sounding, charitable even? No fast heart-pounding, no trembling, no blood flowing through the temples.

"Oh?"

"I'll testify. I just mean that I don't want anyone should know I'm paying for his defence."

"Really? Why? A feather in your cap."

Was the voice a little more alert now, a little more sceptical? They were both men of the world – how else could they have succeeded? They knew one another. They both knew about altruism. Grenoble groped for a reasonable explanation. "Well, you know how it is … it's a duty to a friend, a close friend, practically a son." That didn't sound right. "It's just the way I'd like it done." No, not this way – so lame. "I hate publicity." Not this way either. "All right, I'll tell you. Rabbi Gordon was a close friend. Also he was a very important personage. I belonged to his temple, I was on committees with him, we did a lot of charity work together on Sons of Charity. How would it look if they knew I was giving money to defend his murderer?"

"I see."

The voice sounded sceptical. Grenoble quickly said, "In fact, in some crazy way, I almost feel responsible for his death."

"I see."

He tried to estimate how the voice sounded, what it meant, whether it accepted the explanation. Surely Roy Bleakie was smart enough to know, as he himself knew, that no one ever did anything for nothing. "You see, I was instrumental in their getting together. Even in Harry's going to see him. What happened was, we went to this dinner – Sons of Charity had a fundraising affair – and Rabbi Gordon spoke. He had a silver tongue, a silver tongue. Well, Harry was so moved – you could see that – that then Harry made an appointment with him. Well, I didn't get to talk to Harry about it, but something had happened. 'What happened?' I asked. 'Nothing,' Harry said. But he had this tight-lipped way, you know?" "No."

"Well, I never looked into it, but – come to think of it, it was after that. Oh, why didn't I call Rabbi Gordon to ask? Why?" His voice trembled. "But who knows what goes on in a crazy man's mind? Can he help himself?"

"No."

"I'm sure that if anyone can save that poor boy from – well, save him – you're that man."

There was a little laugh at the other end, almost a bark, really. "That convinced me, Mr. G., Roy Bleakie can do it."

"I'll make out a cheque right away and put it in the mail."

"Be prepared," Roy Bleakie's voice told him. "The newspapers will be coming soon."

"What should I say?"

"The truth. A son to you. A poor sick boy, a driven man. The whole thing," the voice said sardonically.

"It's God's honest truth, Mr. Bleakie."

"Who said it wasn't? See you."

Chapter 5

... and was wakened immediately.

They led Fertig down the corridor to a door. He said he wanted to wash himself, but no one paid attention to him. Martin and Donnell were waiting for him; he wondered why they'd taken him and brought him right back; he was almost relieved to see them. Donnell pushed a door open and they walked, Martin in front and Donnell behind, towards the courtroom. A wall clock said eleven-thirty; Fertig thought he'd only slept a few minutes. His suit was rumpled, his tie askew; he needed a shave; he felt dirty.

An enormous crowd, waiting for Fertig, was there, extending all the way to the back, packed tightly into the huge room, overflowing into the hallway. Max Grinzing, a columnist on the *Afternoon Staff*, towering over most of the people, was holding forth: "The wonder of the case is not that it happened but that it doesn't happen every day. The marvel is that more people aren't outraged at being treated like ciphers in a vast, dehumanized statistical world. And you know who's to blame: the hospitals are to blame; the doctors are to blame."

"Now I've seen some cold ones in my time," the D.A., MacGruder, began softly, making the reporters lean towards him; "but..."

"You know, while he was telling us what he did to the Malabar woman, he was grinning, actually grinning," the commissioner of police was saying.

"... those calm skinny guys with high foreheads are wire-rimmed glasses – you can smellum out..."

An irate little man with frizzed white hair and rimless glasses fussed angrily at his desk, adjusting a stenotype machine. Reporters were shouting and MacGruder was slowly working himself up.

"... who has not suffered." Max Grinzing asked the tops of heads, "the indignity and absurdity of having to fill out forms while we are in pain? The hospitals are a disgrace and everyone knows it. People wait in pain for hours in the clinics. The help is underpaid, therefore negligent. Emergency situations – we know about those. Sterile procedure is a joke. Let me tell you that there are many rejections and at least ten of those a month lead to death. Ten. It is a civil disgrace..."

"... latest methods of crime detection; we constructed the case from the faintest, believe me, but the coldest clues ... What? No, I can't reveal our methods."

"And if it is a principle of justice that innocent men go free, even if nine guilty men have to go free too, why where public medicine is concerned is this reversed? No one cares for the individual as long as the mass is served. Isn't it possible to serve both mass and..."

"One of these days you're going to go too far, Grinzing," Marvin Morgan snarled. "You're inciting to riot."

"There he is," someone shouted and everyone started to talk loudly and look Fertig's way.

"... I'll tell you what he is, he's a hero, an existential hero," Grinzing shouted as the crowd surged underneath his shoulders and away from him. "HERO!" he shouted at the backs of their heads.

The reporters were shouting and the D.A. was deserted by the circlet of reporters as he was saying, "Cunning ... malevolent ... criminal ..." at the height of his peroration, and the police commissioner found himself only with his assistants just as he was telling to whom the reward might go; and he turned to the front of the room where, far above the little man and his stenotype machine, and behind the Bench, brass letters affixed between two Greek false pilasters said "In God We Trust"; risen high above the great hum of voices, above the milling of people, above the reporters and photographers – themselves all over and behind the Bench, on the desks of the magistrate and the court attendant – and above the strident voices yelling for "Quiet". "Quiet". "Quiet". "Quiet".

Words yammered into Fertig's ears; "How did you do it... why did you do it... have you anything to say ... please look this way, Fertig, smile Fertig just another one Fertig did you think that when this way FertigjustanotheroneFertigthat'sit-smile..."

Finally it became quiet.

"Everyone stand," a voice boomed. They started talking again.

Words kept beating at him; he made no sense of them. He tried to adjust his tie; his hands were pushed down; he was photographed. The gavels pounded. It became quiet again. Another little man with a great stiff brush of hair, pompadoured, wearing thick, horn-rimmed glasses, holding himself as tall as he could, his hands under his stomach as if he were holding his abdomen in a black sack, strode up to the little platform and to his seat behind the enormous desk. The court attendant intoned the words in a rapid, concerned mutter; the words rose and fell in a tired litany; the words "County of ... Felony Court ... term ... JUDGE CLEMENTE PRESIDING..." emerged from the ritual mutter.

Donnell got up and gave papers to the man in uniform. The attendant gave it to the magistrate. They whispered. "What's happening?" Fertig asked Martin. Martin didn't answer; he stood stiffly and faced the judge and felt the warming lights of the flashbulbs beating on his grave, proud face. The magistrate waved his hand, gesturing them to come up closer. Feet rustled behind him. Furniture creaked. Voices whispered. Out of the corner of his eye, Fertig could see the photographers all manoeuvering for position, all again creeping up the sides of the Bench till they were standing right beside the magistrate, almost blocking his vision.

"Are you aware of what his happening?" the magistrate asked, speaking gently. Fertig nodded. "Speak up," the magistrate said a little louder.

"Yes, Your Honour," Fertig told him. The magistrate looked satisfied; then he noticed the photographers standing beside him, and so stood up and pounded and yelled, "Behind the railing, behind the railing. What is this, a travesty?"

"Do you understand the nature of these proceedings?" Judge Clemente asked. "Where's your lawyer?"

"I have none, Your Honour," Fertig told him.

"Get a lawyer! Get a lawyer! We can't go on here without a lawyer!" The voice of the judge was sharp again. Someone yelled "Legal Aid!" Someone began to run up the aisle, and returned with a tired, grey man in a crumpled suit. Fertig started to say something. "Hello Willie," Judge Clemente said.

The man nodded at the judge. "I am lawyer Singleton from Legal Aid and am willing to represent Mr ..."

"I know, I know," the judge said. Fertig tried to say something. "Now then," the judge seemed to gather himself in. He sat straight in his seat.

"May I have time to consult with my client and apprise him of his rights?" Singleton asked. The judge was annoyed at the interruption; he started to say something, but the court attendant leaned over to him and whispered something into his ear. The judge nodded. "You may, but make it quick. Don't make a production of it. We have no time. It's high time we brought this man to the bar of justice."

Fertig said, "Your Honour ..."

"What is it?" Judge Clement snapped. "What is it;"

"I don't want a lawyer."

"You have a lawyer? I thought you said you had no lawyer."

"I don't want a lawyer." Fertig smiled. A little sick with weariness, he had to force himself to stand as tall as he could, to say it clearly above the great hum, to insist when the hum became louder. Groggy, he was sure now he hadn't slept for more than twenty-four hours. He really wanted to say so much more, to tell them why he decided not to use a lawyer: "Your Honour, I want to defend myself."

"Listen Fertig, you're not going to pull any fast ones here, no sir. You have certain rights and you are going to enjoy those rights, Fertig –"

"But –"

"DON'T INTERRUPT THE COURT! I know your game. Well, it's not going to work. We're going to have due process here and we are going to cross the *t*'s and dot the *i*'s –"

"But I don't understand, Your Honour."

"QUIET! If you had a lawyer you'd understand. I know your game. You're going to scream that you were denied representation! Retrial. Waste of the taxpayers' money. It won't work, Fertig. We get your sort here every day."

"Your Honour," Singleton said. "If the man says he does not want Legal Aid to represent him, then Legal Aid cannot help him."

Judge Clemente made a motion and the clerk stopped transcribing; he waved to Singleton, who came up to the bench. "Singleton, are you trying to remind me of the rules, right here in my own court?" he asked, dangerously. "You stand by him till we get this formality over with. Don't you worry, he'll have his proper presentation; it'll cost the tax-payers enough as it is. Don't you worry, Singleton." The judge nodded and the clerk resumed his transcribing.

"Fertig, step up here." Fertig stood a little closer. "Are you aware of what is happening here today?" Fertig said yes. "You have been charged with having taken life. You have confessed that you have killed ... killed ... ?" The court attendant whispered into his ear. "All right. All right. Seven people," Judge Clemente shouted, turning to the court and talking over Fertig's head. "Have you confessed of your own free will? No one has coerced you in any way, form, manner, or shape?" Fertig nodded. "SPEAK UP!" Clemente barked; he looked down at Fertig; he saw that the criminal's eyes were bright, dangerous and that he needed a shave.

"Your Honour, I'd like to say something."

"Wait."

"But this trial –"

"This is an arraignment, Fertig, not a trial. You'll get your chance. Now answer the questions."

"No, Your Honour, I have confessed of my own free will." The noise broke out again and Clemente, red-faced and furious, began to pound his gavel. "Now listen carefully, Fertig. Were you told by the police that you had the right to silence till you had representation? That means you could have talked to your lawyer. You didn't have to tell the police a thing. Did they tell you this?"

Fertig said, "Yes."

"You're sure now. Think. There were no … deals of any sort, no … pressure."

"None, Your Honour."

"Do you understand what I'm asking you?"

"Yes, Your Honour. I confessed. I did it."

The noise started again. The photographers, crouching low, ran up together in front of Fertig, stood up, one facing Fertig the other Clemente. Clemente tightened his jaw, lifted his head, and looked towards the top of the back of the courtroom. Fertig squinted and tried, too late, to duck the blinding light. Blinking, Fertig started to continue talking, but Clemente was intoning…

"It is my duty to sit here in judgment on a crime that has been committed, a crime of such gravity, of such a nature as to defy the annals of crime. A crime that pales even the excesses of the Nazis into significance. A crime that…" Someone's sigh sounded through the courtroom. "Are you aware …" Fertig nodded. "WAIT TILL I'M FINISHED!" Clemente shouted.

"What are you, a wise guy? You have been brought here before the bar of justice and stand there, hardened and impenitent. I'm used to criminals like you. We'll show a man like you what you're up against. You'll smile out of the other side of your mouth, believe me," Clemente screamed. Fertig wondered, half-sleepily, why they were screaming at him. He tried to pay attention.

"… killed. Shot in cold blood. This could only be the work of a master criminal who was motivated by a twisted and diseased brain, a brain so warped that it could lead him to do something so heinous, so malevolent, and so many times…" They all laughed behind Fertig. Clemente smiled and looked pleased. "… the work of a maniac, the work of a cold killer, the work of an evil and possessed man …"

Far in the back, Max Grinzing shouted, "J'accuse!" pointing towards the court.

"Throw that man out! Throw that man out!"

"Once more the voices of truth and justice are stilled," Grinzing intoned as he was borne off and out through the court-room doors.

Judge Clemente waited till it was silent and began again in the same loud tone on which he had left off. The phrases came tumbling out of the judge. He worked himself up to a frenzy; there was a froth of spittle at the corners of his lips; he was shouting, leaning over the desk-top, waving his clenched fist rhythmically at Fertig while the court attendant plucked at his robe, trying to pull him back to his seat. He alternated between fits of hysteria and a calm, judicial comportment. He seized the moment and jumbled phrases: the nature of Justice, Crime, Insanity, Man, the District Attorney, the Police Department, the Citizens huddled in terror. He spoke for half an hour while Fertig waited for the moment to tell his story. They calmed Judge Clemente when he was hoarse. The audience broke out into applause and snickers. He composed himself to look strong and noble.

Fertig asked, "May I say something, Your Honour?"

"You'll get your chance to talk later on. If you'd taken a lawyer you'd know this."

"But –"

"Quiet!" Clemente yelled. "I am," Clemente intoned, "going to send you to the psychiatric ward of the City Hospital for observation ..." District Attorney MacGruder rose, outraged.

"I am going to recommend the case to the grand jury and ask that a true bill be handed down."

The court stenographer looked surprised. Fertig was shocked. Why were they sending him to the City Hospital. "May I ask something, Your Honour?"

"What is it? What is it? I told you to get a lawyer. Singleton. ..."

"Your Honour, why am I being sent to the psychiatric ward? There's nothing wrong with me."

"That, my friend, is precisely what they will find out in the hospital. Are you presuming to tell the court what to do? I'll have you for contempt. Kills seven and says there is nothing wrong with him."

Fertig started to say something, but Clemente got up suddenly and went down from the bench while the attendant intoned "Dismissed".

Donnell and Martin took Fertig to the door at the back and handed him over to the Department of Correction. They brought him down the back way, half-dragged him into another van, which drove off.

Chapter 6

Onofrio Candell's dream of golden dust had been disturbed the night before when he thought he saw a familiar face, a face he had seen in yesterday's newspapers. The face had peered at him; the night light and television glow silvered the man's glasses and he tried to talk to him, whoever it was. He hadn't been able to. It had been too much trouble and he relapsed into the golden phantasmagoria and dreamed of precious things the rest of the night. Now he was coming out of it slowly. He looked at the window in the morning, having a moment's drab lucidity, and remembered that the face in the newspapers was the face of Fertig; the face in the dream was something like Fertig's but richer, much richer. Had they brought Fertig down here? It was a figment, he told himself, a rich figment of a tortured dream. For Fertig there could only be the iron prison cell, the trip upstate to the penitentiary after the trial, and the final expiation when they strapped him into the chair, and all the world would watch while Fertig went up burning richly like the sunflames firing all the metal fixtures, all around the room. He shook his head. He could hardly move. The bastards had strap – him in.

He called the ceiling, shouted up at the lights, wired-in for protection from the inmates, "Aw, c'mon Hans. Let me. I want up." He was not ready. All that came out of his throat, even though he said it slowly, clearly, in silver, ringing tones, was a jumbled mass: mud muttered through batting; grunting. He broke into a sweat and shut his still-dilated eyes against the morning light. It was the way it was every morning: the sun streaming in through the barred windows, making everything bright, golden, cheerful, almost happy. Everything glittered because they made all the boys except the black stiff clean up. The ingots on the windows broke up the great beams of light, by prisming the glow into precious fragments and segmented sun gems. It was easier now. Iron-minded Hans, the guard, had been good to him. It was a great fix, very pure stuff. But how, he wondered, would he pay for the next one; Outside, a cloud hovered for a little while and hid all the precious light.

Across the way from him, sitting upright, stiff, and cross-legged, was a slender Negro stripped to the waist; from the waist up the body was turned, the head strained around, the mouth open in a frozen yell, his arm thrust out, a finger pointing, each muscle strained in the direction of the point. When you saw him for the first time you couldn't help looking at what he was pointing at: even now Onofrio would find himself looking, following the finger's lead. The black evil stiff. The Stiff was unmoving, never moving, carved out of unmobile onyx, unhealing and uncaring. Every morning, every noon, and every night they fed him, spooning food into his wide-open mouth. Every night they put him to sleep. He sat, frozen but striving, which was somehow irritating to Onofrio.

Onofrio had his own therapy. He told Hans they should shoot the Stiff full of dust, hook him, and let him take the long horse ride down over golden and green grounds and into the ruby-tinged clouds and through ivory castles; next time the Stiff needed a fix he would come out of it; he would never turn catatonic – that was the word the fat know-it-all Hamisbat, at the other end of the ward, had for him – again. Onofrio knew. They had done it to *him*. He tried again. "Hans, c'mon Hans, let me up." It sounded clearer; but turning to look at the desk at the head of the room, where Iron Hans sat, he saw that his voice didn't have the carrying power. Hans was sitting and listening dreamily, his fat red face almost blank, to some disc jockey spinning out all the old songs. Iron Hans went in big for the old songs.

A lot of beds were empty. Onofrio turned and looked at the bed on his left. Someone had slept in it. He wasn't dreaming and the thought of Fertig *here* began to excite him. He had never known anyone who had made it as big as Fertig. It also worried him because he had seen the fix-hungry faced of Fertig drawn and distorted in a snarl in yesterday's paper: the teeth showed, the brows above the wire-framed glasses were twisted, the eyes stared wildly, full of hate, the cheeks were pulled back – going cold turkey in the hands of the law. He turned back and looked towards the door. Iron Hans was sitting there quietly. Above the door, set on a platform, the television set, shielded in a cage of fine chicken-wire kept playing endlessly; it went on morning, noon, and all night; it was supposed to soothe them all.

Kaprelic was doing his penance, walking up and down the aisle between the rows of beds. He was tall and thin, his flesh eaten away by age and belief. Religious nut; crucifixes and prayer. Kaprelic took great care not to step on the light-bars cast through the window frames; it made his walk jerky and his whole body danced to a rhythm that Onofrio could never understand. "What do you get out of it? What dance do you make?" he once asked the old man. Kaprelic waved a crucifix made out of soap at him and he jumped away. "Loony!" Onofrio called after the muttering, hand-waving skeleton.

"Debased savage. Pig. Low, sinning pig," the old man growled at him and hurried on his perpetual walk.

Another time, Onofrio, beginning to feel his own insatiable call, tried to load *need* on someone else's back and taunted Kaprelic. "What do you want to be when you grow up?"

Kaprelic stopped in the middle of his stride, his left leg half-suspended in the air, his arms still flapping, his institutional pyjamas too loose, ragged, and ruffled, and looked ecstatically over Onofrio's head and into the paled light of the television set and said, "A saint".

Onofrio was impressed. He had prayed to the Mother, God, Jesus, and all the saints when he was a kid; his mother made him. The saints, who were once men and who had done things just as loony as Kaprelic, were now close to God. Men and especially all the women in black like his mother prayed to the saints and gave them money, and that made the saints powerful: them or the saints' bagmen. He remembered all the money that was laid at the feet of the saints. It always disappeared. Maybe it was, he thought, that saints used all the devotional loot to dream always in the golden dust that is the speech of God, the turquoise clouds that are the breath of Jesus, or the sapphire love of Mary Mother. He was mixed up them; it was so unclear then. But he knew this: if Kaprelic made it and became a saint, Kaprelic would have money, more than enough, and perhaps he would spare a little for a poor sinner who also wanted to dream in the golden dust of God.

He shook his head and watched Kaprelic walking up and down and heard his whining voice rising and falling, pleading with God, brushing the lank white hair out of his face with a careless gesture that smudged soap across his forehead. Whenever Kaprelic became too excited, Iron Hans would tell him, "Calm down, Pop". And if Kaprelic didn't calm down, Iron Hans would get up and walk up the aisle till he would stand in front of the old man and hit him once, twice, three times, till the old man understood and prayed in a more reasonable tone. He tried again. "Hans, let me up. Be a good guy." Hans didn't hear.

At the other end, the fat man, Hamisbat, sat at his station, the window. Onofrio hated Hamisbat for knowing everything and having the wise-guy look. Hamisbat was fat but managed to look neat, even in the pyjamas the city provided. He spent his time staring out of the window, looking down at the East River and the Drive or at the buildings over in Queens. Or he would light an expensive cigar and sit, thinking hard till he seemed to disappear in a cloud of smoke. In the evenings he would try to talk to them even after lights-out. "Does Onofrio know why he's here? Does he understand what's happening to him?"

"Sure," Onofrio told Hamisbat. "I know exactly why I'm here."

And Hamisbat would look at him pityingly and shake his head in the tester's wise-guy way, and then laugh and turn away to look out the window.

"All right, if you know so much, tell me."

And Hamisbat would say, "But that would count against Onofrio, wouldn't it?"

What did that mean? Sometimes Hamisbat would sit and sleep in his chair by the window till it was morning. Did he spy all night?

A little further down towards the door, there was a wild Puerto Rican whom they'd brought in a few days ago. He tried to jump off the Williamsburg Bridge after killing his family. He almost succeeded: after jumping and falling, he was only to be caught by a rope someone slipped around his foot. The police, to teach him a lesson, had let him dangle there, high in the air, arcing slowly around and around over the river hundreds of feet below for ten minutes while he screamed and whimpered and struggled as they kept telling him, "Let that be a lesson to you, you bastard. Are you going to try that again?" Not that it mattered. He sat there on his bed, holding tightly to the shining aluminium framework at the head of the bed. He even ate his food now with one hand, holding on with the other. They had to beat him loose to get him to the john twice a day. They were going to send him to the State Bin, Onofrio thought, and he would be better off there.

Around eleven, the sunlight began to pass over the building and the light came down straight, passing between the drifting clouds like downthrust bars probing the earth. The light coming into the ward was reduced to one last ingot deposited at the foot of each window. Kaprelic, having washed himself for the fifth time, diminishing his day's crucifix, walked now in shadow more smoothly. Onofrio called out five or six times more, but Hans was iron and didn't pay attention. He was starting to get thirsty. It was mean of Hans to tie him down that way; Iron Hans knew when he had his fix he never caused any trouble. It was a dirty trick. His body was beginning to twitch a little and, since he was coming back to himself almost completely now, he was beginning to worry. Where was the next fix coming from? At the thought of it his foot jerked a little more, lifting to the limit that the confining strap would let it go.

He had run out of money and now it would really begin. He knew he was safe for a while, a few hours at most, but where, here, could he possibly get funds? He had turned all his money over to his Lip. The Lip subtracted his fee – and then some – and paid Iron Hans some money for a few weeks worth of fixes. And now the horse had run his race. Onofrio suspected the guard had cut the money, a fix or two or three's worth, but that was expected; he would have done the same thing; everyone cut the give. And he had to carry them all on his back. He might permit the night guard to screw him for a little money, but how far was that going to carry him? And if that ape night guard felt like it, he would do it without paying anyway. In the shadows it seemed as though the walls turned green and he longed. He looked at the last of the morning lights playing on the fixtures, the chrome and metal runners, the silvered bedframes, the brown, almost golden window frames, the copper-green sky, the brass frame of the television screen, and the sleek ring half-buried in the fat man's flesh as it caught fire from the last morning rays. He felt hungry, depleted, weak, and wondered how long he would have to wait till a fix, how long he would have to bear the guard's joke, tied up with straps of enduring webbing.

A wordless voice crackled in the microphone over the door. Onofrio turned his head. Hamisbat turned his head towards the other end of the ward. The Puerto Rican held tighter to the bed-frame, Kaprelic pivoted and faced the door, leaning forward, a little, his pyjamas hanging; he held his diminished soap crucifix up. Only the catatonic Negro continued to stare away from this point. Iron Hans put down his paper and stood up to look through the glass port in the door. He nodded and opened the door. Fertig came in. He had been gone all morning. They were giving Fertig the first battery of tests. He was pushed in by two guards.

Two other attendants, following, brought in a small, already decorated Christmas tree on a little dolly and set it up by Hans's desk. Onofrio dreamed of candy-striped packages full of uncut horse. The door clanged shut behind Fertig. He stood there by the desk while the huge hands of Iron Hans went over his body. Fertig held a pad of paper and a ballpoint pen. They were giving him the tell-us-all-about-your-life story bit; Onofrio had been through it before. The slender man moved back a little while every part of his body was touched carelessly, expertly. His pale face was immobile; he started down the aisle towards where the fat man sat, past him, out the window, into space. When Hans finished he walked down the aisle with Fertig.

"Hans, c'mon, let me up. I'm all right," Onofrio whined. He had to control himself. He was tremendously excited. He had to get up. He had to talk to Fertig.

"I'll just bet you are, Candelli," the guard told him.

Onofrio thought of telling Hans he had to empty his bowels, but Hans might take it into his head to leave him there till he made in the bed ... and give him a beating for it. The thought made him want to go. "No. Really Hans. I don't need anything now. I'm fine."

"I think I'll save myself the trouble, Candelli, and leave you there till you feel that old hunger. That way I won't have to tie you again. Isn't that so Candelli?" the guard asked.

"Aw ... Hans," Onofrio whined. They had come to his bed. Fertig sat on the chair beside the bed next to his, looking at him as if he didn't understand what was going on at all. Kaprelic was still poised in the middle of the aisle. Something had got into his mind, some madness; in just a second he was going to come up to Fertig. Onofrio had to get used to Fertig first. He jerked against the straps.

"I don't know, Candelli. I mean you're out of privileges. You understand what I mean, don't you? That means we're going to have trouble with you, doesn't it?"

"You won't have any trouble, Hans, I promise…"

"How can you help it?" the guard laughed.

"I'll pay you, Hans," Onofrio whispered.

"I'll just bet you will."

Kaprelic came over to get close to Fertig, and stood between him and Onofrio. On the other side of the bed, Hans bent down and began to untie Onofrio. When he was halfway through he stopped, straightened, and scratched his head. "Now I don't know if I should, Candelli." He never tired of the game: then he thought of a new variation. The guard looked at Fertig and asked, "Would you give me, say, two to untie him?"

Fertig, startled, looked disgusted and slid his chair back a little towards the wall. "No. Why?"

"Sure, sure. I'll bet you will too. You're good hearted. I can tell. You're contributing three. I can tell."

Fertig looked annoyed. "No."

"And how about Christmas presents for everyone else, Fertig?"

Fertig looked puzzled. He wasn't used to that sneering placating tone. "I mean it," he said, a little agitated.

Hans grinned; he had got what he wanted. He finished untying Onofrio. Kaprelic bent low over Fertig and was peering into his face looking for something. He held up the crucifix. Fertig smiled nervously, leaning away. "I recognize you," Kaprelic told Fertig.

"Now you know you're a famous man, Fertig: you got through to this saint," the guard laughed.

"Hurry up," Onofrio said.

The guard came up behind Kaprelic, jabbed his thumb into his lower part of Onofrio's belly, a little above the pubis and Onofrio gasped. "You just keep that up, Candelli," the guard told him.

"Oh, that Hans, always kidding, heart of gold," Onofrio panted.

"I know you," Kaprelic repeated. Fertig smiled. "Did they hurt you?" he asked. Fertig shook his head. "What did they do to you?"

Fertig didn't answer.

"They tortured you?" Kaprelic's voice was excited, hysterical.

"Nothing really. Tests. Pictures. Patterns. Blots. The usual I suppose. Everyone goes through it, don't they?"

"Endure. Endure," Kaprelic said.

"It's all right," Fertig answered.

The guard came up behind Kaprelic, jabbed his thumb into his behind. Kaprelic, staring into Fertig's face, didn't seem to feel it at all. He kept staring, satisfying himself: was this the man he was looking for? Hans pulled him away, dragged him from the two beds and into the centre of the aisle between the two rows of beds. "March, Kaprelic." Kaprelic began to walk up and down, his hands swinging loosely, his dialogue resumed, peering at something. Fertig took a deep breath.

Onofrio sat up and swung his feet over the side of the bed and sat facing Fertig. "Get off!" Hans yelled. He stood up, weak, shaky, hungry; he had to go to the john; he kept moving his feet.

"I thought I saw you last night. But I said, it was a dream. When I'm turned on, I dream. It gets all mixed up. You know how I mean?"

Fertig nodded.

"Or I see you in the papers. I see what they do to you the other day. You fighting?"

Fertig smiled and looked past Candelli. His feet were pushing the chair, sliding it back. Why was Fertig recoiling? Didn't he know a friend when he saw one? "Then they beat you? They always beat you. Turn you upside down and get all the fall out loot and then they say vagrant. You know how I mean." Onofrio tapped Fertig on the knee confidentially. Fertig moved his foot away. "They get much from you?"

Hamisbat was standing up! He never did that! He was going to come here! He was going to come into Candelli's section. Onofrio had to work fast or they would get to Fertig. "What you got left?" he asked, whispering.

Fertig shrugged his shoulders. "What was left?" he asked, talking not so much to Onofrio but to himself.

Onofrio looked at him carefully. It was hard to believe that this mild man, this slender man, had been a murderer. But Onofrio *knew*. There were all kinds. The thin men murdered as well as the fat beefy ones. Didn't *he* have to kill to get money for a fix? And look at him, too good looking, like a girl, but carrying the biggest monkey ape gorilla on his back. But, thinking about it, there was something of the pusher hooked about Fertig. What was his kick? Onofrio wondered.

"So I said, like in a nightmare. I've seen that face before. But I was under and riding through all the gold dust." He looked carefully to see if Fertig reacted. Fertig smiled that disdainful smile at him and pretended not to understand. Cautious. Good actor. Hamisbat started slowly down the aisle with that casual fat man's walk, arms out, each leg lifted and swung around the other. "And when that scene is on, what can you trust?" he said, moving closer.

"They lied about that picture," Fertig nodded again. "I blinked. That's all. I never said those things they 'quote' me as saying."

"I know. I know. They been testing you?" he pointed at the pad. "The confession bit?"

"They wanted me to write down my history. I've already confessed."

"Yeah, but you can always get that one thrown out of court. Listen, don't do it. Tell them nothing."

"I have nothing to hide."

"Tell them nothing." Candelli was agitated.

Fertig told him yes and slid back an inch and looked around.

"And listen," Onofrio told him, "keep away from those loonies. You know who I mean? I mean that lean saint over there; he killed girls. Little girls. In the worst way. The black stiff over there, he sits, he points, so it doesn't matter," Hamisbat was almost there. He whispered. "The fat one is the one I trust least of all. Looks like a guard; too well fed."

Hamisbat was close. He giggled and nodded. "Onofrio, get Hamisbat a chair. You know he can't stand long," Hamisbat said. Candelli reluctantly got up and got him a chair. Kaprelic was walking and staring at them, turning his head.

"Does everyone go through those tests?" Fertig asked.

Onofrio nodded. "Everyone. They know from them that you wanted to screw your mother when you were a baby. And that is why you ride the horse and carry the ape. That is why you are a maladjusted type."

"It's not that simple," Hamisbat said and smiled. "But when we think about it, every psychological test may be considered to be a lie-detector test." He bowed his fat trunk and pointed to himself: "His name is Hamisbat. May he help?"

"But what if you have nothing to hide? I'm not –" he stopped.

Hamisbat laughed. "Nothing to hide? Nothing?" and he laughed. His scorn was boundless.

Fertig looked alarmed at the laugh. His chair was against the wall; he was wedged between the night table and his bed.

Candelli said, "Sure. All right. The Lip," he whispered leaning close to Fertig's ear, "says it's the only hope. And I know. I paid him enough to tell the truth. Stay cool so the needle don't jump."

"Not that kind of lie detector. Consider; they start with an assumption: he has something to hide. They must find out. 'But I'm telling you *all*,' say. 'No. You're not,' say the tests. 'You're mad,' says the tests. Otherwise, why test?"

"'Be loony,' says the Lip. 'It's the only thing that can save you.'"

"Who is the Lip?"

"Lawyer. Pay him and he'll do it for you. Everything. Money makes it go. Money makes it stop. That's why I won't burn. See how I mean?" And he couldn't hold it any longer. "Hans," he screamed and ran to the toilet. There was no door to the toilet, and mirrors were rigged up so that the guard could watch all the stalls from his desk without moving. Usually he insisted they go in bunches of four in the morning and at night. They resented other times. Onofrio tried to hurry it. What was Hamisbat telling Fertig? His bowels were loose and he couldn't rush. He was trapped in the stink of it, surrounded, shut off, deafened by the rumble of his bowels, and his eyes watered. Kaprelic was moving up and down; Onofrio could see him striding past the doorway ... and all this time Hamisbat, too ... and the round face of Hans in the mirror, watching him. He finished, got up, and started to leave when Hans yelled, "Wash your hands, Candelli you pig," and laughed. Onofrio had to go back, but when he got out, Hamisbat was walking slowly up the aisle back to his place. "What did he tell you?" he asked Fertig. Fertig drew away a little.

The main question was, What was left from it all? Had it all fallen into the hands of the Lips? That was doubtful: after all, seven of them. Was there any left for *him*? He shook a little again and stopped himself. A cool head was needed here. "You have a lawyer?"

"I don't want a lawyer," Fertig told Onofrio. Every time Fertig spoke, Kaprelic's head jerked around and he looked towards them.

Onofrio didn't pay any attention. Softly he told Fertig, "They're *pretending* to test you. They want to find out where you hid the dust. You know?"

"Dust?"

Onofrio could see the bewilderment was a cover-up for great cunning. Of course, that was it! "All those doctors. All that dust. I *know*," Onofrio told Fertig.

Fertig didn't seem to be paying attention. Time was getting short. Onofrio had to find out. "Time to eat soon. These days I don't have much appetite. Dust and food, and they don't go together. Not much more left. Iron Hans is going to be mean., You got some money left?"

"A little," Fertig told him; "they're holding some for me. I think I had thirty dollars when I was arrested."

How easily Fertig talked about his money: was he that guileless… or cunning? "Of course. You don't carry it all with you. You stash some."

"I have some left in the bank," Fertig told him.

"And the rest?"

"A few thousand in the bank. No more," Fertig smiled. "My wife is working now. It won't be so bad."

"But the lawyers. You have to pay the lawyers."

"But I don't want a lawyer. I did it."

"Shh … You don't say that," Onofrio whispered, looking around. Who did Fertig think he was fooling? He looked at Hamisbat. Had they arranged something between them? The walls seemed to turn green in the afternoon shadows for a while and he thought he saw hidden in all the corners black lumps that told him there were dictaphones. "This is the bin. They hear. You know how they come on. Science. Headshrinkery. I'm your friend. They listen. They plant bugs everywhere. They observe. Whisper and rattle paper."

"Sure. Sure. I understand," Fertig said.

Onofrio recognized the tone, the placating look, the selfish-fake compassion, the I-can-withhold, kick-it look, the I'm different smile. It made him desperate and he tried harder to reach Fertig, to convince him of the truth of what he said, to get beneath the veneer of Hamisbat's lies. "Worse. If you pay the guard, he tells you where two, three bugs are. If you pay him more, he tells you where the one-way window is. If you find the bugs, you can make them quiet by laying coins next to them; makes static. But the best way is not to say any thing at all. They watch. They ask. They listen. They give you the trick tests and they have trick ways of finding out where you hid the stuff. He's right – Hamisbat. Lie detectors. I have to give him that."

"It can't be like that."

Onofrio nodded. "Worse. But if you pay off the head-shrinkers, they'll let you off; they won't report. But the best way is to pay the Lip big. Then he gets the pressure taken off."

"I didn't have to hide anything. It was nothing like that."

"All those people? Nothing? What are you telling me?"

Fertig got up, sat down on the bed, leaned back, swung his feet up, and lay down. He lay there, looking at the ceiling.

Onofrio started to tell Fertig he wasn't allowed to do that during the day, but stopped: let him find out, let that bastard, Hans, come over and touch the soles of his feet up a little.

But Iron Hans didn't get up and come over at all. He was lost with his music and newspaper, listening with his face forever set and staring down the ward, appearing to see everything out of his little steel-ball eyes. It was a sign; Onofrio was sure. Everything was fixed by Hamisbat; everything was paid for. He heard the faint rattle and clatter of the dinner cart coming to the ward. It would be time to eat soon. He would have to wait till later, tonight maybe, and then he would work Fertig over and find out where it was all hidden. He felt lonely and left out. He knew he had to control himself long enough to get it from Fertig.

After they had eaten and the guards had poured food down the throat of the catatonic, they all relaxed a little. Fertig didn't eat, toyed with his food, pushed it away. Onofrio ate it for him. Wait. He'd learn. Fertig got up and went into the bathroom to brush his teeth. Hans was at the doorway while his mouth was full of toothpaste.

"Out," Hans told him. "Where do you think you are?"

"I'm brushing my teeth."

"In the first place, every time you want to relieve yourself you call me – if you need to go bad – and it better be real bad if it's out of turn. Otherwise twice a day, and I didn't give the order yet. As for teeth, once a day, at night. Out!"

Fertig started to wash the toothpaste out of his mouth, but Iron Hans yelled "OUT! Jump when you're told. *OUT!*" Fertig left.

What had they said in there? Onofrio wondered. Surely the fix was in.

The shadows deepened as the sun declined and the lights came on and soon the purple sky turned black. The catatonic pointed; the fat man sat; Kaprelic walked up and down, having reduced his soap crucifix to something vaguely diamond shaped. Fertig started to write his history. Onofrio pretended to play with the therapy set, stringing coloured beads on to a waxen thread while he tried to see what Fertig was writing. He couldn't. After a while, though, he was imagining that each bead was money and that it was necessary to string many, many beads on to a string of given length in order to have value enough so that when he got out, if he ever did, he could buy more dust. But he couldn't string more than thirty-three to a string; the beads were inflexible.

Late in the evening the lights went out, except for a night light shining on the desk and the flame-shaped blue, red, and green bulbs on the Christmas tree. The evening guard, as hard as Hans, sat and listened to rock and roll from a propped-up transistor set. The television continued to show shadows, soft, blurred, and meaningless. Kaprelic had gone to sleep in the middle of the aisle. They turned the Negro, unbending as any idol, on his side; all through the night he kept staring ahead, pointing along the plane of his bed, his mouth yelling up at the ceiling. Fertig lay on his bed, sleeping: so it seemed. Onofrio tried to close his eyes and sleep, but he could feel it all building up inside of himself. All the golden and silver dreams, the ivory thoughts, amethyst and garnet clouds, the towering, hazy, crystalline fires, and all the glorious colours of money – green, gold, silver, and copper – devolved finally and ultimately into nothing at all. The walls resolved themselves into mere walls, the floor, and the sound of his own breathing was just the dusty, irritating movement of air in and out of his throat: and into and out of his lungs; his nose ran softly and he had to sniff constantly; his eyes teared a little; his hands kept opening and closing; and his legs and arms did things without volition.

He turned on his side and looked at Fertig. It seemed, for a second, as if Fertig gestured to him in the distorted light, holding money in his hands. Two great coins glittered on the little side table between them; but when Onofrio leaned over he saw Fertig's glasses gleamed: only that. They lay on the pad of paper. What did the writings say? Where it was? Or, was it that the dust was in the pen? They had taken the pen away: you could commit suicide, in the mouth or through the anus, or into the penis … Then was the dust spread out on the paper – in case he needed it at night? Fake words: dreamy words.

He got up softly and stepped over to Fertig's bed and leaned over him. Hadn't he filled many more pages? What had happened to them? How cunning he was, Onofrio thought, to breathe regularly – with the wise-o smile, the sly pusher's smile, fixed – to sleep insultingly while he, Onofrio, felt the great torture starting up inside. A great weight seemed to press him down and from the front; three guards had come running up the aisle, seized him, thrown him down on his bed, and strapped him down again. Dim and soft in the soft light, they held him expertly till he was tied down. It was then that he began to moan and plead and ask Fertig for the money he had concealed. Dirt had clogged his nostrils, stones rained down on him, metal penned him in, and the clownish mask of Kaprelic kept laughing at him till he no longer knew what he was doing. He screamed and swore to tell the whole world what Fertig had done with all the money. He swore and swore by everything he held holy; meanwhile the darkness kept pouring into him, almost choking him. And the last thing he saw was the face of clever Fertig looking at him, pretending to be puzzled, to be scared, revolted, full of mock compassion, sneering behind his soft mask, keeping all that money for himself ... all that money for himself ... all that money...

Chapter 7

Roy Bleakie prepared to go back into the city after spending the week-end with his mother. Shaving in the morning, he tried to taste, with a touch of lather that got into his mouth, the joy of battle beginning. He would like to make this a big case, his biggest yet: he wished it presented more of a challenge – it would probably be his last private case. He stood in front of the mirror and planned the day. A clock's hands, built into the mirror, told him the time. He watched his image between seven-twenty carefully; he postured, assuming his interview poses. To the *Times* he said, "When the lawyer defends the criminal, he defends the principles of Democracy. The law does not state that anyone *except* the malefactor is entitled to the *best* defence it is possible to give."

He grinned and saw the incisive outlines of his face – something like Giulio de Medici's (that hint of corrupt wisdom), yet like a della Robbia angel's – disappear under the lather. Under hands as delicate and strong as a surgeon's, he watched the noble, set chin retake significant shape, like a revelation, part by part, to the swift strokes; the sculpture was economically done – because he had less skin to shave – in two or three strokes, scrape per second, the way they did it in the television ads. He wiped off the disfiguring scraps of lather. His head, now sleek as a stamped portrait on any royal penny, made little motions in the mirror; his eyes remained fixed: Bleakie re-examined himself to see that there were no cuts. *Newsweek* would put it "At the age of thirty-six he has conquered the field of criminal law and is the most sought-after lawyer, a defender of the underdog ..." He brushed back his blond, curly hair. *Playboy* would say: "At thirty-six he is an accomplished playboy and his bachelor apartment is known to many women." Vapour fumes finally obscured the surface of the mirror till only the non-reflective clock hands stood clear. His mother persisted in calling him even though she knew he knew the time. The only thing that spoiled his morning was a slight head stuffiness: cold coming on? So middle class, he thought, the kind of thing that happens to the Fertigs.

He didn't breakfast. He told his mother he wouldn't be back that night but would stay over in his city apartment; he always stayed in the city when he had a big case.

He drove his red sports car from Long Island to his office in Manhattan. "He plays hard: this year he drives a red Mercedes Benz; next year it will be a purple Holocaust." He drove casual his right arm thrown over the leather, curled as if still holding the girl they would give him to pose with. How careful they would be to see that she was short enough. He remembered Friday's triumphs. Morning trees, wet with dew, glittered by along the right of the expressway. To his left, stretches of mud flats, bay and ocean, clouds of gulls, cold white in the clear winter air, drifted by. Beyond, over miles of flat Long Island, he could see New York, spires caught in a perpetual haze which trapped the light, a visible exhalate of eight million people, a solidity of air and building, a sort of amoebic genie-shape: the Opponent screaming for Fertig's blood. The tree-stands thinned and were replaced by small houses and little lawns; three miles of a dreary, small-house development. As he got closer to the city, the old, joyful war tension began to take hold of his body.

He remembered how well he had begun it last week. Before sweeping down to Sara Fertig's rescue one of the first things he did was to telephone Irving Hockstaff from Judge Pilsudski's private office: "Who's Grenoble, Irving?"

"Royboy, not even a hello? Don't you want to hear about my newest grandchild, or even my health?"

"How's..."

Hockstaff laughed. "Don't bother it, Royboy. I wonder sometimes if you're really Judge Bleakie's boy? He was always solicitous."

"Ask mother."

"Don't be snotty, Roy. Your father, even though he had Principles, and was a Gentleman, was a Man; I loved him and you know what I think of you, Royboy. How's mother?"

Hockstaff and his "Royboy" – some day... some day – was Hockstaff sneering at his father? The *Times* piece would read, "... with his three tough assistants, Brodney, Molnar, and Bennick (picture: Roy Bleakie in the centre, leaning over the desk, and the three of them around him looking down at what he was pointing at, the piece of surprise evidence that reverses the lost case), he carries on in the tradition established by his father before *he* became a judge. In fact, rumour has it... She's lovely thanks, and asks after you, Irving. Who's Grenoble?"

"A friend, a lodge brother. Contributes very nicely around campaign time. A friend, you understand?"

"Right."

"And you're going to take on his case?"

"Any friend of yours, Irving... a friend of Roy Bleakie's."

"I would appreciate it as a personal favour that you give him your very best effort, Roy –"

Roy Bleakie quoted himself, "For the hack lawyer case volume counts. The competent lawyer's best is frequently not enough. The great lawyer not only identifies with, but becomes himself, the client –"

"Don't clown, Roy."

"... and makes a cause, not a case out of it."

"And I suppose it would be violating a sacred confidence to ask what it's about?"

"Of course. Surprised at you, Irving."

"That's what I like about you. You're your father's boy all right, you got delicacy and tact and you're discreet like he was, Roy-boy."

"Protect the client," Bleakie said, ignoring the possible insult.

"I mean Jack Grenoble is a friend, a *good* friend, an old, I might even say, a treasured friend. I ask because if I can do anything to help..."

"A holy trust, Irving. You'd be the last to ask me to violate – Harry Fertig was his accountant," he said, having made Hockstaff sweat for it a little.

Hockstaff whistled and said, "Ahaaa!"

"Handling the case. But Irving... ?"

"Yes?"

"He wants to be kept out of it: act of charity – don't let the left hand – friendship – defend the poor, mad, man."

"He's a wonderful man that way – gives heavily to charity," Hockstaff said. Bleakie listened carefully for sarcasm. Hockstaff didn't know anything or he wasn't giving. "Listen, I'll give you a piece of advice. I would be very careful about the way you handle that case. A lot of important people got killed by that lunatic. And... well, money you got and glory you don't need any more, Roy, at least not *that* kind. Get it out of the way quietly."

"I'm my father's boy, Roy Bleakie, Irving. Justice obsesses me."

Hockstaff laughed a long time. "Wonderful. Like in the *Saturday Evening Post*. I'll tell you why I say this, Roy; I got things in mind for you. You have *potential*; you're real, political timber, you can go even further than your father ..." And Hockstaff waited for Roy Bleakie to ask, to plead his case. "What's it going to be, a judgeship or the D.A.?"

"I don't know, Irving. Life is very sweet this way."

"I understand. Take it under your advisement. You can't hang around too many years like this, you know?"

"This is nice of you, Irving," and said no more. How had his father, who could never plead, ever become a judge? It didn't matter: his father had gone no further.

"Don't thank me. After all, nothing is too good for my old pal, Judge Bleakie's boy Roy, right? I'm sure you inherited your father's polit-ical... know-how. And didn't I bounce you on my knee?"

"Can I forget it, Irving?"

"Can you remember it? Think about it."

Bleakie felt good about the way he handled it. Every time you asked for a favour you lost a little political power, and every time you did one you gained: Irving Hockstaff had asked *him* ... three favours, or rather, two favours, once, twice, and even his "exchange" for infor-mation about Grenoble came out in the form of asking a favour of him. Bleakie figured it in a precise political calculus. And so, later, he swooped down on the D.A.'s office feeling strong after having talked to Irving Hockstaff...

The cars were beginning to pile up – being fed into the main highway from the service roads. He weaved in and out, changing from lane to lane, making time, getting ahead faster than anyone, not joining any car flock.

The assistant D.A.'s tried to shake him off, but he made threatening sounds: no grounds. They sent for MacGruder, the D.A. "I might have known. The dandy little vulture's here, boys." They all laughed. They had to.

But where was Sara Fertig? Inside, being gleaned by the D.A.'s men in relays.

"And maybe our little friend can answer the sixty-four-dollar ques-tion: Just how does she manage to live with him and not know?" MacGruder sneered.

"Sure. Never was a murder planned in secret, was there?"

"Planned! Planned! I'll get you there." He could see MacGruder just dying to put a dirty paw on his vest: there was always something irri-tating about that vest.

"Grow up. Psychotics plan too. Next you'll be telling me you never planned a prosecution." Of course no one dared to laugh.

"You can have her," MacGruder said, "but I'll be wanting her again."

"By all means. Don't I always co-operate?"

"And by the way, it will interest you to know who's assigned to this case."

"Roy Bleakie couldn't care less."

"This you'll care about. Judge Jeffries, Bleakie boy; worm your way out of this one."

"Swung it?"

"What do you mean by that?" (*Angrily*; speech-making anger.)

Then Bleakie decided: D.A. He would clobber MacGruder in court and then he would claw MacGruder for the nomination. Judgeship was a dead end. Liebowitz had always wanted to be D.A. You went up from D.A.; it was a tradition. O'Dwyer did it. Dewey had gone up. He would go further than those two schnooks. He didn't bother to answer MacGruder: the answer would come about two years later.

Sara Fertig's own lawyer, a civil-case schmuck, hadn't been able to do a thing for her, not even get her loose from the D.A. He was resentful at the interference, but Bleakie made colleague sounds, big league sounds, and the schnook burbled happily with delight. "I'm honoured..." Bleakie would get Sara Fertig to get rid of him.

Sara was still in shock, unable to function, unable to say anything meaningful, unable even to imagine it, let alone believe it. For a second she thought *she* was the accused and he was *her* lawyer. He had looked at her. She was a little bigger than he was, pale; wisps of hair, having broken loose from her severe pull-back, fringed her face and straggled out from under a misworn floppy-brimmed hat, wrong, wrong somehow for her face; her skin was blotched, discoloured under her cheekbones making them look Slavic; her jaw was clamped making it look strong. She wore stylish shoes, though sensible, not too spike-heeled. Her big hands wore no nail polish, her lips no lipstick; a little bulky in a heavy, almost expensive tweed suit, her wide hips stretched the weave. Her eyes, anodyned by shock and disbelief, stared, but there was agitation beneath the stunned surface – the lips moving, the teeth biting, the mouth smiling too widely or pursing suddenly, grimacing, terrified and puzzled, still not able to grasp it, reactions being tried out, all wrong, off cue, out of phase.

He briefed her quickly in a little side room, told her what to expect when they left the D.A.'s office and what she should say. He gave her his calm, deep, comforting voice; smooth. She was starting to look at him like a rescuing knight. "We couldn't shake them and it's pointless to even try. There'll be newsmen and the cameras; and shouting and jostling and lights flashing and the rest of the circus. Prepare." They left, he holding her arm, pulling her, leaning into the turmoil as if it were an invigorating wind; she holding back, being afraid, but managing it. When they got home they paused on the doorway and turned.

"Give us a break, boys. There'll be an interview as soon as Mrs. Fertig recovers from her deep shock."

"Just a few words …"

"Has Roy Bleakie ever disappointed the press? Give us a break."

"Mrs. Fertig," someone shouted, "how could you live with a man for a year and not even know … ?"

"I had no idea … It comes to me as a complete shock …" Her flattened voice was curiously consonant with those pressed-together lips.

"Do you think the death of your child justifies …?"

"… terrible shock. I cannot bring myself to believe … standing by his side …" And Bleakie pulled her in. Inside, she collapsed into the arms of her distraught, hysterical mother and they wept together. Outside, the turbulence persisted; they were in a state of siege …

The project houses passed, one like the other, evenly spaced, alike in spite of the built-in variations. The sun was bright. He saw himself in the windscreen, a bright figure bathed in light. He roared through a forest of spiky lights thrown off the cars and was entering the great bubble of sunny haze without seeing at what point he entered it. The cars were thick now. He couldn't pass. Everything moved at an even fifty-mile-an-hour pace deeper into the city.

He drove through rows of unimaginative new apartment buildings – Live a Little with Lefrak-red and white bricked, air-conditioned, square, and terraced: Fertig-places, he thought scornfully.

And that panic call from Grenoble in the evening: "Where were you when they brought Fertig up on charges? Why aren't you by his side? What am I paying you for?" The more urgent note of panic confirmed something for him; Grenoble was afraid. Fertig *knew* something about Grenoble. Did Grenoble think Roy Bleakie believed that charity-nonsense, that Gordon-crap? It was a question of finding out. "Don't worry," he told Grenoble. "Leave it to me. Know what I'm doing." Of course, he had sent one of his assistants along to watch the arraignment.

And Fertig had been perfect without knowing why. With that tight smile on his face, he kept discipline – real loony stuff. The genuine surprise … the … outrage at being sent to the bin, … raised voice, but controlled; perfect. It was going to be open and shut… a bore … insane: committal.

He could almost feel sympathy for Fertig. He could admire what Fertig had done – pit himself against the world – if it weren't for the madness that had driven him. Bleakie had no use for the irrational, for the compulsive, had contempt for those who couldn't control. Of course, if the act had been attended by logic, neatness of thinking, brilliant and patient planning, efficiency of execution, as Fertig claimed – *that* one could admire. But the arbitrary choices, that one wild flaw in execution, and Miss Malabar indicated the revengeful madness that motivated it all. Still, Roy Bleakie could understand, envy, almost *feel* the excitement Fertig must have felt when he carried that day's work out. What he was doing was a sort of rectification of that job, an introduction of logic, a direction of the fight against the Opponent.

The cars entered the Brooklyn Tunnel. He saw himself in the windscreen. He was neat, precisely dressed; his black, Italian suit sat perfectly on him, not at all distorted by the fact that he was sitting down. His red vest bobbed along, superimposed on the white wall tiles. In the curved bubble of glass he looked like a boxer.

No. What was he doing, his defence of Fertig, was going to be *more* than a completion, Bleakie thought: it required a greater sense of understanding; larger forces had to be moved than those that had ever been contemplated by Fertig (if he thought about it at all). He would take this case out of the cut-and-dried class and give it a big run for the money – his last big case. But how? What Fertig had done – rising against complexities that mired him down and resorting to a rather simple-minded, monolithic act, the act of an innocent – was only a beginning. Bleakie, carrying the action still further would bring it off, bring it off, and lead Fertig, lead them all, through a complex maze that few could appreciate: the fight against the Great Opponent. Roy Bleakie was the right lawyer for the right criminal; he would organize the direction of the self-interested elements, fuse the random into a coherent body, arrange the scenes. The Opponent – he thought of it (him!) as a confusable but dangerous, slightly stupid giant whose bellowing voice was MacGruder. The Opponent wanted Fertig's blood. The Opponent was seducible; you could make him feel compassion, so that just when Fertig was lowering his backside into the hot seat, Bleakie would snatch him away to the Institution for the Criminally Insane. Much more difficult than killing seven – much more. He yawned.

Emerging from the tunnel, his image faded till only his pale smile was left. He broke loose from the clump of cars. Driving swiftly, his motor roaring, he swerved and curved more sharply than the gentle ramp's curve, shot between two converging cars, cut off another, and beat some cars to a turn-off: he brought it off without scratching a fender or denting a bumper, waved to a traffic cop he knew, shot down the street for half a short block, braked, screeched, slowed to a crawl, light stalled: traffic had stopped him.

As soon as he got to the office he telephoned Donnell, who was on special assignment to the D.A.'s office for evidence follow-up on the Fertig case. Usually he could get some assistant D.A. to brief him, but the word was out. Donnell would keep him informed; other friends would send him private copies of everything in the D.A.'s files. It was standard. He took care to praise Donnell, to tell him there was more money coming to him. Donnell seemed to accept it without crowing: clod or not, the man was a professional. Donnell told Bleakie that he had been down to the bar, Little Mike's Paradise, where Fertig hung out. "I've seen some pits in my time, but this one was worse than I had remembered it, lower than Bowery stuff, you know? I said to myself, How does a Fertig get down here? He didn't strike me as that kind of guy."

"How does a Fertig knock off seven? Nothing's hard if you go off."

"So I asked the barkeep and he clammed up. I said that if he was clean, so to speak, we weren't too interested in him, you know, and I sort of looked around, to show him I knew the kind of place he was running there. After all, Fertig's weapon was a military piece."

"What's that?"

"Armourer's stuff. Mafia stuff. From different guns. You know the bit: barrel – murder in Tampa; stock – a bank job in Galveston; serial numbers filed off; a few armoury touches; a change of parts and venue; a new set of lands and grooves for Fertig. Now who, I wanted to know, gave military ordinance to Fertig? I mean were there certain connections?"

"And," Bleakie prompted: he was used to Donnell's naïve sense of drama.

"The keep, a hairy-eared guy with big choke-you hands, he says he runs a clean place: therapy for hard-ups – narcotics too, I wouldn't be a bit surprised, and what have you – he says he's innocent – 'who *me*?' But he *feels* right."

"What makes him feel right?" Bleakie asked.

"A feel… I can't explain it."

"You go by feelings?"

"The best way. Always right. The keepy, he says that anyone around could have armed Fertig; after all, he can't recognize unsavoury characters, let alone keep them out – which is an understatement.

"'Did the accused,' I ask, 'ever solicit a gun from you?' The keepy, he says, 'Yes.' Like that. Looks me in the eyes with one of those, see, I'm-levelling expressions. Says, in fact, that Fertig asked for a gun to use on his wife."

"His wife?"

"At least that's the way hair-ears reads it. Of course he refused out of hand, not knowing if Fertig might not be some kind of undercover agent – not his usual clientele, you see. I figure it was just cover-up talk."

"How often was Fertig there?"

"He says not too often, more than once a week, but he can't be sure. Not a drinker – a nurser, a brooder: you could tell something was wrong."

"They can always tell."

"Isn't it the truth? 'And how about this slut?' I ask. Well, the gash, she works for him or, as he put it, *rents* a place now and then. This fur is a big-hip girl, wears sun glasses all the time, and it being romantic-dark down there, paradise under twenty-watt bulbs, you wonder how she sees. I questioned the broad, but she didn't give me much satisfaction. Just knew the hero enough so that she could say hello and it is a nice day."

"They never made it?"

"She says no. I pushed it. She denied. I pushed it more."

"Why?"

"I thought it felt wrong. I convinced her of my good intentions, I mean nothing too strong because they're all the time talking about police brutality. And anyway, since the piece was Regular issue', she wouldn't want to encounter any Cosa Nostra brutality. You have nothing to fear, I told her, I'll respect your confidence, but this nooky has everything to fear. I pushed it a little further –"

"Strong hunch?"

"Counsellor, it wouldn't go away; it was as strong as sex smell, you know?"

"But what did something like that and Fertig have in common?"

"Like you said, how does he come to knock off seven? Anyway it's the kind of thing that appeals to some people; get low down, tell it all to the down-and-out cooze, the compassionate snatch, put yourself down real low and find out Truth. There was a guy I knew who felt so low that he went out and found himself this infected black wore, I mean with sores –"

"Fertig," Bleakie interrupted.

"Well, I carried on my interrogation upstairs."

Bleakie thought about it: interrogation by sex: dictaphone in the penis – everything you say may be held against – but tapping was inadmissible in court without a judge's …

"She said nothing new. They had nothing to do with one another but … talk. She said Fertig liked to ask how she got into this business. And she told him she was a virgin princess stolen from her father: some guys get excited hearing this nonsense. And I asked never, not once, for a poor virgin princess; And to show my good intentions, I schtupped her."

"Where in the manual of police procedure is this?"

Donnell laughed. "Above and beyond … So she said she asked him once, twice, but he said he was in mourning. I don't believe her. I think they yenced a lot. Anyway, that was it."

"Keep me informed. Roy Bleakie will be grateful."

Now wouldn't that be a shocker for Sara Fertig when they sprung that in court, Bleakie thought?

He began to work on the Opponent by telephoning a friend with the LIFE people: he might as well begin that process. They would interview Sara – an exclusive with Fertig was the bait. In her way, Sara Fertig should be perfect ... the stricken and innocent wife – it had the makings of Opponent-lulling pathos – and Fertig, the family man, the child-loving man, the peculiar and tragic aspects, the late-in-life baby, robbed by a vengeful and remorseless fate; ... they did it so well ... as tragedy stalked ... and all those Opponent-persuading words. Of course, he said. Roy Bleakie'd be available for interviews and pictures: wasn't he always, and, believe me, you're the first. The LIFE man laughed and made an offer. Don't be ridiculous, Bleakie said: "We're not giving you a cheap case." But certainly an unpopular one for one of these turn-in-the-tide-of-public-indignation stories. They had arranged to have lunch later in the day and talk it over. They'd bargain back and forth, get a little high on drinks, come to a working agreement, and then the real bargaining would begin – what the LIFE people would say – of course, they would be ready to sympathize with Sara, the total victim. But what about Fertig? Well, it was a package deal. It would end, as it usually did, with them getting drunker and having a good-natured contest involving their sexual prowess and a friendly feeling at the end of it all. It could mean a lot of money: it would lead to book on his experiences in court – after all, it was time to draw a fitting conclusion to a decade, he grinned, of defending the underdog, and to inaugurate the opening of a new career as a public servant.

His assistants, Molnar, Brodney, and Bennick, had come in. He would hold a quick conference with them and reassign some of his work to them; he could get postponements on other cases. He unknotted his tie, took off his shirt to change it. He opened a drawer full of shirts: white today to go with the red vest – simple, dramatic – when he remembered Judge Mable Crossland. She had strong contacts with social work agencies, boards of welfare, charity groups, civic-minded penalty abatement groups; she could offset Judge Jeffries' position: she could be a weak link in the Opponent's armour. He telephoned.

Whenever he spoke to Judge Mable Crossland, he imagined her, even though she was in her office, just stirring in bed. Her voice was deep, warm, sleep and sex-blurred – disconcerting, if he let it be. Her large lush body would be coated with that silken black judge's robe, which rendered every wearer except her shapeless. Her big breasts would be pushing at the cloth; her great, round hips, spread out by her chair, would thrust laterally; her large thighs always caught the cloth and showed, as she sat, straight or cross-legged, those surprising curves. He couldn't drive the thought from his head: she was naked under the robes. He leaned forward and looked at himself in the glass covering his desk; the light wasn't right; he couldn't see himself clearly; the stuffiness in his head made him mistake the receiver-static for the hiss of silken legs sliding; that sound could whisper from the bench through a quiet courtroom louder than the creak of unoiled swivel chairs; it could disconcert the plans of district attorneys, the windy summing-up of defending attorneys, however she chose to use it; it overruled the speaker and sustained the objectors at the lawyers' table; it called for order more peremptorily than the clop of gavels.

"Roy, you've not been nice. It's been so long. I've been thinking about you." Her voice more than caressed, it fondled forcibly. Not long enough, Bleakie thought, since she made him stand naked beside her, since they had looked into the enormous mirror – one whole wall – in her bedroom. She was big, great-bellied, big-breasted; her hard fleshed and swelling calves narrowed quickly to incised bone, tendon, tight ankles … motherly, but athletic. Even though she was fifty, her flesh was firm, like warm stone washed smooth by the action of rivers and time. Next to her he was dwarfed, a statuette, neat-muscled, hard, compact. He had been … awed … in her enormous room, all silk and fur and thick with the smells of powders and perfumes and the lingering incense of old lusts and the acrid smell of their just-finished rutting. He had not liked the way he felt. He couldn't control. Somewhere, outside her room, he was sure he heard her husband move.

"Mable, how are you?" he asked, and thought, scornfully, what a ridiculous name for a judge; he wanted to hurt her, but he couldn't; he needed her. They exchanged flirtations, pleasantries. He pitched his voice down to a resonant level and forced himself to speak fully, carefully, not in his usual clipped manner, even though he was in a rush.

"But Roy, why have you stayed away so long?" Did it matter? He wondered. He knew it did. While she had, at one time or another, slept with most of the bar association in her climb to the judgeship, now men slept with her in their rise. Her body had not wholly conquered him; he still owed her nothing, but he was climbing fast himself. She didn't know yet that he was going to be the next D.A.… she would love him more. Of course, for her, it was not merely the matter of sleeping with him but of completing the conquest, of owing her favours. Dropping his voice still lower, he kept the tone somewhere between an insinuation and a virile, courtroom oration: he pleaded the press of business … or had she forgotten Fertig? But who could forget Fertig, that poor man, she said. The case was in all their minds. She wondered if Jeffries was the proper judge. Good! she had brought it up. Of course, he explained, that Judge Jeffries was on his mind too: so old-fashioned and… well, other difficulties, and could a case like Fertig's receive a fair hearing before … and he dropped it.

He told her that of course he missed her but she *understood*, didn't she? Her throaty voice imparted an extra and disturbing dimension of sound into the receiver and tickled his ear as she told him that she did understand, but that was no reason to neglect old friends. Her voice, stimulating his ear along some inner canal, tingled his nose and made his eyes flicker. Was she sitting there, her robes flung aside, showing shoulders and breasts, part of her round arm plunging into the black robe-sleeve? Did her belly press against the grey composition-stuff of her desk, the warm flesh overlapping, just a little, enough to overcome even the sterility of grey aluminium stripping?

"I should be angry with you, Roy," she told him. He told her why she shouldn't be angry at all; he mentioned important politicos he had seen, and had been to party luncheons and important policy-making dinners with: especially Irving Hockstaff. Irving had asked after her, he said. Irving, wonderful Irving, she said. How much they all owed to Irving, she said, and how fond of Roy Irving was.

Bleakie didn't have to mention whether or not these contacts would, or could, do him any good, or had any meaning; whether or not his relationship with these politicians was weak, or strong; whether or not his mere talking to them, seeing them, implied anything other than he *knew* these men; ... he didn't have to. He told her in order to convince her how busy he was ... and just a little more. After all, she wanted badly to be the first woman to chair the Board of Justices and she would understand. He admitted that it took more than her magnificent body to get where she did, and that that sleeping with a large and powerful section of the bar association was not enough: whores did that all the time and were not made judges (or maybe they were! – he grinned at the door to the outer office). She heard the names. Her laugh forgave his absence. The wild note rang in her voice and he saw, again, as she stood before that mirror, the great fecund globe of her belly, the rise and fall of the white, unaged, or ageless, flesh, and remembered hearing, from somewhere far away, the disconcerting movements of her husband or her son. He saw himself in the glass covering the desk. His face was recomposed into a mask that mirrored completely the role he played now: the cajoling satirical lover who held out enticing favours and longed for her flesh; the virile young man on the rise who could inject some of his magic substance into her and ... – was that how she maintained that flesh?

He made a date with her. He would take her out. They would go to some fine night-club', do some of the newer dances, drink, talk in dark places, eat. But this time he would take her to a hotel room, where there was no huge mirror with which to play tricks. Of course they would discuss the Fertig case – who didn't. Perfectly natural. They would be having a fine brandy in a great snifter and he would tell her that, in the name of justice, something had to be done. They would kiss. He would lay her – the hard brutality of an older word suddenly delighted him ... even better, what was the word Donnell had used? *Schtup* – how the harsh word debased her and brought her to his level. As he kissed her throat he would explain his difficulties to her – wave of lynch sentiment. As he fondled her breasts he would discuss pre-judgement in the newspapers. As he bit her ear lobes he might whisper that Judge Jeffries, slipping into vindictive senility, was – at last it could be revealed – anti-Semitic. Her passionate morality would be aroused; her thighs would vise him; her sympathy would make her clasp him to her breasts; for Fertig was, after all, a deranged child in need of instruction, not execution. His voice was crooning: he heard it in the stillness of his office and saw his lips moving in the glass, the clearest thing in the half-observed lewd mask that leered up at him from the desk glass.

Finally, he would appear to be conquered by her flesh, but he would, in fact, be triumphant over her. Over a good-night drink, perhaps kissing the nape of her neck, closing her eyes with his lips, he would suggest that only she could set wheels in motion for Fertig. Of course, if she resisted, he would permit himself to be taken by her again. The passionate stridency of her voice as she agreed to see him reminded him that it wouldn't be easy: he would pay: and so, for that matter, would Grenoble.

She hung up. His fingers fluttered as he arranged his attaché case. He supposed he could have led her into a reasonable attitude by merely pleading the situation, but he preferred the closeness, the possibility that he might not satisfy her, which could make everything just a little dangerous. He got ready to leave to see Sara Fertig... and remembered that he hadn't put on his new shirt. He was perspiring; he wished he had a shower installed in the office. He wiped his armpits with his old shirt and put on the new one.

He left instructions for his assistants, signed some papers on his secretary's desk, drank from a cup of tea with milk she had ready for him, and went, leaving the cup half-full.

Bleakie came to Fertig's home; the news circus was set up – state of total siege: poised pencils, aimed TV cameras, yammering voices, held off by a stolid cop with an apathetic Irish face. Bleakie paused on the stoop and made a short speech to the *jacquerie* asking for a little time, entitled to a fair court trial, boys – as my father used to say – boys, the strangest people are innocent, full interviews for everyone – when had he ever left anyone out in the cold? (the boys knew Roy Bleakie) – but she's had a terrible shock, boys. And he walked in and was met by Sara's mother, who began to yell as soon as he opened the door:

"Can't you let us alone? Savages. We don't know anything, I tell you. What do you want?"

"It's all right, Mama; it's my lawyer," Sara said and smiled at him a wan, awestruck smile, the famous man smile, the we've heard so much about you smile.

Her mother let loose a burst of talk: the phone had been ringing the whole week-end; people saying dirty things, threatening; animals; people offering money for their story and for the things they had in the house, for *his* story; people wanting to sell things, to buy souvenirs; radio people, television people, the reporters trying to climb in the windows, get in the back door, crawl into the cellar. Finally she had to leave the telephone off the hook; they would have it changed to an unlisted number immediately. What kind of human beings were these? Animals!

Sara was apathetic to it, Bleakie saw. She nodded, as if to say, "of course". She looked tired – no, comfortable – no, doped. Probably tranquilizers. Her husband was a killer, but the fact remained undigested. He couldn't do much now.

They went into the living room. She was wearing a blouse and skirt. Her legs were held tightly together, her lower body rigid. Her torso slumped and her arms were drooped over the armrests: her hands, however, were clenched. Her eyes were almost closed; she half-smiled; her face followed him. The blouse was silk or nylon, unornamented blue cloth shimmering over large, brassiere-pointed breasts. Bleakie, restless, walked around the room. The mother stationed herself behind the daughter's chair; her face was hard, set, untrusting; her arms were folded. Tough, Bleakie thought, tougher than the daughter, whose fists were relaxing slowly. Time to wake her.

"Honestly, I had no idea," Sara said to him as if continuing what she must have been saying for hours and hours to the D.A. "I know how terrible it must look – as if I didn't care about him, as if I didn't love him."

"That's all right. Of course you didn't know. We won't talk about it *now*. Relax. You're safe. Don't worry." He stood, nervous, a little tense, pulling at the tips of his shirt sleeves, adjusting the skirts of his jacket, touching his tie, tapping his brass vest buttons. "I understand," he told her softly, sympathetically; "It's all right. You're home. You're safe. Not a thing to worry about. Trust Roy Bleakie…"

"How can I thank you?"

"Don't."

"But I don't understand why you're…"

"Mrs. Fertig. I believe in your husband's –"

"We don't have any money."

"… innocence." She looked surprised. "After all, the sick man is innocent: he cannot help himself." Her eyes were luminous, grey. Not bad, Roy Bleakie thought, not half-bad; older •than him. No beauty. He liked younger women, girls, innocent skins framing corrupt eyes…

The mother kept watching carefully. She talked: "*He* brought this on our heads ..." What could they ever say? Who would have thought it? Yet she always suspected something about him. They always suspected something, Bleakie thought, they always secretly knew, but they never spoke in time to prevent. "I couldn't put my finger on it," Sara's mother said.

"What made you suspect?" he asked the mother politely. Could use her when the time came. He moved restlessly while he heard post-dated statements of sibylline doom compounded out of old, imagined slights, insults, sins of omission.

He looked at the room: not to his taste. Yet, Fertig had come out of this. Swedish-modern furniture. The cloth covering the sofa and the chairs was almost in good taste; Fertig could have afforded *real* good taste. Some pottery was arranged on spaces between books, one or two Early American Antiques. Bright burlap café curtains covered the windows. But there was a dullness, a lifelessness to it all, even in the choice of the framed prints, once advanced in taste, now commonplace: the usual Roualt, Matisse, Modigliani – the colours gone flat in reproduction – a few old-fashioned advertising prints. There were several originals, which indicated that they must have invested in unknown painters, or friends, probably on the chance they might be worth something in time, and arrogant enough to think they had the taste enough to foresee. Daumiers too, the legal series, but everyone had Daumiers: Daumier was obvious ... really an innocent. He walked over to them, moving softly. "Go on. Talk. Don't mind. I'm restless. Think better on the move."

Sara was talking now, telling of her shock, talking about the night they lost their child, what had happened after. She sounded lifeless, repeating a story told too many times to the D.A.

Bleakie didn't recognize the name of the artists. The Fertigs had gambled and lost. Was Fertig somewhere here in this room? Not the murderer, the other Fertig, the usual Fertig – he *was* the room.

"*He* always had an odd look. You'd tell him something that wasn't to his liking and he would look at you in a *certain* way ..." But Bleakie didn't sense that either.

"Ma, please," Sara said. "We took it hard for six months; we had difficulties," she told Bleakie.

"Difficulties?"

"The usual. Arguments. Restlessness. Fights. Terrible guilts. Recriminations. Dr. Anslinger, my psychiatrist, says that these are normal after the loss of a child. I went back to work – I'm a kindergarten teacher – and I went back into therapy; I hadn't gone for about four years. It seemed to get a little better because I began to cope with my problems. Then too, Harry was out of the house a lot. At first he told me he was going for long walks at night… after work."

"Walks?"

"I don't think he came home too late … and … honestly … I was asleep… Then he began some kind of extensive audit of all the firm's books – going back years. He's had day and night jobs like that before; Saturday and Sunday work."

"And how long did that continue?" Had Fertig found something to hold over Grenoble's head? Was that why Grenoble was paying? If so, Fertig hadn't used it. Maybe the case wasn't so cut and dried after all.

"Till he got this infection and was sick – just before they came for him; that was right after…"

"And you didn't know he and Mr. Grenoble parted six months ago?"

"No."

"Of course you couldn't suspect?"

"It was always Harry's therapy to run away from things by burying himself in his work."

What did that mean?

"And you didn't know?"

"Honestly, Mr. Bleakie … Her voice was calm: the fists had reclenched.

"That's all right. Look, Sara – may I call you Sara?"

She nodded, grateful for the personal touch.

"Remember, I'm your attorney: it's closer than being your minister or your doctor. Trust me. Tell me anything you want to."

"I slept a lot; sometimes I went to bed as early as seven o'clock. Dr. Anslinger, my therapist, and I were working it out… I mean I felt we had lost everything… You know the difficulty we had in getting a child – so long – and you feel so… well, not like a woman any more – and we had to work this thing out… I just didn't want to face anything… I just wasn't feeling anything any more, not responding to anything, only unresolved and undirected anxiety, panic now and then, feelings of guilt – for no reason – dreams, all of it. Dr. Anslinger was helping me adjust to myself…"

What was there to feel guilty about he wondered.

"But after a long time… we seemed to adjust. We fell into a pattern. Maybe Harry should have gone into analysis too? Poor Harry."

He looked at her. She was more alive now: he could sense an evasive witness: what did she have to be evasive about? Did she know about the whore? Did she know she was being evasive? He couldn't really probe yet. Win her. "Look. You don't have to talk yet. In a day or two …"

"I want to," she smiled.

Good. First smile. Tired but trusting: tell me, but not them, he thought. She wouldn't be any good to him yet; give her time, he thought.

"Tell," he said and walked around feeling, feeling. Magazines: *Atlantic, Harper's*, LIFE, dreary middle-class stuff; but he was sure they'd sneer at the *Reader's Digest*. He looked away and grinned. Her or him – who bettered themselves? Books anyone with a liberal tinge might read: alarmist books by popular sociologists, sophisticated but popular historians, good novels, Bellow, Roth, and Baldwin stuff; some poetry, Pound and Eliot; travel and exploration books; popular but not too simple science; an enormous section of detective novels – nothing at all that would indicate ... Bleakie smiled: Fertig's textbooks. The smell of the place was wrong for a madman. All too domestic, middle-class, sexlessly bourgeois, no matter what the pretensions – and he was sure it was Sara who pretended – to culture. But Fertig was a man who went mad in these surroundings. Well, you thought of the world of these magazines as being totally outside of you, another world. But she would be entering that world, seeing them with articles about herself and Fertig. Paid too. He kept gathering evidence.

The years before Stevie ... a tale of childless love-anxiety. Why anxiety? And fulfilment after Stevie: more anxiety, though of another kind; more love, another and deeper kind; the last chance for real happiness ... Something here – he sensed it – some special unhappiness. She explained her theory: "He loved Stevie too much. Everybody said so." Did she sound querulous? Annoyed? Jealous? What?

There were pictures on a shelf. Her: old shot ... costume jewellery, beads and beads, great brass hoop ear-rings, intense makeupless look, moody, pensive. Is that what she thought of herself? Obviously taken a long time ago: she looked interesting. He saw a Fertig, dimly seen, dust-covered. Ahh! Dust-covered. But not her picture. Who cleaned now? He wanted to look a little closer, but he noticed Sara's eyes, now anxious, shifting into sharper focus as she talked. Why wary? He continued to stroll around the room, hands behind his back, pulling on his sleeve, ticking one finger against the inside of his elbow, rising on his toes, walking, as if meditatively, as if listening very carefully to what was going on.

On another shelf he saw a few Japanese vases, three cheap African statuettes, two pictures of a little fat-faced blond boy, who with mean and spoiled eyes stared out at the world. Had madness made Fertig do it for him? For this kid? He couldn't feel it, but then, he told himself, Roy Bleakie was a bachelor. Had his father felt that way, that strongly about him, loved too much? Enough to do something like that for Roy Bleakie? If he had been right, his father would have done everything for him ... within the law. If he was wrong ... He remembered the austere features, the perfect sense of right and wrong, the sense that all things worked out in the long run as long as you were eternally vigilant and fought the good fight. But then, he couldn't even imagine his father, like any father, like a Fertig, letting-him take liberties: dandling, playing, being spit upon, having his hair pulled – not Judge Bleakie. But still, was it fatherliness? Roy Bleakie's father could never have gone mad, but then he had understood, to a degree, the way the world went and could do more about things, within the same limitations he set himself, than a Fertig could hope to do. He touched everything while they watched him.

Of course, Sara said, poor Harry (poor Harry? She tried hard to say it with feeling. Relegation to the class of the dead? Or at least gone. Watch it lady, Roy Bleakie will bring him back to life.) had his frustrations and was, in some ways, a competent man, an enormously competent man (competent? The word was an insult.) who, because he couldn't bring himself to express what was inside of himself, was willing to remain in a relatively inferior though indispensable position, which, of course, he must have resented since he could have, on sheer merit alone, risen to the top. Dr. Anslinger, her psychoanalyst, had understood Harry's tensions, his compulsive neuroses, had spoken of blocked aggressions, his repressions, but something like *this*? He himself had risen to the top, Bleakie thought: he would rise higher. She had suggested psychoanalysis to Harry many times… it had helped her enormously. She spoke again as if the whole thing had happened because he didn't listen to her; it was one little note, a touch, really, an undertone of resentment that was gone in the instant she said psycho-analysis had helped her to adjust, to understand the frustrations, the hostilities, to live with anxiety and rise out of the flatness of her affect. Not her words, he was sure, for they were jargon, comfortable talk. He looked at her. Her flat eyes stared as though looking inward but, still, at some stranger; her voice rose and fell, full of the correct stresses as she competently pretended emotion, but it sounded as though it were analysing a stranger. Her lips were slack, moist, almost quivering as though pleading. Pleading for what?

Bleakie became more restless and circled softly, faster, seeking to feel out the ghost of that Fertig who had exploded into madness. But where, in all the smallness of this house was Fertig? What banalities bespoke him? Where were the signs of insanity or, for that unlikely matter, a calculus of will?

Bleakie came around to Fertig's picture again. He quickly reached over and dusted off the coat of neglect. He rubbed his fingers; balled dust and little motes fell to the carpet. He saw the meek face of Fertig fading slowly in the glass, set there by the indifferent art of a studio photographer, staring, lifeless as any graduation or year-book picture. Not the same man as in the AP photos. Madness… the difference. He looked at that colourless face emerging out of the romantic studio shadows – shadows that did nothing to add to, or subtract from – that empty stare, that furtive hovering smile underneath that ridiculous and fussy little moustache. Typical accountant. Behind the picture, on the shelf, stuck among the books, was a black loose-leaf notebook, about three inches wide, six inches long, bulged out to two inches of thickness. Bleakie set down the picture, picked out the notebook, blew the dust off the top rim softly. He flipped through it.

Neat writing on cut-up accountant's paper. The first part contained biographies with pasted-in pictures. There was Rabbi Gordon, but a young rabbi, a long-ago rabbi, a lean and soulful-faced rabbi, full of suffering and holy determination: a temporal lie; a Polaroid snapshot of Miss Malabar, quite new, at work when it had been taken; THE VICTIMS ... ALL OF THEM ... family situations ... work habits ... phrases summing up ... figures, times, dates, numbers, tables, some kind of code, more numbers, something for every day of the week and for each victim so that he could have gone into action on any given day.

He shut it.

There was no point in the D.A.'s seeing this until he knew exactly what it was. Such an apparently logical statement might prejudice Fertig's case badly. On the other hand, it could prove that a psychotic obsession had been going on for a long time. He pretended to pick up the picture again and slipped the notebook into his pocket.

She was saying, "I feel as though I've failed him. Could I have helped him by understanding? Why did he do it? For Stevie? Stevie was dead. What good did it do?" Her eyes pleaded; she looked helpless, almost beautiful.

"Maybe he did it for you," Bleakie said, mind on the notebook, not really paying attention.

"*NO!* she said suddenly, loudly, face harsh, mouth and eye-flesh crease-strained. "I never asked him. What did he tell them? Did he tell them that?"

"No one thinks that," Bleakie said soothingly.

Then she tried to apologize, explain it, calming down fast, flustered and ashamed at being wrenched out of that encapsulation, uncovered; some secret, some shame?

"You have to visit him," he interrupted.

She looked reluctant.

"Have to go. Not to go ... prejudice his case ... stand by his side. Call you tomorrow. Don't worry. Leave it to me. Count on me." He smiled. Troubled, she smiled and looked grateful. Step one. He left.

He drove back to Manhattan and parked his car. He crossed Lafayette Street. The traffic lights changed against him. He danced across the street and evaded cars. He heard the angry shouts float away behind him. He saw his image, fractured, bounce off the polished sides of the cars, jiggle weirdly in the hubcaps, jostle on the spangled chrome, flash for a second in the whipped-by car windows. He trotted briskly up the steps of the Criminal Courts Building and saw himself neatly mirror-framed in the glass doorway. Some idiot cop, coming out through the door, seemed to hurl his reflection far outward. The door was held open for him. Someone murmured "Hello, Counsellor," as he trotted past and in.

Chapter 8

While Dr. Heisenberg, the head of City Psychiatric, waited for them to bring Fertig in, he looked over the reports again. They were very disappointing. Of course he had wanted to get at Fertig right away, but so many administrative duties interfered; he had to satisfy himself by glances through the one-way windows and the reading of staff reports. Then, too, the police had been yanking Fertig in and out; testing had hardly got properly started; then the Christmas and New Year's holidays came and went. When you were understaffed, nothing got done.

Actually, the psychiatric social worker had compiled a fairly complete biography: family contacts, life, business associations, organizations and clubs, no previous psychiatric contacts (a shame because it might have provided an outlet), steady employment – it was all surprisingly dull. It added up to years of rather frustrated living and to three years of extremely happy living until the child's death. Where was the key to the beginning of disintegration? Unless you accepted the premise that several of his assistants offered; Fertig broke down at, or right after, the death of his son. Too simple, too neat, suspiciously aesthetic. He fought against the trauma-thinking and everything it stood for: like life, or its parts, dysfunction was organic, casual, interconnected, evolutionary, not dramatic. If there was a beginning, it had come, probably, at least ten years ago, if not earlier. Of course, after the death – according to the police report – the steady frequenting of the bar, the common prostitute (sexual contact denied) … There is no indication of previous prostitute contacts before the child's death; extra-marital relationships denied.. .. His wife denies sexual adventures too. That's what fooled them: it seemed to begin right after the death. Wasn't it, rather, a new-stage symptom, a lysis sign? And didn't that contact imply a long-standing marital difficulty? Both of them denied it.

Psychology, medical reports, and the preliminary psychiatric work showed nothing special; an electro-encephalograph showed interesting waves, an interpretable deviation but not the schizophrenic's wave, there was really no other pathology, possibly a mild neuritis and a pre-allergic tissue softness of the nostrils. Medical history indicated appendectomy, tonsillectomy – nothing special at all. Fertig ate well and defected without the usual constipative side effects of system-construct retention. The guards, everyone, said he was most co-operative.

Fertig tested in the bright-normal range on the Wechsler-Bellevue scale, no genius at all. High literacy, good musical sense, superior mathematical ability. But curiously, Fertig had poor spatial relationships, slow (but not abnormally so) reflexes, slow motor responses, a touch of clumsiness in manual dexterity. How did this tie in with what the police almost lauded as his "superb efficiency" (a remark calculated to convict if there ever was one)? Heinsenberg would have expected, ... well, almost athletic ability. A profile was not visible, but a sketch had emerged. He was a little aloof from his wardmates and, curiously, his doodles were languid, indicating a passive personality. Obviously there was a pervasive paranoid system, but what kind of objective report could he give to the courts?

He looked at his watch; they were a little late. He was eager to come to grips with Fertig. He checked himself. Eagerness would be a giveaway to Fertig. If only he had time to make a good, long, leisurely psychiatric the way he used to, but he was always harassed; they were pushing him and he never had enough time any more to do much more than administrate.

Now, Sociological Analysis was hounding him for Fertig. The psychological journals were lining up, to say nothing about the direct, high-priority offers from *Time*, LIFE, *Atlantic*, *Harper's*, *Esquire*, and *Playboy*, and all the newspaper chains. *Playboy* was offering the most, but they would make a hash of it: Fertig among the breasts. LIFE was the most attractive. Colleagues from all over, as far away as Budapest, were asking for interviews with Fertig. There would be the spring and summer seminars and conferences at which to read papers. He had been successful in withholding information – except for the inevitable leaks that members of his staff, attendant through professional, permitted – from everyone and keeping Fertig isolated. And of course Fertig's attitude helped; he was claiming the newspapers were out to crucify him. He was going to save it all for the trial. What Fertig didn't know – and it was pointless to tell him – was that it would never get to trial.

They were ready for another round of depth-projective tests; second-generation tests, tests constructed on the information given in the first set. More than the usual Thematic Apperception Test, the Rorschach, the "draw-a-man" tests, he wanted to try a few new and exotic ones like the Cognitive Dissonance Inventory – if they could get the infrared-ray equipment in time – the Anomie Matrix – if Columbia would let them use their computers (it might mean letting them see Fertig). As for his variaht on the Chinese Communist confession-writing technique, he had the first history Fertig had written on the desk before him. As expected it was skeletal, but there were certain areas that could yield clues: for instance, Fertig made no mention of the prostitute – none whatever. Why this omission? The history would be sent back to Fertig with the comment that it was inadequate; he would be asked to amplify the interesting parts. Of course, Heinsenberg couldn't use guilt-generating coercion the way the Chinese did, but if Fertig continued this way it would end right there. On the other hand, he might be enticed by the need to vindicate himself. There was so little time before it came to arraignment, and he had to have a convincing report for Judge Jeffries. So much would be working against him ... public opinion ...

He would hold a staff think-meet tonight to see what they could come up with. Drugs? Total immersion isolation? As usual, he didn't have the equipment. He wasn't allowed to try these tests anyway. Nobody took his department seriously enough: if society did, they wouldn't have to contend with the Fertigs of the world. Someone knocked: Fertig! But it was his assistant with a series of reports to be signed. He scolded the deputy. The deputy apologized, "... but the reports must be in by tomorrow morning." Idiot, Heisenberg thought, what if he'd been in the middle of working with Fertig? What if he'd been in the middle of an insight... forever stifled ...? The assistant left, leaving another set of not-so-urgent papers to be gone through and counter-signed.

He looked over the weekly statistics; they were falling behind, always falling behind. With only limited facilities, how could he concentrate on the Fertig case? It should be his biggest case, the one that should stifle, once and for all, the bloodthirsty know-nothing press and bring to a halt the whole sadistic anti-abolition of capital punishment movement, which focused its most vicious attacks on the very concept of mental illness, calling it the Odysseus syndrome, the malingerer's myth. For the D.A. was bringing in his old opponent the irresponsible (irresponsible because Heisenberg knew him to be genuinely humanitarian) Dr. Bridgeman as prosecution's psychiatric consultant. Usually Bridgeman could make a deal with the D.A. so that he could have relative freedom. Sometimes he would state that a sick man was sane within the cramping and unrealistic terms of an obsolete McNaughten law. And in turn the D.A. would let him save someone seriously ill. But where Fertig was concerned, the D.A. would make no deals – he just wouldn't – he chose to make a reputation on Fertig's illness. But Heisenberg had chosen to fight, for there was too much at stake. If

Fertig could successfully counterfeit the appearance of a healthy man – healthy in the ignorant world's eyes ... No. Heisenberg had coped before; he would cope again.

For Dr. Heisenberg had a dream. He envisioned a universal psychiatric plant where *all* the populace would be tested at various phases of their lives, where all the possible paraphernalia of scientific psychiatric testing would be at hand for use of teams, where, indeed, the Fertigs of the world could be detected before their personalities evolved and hardened into psychosis and they did irreparable damage to society and to themselves. Then the ill could be apprehended, treated with medicine and therapy, or, if science lagged, treatment could be deferred for compassionate custody till science made new strides. Instead they were at the beck and call of the hostile, the ignorant, the anal money-minded legislators, *and* under-budgeted. They were forced to turn the sick back into society and hoped they didn't dysfunction too dangerously. Then when one of them did something horrible, the newspapers always screamed: "Why was he let out?" Why wasn't Fertig down yet. This was why Dr. Heisenberg was thankful he had Bleakie as an ally ... Bleakie, who had made a fool of him in court so many times ... manipulative Bleakie... He stopped himself: after all it was Bleakie's problem, not his.

Fertig was brought up into Dr. Heisenberg's office by two guards. The psychiatrist was looking at the papers on his desk; he looked up and saw Fertig and the guards and smiled. He extended his hand, waving Fertig towards a soft, deep-green leather chair. One of the guards left and the other stood back against the wall. "Someone is always offering me a chair," Fertig said wearily. Dr. Heisenberg smiled, trying to look friendly, not wanting to say anything because he wanted Fertig to ventilate as much as possible before he became involved; the first approach was so important. Fertig didn't smile back: but he had committed himself by his comment on his present state.

As Dr. Heisenberg put the papers into a drawer in his desk, he switched on a concealed tape recorder. There was a button on the floor under Heisenberg's desk; he could tap it softly with his rubber-soled shoes to put a corresponding mark on the tape to indicate those reactions which were non-verbal, significant, revealing. He stood up and went to the windows and drew the curtains. It was very dim but not completely dark in the room. Heisenberg couldn't see Fertig's face clearly, but by now he knew it completely. Heisenberg sat down in his chair and switched on lights that kept him in relative darkness yet illuminated the patient's face without shining directly into his eyes.

They were quiet a long time. Dr. Heisenberg reached into his pocket, took out a packet of cigarettes, pulled one out, lit it, and put the packet on the table. Fertig didn't reach for one of his own or ask him for one. He puffed his cigarette and looked gravely, noncommittally into Fertig's eyes. Fertig looked steadily at him, unblinking. Fertig's finger touched the brass studs set into the leather, followed them around and towards the floor as far as his hand would reach, reversed direction and went, following the arabesque, all the way back; Heisenberg tapped: the psychiatrist felt a wave of warm empathy well up inside of him. They were quiet. Dr. Heisenberg understood. He felt the warmth mount; he felt Fertig involving himself, caught and sick; he noted, for his memory, the untaken cigarette, the unblinking stare, and the compulsive tracing of the loop of studs.

He blew out a puff of smoke. They were quiet. Two minutes went by. He tapped.

"Well, aren't you going to ask me something?" Fertig asked.

"Who are you?"

Fertig looked surprised. "Don't you know?" he asked, and then, seeming to understand, said "Harry Fertig."

"What did you do?"

"I'm an accountant."

Dr. Heisenberg noted the use of the present tense; he also noticed that Fertig assumed the question had nothing to do with his crime. It was a failure to accept irrevocable reality – a holding on to his previous role as a society member. "Where are you?"

"In the psychiatric ward of the City Hospital," Fertig sighed as if bored.

"Who am I?"

"Still another psychiatrist, I suppose."

Did he, Dr. Heisenberg wondered, detect a faint hostility in they way Fertig said it? He wasn't sure. "I am Dr. Heisenberg, the head of the psychiatric section." Fertig seemed unimpressed. "Why are you here?"

"Judge Clemente sent me here."

"Is that the only reason you're here?"

Fertig shrugged and his finger followed the brass studs on one arm. "I don't belong here."

Dr. Heisenberg noted that he used his left hand; the system Fertig had built up and had encased himself in was tighter than Heisenberg had thought. He felt another stirring inside. "Where do you belong?"

"In prison, I suppose."

That Fertig said "I suppose" implied a whole realm of punishments – what else could he mean? what else could satisfy his monumental guilt? – worse than prison. Prison was merely a substitute. "Why?" Dr. Heisenberg asked.

Fertig sighed. "This is all nonsense. You know that, don't you? Why are we playing this game?"

It was out. Good. The resistance barrier was manifest. "Game? But what game?"

"I'm not a child. I'm not insane. I don't belong here. That idiot Clemente sent me here."

Dr. Heisenberg smiled to conceal the sudden surge of annoyance. But he remembered that Fertig was a sick man trapped in the prison of his hate, projecting his psychic state of moral idiocy on to Clemente. It was the classic reversal so necessary to the paranoid schizophrenic: to turn the standard ethical forces into demonic agents of evil. Moreover, he *would*, of course, suppress the heretic insights the mere being here might throw on his reality constructs. He felt again the sense of warmth and understanding return. "Don't you think there might be a *reason* why the judge remanded you here?"

Seeing and noting every flicker of Fertig's face muscles, he could see the annoyance; the lips tightened under the little brush moustache, the head jerked, almost imperceptibly, so that the light gleamed on the glasses and Fertig's eyes were lost to view. Heisenberg tapped. Heisenberg shifted his position slightly so that he could see Fertig's eyes.

"Of course there's a reason," Fertig said. "They think I'm insane."

"And what do you think?"

Fertig didn't answer that.

"Supposing we grant that. What other reasons might the judge have had for sending you here?"

"Stupidity and confusion."

Fertig, he saw, was behaving classically. He tried another approach. "Why do you belong in prison rather than here?"

"I committed a crime. I killed. Isn't it simple?"

Heisenberg tapped twice. He was having difficulty liking Fertig. What was it? Was it that Fertig, in spite of all Heisenberg knew of him, succeeded in looking normal? That he successfully encased the whole psychotic syndrome; he, indeed, gave the annoying impression of a man dealing with children? Was it his trick of tightening his lips and tapping his fingers? Heisenberg could cope with aggression, even hatred. He was used to suspicion. He was used to all the vicious manifestations disturbance made them exhibit, even used to the sneering, supercilious attitudes that the most deranged showed. He had handled the gibbering anxieties of little, resentful men caught in the centre of a vast, incomprehensible crushing complex and driven to kill.... And hadn't the "draw-a-man" test shown it all: Fertig's thinking about his own role? It all indicated explosive repressions that could evolve, as they had, into the grand assurance of a demented prophet: but the psychiatrist had dealt with these too. The healthy man was not, couldn't ever be, like that – didn't they see that? He felt a little better about Fertig.

Heisenberg always assured and loved. And he had been prepared for Fertig. He understood, immediately, what was wrong, understood the warp that cleaved Fertig's personality: the dysfunctions that had gradually destroyed the vital, homeostatic balances; perhaps the fatal programming of the hereditary material; the resultant cramped ducts that permitted only imperfect flows of hormonal juices; the knotted, neuronic wires; the grand and minor imbalances that, malfunctioning the mind and body, made Fertig what he was: progressively degenerating till he had that final outburst of psychic depravity. No doubt he had always been psychopathic, but somehow the tracks of his sickness had paralleled, not conflicted with, the aims of society. The death of his son triggered a switch to divergence, and mere, if that word could be used, psychopathia became ravening sociopathy.

But understanding it all, there was something about Fertig that made him look too normal. He tapped. It made Heisenberg feel ... disturbed the more he looked, the less he was sure ... What was wrong, Heisenberg wondered. What was there in him that made Fertig elicit these hostile responses? What vagrant, neurotic impulse was it that made Heisenberg feel that Fertig should get just what he wanted? Was it the possibility that Fertig was *not* sick that was so disturbing? Heisenberg discarded the thought at once. He would analyse it later. He would examine and resolve his intrusive and revealing feelings – the sub-conscious motives regarding his weakness in thinking Fertig a threat – he would resolve his conflicts. He had difficult, hate-provoking patients before, but they always gave in to resting in a short while. His foot tapped.

"You prefer prison to this place?"

"I don't know. I've never been in prison before; I'm not a criminal ..." Heisenberg noted that. "In a way it's even nice here. The beds are comfortable ... though they don't let you lie on them during the day. The food is – well, it isn't home cooking. The people, on the other hand ..." Fertig shuddered; fastidious revulsion and self-disassociation, Heisenberg observed, and tapped. "But I'm not insane. I belong in prison."

"And you must be punished, is that it? You want to repent?"

"I'm not insane. I must be punished. I'm not sorry for what I did. I was right. I'd do it again. It was the only thing that could be done. It should be done now and then."

The horror of that calm statement, the flatness of voice, the steadiness of the eye ... The insistence on sanity was classic too, of course, but how could anyone say these things and be considered not sick? The insistence on punishment went along with the posture of sanity; only the sane are *worthy* of punishment; this was why Fertig refused counsel at the arraignment. But couldn't he see the vital link between wanting punishment and repentance? "This place doesn't meet the requirements?"

They were quiet for a while. "It's not as complex as that. When Stevie was killed …" Heisenberg noted that version of reality. "… an outrage was committed. An imbalance, call it that, was created. My life ended …"

"How?"

"For me to have killed the three people directly responsible would have been most satisfying, but it wouldn't have meant anything more than my getting revenge. How I used to dream of revenge on those three! How I used to daydream about the different ways I'd kill them … so they'd suffer and suffer!" Fertig took a deep breath; Heisenberg tapped. "You see what I'm trying to say?"

The psychiatrist nodded; he noted the unanswered question but didn't want to interrupt the flow, because a whole, rich vein of fantasy life was implied here – but, meanwhile, a silly and irrelevant phrase popped into his mind, *make your fondest dreams come true*, and he felt ashamed (why ashamed?) for thinking it. He was waiting, hoping for the whole elaborate self-justifying rationalization to be reconstructed for him.

"But there was much more involved in his death. His death showed me a – what'll I call it – an evil. But to merely kill would create another evil, an imbalance, and that imbalance, would finally, have to be paid for by me. The idea was, of course, to do all these things to teach a lesson. And because my life was over –"

"I don't understand how it was over?"

"My child was dead, so it was easy to do, I had nothing to lose. Planning … you know the rest. Now is that so hard to understand? What does the fact that I have such and such an IQ or take so many minutes to place pegs in holes, or tell one story rather than tell another when I see a picture, or I see one thing in a blot in preference to seeing another – what do these things have to do with the issue?"

Dr. Heisenberg didn't answer. The disconnected and arid language Fertig used indicated a significant detachment.

"So you see, I belong in prison. I should be punished. My lesson was learned a long time ago … before I decided to do it. Everyone else's lesson will come in court. What happened should be made public, not confined to your notes."

"But you understand," Dr. Heisenberg told him, "that this is a *prison* ward?"

"So?"

"Think what would happen if you had, let us say, pneumonia while in prison proper. You would be brought here, to the hospital."

"It isn't the same thing."

"Why not?"

"This is the psychiatric ward; I'm not suffering from any mental disease. If I'm here it means that what I did is going for nothing."

"Why?"

"Do you ask these questions to get a response, or do you think I'm stupid, or are you stupid?" Fertig asked. Heisenberg stopped himself from tapping with difficulty: his leg shook. "It goes for nothing because then it is considered irrational, pointless, psychotic. How can the act of a madman mean anything?"

The psychiatrist couldn't help flushing and feeling rage at the calm, pedantic way Fertig asked it. He was irritated to the point of trembling and was glad the lights were there to keep him in the darkness. He started to reach for a cigarette but stopped himself. It would give him away. The room was silent except for the sound of his own breathing and, when he heard that, he breathed more quietly. Suddenly he asked, "But what about the girl? The one you were involved with? The prostitute?" Hoping to surprise Fertig.

"First of all she had nothing to do with it. Secondly I wasn't involved with her."

"But the police reports –"

"Are lies if they say anything else than I used to talk to her now and then."

But of course the Thematic Apperception Test indicated just what Fertig could have in common with a common prostitute. "I can understand your annoyance," he said smiling, "and I sense your hostility. But don't you see I'm trying to help you?"

"You're trying to prove I'm insane."

"Or sane."

"… that's what you're here for. That's your job."

Fertig hadn't heard him. "I can't 'prove' a thing. *You're* the one who does the proving."

"I'm not a child. Don't be a child yourself by acting like I'm one."

Had his tone given him away? Heisenberg made his voice seem reproachful: "You're being hostile to me."

"I'm not. I don't feel anything about you at all."

"Isn't that a sign of hostility?"

"No. This is a waste of time."

"Why is it a waste of time?"

"Because I'm not insane."

"Insanity, Harry –"

"Not Harry. 'Mr. Fertig' or 'Fertig' will do. Not Harry."

"All right, *Mr. Fertig*," Dr. Heisenberg said in his most aren't-we-being-childish voice. "Insanity is a legal fiction. It has no psychiatric meaning."

"All right. I'm not sick. I'm not neurotic, psychotic. I'm well. I'm balanced."

Usually Heisenberg could convince the patient that his interests and the law's interests were not the same and win their sympathy. In this case he was working under an enormous handicap *because* he was the doctor: Fertig's doctor-bias – he preferred prison and the Law to him. Fertig's petulant voice told him how far they would have to go.

"... and, at any rate, you can't prove whatever you want with those tests; they are rational, scientific, and unbiased instruments."

Fertig sighed and began touching the studs. Heisenberg tapped. Time passed. Heisenberg couldn't wait. "Tell me why you did it? Why did you choose to kill *these* people? How did you come to do it?"

"Look at the police reports. I had to tell them six times. I've told a hundred people here."

Heisenberg noted the exaggeration. "I've already seen the reports. You just told them how you did it and the bare why of it. Tell me what happened that night at the hospital."

Heisenberg watched, barely paying attention to what Fertig was saying, being interested, rather, in the flow of reactions. Later, he would listen to the tape again and again. Fertig didn't get excited when he was telling Dr. Heisenberg about the night his son died. He was leaning forward and looking straight ahead, almost into the lights, seeming to see that night and reporting what he saw. Heisenberg's foot tapped several times on the button.

"... and when the doctor and the nurse examined Stevie they were careless. They didn't care at all. Ultimately, they killed him," Fertig was saying.

Heisenberg tapped three times. "How do you know?"

"I saw it, didn't I?"

Dr. Heisenberg tapped.

Fertig continued to tell it, explaining about the three at the clinic, the nurse, the doctor, and the clerk who had been responsible for Stevie's death. Though he told it quietly, tensely, Heisenberg still tapping his foot, could see the suppressed suffering, the damped-down pain, the unbearable pain. Yet Heisenberg wanted Fertig to continue because he knew the telling of it would purge it from Fertig's system again and only then would begin to bring up all the other signs, to ventilate the syndrome that had caused him pain in the first place, to reveal the secret warp that lay hidden at the bottom of it all. He tapped.

"... he died in my arms. They had killed him. He lay there ... twisted ... Sara wailed ... she wailed ... that sound ... and we kept driving to the next hospital while Sara wailed. They killed him."

"But how do you know?" Dr. Heisenberg asked.

Fertig relaxed. "He died, didn't he?"

Heisenberg accepted the logic. They were finished for the day.

Dr. Heisenberg couldn't get to Fertig for another two weeks. He was too busy to evaluate the growing mass of material. Fertig was still writing his second history. Fertig was becoming cavalier about his responses to testing, sometimes working hard, other times obviously trying to get through everything as quickly as possible. Staff was divided; some said this behaviour constituted a psychotic reaction, others said he was tired and they were pressing him too hard. Was Fertig reaction-forming? Should they stop testing for a week? But they had done only less than half the work, technically not enough for a report to the court.

When Fertig was brought in again, Heisenberg lowered the lights and watched him sitting in the easy chair. The tape recorder was on.

But this time Dr. Heisenberg couldn't wait. Time was running out; he had been kept busy with administrative duties. Soon he would be still busier: He was having conferences with the *Time-LIFE* men. He had been approached by editors for a book on Fertig. His department was under fire. So when Fertig would be brought to court, he would then be able to release his articles for publication. He would need to hurry; at least two of his staff psychiatrists were preparing for newspaper interviews.

"Who are you?" he asked.

"Harry Fertig."

"What do you do?"

"I'm a prisoner."

Heisenberg considered the shift in emphasis; Fertig had gone from one state to another, a more advanced state, the pre-martyr position; it was significant that Fertig was still not willing to accept his status as patient. "Why are you here?"

"Mistake."

"What do you mean by that?"

"Killed. Should be in prison. Am not insane."

Was the personality breaking down? The tired, laconic answers and the lack of the personal pronoun indicated a widening rift in the self: was Fertig displacing the character who had done the killings from himself? The extreme calmness was significant, Heisenberg thought. Heisenberg tapped. He prodded Fertig. "Tell me, how did you reconcile what you did with the moral code?"

"I had a moral code once, a system by which I lived, I suppose ..."

"Don't you know?"

"You don't consider ethics much if nothing disrupts your life?"

"What do you mean?"

"I can't be sure. You know this much; someone says to you, 'do this' – change the books a little, for instance; overlook certain invoices – and all sorts of opportunities would arise, so you go ahead and do it. Some of these acts, if you think about it, are good; some bad. There's income tax, for instance; they ask you to play games with it."

This was better: he was beginning to displace back from ethics to emotion-loaded events. "Who?"

"The government. Your boss."

"You mean you always filed a scrupulously honest income-tax report?"

"I mean I never did. I mean I know no one who ever did..."

"What does all this have to do with –"

"Don't you see the connections?"

Was he fusing everything into one world construct? Evil? "I'm afraid I don't."

"Some acts are what you would like to *really* do, but you don't because they're wrong, or you're afraid. Mostly you're afraid."

"Such as?"

"Stealing – but I did that, or helped. I made up for that." He smiled secretly. "Killing – I eventually did that too. Bribery – I bribed and was bribed. Corruption – you always are corrupt without thinking about it; without knowing. But at a certain point – and this is it – you realize what is good and what is bad; and then you know you've always been bad – if you're unlucky."

"Why unlucky?"

"Because your son is killed. Your life is over unless you do something about it."

"And if you don't?"

"The torture is too much to bear."

"Torture?"

"Did you know that itching is a form of pain?"

Dr. Heisenberg had no use for Fertig's *Reader's Digest* medicine. "So?"

"So you don't sleep. Or maybe it's – you know what I thought of it as? An ethical itch. I had to keep moving. To walk at night. Movement stopped it."

Better. The symbolic manifestation. Dermal hallucination. "And?"

"What if Stevie had simply died, had not been killed? I suppose I would have slept well. I would have adjusted, lived, and died... empty, and gone to my grave unfulfilled."

Heisenberg was not ready to concede that Fertig was fulfilled, or to be fulfilled, by execution – not by any stretch of the imagination. He thought of asking what if it had been an accident? He couldn't. He couldn't face Fertig's anger: not that it would be an insane ravening, he was sure. He would even welcome such a reaction. What was it? He free-associated fast. Calmness. Lecturing. Father childing a child.

Logic. His foot tapped. Rational. His foot tapped. This was silly. He wasn't facing it, working it through. "But you say Stevie was *killed?*" he said ironically, and found himself bracing for the... chiding... and tapped his foot to release the bonds of his inexplicable tension.

"Yes. So, you see, if I accepted what I was, then I must accept Stevie's murder and say it was not a murder, it was an accident, something that just happened. Our oldest friends said 'sue'. Was my son's life worth money? Mr. Grenoble..." Fertig stopped.

"Mr. Grenoble? Your employer. Yes?"

"His idea was to liquidate; cut your losses; get out from under; don't throw good money after bad. But this was something you couldn't make disappear by rigging the books. The rabbi, he said pray, join his congregation and pray. I had been – well, he's a modern rabbi so he would hardly use a word like *sinful*. It's too upsetting, that word. It's for revivalists... and the rabbi is a sophisticated man. God gives and God takes – yes, he said that. But the *tone*, as if to say that's the way the ball bounces. It happened. It's over. Adjust. Cut your loss. It happened. I thought, here I am and he doesn't even see me and doesn't even know that he may have been one of the responsible ones. Because I say it was *caused*, something malignant *caused* it, it didn't *happen*.

"How many times did I see newspaper items; people died out of stupidity and neglect, carelessness, indifference. And how many times did I just read the story, shake my head 'terrible, terrible', and then go on to something else. This time it happened to *me*."

"Yes?"

"And I saw Stevie's death was caused. He was murdered... Something that was a part of the way things are did it, and so whatever I learned, whatever I had lived by, all of it, was evil. And at the bottom of his death was murder. It's like doing accounts, you know. Something doesn't balance. You go back and back and you see how each error is connected and how the whole audit was thrown off... *They* were the immediately responsible. That's like saying, 'Oh, yes, this invoice was entered wrongly', but it's more than that, it's more than just a chain of errors, wilful errors, and a chain or responsibility that connects more than only the people who were cruel to me that night. A grand network binds, or should bind us, to *all* these killings." Fertig was musing, thinking about it, going through, reconstructing something he had almost forgotten.

But Heisenberg wasn't interested in Fertig's ethical musing, that was rationalization. "Did you work it out like that, so logically, so carefully?" he asked.

"No. I *saw*. The reasoning came later."

Heisenberg felt the warmth rise now, the understanding. He saw that beneath his calm exterior, beneath the rationale, Fertig was erecting the dreadful tinge of sickness, the mad, visionary fervour, the encompassing and distorted world-view. He leaned back and looked at him, approving, and wished his look had the power to make Fertig see and be healed by seeing. His foot tapped. "What do you mean by *saw*?"

"I could go through it all, point for point, all the things that had meaning, the things ..."

"Insights," Heisenberg said, unable to stand the word *things*.

"Insights. Peculiar things. Events. Moments. Little encounters. It all built up. And then, one day, I *saw* what I had been learning all the time, what I now knew. And I knew that everything was evil, rotten, corrupt from top to bottom –"

"But what showed you that it all worked against *you*?" he prompted.

"It works against everyone. But when you accept, then you are part of it and you don't see it or feel it. But if you step away from it, or are you put outside of it, then you see how it all works against you – the big things as well as the small, the everyday frustrations."

"But was *nothing* right, good, or just?" Heisenberg asked.

"Is anything?"

"And you must set it right?"

"I had to."

"Why you?"

"Stevie died."

"And when you 'saw' you went out and killed ... Did the girl have anything to do with it?"

"Why do you keep harping on her? No."

Fertig's emphasis was too strong. He tapped.

"We just talked, that's all. We just talked. She had nothing to do with it." Fertig leaned back and looked at Heisenberg, exasperated.

"So you went out and killed one day."

"Do you think it's as easy as that? When you see, once you see, you have to decide what can be done.

"Supposing I sued?

"Worse, supposing I sued and won?

"Supposing I went to the newspapers?

"Or walked the streets and said, They have killed my son'? I'd be here anyway, wouldn't I?

"Supposing I learned to write and wrote exposés?

"Who would care?

"Supposing I adjusted?

"Who would care?

"What then?" Fertig took a deep breath. Heisenberg tapped.

"But to kill everyone who was involved in the logical and unlimited chain of responsibility – to kill them all is to kill millions – to make the world *understand*, *see*, you see, I thought of a lot of people who should get it: Stevie's pediatrician for not coming when we needed him, my boss – who was responsible? And I thought, I felt, I came to see, to remove the *unit* that was *immediately* guilty for the death of my son."

"But how does killing solve it if, as you said, everything is rotten, corrupt?" Heisenberg asked. "What purpose does it serve other than to call attention to yourself?"

"It means something can be done. It's in everyone. Everyone can do something. There are two goods. Love is good. Life is good. What destroys them, what beats them down, what is careless about them is evil. So –"

"Just like that? So coldly?"

"Coldly? Who said that? The newspapers are saying that. Cold-blooded? The day I saw Cartwright for the first time my whole body shook with the need to kill him. I'm surprised that his fancy instruments didn't detect it, but he ... he had other interests.

"I read up on symptoms – he was a cancer man, you know – and went to see him with a complete story of illness. He had a beautiful nurse and a beautiful receptionist. He was greying at the temples, but his face was still young, untroubled; it made him look vigorous and fatherly. He sat back in a leather chair, swivelled slowly, nodding wisely while I told him of my 'symptoms'. Very wise. He glanced, from time to time, at a machine that blinked red and yellow lights while dials danced back and forth. In the examination room his voice was gentle, reassuring; ... it's a funny thing to say but his voice was reverent, like a minister's. I began to feel, ... well, helpless: do you realize what a terrible thing that is, to feel that helpless, to need him, and worse, I began to trust him. Trust him! When there was *nothing* wrong with me! I said that the other doctors had told me it was nothing but nerves, for I had lost a son recently: I watched him very carefully. He just nodded. They always nod that way: it means the worst. He told me to wait a few minutes ... he'd be right back. I sat on the cold paper over the leather table in the middle of that tubing cluttering the room, listening to the wise hum of the machines, in the darkness. And I was cold. After about three minutes I got up. The tile floor was very cold. I went to the door and I opened it quietly. You know, I couldn't imagine myself doing anything like that: where did I get the nerve? He was with the nurse; he was seated in his swivel chair, the one I killed him in; she was bent down over him ..."

Fertig sighed. "He's a director of the hospital – he was. What was he doing the night my son died? I shook with it ... Only wait, I told myself ... I had to get out of there fast.

"Another day I was following Blumenthal in my car. He went home. He drove up his driveway and his youngest child, a girl of about five, very pretty, came running out and threw herself into his arms as I was driving past. Then I thought, kill all their kids; they killed yours: that would even it. And I almost ran into a tree thinking, 'kill her'."

Heisenberg tapped again and again.

"So I drove away so fast that I almost got a speeding ticket and I kept thinking, that's crazy, that's crazy, look what they've brought you to. To kill Blumenthal made sense, but not the child.

"The morning I went to see Miss Malabar. She let me in. She whined and cried… And she was only a poor woman, all alone, old, miserable, and I thought, by the time we got to her bathroom, if I don't begin it now I will never do it. Think of the plan. Think of Stevie and Sara. I pulled out the gun. She was talking … Thirty-five years in that miserable apartment and it was lace doilies on the easy chairs and a souvenir of the '39 World's Fair and plastic sheeting on top of lace curtains with window shades down and Venetian blinds closing everything in.… It's a funny thing: I never used to notice any of these things. And it's a funny thing about bathrooms; you hear the echoes when you sing. You know, I could hear an echo sobbing under her nasty way of talking. I knew I was lost. And I thought I'll go on to the next one on my list, but I knew that if I didn't kill her I wouldn't kill anyone: I'd just have to write Stevie off. I began to put the gun away and she turned and saw me.

"The others were easy."

Dr. Heisenberg's foot tapped uncontrollably through the recital, shaking in a palsy while he encouraged, he nodded, knowing that from now on it would be much easier. "You could almost say you considered it an act of love, an act of life?"

"No. It wasn't an act of love. What an idea!"

But Dr. Heisenberg didn't hear him. There he had it; there he had it; there he had it! He could see the whole pattern; the inevitable descent from plateau to plateau of adjustment, coping with frustrations: the early compulsions, the stimulus, the breakdown, the delusional paranoia, then visions of grandeur, the rationalization into saviourism, and that final excess, that significant impulse which triggered the holocaust. All that was missing was the final immolation, which a sane society, which a protective and loving society, must never permit if he, Heisenberg, could help it. It was of such stuff, if directed along the proper channels, that the great dictators were made – the Hitlers, the Castros, the Stalins; it was of such stuff the Christs, the Buddhas, the Mohammeds were built. He could almost have rendered a report without seeing any of the test results.

Heisenberg's foot tapped one two three four five six seven times; compulsion paranoia delusion grandeur protest saviour … GOD! And he loved the poor, low, wretched Fertig.

Chapter 9

By the time they brought Sara into the visiting room she felt tired but calm; tranquillizers insulated her. It seemed as though she had spent the whole day on her feet. And suddenly, for no good reason, she began to worry about the children in her class, though it had been so long since she had seen them. Who was taking over? Was she a good teacher? Would they be well taken care of? She hardly thought about the children since the night they took Harry away ... and now she could vividly remember the trembly feel of the sliding doors of the clothes closet, remember the way Alonso sneaked in and hid among the coats till she missed him, went in, and got him amid the hilarious shouting laughter of the other children: it was an old class joke. She would punish Alonso, but never meant it; he would look abject, but never mean it.

Her shoes sounded on the shiny tile floors, but each click and click-echo sounded not so much far away, in fact, just outside, as unable to penetrate the comforting film protecting her – probably because of the extra dosage (Dr. Anslinger thought it was a good idea). And even though encased, it wasn't as though she couldn't feel each pertinent emotion, it was just diminished, softer, safer, easier to handle.

Her breasts felt oddly heavy, dragging her down – had she worn the wrong brassiere? the one she always wore a few days before she got her period? And how much longer was that going to happen, that painful swelling of the breasts before it began, the intolerable pain of it – like filling up with undrunk milk – causing the straps to cut into her shoulders and shove the tender skin against the binding, balloon disgustingly out over the edges, making her nipples feel sore, marring the cut of her new dress, beginning to unravel her: how long? She thought she had left all that behind after she finished feeding Stevie. It had returned after his death. Lately, for no reason at all, she began to worry about change of life. But she was too young. Yet weren't there cases of change of life even in the late thirties? And wouldn't it be better to get it over with? She could contemplate the terror of it, but it meant the end of humiliation.

She went through the corridors escorted by huge, red-faced men wearing white uniforms. They were a little frightening. She walked down endless aisles faced with nothing but the essential cinder-block till she didn't know where she was or from where she had come. They handed her from guard to guard as they carefully led her through heavy steel doors, clanging them behind her, taking her onward, turning and turning.

When it seemed as though she was on the verge of exhaustion, they delivered her to the visiting room: at least that was what she thought it was. They gave her back her pass and told her to hold on to it. One of the guards joked crudely, trying to be pleasant: they would have to lock her up with the loonies if she didn't have the pass and she wouldn't want that, did she, lady? "Know what makes you different from the *meshugas*, lady? That piece of paper. Only that." And he took it out of her hands and frowned. "What are you doing out here, tootsie? Back to the ward!" And she vaguely felt, far inside, far away there, a striving of something in her head, a muted turmoil in her body, and then the guard gave the pass back to her and laughed. "Your husband's a good boy, Mrs. Fertig, very co-operative. You'd never even know..."

Why not? she thought; it was almost frightening. She had lived with Harry and if he – who had always appeared so sane, so rational – if he was psychotic, then what about... anyone. "No. No. No. No," Dr. Anslinger told her. "It is *his* problem." Dr. Anslinger had departed entirely from his usual psychoanalytic methods for the time being: trauma called for emergency techniques, a kind of psychoanalytic artificial respiration, directive crash therapy to save her... But was it as simple as Dr. Anslinger said? She sat down on a chair in the middle of the room, in front of a table that, running almost to the ends of the room, cut it in half. She was panting as if she had been running. Except for an upright board that reached as high as her chin, the table was bare. She sat in the empty tiled room. It reminded her of taking the children down to the toilet or recess, and she remembered the smell of disinfectant, the children's shouts amplified joyfully off the bathroom walls, and her "If you're not out in *one* minute more, I'm coming after you." Always the boys, only she smiled, feeling as she always did, the sudden irritation, displaced, modified, almost made sweet this time by this tiring comfort.

She waited. Maybe they weren't going to come. Maybe something delayed them. She had put off visiting for so long, that the guilt she felt from not coming increased, and then prevented her from coming when all she had to do, should do, was just go. So simple, she thought, and she smiled to still her... anxiety. Harry might come in any second. She had prepared so carefully for the visit and yet she couldn't bring herself to visit. "You have to confront *yourself* by going," Dr. Anslinger told her. "Why are you avoiding it?" She laid her head on her folded arms and pretended that she was taking a nap with the children at rest time. There was a noise. She looked up suddenly as if being caught doing something she shouldn't.

She saw two guards bring a man into the visiting room. They had brought the wrong man. But he looked like Harry, though she couldn't be sure. He had the same pale, narrow face, wore the same silver-rimmed glasses. He stood, stooping over the same way that used to infuriate her so many times. She had not seen him for such a long time that she couldn't be sure. He managed, through all of it, to retain his moustache. The moustache made him look quite ordinary, quite normal, the way she had always known him. She had a sudden stinging menstrual cramp: impossible; she had three weeks to go. Her lower back began to ache. The pain threatened to upset her – preparedness – she smiled. It was a little ridiculous, she thought, to have that moustache – how many arguments did they have about it in the early days? – and to be flanked by those two huge men. What had she expected? Someone, almost emaciated, bent over from pain (of what? Beating?), the head shaven, or at least the hair turned grey, perhaps even a few teeth missing, knocked out, the lips swollen, trembling, eyes weeping, and the body anonymous in something shapeless and grey – where was the number on the chest? Or perhaps more the stranger because he was a raving maniac, or a catatonic.

But he had his lips fixed together as if he were going to say, softly but firmly, "Sara, how many times ...?" She had forgotten that prim annoyance, those tones he used so much before Stevie was born. "I don't like that dress. Too flamboyant. It isn't you," he might say. And she vaguely felt that answering irritation which had been hers but seemed not to be a part of her at all any more, seemed buried in the past: "Everything is too flamboyant for you." She wondered what he really did know about her. Did he notice that she had slimmed down, that she looked better? For they had taken her to beauty parlours before photographing her. She would have scorned it all once, the muds, the clipping, the steaming, the lotions, the fluttery strategy of finding out her good points and accentuating them, highlighting them with subtle bases, powders, shadowings. ("There is pretty-beauty and there is character-beauty; and of the two of them character-beauty is the best. Almost everyone has it if you know how to bring it out," the famous beautician told her.) And then they would go through it again. Discreet hands caressed and corrected without being vulgar. And a discreet interviewer – someone Roy Bleakie had recommended highly – had begun to ask questions, soothingly, without being vulgar or directive or trying to shape her replies – "should we say that... could we put it... ?"

The guards led him and sat him down facing her and then went to the opposite ends of the room; they folded their arms; they watched. Seated, all she could see was his head and part of his neck. He kept staring at her. Was she garish? Tasteless? Was this the place for... ? She smiled at him. She felt make-up beginning to melt off her face before that superior stare. "Hello, Sara," he told her.

How like Harry's voice it sounded. *How could you live with ... and not know?* They all asked her that. She looked at him. Well, look at him, she thought, you see what I mean? You wouldn't know it at all. She hadn't seen him for three weeks – was it so long? They hadn't been apart for – was it fourteen years? Just under the thinnest layer of skin, her face felt puffy, ballooning, too thick to make expression. She should have dressed simply today, worn her old suit. To give herself a sense of the usual? To give Harry a sense of the familiar? That was it. But this new dress: it's too elegant to teach school in – to get children's sticky hands over her – yet simple enough. *Not* garish. *Not* flamboyant. What was wrong with her? That extra tranquillizer … everything led her back along a tiring line of thinking, self-discussion, while that feeling like menstrual cramps persisted … was she sweating? What would Dr. Anslinger say about this? He looked like Harry, she thought again. He looked like Stevie's father. She strove to remember him … changing Stevie's diaper. Mechanical motions, lifting the feet like levers and thrusting the dry cloth quickly, expertly, beneath the adorable, writhing buttocks – how many times had they kissed those sweet round lumps of dimpled flesh? How many times had they bent over, nose to button nose, lips drawn back in the exaggerated, face-straining, tooth-showing smile to show clearly to that tiny puzzled face that it was indeed a smile? A smile also a little like that monster whose psychotic, rage-distorted face snarled viciously out of the front page of every paper the day after Harry Fertig was arrested.

Had he been so hidden from her all those years? Had she really blinded herself? Fourteen years? Or had his love for Stevie really driven him mad. "I always said there was *something* about him," her mother kept saying; now her brothers were beginning to say it too. Who had she been living with? Dr. Anslinger, as usual, put his sensitive finger on it when he said, "We see everything: we forget nothing. But what does it matter who you were living with? What matters is *why you chose to think you were living with a certain kind of man*; it's that which is the expression of your guilt feelings and constitutes the projection and the contra-reality tropism." Was it so simple? Did she fight facing it? Or did her sense of guilt make her fight having insight into the real Harry and thus the real self hidden under the foamy shield of self-comfort? Her mind wouldn't accept any possibility other than that it was Harry, Harry who had loved her for fourteen years … and whom she had loved – wouldn't let her forget it – had loved passionately, intensely, totally – don't forget – loved most completely *that* night, the night of total release … till… but loved afterwards, too … loved him now, now, this very moment! ! ! And she leaned back exhausted, almost panting again, tired out by that effort to understand and face it (wasn't *this* what Dr. Anslinger wanted?), but relaxing caused the fulness in her abdomen to throb suddenly, uncontrolled by the protecting tautness – and yet, at the same time, she relaxed and permitted herself, now that she was anodyned, to enjoy the pain in a body for which she was not responsible.

He wasn't saying anything. Just looking at her – looking the way they do in movies where the couple separated by a harsh and unjust government have come together for the last time after not having seen one another for some time. Looking – let me drink you in – he, Harry, he looked so soft and desperate. ... Then where had Harry got the energy, the strength, the fury, and the courage? But he had always been able to do what he set his mind to do. He always had a ... smug, assured determination. But something like this. He had been quiet enough when the police came for him. Were a few hours enough to transform him into the raging beast she saw pictured in the papers? Or was it something deeper?

She kept staring at him, trying to concentrate. She widened her smile when she couldn't feel it any more. Her fingers kept rubbing along the smooth black plastic shine of her handbag. "Hello, Harry," she told him. Harry looked as though he wanted to say something. Sara kept smiling; there was nothing else to do. Her finger became more agitated. Her face couldn't change. She felt the vague anxiety inside of her coalescing – the irritation. Her eyes looked at him and then, started to look around the room again – waiting for him to say something, like during the desperate evenings in which their furious arguments were in silence where they felt each other, in which a sign was like a blow, a squeak of the couch a prelude to a whole set of reasons why ... She would sit there, rigid, pretending to watch television, and he, buried in a book, watched her nevertheless, pretending to read, even turning the pages at the right moments. ... What do you want from me? It can't work; it's gone out of our lives, don't you see that? But his reproachful stare: love me, love me, love me again. I can't. And the tears on the face of the TV heroine were Sara's tears while she could feel the hard set of her lips which, if he thought to look at them, as he used to do, would tell him all. She remembered him lying on the other side of the bed, in the old position, his head propped on his hand, violating her body by staring longingly at its curves beneath the cover – much like a rape. Well, I'll get it over, if you can see me through. Wait it out, Harry. What do you want from me? Adjust. Sitting in the kitchen, drinking coffee, staring just over one another's shoulders, she could feel that damped-down but still boiling fury inside of him – so strong a fury that, if she didn't look at him directly, it made him shimmer as though he were heating up the air around him – a fury that was a reproach to her, that made her go through a thousand reasons in her head why it was over, ... well, not exactly over, but couldn't he see what was the matter with her? Didn't he love her? Then she was conceding, permitting, lying under him, patiently waiting it out while he inned and outed and strained and sweated trying to make her explode the way she had that night – the first time in her life – and never never again … Never. Had it happened? That total release? Or was it something she had striven for, believed she should have, and come to believe it wouldn't or couldn't happen? Yet she imagined the way it would be: it might as well have taken place – it *did* take place, their two voices as one, chorus-keening with love and pain, … and she loved him afterwards, loved him … And she owed him so much, but it was only flesh in flesh and done with in just a while longer. But she couldn't keep on accepting even that because she came to feel that the mere violation of flesh was becoming a violation of her mind, so she writhed, trying to get away from him, and he became still more excited as she tried to move out from under him like a speared turtle on its back and he crab-thrashed his insistent way along with her. And then, suck-wrenched apart, the silent argument would begin again till she pretended to fall asleep and slept, leaving him glancing arguments at her back. And sometimes, half-asleep, she would feel movements, as if he were moving towards her, and she would turn – not again! wait! we can't solve anything this way – but the movements joggling the bed would continue and she would fall asleep again, and be wakened by…

One of the guard's clubs banged loudly against the shiny tile-brick wall.

"How have you been, Sara?" Fertig asked.

She smiled and nodded.

"What have you been doing?"

"Nothing," she told him. Her voice was flat, without feeling, empty. She was surprised at how it sounded, echoing faintly in the room. "My mother came to live with me for a while. It's better. She'll be going soon." She had to make a great effort to say what she said. She leaned back and rested.

"Have they bothered you?" he asked her.

She could barely think about it: police, newsmen, the obscene phone calls, offers for her story, the D.A.'s office, the questioning, the humiliation, and Roy Bleakie rescuing her, taking it all out of her hands, firmly and efficiently protecting her from the world. Her mother, her brothers, they told her to look out for him … that it was a shame he was so small, because he was so handsome. How like a hawk he was: those fierce movements, and yet how gentle with her, how protective.

"Not so much," she told Fertig.

"Why didn't you come before?"

She shrugged. "There were so many things; so many things kept happening. They came – the police. I was afraid to go out – you wouldn't believe it – threats –"

"I thought they weren't bothering you too much. What happened?"

"You can imagine."

"I didn't mean for this to happen."

"Are you angry I didn't come?" She expected that furious expression: he *should* be furious at her.

"Angry?" He shook his head. "The anger has gone out of me. I was ... disappointed."

She was disappointed. She twisted the wedding ring; it was loose. She kept talking. "And I didn't know where they were keeping you. Then they told me. I started to come, but the reporters followed me wherever I went, so I went back and stayed home."

"So?"

"But I did come here. I'm here. I came when I recovered."

"Recovered? Were you sick?" He seemed to ask it politely, as though inquiring about some stranger. She couldn't be sure. His face was thin and pale, but it always seemed to have been thin and pale ... and she wondered, as she used to, how Stevie could have been their child; he was so lusty, red-faced, blond-haired ... blue-eyed and adorable ... lovable ... cheerful, somehow, even when he cried. Did she, she wondered, catching a movement out of the left side of her eye, see something? It was the guard shifting his weight impatiently, leaning against the tile wall where the dancing lights dripped downward. Her chair was becoming more uncomfortable; her back hurt a little more; the heavy, down-dragging feeling in her belly increased; gas, she told herself, just a little gas ... and yet she floated and her face kept smiling at him.

"Sick? No. The shock of it ... it was just ... it was such a terrible effort ..." She stopped. She looked at the window. There was a thick, wire netting buried in the glass. The glass was frosted. The dim sun made the window glow. Even though it was still morning it seemed like late afternoon. And she couldn't help asking what she must ask, what she shouldn't ask ... "Why?" To torture herself. "Why did you do it?"

"Don't you know?"

What did he mean, saying it like that, she thought angrily. Dr. Anslinger told her, "Of *course* you knew it all along. It is only your own sense of guilt that made you hide it from yourself. ..."

Hide what? Guilt?

"Once you face it ... which is to face yourself, you will *see* what you have always known and – we must admit – what you, subconsciously, even wished," Anslinger had suggested.

Wished what? Her son's death? Or was it, rather, as the interviewer suggested, that Fertig did it for Stevie. Of course. For Stevie and himself. She shook her head. "It's all so confusing. I mean you learn you've been living with someone you don't know ... only they say that I really knew ... can you imagine how that makes me feel, Harry?"

"I'm sorry this happened to you."

"No, I don't mean it that way, please, Harry ..." But what right did he have to say it that way – forcing her into tiresome explanations? "I came down here the first time and I said I wanted to see you, but they told me they wouldn't let me see you unless I talked to them first. Then they began to ask me questions about you, our life, but they didn't talk long. They were nice for a change. They said they would see me again."

"Who?"

"A couple of people – social workers."

"What were their names?"

"I don't know. I didn't ask." She shrugged. "They're so different in their approach from Dr. Anslinger."

"You're still seeing Anslinger?"

"Why shouldn't I see Dr. Anslinger – especially at a time like this?"

"Of course."

Why was he sarcastic? "They wanted to know all about your earlier life; about our life together; about Stevie. You forget so much. Isn't it strange how you forget? About the first ten years, I mean. But they were nice." She patted her hair. It was coming apart – the smooth sheen cracking, the hair in lacquered clumps, hung. Her nails were dirty. How had they got dirty? She felt vaguely hungry. She wasn't sure if she had eaten that morning. Roy Bleakie came so early and bustled her into his car. He was insistent about the visit. No more delays. Can't prejudice his case. Firm, forceful, charming, surprisingly attractive for such a short man, so much so that while she resented his directing her like that, threatening to penetrate her sense of insulation – first he agitated her with his sudden move, then he exhilarated her with his wild driving, and then he assured her – he made her feel secure. She could forgive Bleakie. Yes, she remembered: her mother made her eat the hot cereal, hot-shot lawyer or not. Harry was watching her. Since when had his eyes become so sharp?

"What else did they ask, Sara?"

How could you live – no, that was at the District Attorney's office. "I don't remember, Harry. Really, if I remembered I would tell you. Things like how were you before Stevie died. Did you have trouble with your parents? Did we have any trouble before? Did we fight? Things like that. Were you unfaithful to me? The usual things they ask ..."

"What did you answer?"

"Did you really do what they say?"

"Yes, Sara," he told her in the old, patient way.

"Because of Stevie?"

He sighed and looked at her. "Partly," he said, and he looked at her a little more carefully. "Partly."

What did he mean by that? She could feel that inside-outside irritation forming, stronger now, threatening to become anger, tranquillizers or not, because of what he was implying. Who asked him? *Partly*. Was she actually starting to menstruate? Was it possible? That one sharp pain, a prelude to the humiliating flow – her thighs began to close to prevent a loss of blood that shouldn't be there.

"Are you sick?" he asked.

"I don't feel well."

"So why did you come?"

Who gave him the right? Why did he ask? She shouldn't let him get away with that question. "But why? You didn't have to. It was a terrible thing to do. You really didn't have to. You know that. It couldn't bring back ... Stevie." And in spite of the fury she felt at him for implicating her, her voice was gentle, tired, reasonable.

Fertig looked down at the table. "I suppose not." His shoulders moved on the other side of the board. He seemed to be doing something with his hands. He looked down as if surprised to see something there. He leaned forward and put his elbows up, resting his face in his hands.

"Put your hands down," one of the guards said. Fertig turned to look at them, surprised, as if he'd forgotten they were there. He put down his hands. "That's the way, that's a good boy," the guard said.

He turned to her.

Why didn't you come sooner? Did he ask it again? The question made her impatient. She thought they had settled it. She became more tired and wanted to go. "I told you, Harry. There was the question of the pass from the D.A.'s office." She looked at him again. She decided that somehow he had changed. She forced herself to look carefully, to understand, to see him. He *had* changed. When?

"What do you mean?"

"When I went there they started the questioning again. They asked about your plans. I couldn't tell him. I knew nothing about it. I never knew. It was a long time, wasn't it? Harry?"

"About six months, everything considered."

"And you couldn't accept it?"

"I *wouldn't* accept it."

"And we all thought you adjusted to it. They're saying that you led a double life."

He looked up at her and smiled suddenly. She had never known him to smile like that before. "What are you smiling at, Harry?" She was afraid of that smile.

"That's what they're saying now. That's why I'm here."

"And you lost your job."

"I left," he said, annoyed.

"And stopped working altogether. You never told me. I never knew."

"Would you care?"

What right did he have to ask such a question? What right! Her anger merged into crampy pain; her thighs pressed closer together. It was all encased again, inside, safely contained and protected. Had she miscalculated? Would she begin to bleed there? Was there a place she could get sanitary napkins? Could she ask anyone? "You kept planning to do that awful thing, that evil thing. You left, every morning

"At the usual time."

"... pretending to go to work and I never knew that. How could you kill those people? Doctors, Harry, and a rabbi. What did the rabbi have to do with it?"

His face changed. His eyes stared at her. His lips were thin and angry. Along the side of his face, she saw little muscles that she had never seen before. The angry little lights glittered along the rims of his glasses; and in spite of that look, he was so pitiful. "Don't you understand anything about it?"

She shook her head. "No. Nothing," she told him.

"They killed Stevie."

And she remembered the ravenous faces leaning over her, the blazing lights. Were the guards looking peculiarly at her? Was she beginning to smell? She was too dulled to even smell herself, but she remembered the faint and permeating blood odour which enveloped her and she wrinkled her hose. It was dirty here; everything was dirty; she was dirty, too. Hadn't Stevie's death been enough? Wasn't his crime enough? This too? "And they even thought I helped you."

Harry shook his head. "But *no* one, no one else knew what I was doing. I told them that they shouldn't bother you. I told them again and again."

"I suppose they had to make sure. They kept me there for such a long time. For hours, I heard one of them ask why they should help that crazy killer's wife?"

Harry looked at the guards angrily; one of them smiled back pleasantly at him.

"And after a while I couldn't take it any more. I almost fainted. Then, your lawyer came –"

"My lawyer? I have no lawyer. I told them in court I wasn't going to use a lawyer. I intend to present my own case –" he said. His voice became flatter, more annoying to her.

"I don't know anything about that, Harry. He says he's taking on the case because he believes in you. He was so wonderful, Harry; he just came in and took me away from them. He's been so helpful ever since –"

"*I don't have a lawyer!*"

"... and he finally got me in to see you."

"Don't you understand? I must not have a lawyer." His voice was raised the way it had been that awful night at the hospital.

She looked at him. The pain stabbed her again and again. Why had he done this to her? He frightened her. She looked around. She looked again for her lost child's face in his. She looked at the glowing window; she looked at the guards and at the wet tile walls and then back to Harry: she couldn't find her baby's face there. He was hissing angrily; the sound rose in intensity, but was stifled in the back of his throat, a muffled shout, really. She had to get out, go home, get away from him before he broke through that thinning skin of drugged acceptance and her pain would make her yell at him. And her voice, someone else's voice, still soft, full of gentle, placating equanimity, said reasonably, "But I was so tired after that. I needed a rest. I don't know what's the matter any more, Harry. I just can't function. I can't sustain any effort. I went home and cried. I cried for a day. It took me such a long time to do even the slightest thing. He kept insisting; he finally drove me down here today to see you."

"What lawyer? What's his name?"

"Roy Bleakie."

"Where's his office? What's his telephone number?"

"I have it here. I have his card here somewhere." She opened her purse and started to fumble around looking for Bleakie's card. Holding tightly to her pass, she pulled items out with cramped fingers scattering them on the table: the crumpled tissues, the unused, neatly folded lace handkerchief, a little leather change purse, the two or three ballpoint pens, a magic-marker, a wallet, and a little bottle of cologne – the cap was poorly screwed on; it fell off. A little liquid spilled and the room was immediately suffused with a languorous odour while she tried to put the cap back on, but it kept jamming and turning downward; it just wouldn't fit right, so she dropped it back in her pocketbook and continued to rummage among the papers and cards, setting aside old, crease-marked photographs taken of the family two years ago, clinking coins and tokens, jangling keys, fretting hurriedly, wanting to get away from this man with the contorted face that looked something like Harry. She looked through photographs of Stevie for Bleakie's card and couldn't find it. She was close to tears. She wanted so badly to go home and go to sleep. The pain was almost through to her now. The seat was too hard. The shame of the blood leaking – she was sure of it – why did he bother her when… she… the sticky thighs, her bloody skirt – and people would point to the stain and says, "*There's Fertig's wife…*" The pains beat against that shell around her and she could watch him because of it, see him almost as a stranger might, acting a part of fury, and feel far away from it. And she was unravelled now, sweaty, sticky, dirty, her new clothes soiled, her make-up dripping down with the sweat.

One of the guards on seeing the quick, secretive movements became alarmed. He was tired of standing there and listening to the low, dull murmur. He had expected something a little more exciting from Fertig, but not this dangerous frenzy; you always had to stop them before they let it go too far. He stiffened when Fertig began to shout. The other guard broke off a yawn – was Fertig episoding? Would he have to ring the alarm bell? Sometimes it was hard to remember that this man was a dangerous, murderous maniac. He saw she was trying to slip Fertig something – a gun, a knife? – and he jumped over and shouted, "Put it all back, lady."

"I'm looking for … she started to say. It angered him more. Jim, the other guard, came up carefully and took great care to smile. "Now. Easy son. We can straighten it all out."

Fertig started to explain it to them.

One guard motioned to Sara impatiently; the other talked soothingly to Fertig.

"Don't talk to me that way," Fertig said, surprised.

"Sure boy, sure," he said cloyingly. "I understand."

Fertig was just crazy-furious and the guard could feel that insane, dangerous, unreasonable, can't-hear-you anger of Fertig's beginning to beat at him. Keep it up, he thought, and he had swift sensations of a fist, a club, and the anticipatory muscular sensation of his shoulder swinging down and the pleasant shock of his hand being stopped satisfactorily by Fertig, the yelp of pain, and that first understanding that the shock always brought to their faces … and then the wild rage that always ended with them in the strait jacket.

"Hurry up. Put it all back, lady," the guard yelled.

"But I'm …"

"It's not allowed, lady," he shouted at her. She looked blankly at him. If he slapped her face, she would understand he thought; her bewilderment angered him … it was a little crazy, too.

"She's just trying to …" Fertig stood up. Jim came up behind Fertig and placed his hand on Fertig's shoulder. He squeezed, forcing Fertig back into his seat, digging in. Fertig was too surprised to fight and let himself be seated, folding his hands in his lap.

The other guard took Sara's bag and swept everything off the edge of the table into it. He gave the bag to Sara, grabbed her arm, lifted her, and led her out. She tripped on the chair, which crashed down; he pulled her over it. She let herself be pulled, not caring, not protesting, looking over her shoulder.

Fertig stood up again. Before she was whirled out of the room she remembered one thing: Harry standing there, his hand reaching or pointing accusingly towards her over the wooden barrier, and she, half-drugged, like half-woken from a sleep, turning, looking, seeing

Harry, his face rage-contorted into a frozen grimace, held by that sleep-wakey moment like a second fixed by lightning into dream-reality, held, almost forever, like a photograph in an album, fixed by the time-distorting power of the pills that placed her anguish beside her and a second or so behind her ... and so forgotten ... standing over her on the bed, his finger pointing to a dark corner where ... what ... who was there? She slept. And so you see, Dr. Anslinger might smugly put it, we are all accomplices because we know *everything*. "But I didn't know," she said and the door closed on him and she hated Dr. Anslinger for making her go through this.

The guard holding him squeezed his shoulder muscle close to his neck; Fertig winced and writhed under the thick, implacable grip. The guard was surprised at how weak Fertig was. "Try it again, loony. You don't have a gun here. Try."

"But she was trying to ..."

"I don't care what she was doing. Nothing like that. Nothing passes between you. Sit there." He was infuriated. What if she gave Fertig a gun? He would shoot up the place. Fertig sat. And the guard went back against the wall and waited for his partner to come back.

Chapter 10

"... and now I think you will find this particularly interesting," Dr. Heisenberg said, and held out a drawing for Bleakie to look at. Bleakie turned from Heisenberg's charts, tables, figures, compilations. It was a drawing of a naked woman which had obviously been started from the bottom, because the lower half – legs, thighs, hips, belly – was large, filling two-thirds of the page, while the upper half was crowded in, almost an afterthought: the head was too small, the lips U-smirking, the breasts almost two perfect little circles.

"Fertig's?"

"Yes. His. Doesn't it speak volumes?"

"You don't have much here."

"And *this*," Heisenberg said, getting more and more excited. The next drawing was neatly centred and occupied two-thirds of the page. The face was clumsily rendered; a man wore a double-breasted suit, a tie, a shirt, and shoes and socks. "Now you can compare these two pictures: The self-image – for such it is – is smaller than the woman's and, you notice, clothed. *Clothed*. Now, if we measure the relationship precisely, in millimetres of deviation from the expected proportions

– I know what you're going to ask: the answer is yes, we do allow an assigned percentage of error derivable from lack of drawing skill (we forget nothing here, you see) – then we have an identification image, which, you will see, indicates a vast repression – placed in the *past*, perhaps in the late thirties, the early forties, when, if other tests were made, would indicate that: it was then, *then*, that the gradual dysfunction began –"

"What has this to do with

"Please," Dr. Heisenberg said and tapped, almost stamped, his foot. "Illness is evolutionary: each step leads to the next step unless there is a remedy to arrest the illness – medicine, therapy. Illness is *not* traumatic (you notice how the word is even a pun on the word dramatic) as Freud so damagingly initiated – even taking his terminology from the classic drama – it is, in fact, at best, only a physiological symbolization. Sickness is, if I may put it so, historical, one caused event causing the next. For heaven's sake, do you know what Dr. Anslinger, Sara Fertig's analyst is saying? He's one of those out-of-date therapists, a pure Freudian – Victorian gingerbread – of whom, alas, there are so many – medieval. Full of those obsolete terms like castration complex, libido, cathexis, id. We don't really have to resort to such exotic theses. It is actually Dr. Anslinger's feelings that because of a certain substitution, Mrs. Fertig was able to sleep with her son through Fertig. Then Fertig, in order to expiate his jealous crime – incitement to Stevie's murder – attempted to project the responsibilities on the father-figures of society, thereby enabling him to rebel and murder in order to be punished...."

"You have to have more than this," Bleakie said, not paying much attention. "Jeffries isn't likely to listen."

"There's much more involved than this arraignment," Heisenberg said.

Bleakie looked through the tables and the conclusions; he looked at a prospectus of tests to come. Cognitive Dissonance Inventory, Anomie Matrix; third, fourth, and fifth strata, directed "confessions"; Thematic Apperception Tests with drawings made up from Fertig's history. He thought of Fertig's notebook. Wouldn't Heisenberg like to see that? Well, he would, just as soon as Fertig was safely binned with the criminally insane and he sold the notebook to the highest bidder. Fertig's statistics, which started as random observations, inchoate, scattered, purposeless, infrequent, almost idly made, became more frequent and little patterns began to take shape: he followed this one, tailed the resident, found himself having a drink in the same bar with Dr. Cartwright and his nurse, went into an exclusive saloon Rabbi Gordon frequented – *that* was an eye-opener : Did Fertig know? Did he think it manly, athletic-club-like, or was he experienced enough to know a fag bar when he saw one? Fertig took on a frequency life and became definitely organized, purposive, from May 1 on: he was concerned with patterns, run-throughs; was very disciplined, very cool, surprisingly. Well, it was easy; the man was crazy.

Bleakie had driven sixty miles out of town, gone to the quiet glade where Fertig practised being what he was not, a gunman, a hero by the numbers. The woods were now trampled over by newsmen, state police, curiosity seekers, who had left a debris of cigarette butts, gum wrappers, crushed branches, wheel grooves in the soil, oil-pourings, some condoms, and almost every tree with bark gouged out as they tried to eviscerate every bullet Fertig had practise-fired. There had been thousands. Fertig was thorough. He kept a record of his performance: the amount of time to shoot and the hit-accuracy of every round. Towards the end he was ninety-eight per cent accurate.

"Why play games? He's gone. Open and shut. Just get the right kind of report ready," said Bleakie, lighting a cigarette.

"You're not really interested in any of this unless it serves your purpose?" Dr. Heisenberg asked Roy Bleakie. "I must admit that I view your involvement with this case as a mixed blessing." He tried to smile but looked at Bleakie's plumage, an orange vest, with hostility.

Bleakie shrugged.

"But I'm glad we find ourselves together, especially on so important a matter. But frankly, why are you doing this? And for no money, too! – so I'm told."

"A criminal has the right to representation no matter what the nature of his crime; he must not be condemned out of hand. He is guaranteed those rights by the constitution. The law doesn't say anyone *except* a Fertig."

Heisenberg's face didn't change.

"You don't believe me."

"*You* said that."

"You don't believe me."

"Let us say that man rarely acts out of motives of nobility."

"And I ...?"

Heisenberg brought his hostility to the surface, ventilated his feelings to let them dissipate: "You've made me look silly in the past... I confess it –"

"Job. The give and take of trial combat. Nothing personal."

"... but now, more than ever, I ... we need you."

If they needed me, it was always "now, more than ever," Bleakie thought. Heisenberg was going on. "The quality of his sickness dictated that *reasonable*, that is to say, consistent goals of revenge be set up. And therein lies, you see, the confusion; there seems to be so much sense to what he did, such connectivity, such a deceptive limitation of the victims chosen. This is why everyone, the layman, the outmoded judiciary, thinks Fertig is such a particularly vicious and volitional murderer. No such thing. It is one of the signs of paranoia that the reasons for acts are provided carefully. In this case the very reasonableness constitutes the additional and masking dimensions. Our sociologists tell us that the reaction to Fertig is mounting to a new pitch, the Keep Capital Punishment movement is more vociferous than ever: How can we permit a confessed murderer to laugh at us? If he gets away with it ... You know the chant, Bleakie."

"Roy Bleakie knows. Fought it before."

"... a barbaric laity is prejudging him."

"You need sociologists to tell you that?"

"... and the worst enemy of all is Fertig himself."

"How's Fertig a threat? Fertig's out of it."

"I've never known anyone to maintain discipline this long. Of course it's a part of his reality construct to view me as a representative of a world of madness from which his sickness makes him dissociate so completely. It indicates the pervasive depth of his illness."

"The wonderful world of Fertig."

"There are difficulties, but given time, I don't think they're insurmountable."

Heisenberg went on to outline the attack that sought to abolish the very concept of mental illness. "It threatens not only to destroy the gains of a hundred years in psychiatry, but to throw the whole science back to medieval days. Why supposing you used their logic, you might grant that six of Fertig's murders showed ... rationality (I could gag over that word in this context)..."

Fertig's notebook showed rationality enough, Bleakie thought: the driest piece of murder-bound logic going.

"... but the fact that Fertig only admitted it, but also showed no repentance..."

What did repentance have to do with it? Bleakie buttoned and unbuttoned the black bone buttons of his vest.

"... and not the pronunciamentos of the psychiatric Right are being taken up by conservative and fundamentalist elements, simplified and perverted in order to cut through and solve the complexities of life by a negation of scientific finding, which, in itself, constitutes a paranoid manifestation. And poor Bridgeman in his drive for ego-gratification – where was he until he came up with these misguided theories? An obscure and second-rate practitioner, a contributor to the *Reader's Digest*; you know, the be-glad-you're-neurotic kind of thing – is becoming a spokesman for them, an innocent dupe."

Bleakie was bored. The tests showed nothing. The "confessions" were dry, nothing special, not even the stuff in Fertig's notebook ... a homosexual, a philanderer, a diverter of moneys, and Grenoble – his instinct was right – was on and off the list twice. What had Grenoble done to Fertig? "Has Fertig mentioned Grenoble at all?"

"Who?" Heisenberg, looking at Bleakie, was puzzled for a second.

"Grenoble. Fertig's boss."

"Not particularly," he said and went on.

Fertig's pediatrician had made the team, had been on it for two months, and was finally scratched. The rabbi fluctuated on and off in the build-up period and then stayed on till he was killed. Bleakie remembered the stapled-in photo of the rabbi, an old picture, a soulful face, holy. But why had Grenoble been on and off?

"Look at this," Heisenberg said. "It's one of the pictures I had made up from Fertig's material for the next generation of tests." Heisenberg showed Bleakie a stylized drawing, murkily rendered, full of India ink shadows. A street lamp shone down on a girl who leaned against the lamppost. She was big-breasted and wore a skin-tight nylony blouse: peasanty. One shoulder showed over the cloth and gleamed off highlights. The cleavage between her huge breasts was clearly marked. Her hair was glossy black, full of oily highlights too; her lips were brilliantly painted, moist, seductive. Her obviously stained eyelids drooped enticingly, one lower than the other in a half-wink. One skirted hip was pushed out in the direction of the shadows. A man, half-seen, not clear at all, lurked in the shadows. He seemed to hover between coming out and staying there, indecisive. It was to him whom her invitation was directed.

"It's a little romantic. They don't hang around in the streets any more," Bleakie said, "and they don't dress nearly as obvious. In fact, the style is, these days, to look young, innocent, childlike ... Did he sleep with her?"

"He denies it, but everything points to it. Not only was he a *man* in respect to this girl, this common prostitute, but she became a wife-mother substitute, economically and sexually controllable."

Was Heisenberg taking this prostitute business as one of the manifestations of madness? Well, it would help when MacGruder tried to spring the whole thing – the sinister double life, the evil man, bad associations – on Roy Bleakie in court. Roy Bleakie would be doubly ready.

"Of course people like Fertig tend to consider surface estimations of the self as valid – under the heading of taken-on responsibility, extremisms, "witnessings", holy rollers – so he felt he led the victims of forces, the victims of the Grand Conspiracy. When he came to decide on this course of action he proved to himself he was more than a man, he was a chooser of his own destiny, a destroyer of the forces working against him in this now oppressive society, a leader, a scapegoat; all very messianic, most integrated, and therefore the most suicidal front – as you have seen –"

"Haven't talked to him yet."

"You haven't talked to him? Why not? I don't understand." Heisenberg was agitated.

"Leave it to me. Roy Bleakie knows what he's doing. I'll get Fertig off."

"I'm sure you will, but I can't understand why you haven't seen him."

"Don't have to."

"Is that right? Isn't that high-handed?"

"Look, you want something. I want the same thing. Why worry about my method?"

"But you should talk to him."

Bleakie touched the psychiatric material: "Slim stuff here, Dr. H. Nothing conclusive."

"But it's obvious. You can see the whole grand structure of the delusion. Look. It is a desire for ego-gratification – to use the language of physiological symbolization – the old infantile revenge fantasy, the old I'll-show-them merged with the elimination of the witnesses, the so-called causers of his inadequacy. Think how the people he killed represented a microcosmis totality of the oppressive psycho-social system." He accompanied each statement with a decisive tap of his foot. "The receptionist-clerk was a mother-authority figure; you had, in effect, to justify yourself to her, that is, to give information that proved you were indeed you, which brought you into her and society's good graces: I've been a good boy.

"Old Dr. Curtius represented the father. Removed. Godlike. Timeless.

"The administrator symbolized the economic system.

"The nurse, who, I am told, was good looking, was a sexual figure, a Lilith (as against Sara Fertig's role) who he could never live up to in a free-competitive situation.

"Dr. Cartwright was a rival-sibling figure, who, by his dominance over disease, was no longer bound to the body.

The rabbi represented Fertig's shame at being a Jew: In killing the rabbi he symbolically freed himself from the ethos that bound him to what he subconsciously deemed an inferior position." Heisenberg paused.

"And the resident?"

"A youth-figure, an uncontrollable son, supplanting Fertig's virility. The young doctor and Cartwright are a gemmation symbolic of the basic sexual difficulties, but they, plus the old doctor, another symbolic life-construct – a typical reinforcement – represent a trinity. Of course much is hidden, but given a little more time, time, Mr. Bleakie ... We have a saying in the psychiatric field: *From him who has eyes to see and ears to hear, no mortal can hide his secret; he whose lips are silent chatters with his fingertips and betrays himself through all his pores.* It's all pretty apparent to an expert."

"That's no expert on the bench. No significant deviations – that what you call it? The D.A. is no expert. It doesn't matter: Roy Bleakie – Send me a copy to look over."

"I'm not supposed to do anything like that, Mr. Bleakie."

"To be sure. But, after all, we want the same thing. Need any and all ammunition."

Heisenberg agreed to send a copy of the report to Bleakie. He was about to continue talking, but time was running out on Bleakie. He stood. "See him?"

"Of course. He's being tested now. We'll be through soon and –"

"I want to see him – not have him see Roy Bleakie."

"But why? I don't understand. It's a rather strange request."

Bleakie noticed that Dr. Heisenberg took great care to keep his face totally bland, devoid of comment, which in itself was a comment of the most dangerous kind – that suppressed smile, that ... psychiatric superiority. He didn't explain. "The feel, Dr. H. The feel. You will leave the strategy to Roy Bleakie."

Dr. Heisenberg had to agree. Bleakie bothered him, but Bleakie was probably the best man: enormously self-seeking, manipulative, even infantile, but intelligent. Bleakie suffered from the usual paranoid feeling that short men had, but he over-compensated furiously, for instance, by using the third person to refer to himself – a mild megalomania – and this air of mystery.... Bleakie was taken to see Fertig.

He was led down a short corridor. The guard unlocked a door for Bleakie, reached inside, and switched on some dim lights, which illuminated a very narrow passageway. Bleakie followed the guard in. They walked for about twenty feet. The guard, being wide enough to scrape the walls, got smudge marks on the shoulders of his white jacket. Bleakie avoided wall contact. The guard turned a corner; it was dark. "Watch your step. Chairs." Ahead, the passageway ended in a wall. There were some chairs lined up, facing one side. The room smelled close, musty, airless. Following the guard, Bleakie walked in front of a glass panel and, reacting instinctively, jumped back: but he was caught... unprepared.

Waiting, Fertig stared at the wall behind the psychologist. The psychologist was taking a long time to write. It was the third round of tests and Fertig still hadn't got rid of that silly, that unexpected, that old feeling of taking school examinations and having to do well on them. He felt something and stared harder: was the psychologist watching him? The psychologist flipped a page of his pad and continued to write furiously, trying to keep up with Fertig's swift, flat delivery as he concocted a story about the picture he held in his hand. Even though it was cool, the psychologist was sweating with the effort: no, too busy to watch him. Who was watching him? Was he getting jumpy? What had he said to the psychologist to make him write so much? What was he doing wrong? He couldn't ask. They never answered him, only kept writing ... and did that mean ... what? Points off? He kept staring at the wall and shifting his position, and the psychologist, noting the movement, wrote more.

The glass over the figures beyond reflected Bleakie's image as if he were floating so that Bleakie, watching it, looked to himself like a stranger caught in some strange posture by him whom he was pursuing. Two men sat just on the other side of the one-way mirror. One of them looked up, right at him. Fertig. And he had that sense of – what was it? Anger? Revulsion? Discovery? It was as if the one-way mirror worked the other way round and it was he who was seen and Fertig who, curiously invisible for a second owing to Bleakie's reflection dancing on the glass in front of his eyes, was the seer. It couldn't have happened if they were face to face. That feeling, that almost *physical* feeling of antagonism wouldn't have been startled out of him. It was the first time in years that anything like that had happened. He moved to the side so that his reflection moved away from Fertig's eyes, and, because he *had* to move, had a feeling for a second, not only that he had lost but also one of the most intense and unprofessional hatred. "You idiot," he whispered to the guard, who was blundering around among the chairs and didn't seem to hear him.

Fertig stared his way as if smoothly, smugly, summing *him* up. Bleakie knew the look; encountered it all the time. The hostile-witness look. He was an expert on the hostile witness; he had cracked enough of them. You could almost say there was a physiology to the hostile witness – his father, for instance; the only thing that had kept his father from being a witness was the fact that he was a judge and never cross-examined. He recognized the look, had grown up with it, and could write a book about the hostile witness: prim-pressed lips, a know-it-all air, a high, narrow, almost bulgy forehead, intelligence, a stubborn stare behind glassed eyes – a not-too-clearly-seen stare because of the lenses – a narrow, set jaw, long, recalcitrant nose, and ... the wrenchable neck – don't forget the wrenchable neck. You won them to your side or, finding some opening, some psychic flaw, pried them open, caused them to hang themselves ... One hair of Fertig's moustache curled upward – did it tickle his nostril?

He brushed his nose and continued to stare over the psychologist's shoulder – distracted by what? feeling what? Boredom? No. Something else. Was it true, as they insisted in the ward, that there was a one-way mirror there through which they watched him? He noted that the psychologist was holding up another picture, waiting, eyes on the clock, on him, on the clock, making notes, so he picked it up hurriedly, looked at it, thought about it while the psychologist wrote ...

The window seemed to magnify Fertig so that Bleakie had the impression that Fertig was huge. Then he saw that the further away everything was, the bigger it seemed – like seeing it on a television set. Fertig's lips moved as if he were talking to Bleakie – television panel show with the sound turned off: now, Mr. Fertig, he thought, tell us how you compiled those fascinating and informative tables that enabled you ... Fertig's face, lean, studious, older-looking than he had imagined, a non-entity, a settled, housing-development dweller, he mocked.

"There he is, Counsellor, our very own star," the guard said. His voice exploded in the small room, and it was surprising that it didn't seem to jump through the glass and into the room on the other side.

"Shhhh!"

"It's all right. They can't hear us."

A look of pain seemed to pass across Fertig's face, but it must really have been concentration, and the lips moved slowly, paused, as if in answering something. It looked as if he could really hear Bleakie and the guard, but was avoiding giving any sign. There he was, Bleakie thought. The lips moved. The body moved. The lack of sound made Bleakie feel, in the silence, that there was between them a misleading interposition through which, oddly enough, they could understand one another; and, after all, hadn't he seen, though it wasn't thoroughly evaluated yet, Fertig's notebook? But it didn't mean that Fertig knew anything about him. There he was – it taunted Bleakie – more unprepossessing than the photograph in Sara's house, more insignificant now that the harsh reality had stripped the romanticism from him entirely.

Bleakie took out a cigarette, lit it, and blew smoke towards the window. The cloud hit, spread outward in a doughnut shape, half-obscuring Fertig's face. Bleakie began to revel in invisibility.

Fertig's lips moved; his head shook; his eyes turned downward. Oh, no, Bleakie thought, you don't avoid me that way. I know all about you.

"Sit down, Counsellor, enjoy it. I'll turn on the sound. Like in a movie."

"No, no. I always liked the silents."

Fertig's lips moved again. A lit cigarette was moved to the lips and.

they sucked inward and pursed slowly, parsimoniously letting out little puffs of smoke.

The psychologist was writing. Did even this count against him? He hurried on and then realized: what was he rushing for? Why please them? Was he being watched?

"Real pleasure in a thinking man's cigarette," Bleakie said and the guard exploded with laughter. Bleakie couldn't help being startled again, but since they didn't react in the testing room, he found an odd enjoyment in the very loudness.

Fertig toyed with a pencil. The questioner looked at his stopwatch. Infinite reaction-time, Bleakie thought, definitely a nut. Bleakie could just see Fertig bending over meticulously making an entry into that notebook in that neat bookkeeper's handwriting. Did it follow – how could a man like Fertig, a man who had done nothing all his life, begin to act like a gumshoe? Madness. Had he been that good at it? Had they suspected – would they have any reason to think they were being followed? No, Bleakie thought savagely, who could suspect any Fertig since, even if you turned around to look specifically at him, he was insignificant enough to fade into the mob as you looked at him. But not insignificant enough not to kill seven; he couldn't forget that: crazy. These considerations, though – the motive maturing into the deed – didn't even appear in his book at all, so Bleakie thought that when he had time to consider it enough he'd find it out, prise open Fertig's stubborn clenched lips – yes, certainly about Grenoble and his little games – because he had the notebook and it was going to be worth money and all the world was going to know about it in time when he sold his story.

No. He just didn't look capable, Bleakie thought; he just did not look the part. It must have been *some* education, right Fertig? Some fuel for the madman. And, at this moment, Fertig looked up seemingly into his eyes again, and Bleakie felt that wave of – what had it been? – exposure … anger … hatred …

"He's not so much," he told the guard.

"No. He's not."

"Are you sure they can't see us?" he asked the guard.

"Feels like it, don't it? No. But they *know* though. I mean there's no leakage soundwise or lightwise. I mean instruments can't detect any, but they get that *feel* very soon. Hard to explain. They never know *who*, but they always know when someone's here watching. Them scientists, they don't know everything."

"How's he behaving?"

"He's all right. Standoffish, like everything stinks, but no trouble."

You'd never know, Bleakie thought, that any schnook like that prissy man sitting there could train himself to put those wild dreams into action and have that *one* supreme day in his life when he didn't melt into the crowd. Could you train for greatness then? He doubted it: you either had it or you didn't. But Fertig? He was mad, remember that and keep remembering it and because he was mad, he *had* it. Didn't look the part. Look crazy, he thought to Fertig; save yourself.

Was he talking too much? He never knew. They never told him. On the other hand, was there such a thing as talking too little? He stopped telling the story of the whore in the picture – but who said she was a whore? Why had he assumed it? Why give it away? Be careful. Like seeing too many vaginas in the Rorschach – couldn't help it – or drawing the child big as a man, but naked, diapered. Did they take it into account that he was always a bad artist? Could they see signs of madness in that? Watch it. He looked over the psychologist's shoulder and tried to bring his little story to an end. He leaned closer and lowered his voice so that only the psychologist should hear. But why?

"In fact," the guard said, "he's kind of popular in the ward."
"Popular?"
"Maybe that's the wrong way to put it. They respect him. Maybe because he's crazy in a different way … He tries to keep to himself, but they flock around him. Still, they always hang around the newest member."
Bleakie looked at Fertig in his direction and watched the economical way the man stubbed his cigarette out. Just like any sane man, and it made him angry to see Fertig acting so normally, so much the nonentity. Why should it make him angry? That nothing? It was going to make his case harder – no, that didn't bother him; he welcomed difficulties. He would move them all through their paces. Then why feel bothered?

If Fertig is sane, I must look at things in a different way, he thought. That would be amusing. Make the case properly hard too. Sara, for instance, what did she know or understand about this man? Did she know about the notebook? Having seen its contents – the extensive preparations – how couldn't she have noticed? She claimed to have known none of it, not even the whore. Or was she hiding something from him? Yes. Did she know it? Hostile witness? No. An unconscious one? Maybe. She visited him now twice a week. She told Bleakie about Fertig's explosion. No trouble, no reluctance now: Was he planning something? No. Crazy moment. Episode. Save it for court, he thought; act a little crazy. She reported that he was insane – not that he acted that way, but – She was loving, compassionate, understanding … no trouble at all now.

Bleakie stood there for a long time looking at Fertig and watching his movements. The feeling that he was seen – caught – went away. Something bothered him. What was it? He watched Fertig take another cigarette. He stood up. No, he told himself, Fertig was mad and that was what made it easy. And yet ... why was that answer too easy? All right, he was sane now, Bleakie thought, now that it was over. Nevertheless, Bleakie would still end up pleading that Fertig could not understand the nature of the charges at the arraignment.

Hateful face, he thought; hard to like a man with a face like that. Wants a trial: won't get it: I'll save him in spite of himself, thought Bleakie. The newspapers might scream, "never before in the history of crime..." "another Oswald, even worse..." What the newspapers and what Fertig wanted didn't matter at all; the power was in Roy Bleakie's hands.

He turned. The guard started to lead him out. Wrenchable neck, Bleakie thought – how did she live with him all these years? – thin, ramrod neck set forward tenaciously, stubbornly, he went along his trail to ... "Listen," he told the guard, "just get the word to him that I was here watching him."

"I don't think that I should do that."

"Here. Buy yourself something and let the word slip," said Bleakie giving the guard a ten-dollar bill, "but no more than that. Got it?"

"You were here and we sat and watched him and talked –"

"Don't make a Federal case out of it. I was here. I watched him. I left. Just that."

"It's your money, Counsellor. Maybe you belong in there." And the guard laughed and led Bleakie out.

After testing they took Fertig back to the ward. Hamisbat, when he saw Fertig, half-stood up and waved to him. Fertig felt tired and just wanted to sit a while, but Hamisbat waved again. When Hamisbat stood, it meant extreme excitement; well, Hamisbat was harmless. He hesitated, but Hamisbat waved, this time holding a magazine. Fertig went down the aisle.

"It's begun," Hamisbat said loudly before Fertig got close, and smiled happily.

"What?" Fertig asked. Onofrio and Kaprelic were coming behind him.

"The drama!"

Fertig waited; he was getting used to Hamisbat's ways.

Hamisbat fluttered his lips and made a high sweet sound like trumpets belling far away, and then a phlegmy drumroll in his chest and held up, with the air of a master of ceremonies presenting a surprise, the cover of the latest *Time* magazine. On it, there was an

Artzybasheff painting of a silver-armoured knight leading a streaming rout, a ragged and fanatic group, all twisted, all sick, along a curled and infinite road. They carried tattered banners and crude placards; all were mad-eyed and rave-mouthed. The face-defining shadows on the knight were red – bloody; and suddenly, frighteningly, Fertig recognized his own face beneath the raised and slotted visor, underneath the murderous black plume made out of tiny numbers. The banner that surmounted his barbed lance said "FERTIGISM". On all sides the doctor fled. Fertig pulled it out of Hamisbat's hands and looked closer. The face was like the face in the AP photos. Fertig flipped through the pages till he came to the article. "The Revolt of the Patients". There were two photographs accompanying the article. One was a picture of Fertig taken some time ago; the face was serene, even vapid … he remembered the photograph … it was quite old. The other was a shot showing policemen standing around with some white-coated doctors on a debris-strewn floor. The caption read, "A little riot in the Flatbush HIP: the latest incident of Fertigism."

The article began with a quote of a letter from the *Daily News*.

"It is about time someone showed them Drs that they can't get away with it forever. The prices they charge. You can fool some of the people. Now maybe they have learned their lesson. Now maybe they will shape up. I know that this is an unpopular opinion but the truth will out. Three cheers for Fertig! ! ! I dare you to print this." It was signed ROOKED AND LEFT CRIPPLED. The article went on to trace a series of incidents in which Doctor-patient violence had taken place. In collating those events that had happened over the last ten years all over the world, it peaked the Belgian and Canadian doctors' strikes, with their attendant excesses, crested the rising tide with Fertig's crime, united the disparate events into a growing, messianic anarchistic movement that it tilted *Fertigism*, and concluded with a report of an hysterical office-wrecking little riot in the Flatbush HIP offices which it called, ominously, the latest episode in the rise of Fertigism: The implication throughout the article was that these were a series of related events building to a final clash that was to come in the future. The first clear anarchic proponent of the movement was Fertig.

"So what. They've been saying things like this all the time," Fertig said, giving the magazine back to Hamisbat. Kaprelic strode forward and took the magazine from Hamisbat and stood, looking at the cover reverently.

"But now they begin to invest Fertig with proper importance, so that the next phase of the drama begins. Fertig's skinny – a shame: old mould, old tradition. Hamisbat is fat: true mould, older tradition."

"I don't know that it's a drama," Fertig said and yawned. Soon they would be taking him for another round of testing. How pointless it was to talk to any of them, he thought, how they distorted, how they changed your words. He should be angry, he thought.

"That's bad; it could count against you," Candelli said. "Should have got money for it. You got to make them pay for what they write about you."

Kaprelic had left and was walking up and down the aisle with the magazine in his hand, looking at the cover.

"You got a convert, Fertig," Candelli said.

Fertig looked at Candelli angrily. Hamisbat laughed. "The first disciple. It's always the way. First the deed, the miracle, and then the reviling, the anger, the hate, and then the march to the crucifying ground, and, finally, the turn of the tide, as it were, the world acceptance, the adulation, the veneration..."

"It's nothing like that," Fertig said; but he couldn't help remembering his dream of the speech in the great courtroom.

"When they begin to love him, when they begin to write about him with compassion and beat their breasts for their cruelty and wish that they had been more understanding and worshipping, then he will know that he has been crucified, that he has marched along the long planned road...."

"There's no planning."

Hamisbat's smile pitied and Fertig knew better than to argue with him; he had learned that much.

"When are we going to eat?" Candelli asked and, looking down the aisle, said, "Look at that nut now."

Kaprelic had gone to the little table beside the bed, had propped the magazine on the table, and was kneeling before it holding up his soap crucifix.

"He shouldn't do that," Fertig said, beginning to go to Kaprelic.

"Can Fertig stop that ancient machinery?" Hamisbat asked. "He is on stage, man: it is too late to change the plot."

Fertig looked at him, not understanding.

"Make the peripeteia his own."

"What's that?"

"Reversal of intention."

"I don't understand."

"The reversal of intention reversed."

"It's a good idea," Fertig nodded, humouring Hamisbat.

"Why must it always be this way? Is it the only legend? Myth?" Hamisbat shouted angrily. "Is our imagination really so limited? But, he says, each age gives us the man of its time; the business man, the robed medieval, the beatnik, but it is always the same face that confronts us – only from different clothes."

"Shut up, Hamisbat," Iron Hans shouted.

Hamisbat smiled. "You see?" he asked, satisfied. "Let him tell him something," he whispered, leaning towards Fertig. Ask himself. Why is it always that emaciated one writhing so obscenely so that you can see his disgusting musculature? Has he ever seen, or heard ..." he paused and breathed deeply, as if gasping for air, "or *thought* of a fat one? Anywhere? Or any time at all? When the truth of the matter is that he was quite fat, bull-necked even, thick-wristed, joyously fat. And when they nailed him – Well, why go on. You know it all. They don't want it that way, do they?"

Fertig suppressed a yawn. "I don't suppose they do," he said politely and waited for Hamisbat to continue. But Hamisbat turned away and was looking out of the window. Fertig smiled. Hamisbat wanted the role for himself. Let him; he wanted no part of it. Fertig turned to go back to his bed and saw the sneer on Candelli's face and looked past him to where Kaprelic kneeled before the drawing on the *Time* cover, praying to it. His stomach rumbled; he was hungry.

They took Fertig into the visiting room. Iron Hans waited with Fertig till the other guard, Jim, came back with a man. "Not long," Hans said.

"A minute," the man said, and shook hands with Jim, who looked proud and pleased. Jim pocketed something and smiled at the man, who looked evaluatingly at Fertig. Tag ends of columns ran through his head – leads: *No longer clinging to visions of escape, Fertig, the mass killer ... and I didn't think he looked so hard. But do they ever, these baby-faced butchers ...* or *Under that deceptively mild exterior ...* After looking for a second, he smiled cynically and thought that yes, Fertig, after all, was not so much. They never were. The quiet ones, they were the ones who blew up. Look at Unruh or – they were the ones who had the discipline to make the best agents; look at Abels, look at Oswald. He walked over the end of the table and came around to the side at which Fertig was sitting. "Hello Fertig," he said and smiled. He peered sharply at Fertig; the knife-like face contradicted the easy, expedient smile. The long nose kept sniffing. He missed nothing. No fact escaped him. He saw the dismal shiny walls and the unbreakable frosted-glass window, the long table, the satisfied smile of Jim, and the hungry look of the second guard, who edged, imperceptibly, towards him. "Hello, Hans," he said; "getting much?" Hans laughed. It was an easy laugh, distorted by the slightest echo off the tiling, and strained a little by anxiety.

"How could I?" the guard said. "They put me in the men's loony bin. Loony like that I'm not. Now if it was the women's ward!" and he winked, broadly, clowning. Feeling that Hans had earned it, the man gave him a bill. Both guards went to the ends of the table and stood, watching, listening. The man, sitting on the table next to Fertig,

looked down at him. He tilted his rakish hat back. His receding hair-
line made him look, somehow gentle, almost intellectual, soft. Fertig
looked up at him. *What makes a man do it – madness or cunning? They
always...*, the man thought. "Do you know who I am, Fertig?"

"Are you my lawyer?"

"Don't even know your own lawyer? Man, are you that bad?" the
man laughed. He continued to stare at Fertig thinking, this little
man, this pale nonentity, had done it. How mad he must have been to
overcome his mildness. An accountant, he thought, sneering a little,
or... How could an accountant be such a big murderer? *Man kills seven.
Grand plot suspected. Communist conspiracy*, or... Here was the "Grand
Plot". *The twists and turns of the demented mind. They were all criminals:
Bluebeard and Gilles de Rais, and Fertig...* but he wasn't dumb, the man
thought; he could see that Fertig was not dumb. First sabotage of the
healing-power pool? "Your lawyer's Bleakie."

"Who is Bleakie? Why is he defending me?"

Hans came over and whispered into Morgan's ear. Morgan smiled.
"Really?" and he followed the guard's nod towards where the one-way
mirror was. "Still around?" Iron Hans shook his head.

It was wonderful how bewildered Fertig could make himself look,
the man thought; and he began to believe for the first time, public outrage, shock, indignation, or not, Bleakie might bring it off for Fertig:
that made him angry but he played it as cool as Fertig. "Good. Good,"
he told Fertig. He reached into his pocket and took out some cigars and
offered them to Fertig.

"No thanks," Fertig told him. Fertig took his own cigarette.

"Dollar-a-shot Uppmann's? Go ahead."

"No, thanks."

"Come on, take them. Give them to your ward buddies."

Fertig didn't answer. The man thought it was a wonderful touch. He
lit one of the cigars. Rich, acrid smoke rolled out in round clouds. One
of the guards, laughing, pointed to the No Smoking sign. He tossed a
cigar apiece to the guards.

"I don't want a lawyer."

"Why not?"

"Who are you?"

"Don't you read the papers? Don't you recognize me?" he asked and
wondered why some men wore that little moustache; didn't they know
it made them look ridiculous? He would just bet Fertig wore rubbers in
the rain and knit vests in winter.

Fertig looked up at him, folded his hands in his lap, and sat back
to wait.

"I'm Morgan, Marvin Morgan. Of the *Examiner*. You read my
column." It was a statement rather than a question.

"I don't buy the *Examiner*." Fertig told him.

There was something about the way he said it something prissy. It infuriated Morgan; it was too righteous. Who was Fertig, Morgan wondered, looking at those ridiculous slumped shoulders, to cast the first stone? He contained himself.

"Listen. I'm empowered to give you ... two thousand for your story. Two thousand is a lot. It almost even buys a lawyer like Bleakie." One of the guards laughed. Morgan could go as high as five thousand.

Fertig thought about it. "You wouldn't tell it right and I don't want a lawyer," he told Morgan.

"Why *not?*" Morgan asked. If he got Fertig talking he might get enough for a few columns without paying: *Fertig mad, suicide bound, or very cunning indeed...* He could then bill the paper for five thousand anyway.

Fertig didn't answer.

"After all, they extorted the confession from you; beat it out of you; got it under duress; didn't tell you what your rights were, right ? " Morgan smiled.

Fertig didn't answer.

"Or, if you did it you were insane. Mad as a hatter. Didn't know what was happening?" Morgan grinned.

Fertig looked angrily at him. He started to speak but stopped himself. Iron Hans was leaning forward, lapping it all up. Fertig sat more rigidly in his seat. The light, gleaming on his glasses, made them look like discs, hiding his eyes from Morgan's sight.

"Look, Fertig, you're in trouble. I understand. Don't you see that? You know, it's not the first time the hospitals have turned someone away and they died, not the first time at all. Something like that happens all the time. I should say that someone sick, seriously ill, is refused admittance almost every day from some hospital: you know I'll bet at least ten people a month die because of neglect. A lot to answer for. Or the doctors with their air of infallibility ... and the prices they charge ... and their self-righteousness ... You had grounds, you can see that. Just the other day someone fell down in the street. An old man. In Bensonhurst. He broke his hipbone. It was raining. He lay in the rain for one hour" (*Stricken man lies in rain for hour before help comes. Hospital pleads innocence...*) "till they came with the ambulance. And imagine, they even had to argue with the hospital to get them to send an ambulance. The hospitals want it all their way." Morgan spoke softly, insinuatingly, trying to mollify and persuade. "But you may have changed all that, Fertig. Now they think twice, right?"

Fertig didn't answer. His pale face had become red, suffused, and he began to perspire. He leaned back, trying to avoid the smell of the cigar. Morgan saw he was on the right track. They were silent for a second. One of the guards shifted and his club banged against the tile. Fertig didn't answer.

"Or think of your wife. I saw her last week. She doesn't look any too good. I understand you used up most of your savings too. Two thousand *five hundred* will come in handy." He paused. "Never mind the lawyer. Never mind Bleakie. Think of your wife. Listen. Publicity. Her plight. People are funny. You have no idea how they'll kick in. Think about it."

Fertig turned around and looked at Hans. Hans smiled and made a broad, patronizing motion and smiled; it said, be a good boy and talk to the nice man. "Who gave you permission to see me? I said I didn't want to see any newsmen," Fertig said. "The D.A.?"

"Yes, of course," Morgan told him; flatter Fertig, he thought. "Look, you're very important. To put it bluntly, you're the most important murderer since I don't know when. It becomes a matter almost of necessity, of public duty, that the world know something about you, your reasons."

Fertig considered it. Morgan thought he was on the right track; he had Fertig thinking. "Think of it. We present your case to the public, slant it your way. They wouldn't burn you then. Insanity. The public will see, understand, and forgive. I can help make them do that. I can do a lot for you."

"Can you tell them the truth, simply the truth?"

"Listen: my column; a separate story of your own, an as-told-to; two or three analysts commenting on it; a big spread, the biggest. Harry Fertig's exclusive. How about your whole life story, a column of your opinions twice a week for a month –?"

Fertig tried to interrupt.

"... all right, three times a week?"

"But –"

"... including Sundays; there are a few million more circulation on Sundays. What do you say, Fertig?"

"But why have you been writing that business about communism and Castro?"

"That's nothing, Fertig. Drum beating. Arousing the public interest. Thrills for the plebes. Nobody important believes that stuff, but it sells papers."

"Or why did you people print that picture of me? The one when I was arrested? The flashbulbs made me jump. Then you label the picture, 'mad-dog killer at bay'. Was that honest? Was that the truth?"

Morgan spread his arms. "I had nothing to do with that. It was an AP photo. A caption writer does these things. I have my own standing. I'm independent. I'm syndicated. The whole country knows. I write what I want. The newspaper prints me because I sell papers; because I sell,

I have my say. I'll give you a better deal than *Time*, or any of the magazines. A lot of people buy the rag only because of my column. I can be for you. Besides, every paper printed that picture, even the *Times*." A sympathetic look made Morgan's face soft, interested. He pushed his hat higher, showing more bare forehead. "Yes, I can be for you, or against you." He kept looking for the essential Fertig, the Fertig to whom he could appeal. *Beneath this mild accountant's look ... Why do they do it, these little men, these frustrated men?* he thought. Fertig would come around. How could he, a cipher as anonymous as the neat marks put on an accountant's sheet, have worked without wanting somebody to know his name? That was probably why he did it in the first place: publicity ... or – No, then he, Morgan, couldn't rush the political. If Fertig were an agent, he'd be disciplined enough to resist it. He would make Fertig immortal. Fertig would come around. Not even a spy could resist publicity and money.

"The hue and cry is on. *Three thousand*. Everyone is screaming for your blood. Four times a week ... all right, Front Page. There hasn't been anything like it since Murder, Incorporated," he said gleefully as if they were already collaborating because he could see Fertig rising to it; he was sitting with his hands by his sides, holding on to the edges of his chair.

"It's not the same thing."

The way Fertig said it annoyed Morgan. Fertig had an exasperating trick of clamping down his lips in a certain way. *Abe the Twist Reles, or Harry Fertig*: "In effect it is, isn't it?"

"It's not the same thing at all," Fertig replied, shaking his head stubbornly.

"How is it different?" Morgan asked. "Except possibly you make them all look like pikers. You know, I never knew how easy, really easy, it was to kill,

"It wasn't easy."

"Wasn't it? What do you mean?"

Fertig didn't answer. Suddenly he looked up at Morgan. Morgan's leg began to swing from the upper edge of the table. Fertig's glasses caught the light again. Under that ridiculous moustache, tinged with grey at the edges, Fertig smiled. "No," he told Morgan, "I'm not going to do it. I'm afraid I couldn't trust you ... I don't mean it personally ... " It sounded so weirdly polite. "But I'll tell my story to the judge at the trial. I'll get my chance in court. Then you people will have to print the truth."

"But what makes you think that?"

"Because everyone will be there. They'll hear – all the papers ... together. Say what you want now. I will say nothing at all." He kept shaking his head.

Morgan's face became hard. He tried to keep the smile, look friendly, but it made him look foxlike. He snapped the brim of his hat further down on his forehead. He puffed hard to calm himself. The room was filling up with cigar smoke. Fertig lit another cigarette from his burned-down butt. Morgan took out a key chain and played with it: wrapping it and unwrapping it around his finger, pressing the tiny links into his flesh and then unloosening it and looking at the marks in his flesh. "I don't understand your attitude, Fertig."

"There's nothing to understand. I killed them. Leave it at that. You know the story. You had it from the police. You all distort anything I said. You won't do it better next time. Fertigism! If you want to know, wait until the trial. I don't want to talk about it any more." He coughed.

"Fertig, you smoke too much. Now with cigars you don't get lung cancer." Morgan took the key and scored little parallel scratches into the table beside Fertig's hand. "You don't understand. I'm on your side. You need all the help you can get. Except for the bleeding hearts, the liberal columnists, the Grinzings, whom nobody reads anyway," Morgan sneered, "the newspapers are having a field day with you. They are going to crucify you. The public wants your blood. That old fart, Judge Jeffries, has been appointed your judge. It's not as if you're going to have one of those cure-not-punish ladies like Judge Mable Crossland to put your head on their soppy tits.

"I wouldn't want a judge like that."

"I'll bet you wouldn't. Know anything about Judge Jeffries?"

"I would rather not talk about it."

"Judge Jeffries has no use for the popular psychiatric dodge. Kill and you're guilty. It's as simple as that to him. Before, he had to play ball and go along with the popular trend, up to a point, but now ... Now Judge Jeffries is too old to give a damn about votes. He's going to retire soon and he's going to give it the full treatment. He has nothing to lose; he's responsible to practically no one. Do you think anyone is going to come along to save you? You're the D.A.'s meat. This is one time Bleakie won't be able to put the fix in –"

"What do you mean?"

"Has Bleakie been to see you?"

"I never hired him."

"You have a lawyer of record; of course the phony is giving out with that justice, fairplay, and no-fee juice, but he's only going through the motions. And it doesn't matter if you didn't hire him: your wife retained him."

"My wife?"

"And he hasn't had a conference with you?"

"No."

"See! Did you know he saw you this morning? Do you know he

was out there, watching you?" Morgan pointed dramatically towards the one-way window: the reflection pointed back to Fertig and him; the two guards looked at the reflection, impressed. "Why is Bleakie playing these mysterious games? Ask yourself that."

Fertig looked agitated.

"Let me help you. Only the newspapers can help you. Everyone knows Marvin Morgan."

Fertig didn't answer.

"Don't you realize that I'm the only one who was able to get to see you here? Doesn't that mean something?"

Fertig stood up. "Thank you just the same, Mr. Morgan, but I don't want to talk about it." Jim, the guard, came up behind him, seeming to be there without having crossed the room. "Talk to the man," Jim told Fertig, nudging him with his club.

"I'd rather not," Fertig told the guard.

Jim took Fertig's elbow in his hand and squeezed. Fertig gasped. "You're so much trouble. Talk to Mr. Morgan. It doesn't hurt to talk."

"I can report you for this, you know," Fertig told Morgan.

The guard took the cigarette from Fertig's hand. "You know you can't smoke here." The last of the smiling mask was gone; the hat brim was snapped low over the face. He saw Fertig now, with all his pretensions gone. No longer would Morgan admit Fertig his view of himself. Fertig was the cunning killer, lying to save himself, monstrously arrogant. Who knew what other mysterious connections there were – that sly, conspirator's look. A man doesn't do a thing like this himself, not a man who looked like this, not a mere accountant. "Report *me*? You don't understand. You're a madman," he drawled the word out mockingly, making the first part of it sound like a bleat. "You're in the psycho-pen, I'm not here. I'm a mere figment of your imagination. I'm not here, am I, men?" Morgan asked the guards.

The guard Hans laughed: "Hallucinating, like they say."

"Delusional," said Jim, who was standing behind Fertig and squeezing his arm tighter.

"Paranoid. Visions. An episode," the other guard responded.

"Please, take me back to the ward," Fertig told them.

"Find it restful? You're in a rush to get back to your buddies in the bin?"

"Can't stand the active life? Like those long hours of thinking? He's a big thinker, you know."

"Personally, I think he's lazy. Sits all the time. Won't even *try* his occupational therapy."

"He's found a home away from home."

"Why don't you talk to me, tell me all about it. You'll feel better," Morgan said.

"There's nothing to tell. You know all there is to know."

"Is that what you're going to stick to?" The sound of Morgan's key sawing into the wood rasped. Fertig wouldn't answer. "All right, lose your chance for salvation. Don't blame me. I can't stand between you and them. They are going to have your head. Nothing can save you. You understand?"

Fertig kept looking into Morgan's face.

"Maniac," Morgan whispered to Fertig. "They'll burn you; they'll burn you; oh, you'll feel the shock of it in every part of your body." He leaned close to Fertig, so close, that his breath was moistening Fertig's glasses. "Just before you die, Fertig, you'll twist and turn and there'll be no way out while you burn."

As the guard squeezed, pinching into Fertig's elbow, Fertig twisted, danced, jerked uncontrollably, trying to get away from the pain.

"Every part of you will burn. You'll smell your hair burning; your flesh will burn; your body will dance with the pain of it, understand? I'm the (only one who can save you." Morgan yelled at Fertig. The guard swung Fertig back and forth, handling him as easily as if he were a little child. "Is that what you want?" Morgan screamed.

Fertig wouldn't answer. His glasses swung loose and hung by one earpiece, arcing violently each time the guard shook him. He tried to reach for his glasses when the other guard slapped his hand away. "Easy, that's a good boy. Now take it nice and easy."

"Four thousand."

Fertig panted.

"Four thousand five ...

"Four thousand seven ... fifty...

"A column every day... your opinions ...

"All right then, all right ... all right. Let him alone. Four thousand nine hundred dollars."

Fertig didn't answer.

"You'll burn," Morgan told Fertig and went out of the room. The guards pushed Fertig out of the other door and took him back to the ward.

Onofrio Candelli was sitting on his chair between his and Fertig's bed when they brought Fertig back. When he came through the door and passed the desk, Hans patted him on the back. Fertig turned. Iron Hans grinned to show there were no hard feelings now; the relief guard got up. Hans sat down at the desk. He unlocked his drawer and took out a pocket transistor radio, propped it up, and began to play his sentimental songs. Fertig adjusted his glasses and looked at Hans. Aside from the fact that he was huge, bull-necked, he was actually a young man, a little more than a boy. He had never noticed it before. He walked to his bed. He wished he could lie down and sleep and keep from having anything to do with them. Candelli was waiting for him. Kaprelic was waiting for him. Hamisbat was waiting for Fertig too. He wished he could keep aloof. He sat down.

"I hear Morgan was here to see you," Candelli said.

"How did you hear that?"

The little face was wise and hard. "I know. I know. What did he want?"

"Don't you know that too?" Onofrio shook his head. Fertig thought a while and said, "He offered to save me."

Onofrio understood. "Did you hold out for a lot?"

Kaprelic came up behind Onofrio, who didn't notice him. He was leaning excitedly over Onofrio's head, looking at Fertig, listening. Kaprelic could see that they had scourged that man; the pale grey eyes behind the glasses were misty with pain; lines had been etched in that man's face since morning. Had he withstood, Kaprelic wondered? And he could see from those hard lips slowly softening into meekness that Fertig had prevailed. Fertig smiled up at him over Candelli's head. Far down the aisle, Hamisbat now looked in their direction, appearing to hear everything. He heard: Kaprelic knew.

"He wanted to save me. He offered me four thousand nine hundred dollars and lots of publicity," Fertig told them and got up. He wanted to get away from them and he walked down the centre aisle towards Hamisbat. They walked beside him, flanking him, and sat down around Hamisbat.

"You're in. You're in," Onofrio bubbled. "Morgan has the power. You're in."

"I refused."

"You refused?" Onofrio couldn't believe it. "You refused forty-nine hundred?" Kaprelic straightened out and folded his hands over his soapy crucifix. He looked up at the ceiling lights. His emaciated face twisted into a smile of thanksgiving. "You're crazy," Onofrio told him.

"How can he save me?" Fertig asked. The answer made Kaprelic happy.

"If Bleakie or Morgan can't save you, who can?" Onofrio asked.

Hamishat began to laugh. His great belly shook; his whole body quivered; tears ran down his cheeks, such jolly tears. Hamisbat's white eyebrows arched high; his eyes were comically round.

"What are you laughing at?" Candelli asked angrily.

"But doesn't Candelli see? It is prepared. The script is written. Fertig will suffer and they will take him to their heart?"

"He'll burn," Candelli said.

"He will prevail," Kaprelic told the back of Onofrio's hateful head. He saw Fertig's gentle smile. That man even forgave that little beast. He wrung his hands and felt the good feel of the soapiness come off in them. Across the way from them that black idol mocked on his haunches; he found himself glancing the way he pointed. The gibbering Puerto Rican, his crystal eyes bright with terror, held to the metal head of his bed. Kaprelic gestured towards them with the cross, keeping evil on the other side of the shiny, flowing linoleum.

"Money. Money. Money. Money. Money makes it all go. Morgan's paper backs him. They buy and sell judges. Without the newspapers, no judge gets elected. The papers give them the publicity and, in turn, they get favours from the judges – inside tips. How do you think Morgan got to see you? Then with the money you put the fix in with the judge," Onofrio told Fertig. He was so excited that his voice was high, almost tinkling.

Kaprelic was getting angry again. He would kill this little man, kill him.

"It's the only thing that will save you," Onofrio said and bounced up and down.

"It's not a case of being saved."

Kaprelic was nodding violently. Down at the other end of the aisle, Iron Hans was watching them all carefully. The sun had begun to decline, leaving the last few blazing bars of light on the floor. In the shade it was cool, and dancing figures on the television screen danced more violently. Kaprelic could feel the wonderful agitation this man exuded. It filled the warm upper air and the cooler lower layers.

Onofrio was smiling scornfully. Kaprelic was happy that the nature of the beast was coming out.

"Burn yourself, man, burn yourself. You're just as loony as the rest of them."

"Burning is not the issue," Hamisbat said. "Candelli sees things simply. There is the drama at the centre of which is Fertig."

"Why me?" Fertig asked reasonably.

"It was decided long ago." He looked at Fertig. "Fertig doesn't believe Hamisbat. Fertig thinks he's different, he's not mad. Of course, the thing is to convince Fertig he did not do what he did. He will play his part better."

"How can they do that? What I did I did."

"Shh..." Candelli said.

"How can I be convinced I didn't do what I did, what is done?"

Hamisbat tells Fertig that the issue is not sanity. What's sanity? A word. Who has it? He who tested you this morning. Fertig had it months ago. They have it there." He pointed to the stream of cars. "Fertig's here. He hasn't got it." Hamisbat laughed again.

Candelli said "You fat fool," got up, no longer able to stand it, resisted and bested by them, and walked away.

Kaprelic changed his seat and sat down in front of Fertig where

Onofrio had been sitting. His long, bony knees kept jabbing Fertig's knees. His great, skeletal hands were entwined, twisting and squeezing together, writhing, giving off a faint sound of crackling, as though they were filled with sparkling static. The rags of his pyjamas fluttered all over, gay streamers on his thin, agitated body. He couldn't get out what he wanted to say. His mouth kept opening and closing as he tried to say it all quickly, completely. His eyes burned. He opened his hand and held out the crucifix. He leaned far forward. Fertig tried to stiffen himself, but it was too much trouble; he was getting used to Kaprelic's stink. He smiled. Fertig was all love; Kaprelic could see that. The stench of something decaying in Kaprelic enveloped them both. Hamisbat turned away, leaned his head on his fat fist and looked out the window.

"I used to have so many of them," Kaprelic told Fertig. "They saved me for a long while. It saves. It saves me every night. But sometimes they come and say, 'Kaprelic, you are a dirty man.' Then they take me and force me to bathe. When that happens, Christ's cross is worn down a little, bubbled away. I used to have many crucifixes when I was free. I carved them myself. You understand?" He looked at Fertig. He didn't look at Hamisbat. Hamisbat was the voice of the devil, the lord of misrule. Fertig nodded, encouraging him. "I used to be a janitor. At least that is what I've told them. But really, all the time I prepared the way for one who came after." He smiled at Fertig. "For the world will go down in a bath of flame because all of it is evil. You understand that, don't you, you of all people? Washed in … You know it. Why should I tell you? I had an Ivory cross. I had a Lux cross. I had a Fels-naphtha cross. I had a happy-little-washday cross. Nothing as inferior as this," and he held up the strong-smelling, brown soap. "Once, I even took detergent flakes, wet them slightly, bonded them. They looked like galvanized iron. A beautiful cross." He looked down at the worn soap. "When he is gone I will fall into the pit. *Look!*" His hand shot out past Fertig's ear. Fertig couldn't help turning around. Kaprelic was pointing towards the television set, where the catatonic was pointing. He leaned close and whispered, "Each night when the light is right – for, you see, that light that burns over the door at the end of the hall has X-rays in it (they permit me to see through) – I see that there are millions of people burning and drowning at the same time because they haven't prevented themselves from their doom. They are unclean. The unclean and unlathered burn. Believe in this," and he held the soapen cross. "Washed in the blood …" Kaprelic said and began to laugh.

Fertig forced himself to pat his hand. Kaprelic calmed down. He felt the enormous calming power of that touch, something electric, recharging, flowing through the hand into him from Fertig. The last afternoon light shining on Fertig's head made it blaze with holy light. "Don't listen to Onofrio; he has the mark of the beast on his forehead.

That is why he howls when he cannot get what makes him human. His power is running low. They give him little any more. He is enslaved. They are all against us, Fertig. Do you know, when you came in, I saw something. I knew. I had thought I was alone and they were laughing at me." He motioned Fertig closer till he was whispering into his ear. "They are the ones who foment decay. They are the evil ones. All my life they have plagued me. You did right to kill." He looked around. No one was listening. "I prayed for many months. I put pine needles and burning autumn leaves on my cross shelf. But the evil entered into me. I heard the laughter of girls drown out my sweet voices. I am God's man, but also, Fertig, I am human. You see that. I had a wife. I had three sons. All strong, strong as merely flesh and bone can be. The evil entered me. It stayed there." His bony finger pointed between his legs. "For six months the evil stayed within, bursting through, making me ashamed. I taped it to my skin. I beat it. Nothing would drive it out. You understand. Even the cross washing it only wore itself down. I could feel it going through my body. I began to become fat. It glowed in the dark. I called for help, but no voices came to me. Only the laughter of the girls who kept peering through the window into my cellar.

"One night I heard them laughing and I ran into the streets. I showed them. *'Take back your evil,'* I yelled. They laughed and I attacked the harlots.

"And then it was peaceful for a long time. I could hear the voices singing to me, soothing me, sublime, and the evil, the touch of the beast had flown out of me, flown into the air. I could see it depart, an evil, white mist flying upward; and I thought *that* has been in me for six months.

"You did right to kill. Witches. Priests. Evil counsellors. Seven beasts. You did right."

"I suppose I did," he told the old man. "I tried to."

"And now you must get us out of this evil place, out, up, and away from here. You must kill the four of them."

"The four of them?"

"Wave your hand. Kill them."

But Fertig merely smiled at him gently and Kaprelic saw that he had not yet understood Fertig completely. His lips moved. He prayed for patience, for understanding. He could feel his sins destroying him, destroying him before this man. He waited for the voice to help him. "We are lost now. Your trials have just begun. They are going to test you."

"They have been trying to test me all the time," Fertig told him, smiling.

"They have been rehearsing Fertig all along, believe Hamisbat: and Fertig has been learning beautifully for their play," Hamisbat said.

"Don't suffer it."

Fertig spread his hands apart and smiled a little, shrugging his shoulders.

"No. No. Don't let them do it to you."

"No one's doing anything to me, Kaprelic. Don't be afraid," Fertig told him. Kaprelic looked around. He looked at the mocking smile on Hamisbat's face.

"But they will, they will, they will. Because … you *know*."

Fertig nodded. "But I will stand them off, old man."

Kaprelic began to weep. Fertig patted him on the shoulder.

"Don't worry, Kaprelic, you're in good hands."

"What are you telling him, you crazy old man?"

Onofrio stood grinning by their side. Kaprelic held up the soap crucifix and said, "Behind me, Satan. Kill him, Fertig. Wave your hand and make him disappear."

Onofrio pointed to the *Time* magazine on Kaprelic's table and said, "Pray to St. Fertig, old nut. Dirty old nut."

Kaprelic ran down to his picture and saw that Candelli had brown-smudged in a moustache and beard; it smelled of ordure. Kaprelic ran back and had Onofrio by the throat, threw him down on the floor, and was choking him. Bells rang. Fertig watched it, detached from it, thinking that he should go and get between them. Iron Hans was running up the aisle. More guards were pouring in through the door. Onofrio and Kaprelic slid across the waxed floor and smashed into the catatonic's bed. Holding his position, his legs still folded under him, the catatonic fell down to the floor: his head lay against the floor, bleeding; his neck was still rigid, unbent; he was unchanging, indestructible; his eyes kept staring; his mouth still yelled into the floor; and his hand pointed along the shining wax. The Puerto Rican was clinging to the bedstead and screaming wildly in Spanish. Guards grabbed Kaprelic and hustled him out of the door. His cross went sliding across the floor. Guards grabbed Onofrio and threw him on his bed and strapped him down. He began to rear and hiss at them, throwing himself upward against the straps, yelling over and over again. After a while he stopped and lay there panting, and soon he fell asleep.

Fertig shook his head; he went back to his bed and sat down. It was horrible, he thought idly, and wondered why it hadn't frightened him. His stomach was bothering him. He had become constipated; the food was all wrong. He was restless, uncomfortable, bored. There was nothing to do. He got up and walked. He thought of going to the bathroom, but Hans wouldn't let him. If he didn't defecate soon, they would give him an enema; he couldn't stand that humiliation. If they only had decent food here. He sat down. He tried to lie down and sleep. There was still an echo of screaming and shouting in the room;

it beat and beat like a pulse. Fertig's eyes opened and closed. Hans yelled down the aisle at Fertig, telling him to get off the bed. He sat up, He noticed that the catatonic was still on the floor. He watched for a moment and saw that there was blood on the floor. He was tired; he didn't sleep enough, he was hungry; and he looked at the poor black stiff lying there. He might lie there all night. He got up, and went over to try and pick up the Negro, but he couldn't do it alone. He called-to Iron Hans. Iron Hans took a long time in coming and Fertig was getting more and more excited. "What's the rush?" Iron Hans said, coming up. "He doesn't feel it anyway, the silly nigger. You know, hard heads." Together they picked him up and set him sitting again. The guard went to send for a nurse to patch up the bleeding wound.

Fertig went back to his bed and lay down again. Hans came down the aisle and stood over Fertig. "Once more! Don't let me tell you again." Fertig got up. He looked up and down the aisle and shrugged his shoulders. He sat down on a chair and closed his eyes. He slept a long time.

A few hours later Hans woke Fertig. "You missed your meal, hero." They took him out again. "You're popular today, Fertig."

"I don't want to see anyone."

"This one you have to see. Another headshrinker, a visiting fireman," the guard told him. At the door they were joined by the inevitable second guard. It was a new man, who looked carefully at Fertig.

"Is that him?" he asked. He seemed disappointed.

"That's him. Fertig, the fiendish killer. Don't let the appearance deceive you."

Fertig started to say something, but he was pushed along down the long corridor.

They brought him to one of the psychiatrist's offices. The room was bright and bare. There were several diplomas on the walls. A white-haired old man, seated in the chair, looked at him pleasantly; he kept his hands in his lap, behind the desk, to conceal their trembling: he was afraid of the insane. He looked into the cunning, the malevolent, the malingerer's face, quite calm now, as Fertig was seated in the leather chair. One of the guards stood to the side and behind Fertig's chair.

Making every attempt to be pleasant, reassuring, he greeted Fertig. "I'm Dr. Bridgeman. I want to ask you a few questions."

Fertig looked annoyed. Dr. Bridgeman, who had been sent to interview Fertig by the District Attorney, could understand Fertig's annoyance; they were giving him the full treatment here. He knew the whole approach. Fertig looked calm. His respiration was normal. He seemed rational. "Oh, this is going to take only a few minutes. No more." He laughed easily. "All right?"

Fertig shrugged his shoulders.

"What is your name?"

"Harry Fertig."

"How old are you?"

"Forty-four."

"What did you do before your arrest?"

"I was an accountant."

"What did you do to be arrested?"

"I killed seven people," Fertig said it wearily. "Aren't there enough people asking me questions? Are you a new addition to the staff? Don't you people consult one another's notes?" Fertig's voice was tired, almost petulant.

Dr. Bridgeman saw that Fertig was calm, reasonable, and ordered. There was nothing odd, so far as he could see, about Fertig's replies. Was the weariness out of line? Dr. Bridgeman wondered. No; they were working him over, building an escape case, pinning seven deaths on "illness", because they didn't want to face hard fact. And constant repetition of the story would make anything, any trauma, murder, commonplace, he thought. Was there anything he was missing? He doubted it. His fear was gone; he was at ease; Fertig was *not* insane – for he had a motto: "From him who has eyes to see and ears to hear, no mortal can hide his secret; he whose lips are silent chatters with his fingertips, betrays himself through his pores." Fertig must show him everything. The shaking of Dr. Bridgeman's hand stopped. He put one hand on the desk top and leaned on it a little.

"Now this is important, Mr. Fertig. Did you know what you were doing at the time?"

"I did."

"Did you get the impulse to do what you did suddenly, or –"

"I planned it a long time."

"Did you know what you were doing all the time?"

"I did."

"Did you know what you were doing was wrong?"

Fertig frowned. "Wrong? I'm not sure, ultimately." He appeared to be thinking about it. "Do you mean wrong according to the usual standards? Wrong according to law?" Dr. Bridgeman nodded. "Yes," Fertig told him. "I knew it was wrong. But that was its purpose: that it be wrong, as a protest; but –"

Dr. Bridgeman could see that Fertig was becoming a little excited. "Just a few more questions, Mr. Fertig."

"But I want to tell you about it."

"As soon as I finish I want very much to hear. All right?"

Fertig relaxed and nodded.

"Did you know at the time of the killings the nature and quality of your acts? By that I mean, did you know that what you were doing and the fact that you were doing it, firing the pistol, I mean, would lead to the death of those people? Did you understand that?"

"Yes. I knew that. As I said, that was the purpose of the whole thing: to lead, as you put it, to the death of those people. How calmly you state it," Fertig said.

Dr. Bridgeman put his other hand on the desk. He leaned on his elbows. "Now, and this is important too, did you at all times have full control of your sense of volition? Were you labouring under an... impulse?"

"Of course I was labouring under an impulse. I had to kill them. It balanced things. My son, Stevie..."

"I mean, Mr. Fertig, was that impulse irresistible? Was it of such a nature that you couldn't control it?"

"No. Of course, I could control it. I could always control it. It was a *decision*."

"Now, one thing. Do you understand that you have killed and so are – shall we say – guilty?"

"Of course," Fertig smiled.

Dr. Bridgeman smiled back. Obviously Fertig was remorseful. "Have you ever been institutionalized?"

"No."

"Has any member of your immediate family been institutionalized?"

"No."

"Ever had a nervous breakdown?"

"Of course not."

"Were you ever just nervous, jumpy?"

"Do you mean to an excessive degree?"

"Yes."

"Only for a while after the death of my son."

That seemed reasonable. "Well," Dr. Bridgeman closed his note-book, "you seem fine enough."

"So why am I here?"

"For observation."

"But if I'm sane?"

"Exactly," Dr. Bridgeman said. He looked at his watch. "Well, thank you. Thank you very much." He stood up. "I must run now."

"But don't you want to hear what happened after Stevie's..."

"Some other time. Soon. I must go now." He left. The guards brought Fertig back to the ward.

They had their supper. Fertig managed to eat everything they gave him – the cooking was bothering him less and less. He fed Candelli because Hans wouldn't untie him. Then, they sat around till it was time to go to sleep. He still couldn't defecate and for a little while after he had eaten, the pain was acute; he was still bothered by the idea that he might be watched on the toilet.

His second history had been returned. Several sections contained pencilled notes asking for further amplifications, pointing out contradictions, not only in this version, but in his story changes from the last version. Of course, he saw, it would be easy to clear up; he just hadn't been thorough enough. He started to write but then stopped because he was too tired. They kept on harping on Lucy. There was nothing really to tell – anyway, he wouldn't embarrass Lucy … or Sara, for that matter, and what did Lucy have to do with this anyway? Or, well, of course the question of the first impulse – well, who remembered when it really began? One day – But what day? Her back had been towards him and … how could he talk about that? Or, after the night he went back to Mercy Memorial and …

He couldn't sleep. The lights were out, except for the bathroom lights, which stayed on all night. They had brought Kaprelic back from hydrotherapy, still wearing the dripping rags, and faint lights played on his emaciated face, making it look as though it were some stone's face; the flesh was washed down almost to bone and sinew, laved of dross, flickering in the light. The eyes were open and stared ecstatically at the ceiling. The catatonic slept; an ever-exhorting statue, pointing to the unseen horror, warning them all. Hamisbat still sat at the end of the ward, looking like a mound, soft and shapeless, covered, dark, a wave thrown up by a soft sea, frozen into a position of rest near the window. Now that it was very quiet Fertig could hear the faint and perpetual hum of cars going by along the East River Drive. Onofrio, caught by his nightly horrors, moaned softly and moved against the straps. The television flickered and the night light shone. The lights from the little Christmas tree they hadn't removed yet went on and off, green and blue and red, all night.

"Make a miracle again. Kill them," Kaprelic's voice burbled. He saw Fertig's calm face as through a film and saw, after a while, that Fertig wasn't looking at him but seemed to be sleeping and smiling beatifically. Kaprelic slept.

But the gas pains in his stomach and the terrific pressure in his lower abdomen wouldn't let Fertig sleep. He got up and went down to the guard who was sitting and listening to an all night disc jockey. He said he had to go to the bathroom. The guard thought about it a long time and asked if he hadn't gone before. Fertig said yes, but – The guard considered it again and said all right, this once, but not to make a habit of it because all order would break down and before you knew it everyone would be going whenever he wanted to and soon you'd have anarchy, or have to station a guard in the john and – was he going to be a good boy if he let Fertig go just this once? Fertig mumbled something that the guard took to mean agreement.

The lights were bright in the toilet. Fertig was happy to be alone for once. He sat on the seat and looked towards the door. He knew the guard could see him, or any of them, but the bright lights in the toilet made the ward darkness seem complete, a wall to shield him. The pressure was downward against the tension of an unyielding and ashamed sphincter, but he struggled hard because otherwise the guard would come for him soon. He managed to defecate a little; he would have to do better or they would give him an enema – he couldn't stand that – he had heard of people being poisoned from not being able to go – he imagined all that waste dissolving into his blood, being carried along through every vein and artery into every part of his body ... He finished and left.

He lay there and couldn't sleep. He turned on the night light, slanting it away from Candelli, and picked up the pad and pen. What was there to say? He had seen Miss Malabar through the dusty window, her yellow hair like a mane, bent over, still writhing, while he had to wander down the lone streets, the pain in him – and Sara, with her back always towards him now, grieving endlessly for her lost son. Miss Malabar wrote entries; she wrote entries; and they permitted her! He thought of running in and grabbing the pen from her hands and ... madness.

And in the long run he went home. It had been four o'clock in the morning and he should have been tired enough to sleep, but as soon as he lay down the pain began again. And he thought of her again, that yellow wig, that spiteful face, he saw her in a murky yellow light where, garnet and gold, amethyst and emerald – she gleamed! It seemed odd to see Miss Malabar going about her business in the blackness of his room (but he willed it, he wanted to see her, he remembered that), detached from her surroundings, talking to nonexistent patients, writing in absent ledgers. And he had been pricked by silver pins all over his body and he pulsed to some great beat.

He stood up on his bed and pointed his finger at Miss Malabar; she became aware of him and cringed away. His finger tingled. Slowly, the light went out of her till she looked flat in greys and blacks, like in a movie. And her body began to jerk in horrible agony and she crumpled to the floor and died. He was triumphant, throbbing with power as he stood on the bed, towering over the blackness she had become, and he felt his swollen finger draining the pain in his body, return to its normal size, then crumpling as though it had been in water too long. And his pulse now beat slowly and serenely.

Kaprelic pleaded again, his voice clear in the darkness: it was wordless and anguished.

Fertig stopped. How could he tell them something like that? He sat down in bed. How could they understand? Was it crazy? No. No. The dreams you have – well, he *knew* it was a dream, a fantasy ... and it had gone flat in time so that ... what power we wish for, he thought, how different it was from dreams. He could explain it carefully to Dr. Heisenberg ... Madness.

He smiled. He saw what they were after. He crumpled the paper, started to throw it away, stopped, and began carefully to shred it. He kept tearing and re-tearing till there was nothing but fine confetti-slivers, which he tossed into the basket by his bed.

He smiled. Yes. He saw what they were after and he knew what to do about it. He would take no more of their tests; he would sit there and look at them and, politely, refuse to answer. Refuse and refuse till they brought him to court. Then ... *then!*

He lay back. He relaxed. His bowels rumbled. He broke wind loudly. And, instead of being embarrassed as he always was when other people were around, he laughed. "Quiet there," the night guard yelled. He lay there still active while the tightness in his belly slackened and he began to feel quite good and fell asleep.

Chapter 11

As Bleakie's car bumped over the boards of the little drawbridge over the Gowanus Canal, he could see where a half-stink barge decayed, and rings of lamplight were reflected by the still, oily water. In spite of it being very cold and clear, he could smell something chemical in the air. It was eleven o'clock and he was driving to Little Mike's Paradise Bar. He had spent the evening talking to people, working to nail down the nomination for D.A., but keeping it quiet: let MacGruder be surprised. Why was he bothering?

He turned off and drove along narrow streets; he passed a torn-down section for a low-rent housing project where rubble steamed up plaster ghosts into the clear night, ghosts given radiant solidity by the moonlight. Beyond the dancing fumes, Mercy Memorial Hospital loomed high, its towers and turrets and roof tiles, the whole assemblage of different architectural styles shining in the moonlight. Fertig's range, he thought: Fertig stalked around here, skulked down these lonely streets, into Mercy and out again, wrestling with his conscience, to Mercy and back to the Paradise and out again (at least that was what Donnell's report indicated), invisible then, a nothing ready to commit his gigantic act. And off to the side, up the long slope to the high apartment houses quite sharply limned in the clear and cold air, there was Sara, up there, sleeping. Did she wonder where Fertig used to go?

He parked the car in front of Little Mike's Paradise and stepped out. The streets were deserted; except for the light from the bar everything was dark. The pavements were slate with patches of crumbly concrete; slate kerbstones sank slowly into the sub-street ooze. The streets were cobble-stoned with wood, except for where disused trolley tracks were asphalted over. From far off he could hear the perpetual buzz and hum of the city traffic, the rumble of subway and elevated trains, machinery. Fertig's notebook didn't mention any of this. Scene against careful entries in a schedule: film clip: Fertig alone: show the jury: "Driven, haunted by the death of his child, he descended, ladies and gentlemen of the jury, to … this …"

The bar-name, Little Mike's Paradise, was announced on the window in gold lettering. Gay nineties stuff: some of the letter tails were chipped off. The flaky and pitted metal framing the window was painted over in bright red with bright blue trim over the corrosion. Above the bar were two storeys of a house with a fairly new asbestos façade, made to look like brick. A store flanked the bar on one side; on the other side was a burned-out house. Bleakie went in.

The air was thick, heavy, unmoving, full of warm smoke and the smell of beer, hazy, palpable as a gel in which everything and everyone hovered and shimmered. His eyes teared from the temperature change. A big Santa Claus Bubble, whose belt said "Drink Schaeffer's Beer", had been left up behind and over the bar. Red and green jukebox lights twinkled constantly and amber bubbles cauldroned up and a tenor voice almost drowned by the bass sang some sad song of love. Stools were set along the length of the bar; there was a lunch counter on the other side. The walls above the lunch counter were muralled, but darkened, invisible.

It was pretty full for so late at night and for the middle of the week. People turned to look at him: young, hard, old, soft, sad, tough faces turned to stare at him. The shock of the air made him dizzy for a second and he had the impression that the bar tilted down to a trellis and beyond that to smoke, and he was looking down at all of them, and the faces looked up at him from the wavering fuming light. Negroes, Puerto Ricans, hard Irish faces, white and dark, brutal and brutalized faces giving him the expected and cold look-over; you got it in the poor bars; you got it in the rich bars; it was always a little menacing. How did a Fertig have the courage to come down into a place like this? By being crazy, he told himself.

Three young hoods, leaning with their backs to the bar and with drinks in their hands, turned their heads his way. He walked further in; the only free place was in the middle of the bar. He strolled past their stare. He stood in the free space. The bartender saw him and came down the length of the bar and whispered in the ears of the man sitting next to Bleakie; the man got up leaving his stool. It was almost as if they were expecting him. He sat down beside a cut-out of a little crippled girl with a clear-plastic collection box stapled on to her chest.

The bartender gestured and put a glass in front of him. "What'll you have?" The bartender appeared to be as short as Bleakie, but he had fat forearms, thick wrists, big hands. He had a round bulge-domed head and his features being compressed into the lower third of his face gave him the look of a good-humoured and intelligent baby. But his ears were very hairy.

Bleakie sat on the stool and looked around. The others sitting and standing along the bar were looking at him. "Bourbon and Branchwater."

"The only branch we got around here is the Gowanus."

"Sparkly, tangy, zesty. A real taste treat."

The bartender laughed. Towards the back, past the free-lunch counter, an old man sat perched on a stool and played an accordion, but Bleakie couldn't hear what was being played because of the jukebox. Gradually, they all seemed to draw away from him, isolating him. He looked around.

"Yeah. This is the very place where the killer planned his dark deed. I recognized you from the newspapers."

The violent masks of girls' faces leered, hovering above bare chests: old women's face reddened and lined by whisky-bloating stared at him. "You could make this a tourist trap. A short itinerary. Little pointer talk. Display cases with some of his effects. Charge admission. Make a lot of money."

"I don't know if we'd like that, Mr. Bleakie. We run a simple, family bar here," the bartender said, and Bleakie had to laugh.

"You don't mind if I look around, do you?"

"Look. It's still free." The bartender poured a shot of bourbon from a bottle he took from under the counter.

The bar was grimy; he felt dirty; he'd have to change his shirt soon, take a bath. Men kept coming in and going to the back with the girls; men and other girls kept coming out. An old couple – she, Negro, greyed by dirt; he, white, blackened by dirt – drunk and ragged, entwined, danced up and down the long room, weaving from the trellis in the back to the door and back again. He could smell them as they danced past; he turned his head away from their sour stink to his drink. A tenor's voice, reedy, barely audible, came through the enormous bass beat, singing "... we will never be aaaaaapart."

The old woman held a glass full of whisky in her hand. The old man's hand held her outthrust wrist while he leaned against her, his face buried in her wrinkled neck, seeming to smell at her straightened white hair. Drooling, his lips nibbled at her neck, sucking, while she, looking pleased, her face frozen into a feeble, toothless grin, tried to prevent his reaching the drink and taking it away from her. They fought for the drink without spilling it, waltzing, fox-trotting, polkaing, twisting up and down. The hoods were laughing at the dancers, tormenting them with remarks. The dancers stagger-danced around, not caring, never stopping, while that little hand struggle for the glass of whisky went on.

The bartender said, "Cute, ain't it? They never spill a drop. The boys," the bartender nodded towards the three, "provide the drink. If they get enough laughs, they buy another drink. You know the way the young are these days; no consideration." He shook his head; he looked like a wise baby. "They never spill a drop."

"And Fertig came down for the laughs?"

"He even bought them drinks now and then, only with him the condition was that they don't dance. I told him that there is no end to their thirst and you just haven't got that kind of money; no one does. Well, you're a bartender, you see a lot of things."

"I imagine."

"This isn't the worst. You hang around you see a lot of things." The light gleamed on his high, bulging forehead.

"You saw Fertig."

"I saw Fertig. He didn't seem like the worst. He sat there, right where you're sitting now. He used to brood a lot. You could tell something was coming off in him."

"You could tell that?"

The bartender told Bleakie how Fertig was after him for a gun all the time.

"All the time?"

"All the time."

"And you didn't call the police?"

"Are you kidding?"

"What was it for? Did he say?"

"His wife. See, the first time he was serious; after that we made a sort of joke out of it. He'd come in –"

"Any set time?"

"No. He wasn't regular. Afternoon sometimes, nights. He'd come in and I'd say, 'Well, Mr. Fertig –'"

"You called him Mister?"

"Why not?" the bartender frowned.

"How many of your regulars do you call Mister?"

"I see what you mean. You know, I never thought about it. You see, there *was* something –"

"Sure. Sure. And –?"

"I'd say, 'Well, Mr. Fertig, did you get your gun?' It was a standing joke."

"But you told the police he only asked once."

"Them? Come on. Did I know what he might have said to them? I played it safe."

"Did he seem crazy to you?"

"Well, he had a *look*, if you know what I mean."

Another post-facto prophet, Bleakie thought. Near the lunch counter, a man with wild eyes drank steadily and crammed food into his mouth. He had sandwiches in wax wrappers and was eating them and packing free lunch into his mouth. His hand darted out, undecided, trembling over the meats, the relishes, the salty breads, unable to stop. A dog sat by his feet and licked hungrily at the food that dropped from the man's mouth; sometimes licking at the crumbs on his shoes, the dog seemed to bite into the leather. He saw Bleakie looking at him and his eyes became wilder; his hand waved for a second and he talked, but he was still eating and his food sprayed again, so he stopped talking and ate till his eyes began to run over and he wept, unseeing, eating, swaying his thin body.

"A look like that for instance?" Bleakie asked.

"Not as bad. I recall, he'd sit there, right where you're sitting now, and look out the window at the hospital there ..."

Bleakie turned and looked out of the window; he couldn't see anything but the reflection of the bar-room in the window and a few lights floating out there in the night.

"... and he'd be drinking..."

"A lot?"

"Not too much. A nurser, if you know what I mean, a brooder."

"Too bad he didn't drink a lot."

"Maybe moren'd be good for him."

"Your memory will be valuable on this thing," Bleakie said.

"Definitely more than he should have been drinking, more than a guy like him is used to drinking. A man of sorrows; you know the bit." The bartender thought. "But not enough to be a rummy."

"Yes."

"And now and then he'd hop up and walk out, kind of muttering to himself; you know?"

"Muttering to himself? That's good. Where'd he go?"

"Search me?"

"There?" Bleakie asked, nodding towards the window, towards the hospital.

"It's a possibility."

"You're giving me valuable help."

"I'm glad I can be helpful. As a matter of fact I know he once went

around to the hospital. Once we had a little discussion down here –
you know, bottle against barstool. A head was cracked and Fertig took
a ride in the meat wagon down to Mercy."

"Where's the girl?"

"She's here. At the back. Be right down." He looked at his watch.
"Say five minutes more. Looks like a three-minute man.

He bangs. Spends the rest of the time telling her how lucky she is to
have a guy as good at it as him. You know the kind?"

"I know the kind. And what's her memory of Fertig?"

"Why don't you ask her?"

"I will. But what did she tell *you*."

"Not another John; not another lay for pay; not that kind of thing.
They used to talk a lot and a lot of times he paid for that privilege. After
all, she's a working girl. The way I figure it, some men, when they feel
down, they have to talk to the lowest. You know the kind."

"That kind I know."

"Unless she's lying about it."

"Why lie? Things like that?"

"You know the kind they are; whores are the most sentimental –"

"And have hearts of gold. Old story."

"They like to think they have a man crazy over them, someone who
likes them for something beside the old cooze, you know? She said he
was nice, never laid a finger on her."

Bleakie tried something. "Not what the police say. They say all the
time. Doesn't that machine ever stop?"

"A little music makes the place more home."

"And the gun? He got the piece here."

"So he says."

"A Mafia piece."

"So the police say."

"From her?"

"Lucy doesn't know from buns. She's a good kid."

"Look, I'm not the police. I'm not prosecution."

"Excuse me. The citizens are thirsty." And the bartender moved
along the length of the bar filling glasses and collecting money.

Bleakie got down from the stool and stood. He felt itchy, and an
unbearable feeling around the skin, especially on the inside of his
arms and along his sides. Was there a faint rim of dirt along his shirt
cuffs? He kept his coat closed; he was beginning to be hot, but if he
opened it he was sure he would get his bright yellow vest smudged.
He kept his gloves on. The music never stopped. Men kept coming
and going. The girls kept going from the bar to the curtain beyond the
trellis and coming back. The bartender returned.

"Look," Bleakie said. "Understand anything about the case?"

"I read a little – headlines. Looks bad. People are in an ugly mood."

"Things are not the best. Popular opinion's against. I mean doctors – holy – and a man of God – very popular religious leader. Even the Bishop of New York laments. Not good."

"So –?"

"But he was a sick man. He could not help himself. They are trying him and judging him and condemning him in the papers. What chance will he stand later? Will justice be done?"

"No."

"That's why I'm taking it on for nothing. For justice. All right, a little glory too: I'll admit it."

"Sure. Everyone has a motive. Nothing wrong in that."

"Still, I'd even sacrifice a little something from my very own pocket to help, for right, for truth."

"Sure," the bartender said, smiling broadly, his infant's face making him look absurdly pleased. "We all have to make sacrifices."

"We do."

"Well, those beauties, they come around and they question, but they already *know*. Now it is my theory that when you deal with a bull who has made up his mind, you have to give them a piece of what they're looking for or they're mad. Lucy, she earns a living taking it from any client she can find, so naturally they assume that all the talk Fertig has with her is in terms of grunt and groan. Object? Pleasure and a piece. Get it?" He laughed.

Bleakie nodded. "Opinionated."

"Takes the pressures off other areas. Now I know for a fact that Lucy don't know from guns. But with the police it's a case of gun plus the lay. It angers them to think it could be another way. But she said no. I'm pretty sure. So if the police say that, well it's because they have this theory."

"*Cherchez la femme!*"

"You know it. But we deny. If they want to *think* that, well fine, but so long as they don't act on it."

Bleakie looked around and saw a stand-up cardboard sign on the bar. "I'd walk a mile for a Camel? You're behind the times."

"Listen, I've got signs in the back which sell Lucky Strikes in a green package."

"The good old days."

"Nothing is right any more. I have a theory that it began to go bad when the green went to war. Casualty."

Bleakie took out his wallet and pulled out a few notes. "I'd like you to contribute this to your favourite charity for me."

The bartender took the money.

After about eight minutes a girl came through the crowd; she was followed by a big, sack-bellied man, who, as soon as he passed the trellis, began to stuff his shirt down tight under his belt, doing it conspicuously, raising his shoulders high, looking around smugly, pretending that there just wasn't room for shirt and genitalia – side-step motion, swinging that tool free, hand-stuffing past the belt – old gesture – meant that he could go for another round easy but she, that lucky girl – who was he telling it to? The other girls? They didn't care. The other men? Himself? What a fuss over business, Bleakie thought.

The girl sat down near Bleakie and oscillated slowly on the red plastic and chrome stool. She was wearing green bulge-sunglasses that hid her eyes. She seemed to shine around the edges under the hot, yellow lights that simmered down from the dusty neon lamps. The man, coming up beside her, ordered a drink and took his shot quickly, throwing it down his throat and sighing, almost belching, and wiped his mouth on the meaty part between the thumb and forefinger, making it seem like he needed that drink because he had really put everything into it. He looked at the girl, almost benignly now. She didn't look back but moved herself from side to side with her toe. The man said something into her ear, grinning, and threw back his head and laughed loudly. Her orange shining lips had a purplish undercoat; they stretched into an easy grimace; a gold tooth reflected hungrily. Her face turned a little towards him, but two points of light from her sunglasses reflected towards the mirror behind the bar. The man mistook the smile for a thankful look.

Her skin, even in the yellow light, remained white, stiff; cracks were drawn into it, alongside the mouth and radiating from the eyes and circling her neck. She wore a choker of glittering stones and tiny bright sequins were sewn into her dress. There was a fringe on the bottom; her knees broke the strands apart. Fertig went to bed with this? Or even bothered to talk to this? Maybe there was something to the dregs theory after all, Bleakie thought. "Hello, Superbia?"

The face turned towards the bartender, who was standing in front of them. The bartender beamed and nodded. "Don't call me that. Lucy. Let's go," she said, tossing her head towards the back.

"Sit. What's the rush?" "I'm losing time."

"Let me buy you a drink."

"Buy," she shrugged her shoulder. While the glutton ate, he stared at her. Men drinking stared at her. The old dancer looked at her over his partner's shoulder. A man bundled in layers of plastic raincoats talked about a contaminated God who suffered from radiation burns while taking quick looks at her. Another girl came walking into the bar swinging her hips; they talked to her, shouted, touched her as she passed – putting hands on her shoulders, waist, breasts, behind... She walked through, uncaring, passing Bleakie and the girl.

"Where's your boy friend tonight, Angie?" Lucy asked.

"He's going to commit suicide," she laughed, "because I won't marry him." She went on and passed through the trellis.

They all seemed to be closing around Lucy. Her bed-companion had another shot but kept looking the other way.

"I can't stay here all night. Let's go before *they* want."

"Popular girl?"

"There are nights, buddy," she told him.

"I'm not here for that."

She looked at Bleakie and then to the bartender, who was back from serving the others. The music jangled with the sound of wavery voices and massed electric guitars, but the beat remained the same. The bartender smiled benignly; a cherub.

"Remember your old friend, Harry Fertig?"

"Again? You're small for a cop. All right, come on."

"No. I'm his lawyer."

"That poor guy; he doesn't stand a chance."

Stupid slut, he thought, stupid little whore, what did she know? Fertig would get off. "A few questions."

"I have no time for questions. I have to pay the cop or I get arrested. As it is he takes me in twice a year. I have to pay my boy; he has a big habit. I have to pay the landlord," she nodded, looking at the bartender. "I have to eat once in a while, though lately, I'm losing my appetite. I go because otherwise they say, Lucy, she's stuck up, and then I won't get business. Besides, I like it. You meet all kinds. You, for instance, you're different."

"And Fertig, he was different too?"

"In the beginning, one way; later, another way. I can't talk all night."

She's making a production of it, he thought, a moment of glory. "Fine. Let's go back." "You don't understand..."

"I wouldn't think of wasting your time."

"Come on." And she led him through the bar.

They passed the waltzers. They passed the girl Angie, seated in the darkness beyond the trellis, drinking, humming to her-self, tapping a red-tipped finger to the music, nodding her head, waiting for her customers; long rhinestone earrings swung. Lucy led him past the men's room and the women's room. She pulled the curtain aside; he followed; she led him down a long, narrow corridor that smelled of stale urine, as if they used the passageway instead of the toilets. The creaking linoleum-covered floor tilted slightly downward. There was a wooden door at the end. She knocked on one of the red-enamelled panels. A key rattled in the door; it didn't seem to work. Another key was thrust in and the lock turned. Lucy kept tapping her foot. She looked behind her, past Bleakie, down the long corridor. Bleakie turned around and looked through the bulb-lit bands of light: there was no one there. He was used to girl's like Lucy, but of a better class. He had never been down to a place like this, but, after all, Roy Bleakie knew the world and its possibilities. But what about Fertig? Nothing in his past indicated that he knew such worlds; yet he had ended up down here. And risen, Bleakie thought, risen. Unless they were all lying and just didn't know. The secret life of Fertig. Was Sara lying to him? Those happy-days-be-fore-we-fell-on-tragedy jazz?

The door opened and a huge man stepped out; he was dressed in grey. The face was twisted, ravaged, destroyed by an old acne. "Is he with you?" the voice, almost human, asked. Bleakie jumped: How it must have terrified Fertig! he thought.

"Yes, Pete," she told the man. The man squeezed back to let them through. Bleakie followed Lucy. They walked up creaking stairs.

"Inner Sanctum stuff?" Bleakie joked. She didn't turn but said "What?" Her behind, barely visible in the dark, swayed a few inches in front of his face, receding and ascending in crude side-to-side jerks.

"Nothing," Bleakie said. Time and poor lighting had turned everything black with decay. Someone had tried to mask it over with thick coats of black enamel, but age had shattered each coat, making the cracks gleam – an endless covering web. At the top of the stairs there was a white-enamelled door; the brass figure of a One hung loosely on it, swinging by one nail. They passed down another cor-ridor, through a smell of dead, musty cloths, once wet, now dried-out; Bleakie was reminded of the inaccessible sections of old-records rooms and his nose tickled. They passed five doors. Next to each door there was a little alcove with a rust-streaked sink into which water dripped. He heard muffled sounds, the creak of springs, coughing, the click of her heels, the sound of far-away blues-music, a static-y radio-scream, all blending to sound like a machine beat.

Her room was small, square-shaped, high. There was only a single bed, a cheap chest of drawers, a portable closet made of masonite. The walls were papered with pine trees beyond which, half-faded, Bleakie could see mountains: it was all wrinkled by narrow tongue and groove boards underneath so that the trees and mountains were seen through waves as if heat shimmered the air. It was stuffy in the room; the window was soldered shut with dirt. On one wall hung a plaster horn out of which oily red, yellow, and purple fruit poured and blazed in the dim, forty-watt light. A blue, red, and white luminescent statue of a styrofoam Christ hung on the opposite wall. She had tied a tiny piece of black cloth over the eyes.

She sat down on the bed and crossed her legs. The sound of silk against silk, the sound of the flesh of her thigh rubbing the flesh of her other thigh hissed through the room. There was nowhere else to sit; Bleakie leaned against the chest of drawers. How different she was from the women he knew; how stupid; how cheap. The expensive ones always dressed simply, let you see their eyes, looked pure instead of like whore caricatures; they were a case of evil beneath the clear, untroubled skin, the youthfulness, the frank gaze, the gleam of shampooed-and-hundred-brush-strokes-a-night hair. What had Fertig felt? Moonshine: the purity beneath the sordid casing, the fallen woman, the woman of mystery, the woman in the depths, the whore with the heart of gold, both suffering – old story; the kind of story innocents believe and innocents tell of themselves. Could it have been that kind of innocence that drove Fertig up to this room to listen to her stories? Why did she dress like that? Maybe it was a matter of advertising one's shame: or down here they might want things labelled clearly; pure food and drugs; let the buyer beware. Evil is evil and sin is sin and everything else is your wife, or a boy, or your hand. Very simple: very satisfying.

"Did he come up here a lot?" Bleakie asked. He was warm.

"You have to pay seven dollars for the room," she told him.

"That include –"

"No."

"Rent, operating expenses, depreciation?" She was jacking the price up.

"Sort of."

He gave her ten dollars; she didn't give him change. "None of it is for me."

And she stood up and slipped her dress over her head before he could tell her she didn't have to do that. She was wearing nothing underneath. He looked at her clinically. She wasn't much. She had heavy, wide hips, thick legs, a little knock-kneed, heavy without clean indentation marks for knee and ankle, as though her legs were hewn out of one piece, crudely, almost no definition. She stood, holding the dress loosely in one hand and teetering on heels. Her black, spider-textured stockings were rolled, cutting deep into the puffy smoothness of her thigh. But her torso was thin, she was long-waisted, her small breasts drooped slightly, pointing into cones low on her chest; she was narrow-shouldered and her clavicles showed; her thin arms were smooth, without muscle tone: two women joined together, a girl growing up out of a woman, still like a clumsy adolescent, and he realized that she was young, in spite of the cold face and the expressionless sunglasses: his rounded face stared back at him, amused, out of each green beetle-back glass. The garnet and gold, the rhinestones and marcasite, the green glass and glowing ruby choker were brilliant against her parchmenty skin, except for where she had lacquered her heavy undifferentiated nipples and aureoles into a state of red attention. A sharp-pointed ebony cross on a long, very fine silver chain dangled low, beneath her diverging breasts and just above the child's jut of her stomach. Below, the hair of her bulgy pubis was almost all shaved off, except for a fine line. Bleakie pressed back against the chest, felt it slide back, come against the wall; the knobs painful, satisfying in their pain-giving, jabbed into his back through the coat. Not much, he thought; he was used to much-better-looking girls.

She remembered something and turned, holding the dress in front of her, genuflected and crossed herself in front of the styrofoam Christ. Her big bare behind faced Bleakie; the stretched skin smoothed out of the web of tiny fat bulges. She stood up and went to the closet and hung her dress up carefully.

She had decided to play it this way; up to a point he would go along with her. "Why? He can't see," he told her.

"I know, but sometimes I have the feeling he's peeking from under the blindfold. I've adjusted it a hundred times, but I always get the feeling he can see. I always feel it isn't right. I used to put more cloths over the face, but that blacked it. You have to see the face or it doesn't count."

"Maybe he should see?"

She was sitting on the bed. Metal silver and red flowers gleamed in her hair. Hot tropical smells filtered in through all the cracks in the wall and past the door. He could smell bananas and plantains being cooked, the reek of boiling greens, slightly spoiled meat, those odours strange, slightly nauseating. How many times did a fastidious Fertig recoil from this?

"Why don't you sit down here?" She patted the bed beside her.

"I'm fine. Been sitting all day."

His image was centred in the green eye-globes; she was looking at him. "Take off your coat. You must be warm."

"No. I'm fine. Only going to stay a little while."

She shrugged; her breasts jiggled. "What do you want to know?"

"Was he up here much?"

"He came up a few times. We talked," she looked at him, inquiring.

"I'll pay you," he said. He had no intention of hitting the sack with her to get information. "Did he ever talk about home... about his wife, I mean, unhappy marital life... anything like that?"

"No. He told me he lost his kid. He told me he had a wife. Didn't give me any of that pure wife crap. That. No more. I didn't know the kid's death was bugging him. He treated me nice, you know. He was always a gentleman. They're not all gentlemen. Most of them are pigs."

"What else did you talk about?"

"I told him stories. Like I'm telling you."

What did she mean by that? Was she putting him in the class of a madman who had to talk to a ten-dollar whore? He kept his mouth shut. He couldn't antagonize her. He might need her. He wouldn't give her the satisfaction.

"You know the kind," she lay down and stretched her arms over her head; her breasts flattened and the top of her seemed almost boyish. Her face, he noticed now, was oval too, too young, almost unformed, white-skinned against the yellowed sheets. "They always want to know about your life, so I tell them things. How I got into this. Why I stay in it. I'm a princess, you know, a rich man's daughter. I was stolen away by the gypsies and sold to a pimp. If you take me away my father will reward you beyond your fondest dreams." She turned towards the wall and looked up at the plastic feet of the Christ. "It's true, you know."

"Did you ever –"

"No."

"Really?" He smiled at her as if to tell her she didn't have to lie to him. The glasses pointed in his direction. It was hot, getting hotter here. "Could we open the window?"

"Take off your coat."

"I'm fine."

"No," she said, dreamily, "not really."

Not really? What did she mean by that? Was she smiling? He wasn't sure when she wore those glasses. "Don't I get to see your eyes for my money?"

"Does it help your case?"

"No."

She said, "I thought so," and sat up again. What did that mean? He was breaking out into a face sweat. "So why ask?" she said.

"Curious."

She looked up at him. Her fingers were holding the ebony cross, kneading it, moving up and down the upright of it. "I read the papers. You're good, but he's going to lose it. They never give you a break. It figures. No one can help him."

But Roy Bleakie would help Harry Fertig.

"He was a sweet fellow, but a little crazy."

"He seem crazy?"

"No. But he must have been."

"Say anything crazy?"

"No. One thing. Once …"

"Yes?"

"But he was drunk …"

"What was it? About his kid? Anything about his boss?"

"He comes in one day and says I saw your father. He showed me this picture and asked me if I recognize him. I said no. He said that the guy was a rabbi. My father. I'm no Jew, I told him. But he was excited. He said he had just seen this guy, been watching him and on his way down here something clicked in his head, he said. A Jew. Well, I started to tell him no, but he kept on talking about the long-lost father and the long-lost daughter and before I knew it he grabbed my arm and took me over to the phone booth and was calling this guy. And I thought it was funny and I was laughing at it, you know; he tried to make an appointment to see the guy."

Bleakie pulled out the notebook and turned to the picture of the rabbi. "Was this the man?" He was excited.

"I think so. That was the guy he killed, wasn't it? Crazy. Why did he think I was his daughter?"

A laugh, Bleakie thought: The rabbi's daughter. "Well, you said it: crazy. Or maybe those stories you were telling got to him. After all, the man is, was a prince of the synagogue."

"But I'm no Jew." She shook her head. "And I mean, the gun, and all... I never really thought –"

"... when you got it for him it would lead –"

"No. Not me. Just you remember that. Not me. I told him he might get a gun if he hung around, got to know people. But I never got it for him."

"I'm not from the police."

"No," she said, her face looking up at him. She sat up. She put the upright of the cross into her mouth and moved it in and out, sucking, looking at him challengingly. She crossed her legs and leaned on one elbow, turning away a little from him, showing him more of her haunch and behind. He squinted, trying to see if he could see her eyes through the sunglasses. Stupid slut, he thought, did she think he was a Fertig? They couldn't stand it. Try it and they say you're always after it. Refuse it and they can't keep away. Rule of the thumb. He could feel the dankness film between his clothes and flesh. He had to finish soon. His eyes teared a little; the smell bothered him. The cheap perfume aura was grabbing him: he would stink for a week. Just try and see Mable Crossland this way. Needed a steam bath, shower, get rid of his clothes. What did she think she was offering him? Roy Bleakie could get a thousand girls like dream-virgins to look at, lovely girls with beautiful long legs and innocent eyes, not whore parodies. Maybe a Fertig might be moved by her ... maybe a Fertig with a wife who wouldn't let him touch her ... a Fertig whose wife couldn't hear his cry of pain ... was that it? ... make another baby? Keep away. Was that it? Was that what drove him down here? He didn't look like the kind of man to be driven by a hard-on, not Fertig, not the cool killer, not that little man, that fastidious man next to this. ... He saw twin images of himself looking contemptuously. ... Did her face harden? Watch it, he told himself. She looked like a child now, the cross sticking out of the corner of her mouth while she waggled it up and down with her teeth.

"How often did he come?"

"Enough."

"What's enough?" He took out his handkerchief and dabbed his face.

"Now and then."

"He spent all that time with you?"

She uncrossed her legs, sat up, bent forward, crossed her arms on her knees, and looked up at him; her breasts dangled on her forearms; one hand swung the cross chain; it tapped down against her shins and swung up suddenly and tapped against one eyeglass. "Is that so hard to believe?"

Yes, he thought. His hands were wet in his gloves. "What else did you talk about?"

"We talked. You don't believe me, do you?"

"No, I believe you." And he wiped his face carefully, unfolding the handkerchief this time, wiping the sweat from the ridges around his eyes and his eyelids while she talked.

She went on about a whore's life and how she became bitten by the glutton's dog, and she turned to point to a small, scabbed tooth mark shivering on her big behind, and how it was swagger in and bang, and swagger out, and...

An old story. Roy Bleakie could have told it for her and told it better: because rich or poor, ten dollars or two hundred a shot, it was an old story.

"I once had a guy who killed somebody about twenty minutes before he came up with me. I heard that he always went and tore off a piece after he killed. You know, I wish Harry had come here after... he never did... This guy, he was a Mafia man, and he came in here and – well, there was something about him, you know? Like it made him longer and thicker and he had me screaming out of my head, just out of my head. I told Angie about it and she said it was just that he put the blood of the deed into it and into me and..."

Bleakie was smiling.

"You don't believe me?"

"No. I believe you."

"There are all kinds, you know. Some do it. Some talk. Some talk about it. Some sit and look at you and think about doing it. And some look at you and think about someone else doing it."

She leaned against the wall and put one foot up on the bed and clasped her shin with her hands. The stocking roll cut deep into the back of her thigh; it has shifted a little to show red marks in her flesh. The face turned towards him; the image danced on the surface curve of the glasses and she seemed to make some decision. If he could have seen the eyes… She spit out the crucifix; it shot out, wet and gleaming, back to the end of its fine-linked chain and bounced against her stomach. Something had happened to her voice. It was more assured, amused, but he couldn't be sure unless he saw her eyes. His instinct told him something had happened, something had changed between them, but he wasn't sure where it happened, or why. What was he thinking of when the change took place?

"You're hot in that coat," she said, gloating.

"No," he told her.

She shrugged her shoulders; she got up, went to the closet, took out her dress, and turned around holding it. "Well, we're about through."

Bleakie moved away from the dresser and put his hand in his wallet.

"Of course," she said, "like I said, now and then someone comes around and he doesn't roll you like a pig and he surprises you because he turns out to be pretty good. I mean, let's face it, if someone can give you a good time, a girl like me, he has to be good. There are those. They happen once in a while. It's a crazy thing, but it happens."

"I'm sure," Bleakie smiled. "Like Fertig."

She didn't answer.

"I said, like Fertig?" He was standing free of the chest of drawers; his hands were wet in the gloves now. He looked at her. He should hit her. That she would understand. He couldn't yet. The glasses watched him. He leaned a little closer trying to see the eyes. She smiled a little, looked contemptuously at him, and put on her dress. He watched the white flesh disappear as the gorgeous, flashing cloth slipped down; it took a long time to work the cloth over her hips and down, engulfing, finally, the bulge of white flesh above the black stocking roll and hang, the fringe swishing on the plump knee.

What did the look mean? An old come-on. Rule of thumb.

She took a cigarette out of her little bag and put it into her mouth and sat down on the bed again. She looked up at him again and blew out smoke, her mouth in an o shape. He reached over quickly and pulled off the girl's sunglasses. She blinked and grabbed for the glasses, but Bleakie stepped back. Her eyes were heavily limned with make-up: green lids, a stylized pencil-arch over her eyes instead of eyebrows, thick lines painted under the arch of her upper lids and continuing out for about half an inch, but straight, not contiguous with the line of the lid at all. "Give me those, you bastard," she said.

"Blue eyes," Bleakie said. "I always liked a girl with blue eyes. It's a sign of candidness. You shouldn't hide eyes like those."

"Why bother me, little man, I told my story?"

The "little man" didn't bother Bleakie: he had been through it all his life: he had prepared himself for it and so there was never any surprising him with it: you lived with it and made yourself big in other ways. More important people had looked "little man" at him. Had it bothered Fertig, he wondered? Had she got into bed with a "little man"? "How much?" he asked, quietly, taking great care that his voice be normal, steady, even a little warm, that his face not be different in any way. "You've been very helpful."

She nodded. She seemed to have made up her mind. She started to take the ten-dollar bill, when he pulled it back. "You didn't answer me."

She puffed again and waited.

He gave her the bill. The bitch, he thought. She's lying. She's lying. She never went to bed with him. What had he, Bleakie, done wrong? When had he not paid attention and it slipped past him? "You're lying," he told her.

"I didn't say anything."

"But you're trying."

"I mean, now and then he'd be a little down in the dumps and I'd say, Harry, why don't we? Well, once he did."

"When did he?" Was it the night after the murders?

"Spring, I guess; I'm not sure. End of April, beginning of May."

No. Wrong date. Yet … something nagged, … loose connection … but she was lying, the taunting bitch. "Why didn't you tell it to the police?"

"Because then they'd bother me about the gun."

He nodded.

"Was I helpful, sweetie? Did I tell you what you wanted to know?" she mocked.

He wouldn't push it any further. He gave her back her glasses. He turned to go and saw the window. The crust of dusty accretions appeared never to have been washed. Whatever lay outside was dim and distorted by the layers through which the light had to filter. He could see, as though far off, mystical, romantic, the spires and towers and mansards and gables and one plate-skin cube of the Mercy bathed in light, seeming, even, to emanate light. He left and went down. She followed him, her heels hard and mocking on the wooden floor, each creek following him and laughing at him.

He stopped to talk to the bartender.

"Was she helpful?" the bartender wanted to know.

"A pool of information."

"She's a good kid, one of my best."

Bleakie turned. She was sitting at the bar, beside him; her green-glass domes staring across the bar-wood, at the Santa Claus the way she had when she came down with the other man.

"Ever notice if Fertig did any writing in a notebook?"

"A notebook?"

"Like this," Bleakie said, pulling out Fertig's notebook.

"Now that you mention it…"

"Ever ask what? Ever ask why?"

"No. Looked like figures."

Bleakie nodded.

"Adding his accounts?"

"No, writing poetry," Bleakie said and left.

The air was clear, chill, but the chemical smell persisted; he bundled his coat close around him. There, across the street and over the low buildings, he could see the Mercy Memorial. The entries in the notebook indicated Fertig had come down here a lot. Where did he come from? His house or Little Mike's Paradise Bar? On foot or by car? Instead of getting into his car, Bleakie began to walk to the corner, turned, and walked towards the hospital; it was only three short blocks away. How many times had Fertig walked down this street? Bleakie imagined a man flitting from door shadow to door shadow, just ahead of him. He laughed at the romantic image: why not walk down the centre of the sidewalk: what did he have to hide then? There was no one in the streets. It was lonely here, but that must have felt … well, good, pure. He almost wished Fertig had written it all down in notes instead of in figures. He had entered only bare numbers for visits to Mercy, never the streets walked down, nothing about his feelings.

Maybe that was how he came to Little Mike's Paradise in the first place: drawn to the place where his child was rejected, led to the source of his pain, or running away from it, purposeless pure movement, growing into purpose as he walked at night around the hospital, passing the bar, needing a drink, going in … He wouldn't have known what he was looking for at first – otherwise the entries in the notebook would have begun earlier. … And later, the notebook indicated, the odd visits became scheduled stops: the plan. He came to Mercy.

Bleakie stood under the wind-wavered lamps and watched the few scattered lights still shining out from the disparate and oddly shaped windows. Mercy was first built in the nineteenth century. It had been added to, decade after decade; styles were piled on styles; it was constructed predominantly in an ugly red brick with the graceless long windows used for factory buildings in the late-nineteenth century. False turrets had been put on some of the extensions. When he passed along the front, he could see a soft light shining down a long, low-ceilinged hall He looked at his watch: it was one o'clock. Why was he wasting his time? He had to be in court early. He could always get a postponement. He went in.

There was no one at the reception desk; he walked the silent halls. No one stopped him. He saw nurses, doctors, attendants flitting by, white against the brown walls, in the soft, late nightlight. A heavy smell of antiseptic permeated everything. The only thing he could hear was the click of his own heels against the waxed linoleum floor. He thought he saw a patient wandering, far away, looking irrelevantly gay in a bathrobe of vertically striped colours, but he couldn't be sure. A nurse came out of a side corridor and passed Bleakie; she smiled at him. He smiled back. He was neatly dressed; maybe she thought he was a doctor. He was feeling a little tense – excitement of the hung; it was so easy. He walked down to the emergency room and looked in. There was a uniformed guard there, but he didn't pay attention to Bleakie. Some white-covered forms lay on stretchers. He went on strolling. He found out where, after a short search, the residents' and Interns' quarters were, and went up. How easy! At first Fertig might not have even known why he was here. Then, when he decided, Fertig would have feared, *There's a catch to it*, and he would have thought ... *when I come to kill them they'll be waiting.* After all, Fertig was untutored, an amateur. He *had* to fear something like that, worry about it, didn't he? But even now, now that it had been done, now that they knew how simple it was to come in, they didn't guard. He turned and left.

He walked the windy streets to his car; it was getting colder. He looked up. The moon was beginning to haze over; it would probably snow tomorrow – the first that winter. He came to his car, got in, and drove off.

Instead of driving back to the Gowanus Parkway and into Manhattan, he drove up the long hill towards Fertig's house. The streets were deserted, looking harsh in the lamplight. He probably would have walked along here; it was the straightest way. But why? At first, irresolute, he might have just wandered. Bleakie began to drive up and down the side streets. The whole area was decaying slowly. The cold had driven everyone inside. How could Fertig have wandered such a desolate neighbourhood? He saw a bicycle tyre hanging from a lamppost and thought he saw a crowd milling in the distance. When he had driven there he only saw dirt wind-whirled under the shuddery fluorescent bulbs. He saw a blaze of light and roared down the street towards it and saw the man with the plastic raincoats and plastic rainhats running in and out of the pools of light, which hit the opaque sheen of the man's silhouette so that it seemed to radiate a great silver, almost blinding translucent gleam. He drove close, rolled his window down, and called – he must have spoken to Fertig – but the man began to run away. Bleakie followed, calling, trying to reassure, but the man turned down a side street: it was a one-way street – the wrong way. Bleakie screamed around the block, but the man was gone.

He drove back to the main street and began to drive up the hill again. He came to Fertig's house after five minutes: a half-hour's walk, he figured it. Looking at the neat little two-storey houses here – it was a different, a self-contained and smug little world; and only a few minutes brought Fertig down into that other world. The air was fresher here, high on the hill; it was near Prospect Park.

He parked the car. There was still a light on in Fertig's house: wasn't she sleeping? Were they here, her family? He didn't see any signs of the police. Things had calmed down; they had taken the guard away. He lit a cigarette and sat, resting, smoking, tired out, looking at the house. He took off his gloves. His hands felt sweaty, dirty, they were chilled and trembled a little – that degrading, rheumatic pain. His body was wet, dirty, stinking, he was sure; itching. Soon, he thought, soon she would sell the house and be out of it altogether and living a new life, away from Fertig, those memories ... The other one, that lying slut down there, she would already have forgotten Fertig if the police, or he himself, hadn't come around asking questions. He kept the motor running and the heater on, but he had to put the wet gloves on again because his hands were getting colder.

And suddenly, watching the house, smoking his cigarette, lazy in the warmth of the car, he got a sudden and urgent erection ... like some uncontrolled adolescent. It doubled him over; its urgency pained him; he put his hands on his lap to cover it; and then grinned at the reflection of the bobbing cigarette coal in the windscreen. That bitch, he thought, that bitch. She was lying, she was pulling his leg, she was building up her part. Fertig was not the man to sleep with a slut like that. He opened the window. The chill air blew in. His hands were freezing. He put them back on his lap. It wouldn't go away.

He turned the motor off and got out of the car. He went to the door of Harry Fertig's house and rang the bell. There was no answer. There was no answer for a long time. He rang the bell again. There was a sound of someone on the other side, the rattling of the chain being put on the lock; the door opened. She looked at him. She was still dressed. She hurried to unlock the door and let him in.

"I'm sorry," he told her.

"That's all right. What..."

She was different. What was it, Bleakie wondered? She smiled at him. She shook his hand. Her grip was strong. Her face was thinner. Her hair was cut differently. Was she more confident? She kept smiling at him. She had changed: she was changing. How glad she seemed to see him. What should he say?

"I couldn't sleep ... I keep worrying about your husband's case." He fought to stand upright; the pain of it was bending him over. Thin, tasteful bangles, Amerindian silver with turquoise inserts, clicked above her strong, firm hand: the fingers were a little spatulate and the nail polish red, but not too bright, almost the only touch of colour aside from the bracelets. How did her hair manage to shine so? What were they doing to her skin? Lotions, ointments, polishes, packs, massages... Was it possible, this youthful glow? Even her breasts seemed to have lifted and were now somehow, younger, firmer, too. "There's so much going against us ... I feel as though I'm failing you...."

"No," she said, and squeezed his hand. The smell of that cheap slut was strong and clung strongly to his clothes. Hadn't Sara noticed it when Fertig returned from his 'audits'? He moved closer, introducing it as surprise evidence. "Not really," she said. He squeezed her hand back. She moved closer. The perfume smell was something palpable now, jelled, compelling, vibrating between their bodies, binding them. The treacherous bitch, the lying bitch, he thought. They kissed. He pulled her down, threw his coat open, unzipped his pants. Unsheathed, it sprung free, shooting out. He pulled up her skirt, pushed her gently back, was on top of her on the floor in the hallway, murmuring how hard it was, how he was afraid of failing her, and she, moaning, no not at all, whispering what respect she had for him, what faith she had in him, and it would come out all right because all the world knew what a fine lawyer Roy Bleakie was.

And his strong hooked forefinger raked her underpants aside and he tore in. They sighed for a second at the easiness of it, the very simplicity. And he slammed quickly, savagely, two, three times. She strangled her short scream, her body fluttered in his fierce grip, her thighs buffeted his cold coat, her buttocks bounced on the floor, her hips thrust up to take his pierce, one hand flapped around his neck, the other raked the wool, she shuddered as he, surprisingly quick, ejaculated and it was over. The both of them lay there, utterly satiated. And he smelled that cheap rut-perfume and grinned to think of that slut: tough luck, he thought, you missed it, bitch. He withdrew, taking great care to keep himself from staining his clothes, especially his vest. He kneeled there, exhausted, drained, while she, her knees high, lay there and looked at him, consciousness coming back to her slowly, shocked at what she had done, beginning to become embarrassed.

Then she laughed, a harsh, bitter crow, throwing her arm over her face, and he thought, now we're in for it, they can never do it without a whole scene. Recriminations, breast-beatings, remorse, I didn't know what ... And he would say ... in the grip of overwhelming passion ... The smell was stronger; wouldn't she notice it? Remember it? She gave no sign. She kept laughing. He thought of slapping her: old gesture – they learned to expect it from the movies, grew to want that old therapy, rule of thumb. She stopped and looked at him and got up slowly... to her knees and took his hands, still looking into his eyes.

"How ironic. Do the gods laugh at us? Do they sneer? Do they give us one thrilling moment before disaster? You go all your life," she said; "and it never happens as you hope and pray and work for it, and when it finally comes ... – well, it did, once before ... Does this mean that something terrible is about to happen again? Does it, Roy?"

He tightened his grip on her hands and she calmed down. He watched her breathe dramatically, guilt-stricken for what she had done, making a production out of it, working her way up to the-in-the-grip-of-something-greater-than-the-both-of-us, a-love-that-must-not-speak-its-name. "How easy," she babbled. "How many years I waited to find out it can be so ... easy ... so good, so ... pure, Roy. Oh, Roy, something terrible is going to happen."

"Nothing is going to happen. We have to be ... careful."

"It happened last time. It's ..." She smiled. "I was going to say punishment. Guilt makes you believe terrible things, doesn't it?"

She sighed. That unsmelled scent fumed all around them. Why didn't she notice it? She pulled him close. She kissed him. She smiled lazily, and rubbed her cheek against his cheek. "Do you sleep with all your clients?" she oozed cosily to Bleakie.

Chapter 12

The secretary led Bleakie from his office to the late Rabbi Gordon's office. He was a blond young man, tall, good-looking. Bleakie remembered Donnell's growl: "I can smell fag every time. I hate the little suckers. Hate them."

"They say that's a sign you're one yourself."

Donnell didn't answer that: his fists balled; the next one Donnell caught would be in real trouble. But Donnell found out nothing more than that Fertig had been to visit the rabbi once. That came under the heading of reconnaissance. Bleakie was feeling a little better. He had caught a cold, but kept working anyway – when did illness stop Roy Bleakie? – drugged, the nose dammed. Taken some pills; histamines, fever seemed to have gone down. Needed a rest. Pressing too hard. Fat Fertig file growing all the time. Other night, dashing around in the cold ... with Fertig's widow ... wife ... it was finally snowing when he went home. Bleakie longed for warm places ... Florida, the Bahamas, Riviera ... vacation, rest, all the girls in their bikinis, their brown skins, shining and the secreted white parts just showing, hinting ... away.

The secretary stood aside and invited Bleakie in with a wave of his hand. "Rabbi Gordon's successor is using the office down the hall. We're thinking of leaving it all just as it is – a sort of shrine to his memory."

"We?"

"The Board of Guardians of the temple. Of course, we don't go in for shrines in our religion … but there will never be another Rabbi Gordon."

Bleakie moved into the room. Sanctum sanctorum. The walls had been pasted over with white linen and halfway up and running around the room a narrow, illuminated blue scroll showed Hebrew characters picked out in silver, interwoven with little brass birds, beast, and fish. On one wall there was a huge oil painting of the rabbi – idealized, gaunt, suffering, like the photographs in Fertig's notebook; he hadn't been that way in years. Behind the rabbi's desk was an enormous painting out of which seemed to loom something great and threatening made of swirls, vermilions, ochres, starbursts, sheaves, greys, spirals, nebulas, clouds, and stark-black. Bleakie looked up at it and whistled.

"Isn't it wonderful? The rabbi had quite an eye for art. Better than anything de Kooning ever did."

"I see."

"It's called *Where wast thou when I made the world?*"

"Well, it's certainly not a graven image."

The secretary laughed and moved to a pastel-yellow filing cabinet. He opened it up and reached in for a folder. "Honestly, the police had bothered us again and again. I mean you get so tired of saying 'Yes, he was here. No, I don't know what they talked about. No, only one time. No, I never saw him before.' Honestly." The secretary shuddered. "Why, he might have killed me too."

"Might have. Doubtful. You're not on Mercy's Board of Directors. Single-minded man, that. Will you be able to hear when Mr. Grenoble comes?"

"When he opens the front door, a light goes on here." The secretary pointed to an intercom box on the rabbi's desk. He opened the file: it had one card. "Here it is. 'Visit, April 31. 8.45 to 9.05. Lost son. Bereaved. Non-member. Grenoble's employee. No temple affiliation. Short talk. To return.' He never did, you know." He gave the card to Bleakie.

But he did return, Bleakie thought. He looked at the soft, spidery handwriting. April 31. The date reminded him of something. What? Fertig's notebook; first definite organized following of the victims began May 1. Something was falling into place. Bleakie shook his head. Drug buzzes; histamine rattles. When had Fertig gone to the fund-raising dinner?

"A few weeks before. I could look it up."

Had he asked it out loud? Those pills, but his body felt a little better now: easier to breathe; he tended to sweat, though … – a sense of sweat-film, grit-filled ... bitter taste ... He picked up an antiquated little green bronze of Mercury poised on one foot and running, one finger jutting into the air. Put it down. When did he quit the job with Grenoble? Mr. Grenoble, I've comptrolled my last for you ... A low bookcase ran around the room under the scroll. Books bound in blue, purple, and scarlet linen were stamped with golden Hebrew characters. Little statues stood on the shelving above the books. A clock under glass had four revolving globes, which hit the light and shot off the bright, brass minutes. Bleakie moved around the desk and sat down, leaned back in the reclining chair before the secretary could say anything. The young man's handsome face looked silly, his pouting mouth, petulant, very handsome. "You shouldn't do that. It was *his* chair."

The sacred naugahyde defiled, Bleakie thought and leaned his head back and closed his eyes for a second. He felt as if he were lurching off balance, sudden nausea: he opened his eyes. A little censor contained a half-burned stick of incense smoking on the desk; fumes tickled his nose and penetrated to his brain. St. Cunegunde in the Caribbean; definitely. "I'm tired. Cold coming on. Wouldn't begrudge me, would you? A mercy..."

The secretary looked at him angrily.

Bleakie swivelled around in the chair slowly; monstrous shadows were cast in the painting; it seemed to represent a great cloud now, travelling fast, from one end of the frame to the other. "What did the rabbi talk about that night?"

"I told you, I wasn't there."

"I mean the night of the speech. Have a copy?"

The secretary went to the filing cabinet and brought back a little pile of index cards bound with a rubber band. "The rabbi never had a set speech. He worked from the cards with variations, depending on whom he was talking to and what the occasion was and what might have happened in the news that day. He was very good that way." He gave the cards to Bleakie. Bleakie riffled through them quickly and tapped the desk with the pile; He read. "*We are gathered here tonight on a mission of mercy....*" Old stuff.

"The rabbi dreamed of a great new healing centre, the Gordon-Mercy Memorial Centre. It would be the showcase of a nation, the healing centre of the health galaxy. The rabbi envisioned the help thousands would get – oh, I could go on for hours – the latest equipment, research machinery, university affiliations, computer diagnosis. And he managed to convince many fine businessmen – they tend to be conservative, you know. They have to be shown that healing can be a well-paying proposition. Mr. Grenoble was his closest associate and in the forefront of the fight; he brought in many from the business community. Mr. Grenoble has caught up the standard from Rabbi Gordon's dying hand. Rabbi Gordon used to tell me, 'Harold, Grenoble is my special convert ... If I can make a barbarian like that love, then there's hope in the world. Well, we don't have a stronger disciple in the business world.'"

"Was he a partner?"

"I know nothing of the business arrangements," the secretary said, and looked annoyed.

The light blinked on. "Grenoble's here," Bleakie said.

"I'll go and show him in." The secretary turned to go.

"You're sure there was no other contact?"

"No, I've said it a thousand times ..."

"Did he ever call up and say anything like – I know it sounds funny, but did he ever call up, or come in, and say anything like – he had found the rabbi's daughter?"

"The rabbi's daughter?" The secretary giggled. "No ... Wait ... Some disgusting drunk *did* call up one afternoon ... I don't remember when – probably some time before the dinner – and said he had to talk to the rabbi. A matter of life and death. Well, of course, I couldn't let him come in, just like that, you know, without knowing who he was. I asked who it was, and so forth, but the man kept on saying a matter of life and death. And he was laughing and I heard music in the background. Well, I told him in no uncertain terms that the rabbi is a busy man – you know, it was on a Saturday. Well, honestly, Saturday, the nerve of him. People are always playing jokes on people in prominent positions. And then he said he has something of the vastest importance to tell the rabbi. He had found the rabbi's daughter. Well, I just hung up on the fool. An important man like that is always getting obscene phone calls –

"Was that Fertig?"

Bleakie nodded. "Probably."

"Well, what do you expect from a madman?"

Bleakie pulled a miniature chest towards him across the desk blotter. It had poles hooked on to the side, as if meant for carrying; it was a tiny ark of God. He touched one of the poles. The chest's lid opened; there were cigarettes in the chest. "Clever. You should have listened to that cry of distress."

"Well, how was I to know? I mean we get all sorts of people, cranks, who have to, just simply have to see the rabbi right now, right this instant or they'll *plotz*. He was a very important man. A lot of people think he helped to save them in times of spiritual crisis. A saint."

"I'm sure. Drunk, you say?" And Bleakie pointed to the intercom light.

"I'll be right back."

Bleakie leaned back. He closed his eyes. He was calm; the pills were making him sleepy, but he was on the edge of something. The chair was comfortable enough to sleep in, but he forced himself to think. Hard to do. May 1. The rabbi's daughter, the slut Lucy, she had said something about it – the rabbi's daughter? What an idea? When had Fertig told her that? Before or after the visit to the rabbi. Have to see her again. She would lie there, naked, posturing, pushing her fat snatch in his face, lying about Fertig, the big lay, blood of the deed – he knew better, now, and he smiled lazily. He would have to be more careful to get what he wanted out of her. But if Fertig began the systematic and murderous book-keeping right after he talked to the rabbi, what made him decide to kill? What did the rabbi say to him? Ridiculous; he was spinning mystery stories for himself. He looked at a silver-framed desk picture of Rabbi Gordon and the Bishop of New York, looking quite alike, their arms around each other's necks. What could a man with a face as corrupt as that have to tell a Fertig? Did Fertig see the corrupt face or the pure face in the notebook snapshot? There was no sign that Fertig believed in God. Why come to a rabbi if you don't believe in the nonsense. Desperation? End of the line? Almost six months after the death of his son and probably that time of no more hope – why no hope? Sara? Sara! He remembered her on her knees, her eyes wide, love there, innocence, love-simper and simpering livingness... inno-cence... revirginized, The-Love-That-Must-Not-Be, The-World-Must-Never-Know ... harsh, ironic, laughter – once-in-a-marriage orgasm? Too pat. How would he get it out of her ... what she might not even know she knew?

Of course Fertig was crazy; saw anything in everyone – any hope. Must have barged in here saying, give me your secret, give me hope, explain, save me, and the Beloved Man must have muttered pious platitudes: go home and pray, my boy. His head spun for a second and he compensated with a jerk of his body in the swivel chair (it creaked). Go away. Sleep on the beach at Biarritz, Cannes, too sick for Saturnalia on the slopes around Davosplatz. She knew. Did he smell smoke from Grenoble's cigar preceding him? Potent incense, oily Uppman Panatella – cloud offering up to the nostrils of God. And whatever he was on the verge of understanding fell apart in his mind and the pieces lay there – he, too tired to reassemble Fertig's fragmented experience because the head-addling drug fought the alien virus the eight-fold way in his sick body.

The secretary stood aside with his half-bow, the light shining off the top of his blond head; Grenoble followed.

"Why do we have to meet here? Your office, mine, the club ..." Mr. Grenoble said. Obviously he felt uncomfortable, made clumsy by rev-erence. He sat down in the chair across the desk from Bleakie. The sec-retary stood with folded arms, waiting.

Grenoble wanted to meet him in one of the downtown men's clubs, the Hercules Health Club. Beakie knew the place; he had been there before. He went whenever he had to meet clients with exotic tastes. Lusts did not surprise him, but when they were used for the advancement of other purposes, he thought them superfluous, even handicapping. If they had his body anointed by the sensual businesslike hands of girls, it was an unexpected form of interest-payment for services: unctuous gratuities. A man always tries to pay with treasures valuable to himself: rule of thumb. He was supposed to feel so grateful while a girl's hands reduced him to an emotional jelly so that the client, presumably untouched, could gain dominance over him. Then, too, there was the peculiar camaraderie of being naked together; very intimate, blackmailable. But it was the client who always succumbed; after all, it wasn't Bleakie's special lust. Shame too: he could have used the steam, to sweat out the sickness, to wash out the persistible sweat-film, but to sweat with a stranger – with Grenoble – disgusting.

"Hate to meet you so late ... here, been collating Fertig's actions, been asking a few questions. And if we're looking for something – evidence – well, on the scene is best. Combine our businesses. Besides, it's nice and private here. Relax a little. Can't drive all the time, Mr. G. You have to untense. Heart attack. It was you who recommended him to the rabbi ..." Bleakie looked at Grenoble's alarmed expression; the fool thought he was going to give him away. Bleakie riffled the cards.

"Let me assure you," Grenoble started to say to the secretary.

"Please, the rabbi himself would have forgiven Fertig. If he were alive, he would be in the forefront of those pleading for mercy for Fertig.

"It's more than I can do," Grenoble said. "What that man – it's made me bitter. Bitter."

"But this isn't the place – I mean *this* office – no bitterness," the secretary said.

"I've been up here many times. What a man he was, Mr. Bleakie! Did you ever meet him?"

"Once or twice. Now, as I get it, you got Fertig to go to a fund-raising dinner, something like that? Why?"

"I thought it would do Fertig good to hear the rabbi talk. He wouldn't accept. I thought the rabbi could give him some comfort."

"Rabbi Gordon has comforted many bereaved," the secretary said. "He had a certain touch."

"He will be missed." Mr. Grenoble said.

Bleakie looked at one of the cards: It read "Start it low. *Heavy is the way of a follower of the Lord. His festive garments gleam*. Rise slowly. *Because he is the servant of the Lord and he aboundeth with good deeds*. Triumphantly. Mournfully, regretfully, a little trembly, *But his heart is* like lead because he must chastise, and chastise again, the whited sepulchres. Ring out the *But would you know about that, you good men?* Ironic end. And then, with trembling voice underscored by an aching soul say *The Lord Giveth and the Lord Taketh Away.*"

"It was a charity dinner, by my organization, the Sons of Charity. I'm very active on the committee."

"Mr. Grenoble has been one of our stalwarts," the secretary said.

"I've done my bit."

"Few have done as much," the secretary said.

"It's a duty," Mr. Grenoble said. "I mean I just used to give and deduct it from my income tax; I even made money on donations. I admit it."

"Rabbi Gordon once said *For your names will go down not only in God's book, but in the books of the hospitals as contributors and saviours and in the good books of the tax experts for rewards beyond the price of pearls and the race of God.*"

"I remember that," Mr. Grenoble said.

And having been schooled in charity was why Gordon gave so much for Fertig's cause, Bleakie felt like saying.

"Listen, I'm a hard-nosed businessman, but that guy," he waved in the direction of the picture on the wall, "got to me. Most of the time you contribute because you have to. It's good business; everybody in the industry puts pressure on you because they know just what you can give and what you can't. I admit it. But this guy, he really got to me."

"What were you raising funds for?" Bleakie asked.

"For the hospital, the new Mercy. We're going to call it the Gordon-Mercy."

Bleakie knew those dinners. The speakers were always saying "Open your minds, open your hearts, open your pocketbooks, give." A priest would donate a few jokes about the Catholic priesthood to show them all how human and quite like other men priests were. A minister would contribute some joke about a minister and ask for funds because disease was non-denominational. Then, when the coffee, cigars, and Cointreau came, the waiters edged back a little and stood dimly against the walls, the star speaker would come on and the lights shining down on the dais would be more radiant. If he were good – and the Rabbi had been very very good – the speaker would stand there, just stand there, waiting for the clink of the cups on the saucers and the tinkling of the silver, inadvertently shoved, to die away.

"And how did Fertig react?"

"We were all moved. I can't begin to tell you. Fertig was in tears. Tears, Mr. Bleakie. Oh, how that man could speak, how he could make you feel it! And he was a real man, Mr. Bleakie, not one of your milk-and-honey characters; a real man. He hits you…" Mr. Grenoble said and made a vague gesture towards his stomach.

Bleakie looked at a card, "*But where are your hearts, you hard men, where are your hearts?* Pause. Long Pause. *Softly. Alas, I am an impractical man.* But hit them again with *Do you hear, you hard-hearted men?* Loud, out to the end of the hallway, RINGING *Oh, I know you, I know you of old.* Dead stop. Long wait."

"Fertig was – he looked – cheered up for the first time in months, in months."

"Took his mind off his work?"

Grenoble trembled but kept on talking. "There was hope in his face and he said he had to see the rabbi, just had to. I arranged it. I admit it…"

What was there in the rabbi's speech to make Fertig come to life that way, to have hope for the first time in a long while? It read like another tired fund-raising speech. Or does a man look for hope to keep him from doing something he has made up his mind to do?

Bleakie read out loud, "*Will it have the same effect in the temperature charts, in the table of the cured as, let us say, expensive penicillin? Will love heal and make hale as the golden glow of aureomycin? Will the arthritic joints locked by pain respond to love as they respond to cortisone? Wherein lies the medicinal value of a caress, a kiss, a touch? What is the effect? Has the research biologist isolated its virus under the microscope? Will the drug companies encapsulate love and issue it under a new brand name? Or is love itself a virus? Do we, in these hard times, consider love a cleansing virus, a saving virus, a miracle virus?*" Good. Good. Glasses would clink, cups, saucers, and masonic rings would click and their chairs would creak as they shifted. Bleakie turned to another card.

"*And if you love … then you will be more endowed than corporations, have greater income than cartels, and can outspend the Aga Khan any day in the week. And your hearts will open of themselves and overflow all the wards and the children will have love taken into them, correcting deficiencies that the most brilliant of biologists, the most clever of chemists, have not uncovered.*" He poured it on: Roy Bleakie knew how.

A great choked sob rumbled next to Bleakie. "Every time. He did it every time. It hit you. It hit you right here."

Bleakie looked at the fat, pained face. Grenoble meant it. A cloud of cigar smoke flew up high to meet the painting, where it wreathed a great figure manufacturing itself out of curves and colours, looming out of the chaos, pointing an indicating finger-dab.

"It isn't the words," the secretary said. "It was the special way he said it."

"But what happened the night the rabbi talked to him?"

"I said I don't know. I was outside," the secretary said.

"He had to pass your desk to go in and come out. Say anything? See anything?"

The secretary shook his head.

"Not a thing? How was he while he was waiting for the interview? Did you talk to him?"

"Just got routine information for our files."

"Was he agitated?"

"They all are, you know, when they have personal problems."

Was that all there was to it? After all, Fertig followed the rabbi while fitting him into his schedule; he must have known. Of course he couldn't see it right away, but he had come to know, as the notebook indicated, implied … did Grenoble know? "Could Mr. Grenoble and I have a few words in private. I'd like to ask you a few questions afterwards, if you don't mind."

The secretary hesitated, looking around.

"All right. Won't touch a thing."

The secretary went out.

As soon as the door closed, Mr. Grenoble said, "Did you have to say that?"

"What?"

"About my recommending him to the rabbi?"

"They already know. Besides, I won't breathe a word about your good deed."

"That's what I've been wanting to talk to you about. This can't go on!"

"When did Fertig leave your service?"

"I don't remember exactly. Early May, something like that. Did you hear what I said, Mr. Bleakie? It is not going good. I can't afford to throw good money after bad. I'm through. This is an especially hard time for me."

"But it's going beautifully. Events are being shaped. Trust Roy Bleakie: faith. Say May the first?"

"What? Oh, I'm not sure. I could look it up. Around then. What do you mean, good? The newspapers are crucifying him and you ask for more money and nothing happens –"

"Behind the scenes…"

"Listen, my lawyer told me it'll come to a trial. And then public opinion will do the rest. Fertigism! Did you see that? They're calling him a saboteur and Communist and anarchist. If it comes to trial all kinds of things will come out."

"Like what?"

"Like I'm paying for his defence."

"No fear. The right hand will not know what the left hand is doing. Darkest before the dawn. Have faith in Roy Bleakie."

"So he went to hear the good rabbi speak and he got religion. Last resort. Thought he was getting an answer when, in fact, he was getting a tired, fund-raising dinner garnished with platitudes –"

"*Listen*, you don't know what you're talking about. You never heard him speak. He could recite the telephone book and make you cry." Grenoble was furious.

Was Roy Bleakie a better speaker than Rabbi Gordon? He wondered. Probably. Different subject. "And he hears this inspirational message aimed at *him*, and him alone. Comes here. Turns out to be the same old soft soap..."

"Listen, I don't like your attitude, Mr. Bleakie."

"Lord giveth. Lord taketh. Abraham for whom no ram ... all that junk – he feels he's been betrayed and then rushes out of here with murder on his mind. You know you were on Fertig's list?"

"Me?"

"Changed his mind several times. On and off."

"I ? What did I do? I was like a father to him."

"Don't you know what you did?" Bleakie asked, insinuating all. A quasi director of Mercy. The new Mercy. Silent partner. Where did the funds come from? Overspent? Ahhh ... Fertig saw the money embezzled, milked, whatever it was that Grenoble did, but the fact that Fertig didn't know where it went saved Grenoble's life ... "Don't understand. Man's sick. Took offence. Listen, he's got something against you. For some reason he must have associated you and the rabbi in his mind."

"I'm proud to have our names linked..."

"You, the hospital – the Gordon-Mercy – and maybe even the death of his son. Linked."

"How am I responsible? Such things wouldn't be able to happen in the new hospital."

"Thought, maybe, that your advising him not to sue was a sign of, shall we say, interest."

"He didn't know anything about that."

"Wasn't sure whether or not to knock you off..."

"Instead, the bastard..." Grenoble stopped.

Bleakie grinned. Instead Fertig had probably gimmicked Grenoble's books – something like that. "I'm having trouble keeping him isolated from the news media. Know what I mean? People like Max Grinzing would like to talk to him. They talk one another's language."

"But I'm trying to *help* him."

"He doesn't know that."

"Tell him!"

"Well, in fact the rumour has got to him that you are behind his defence. Made him angrier than ever."

Grenoble glared at him.

"Not *me*, Mr. Grenoble. Roy Bleakie keeps his client's affairs secret. Ask anyone. Everyone knows Roy Bleakie. Silence is my middle... Have you talked to anyone about this? Wife?"

Grenoble shook his head.

"A friend? Mr. Hockstaff, perhaps?"

"What does he have to do with it?"

"Well, word gets around, you know."

Grenoble didn't say anything but blew out cloud after cloud of smoke from his annoying cigar.

"So it's going to cost another five thousand dollars... at least."

"FIVE THOUSAND FOR WHAT!" The bellow rang through the room.

"Please, you'll bring our friend running in; don't disturb the shrine."

"What for? Just tell my why I should continue to pour money down a well," Grenoble whispered fiercely.

"Because these things cost money. Public opinion has to be veered away from its lynch mood. I need a publicist to plant a big anti-capital-punishment campaign. Many disinterested psychiatrists have to publish think-pieces to offset Bridgeman's nonsense. Paying for their writing time, publication, *amicus curiae*, to negate the Fertigism nonsense. Do you have any idea how many witnesses are needed? How carefully a whole chain of evidence must be built up in a case like this?"

"Bribes?"

"Nobody does things like that, Mr. G. Circumstances shaped into evidence, a coherent picture. But memory is sticky; needs to flow; memory costs; someone vital might be in Rochester; have to bring him here."

Grenoble didn't say anything.

"Five thousand dollars," Bleakie said.

"Charity goes just so far."

"Biggest charity of all. Not deductible, but what a good deed. Books of God." He stopped himself. He was drug-giddy. No point in outwardly antagonizing Grenoble and forcing him into a corner. "What would the case be in the hands of another lawyer? Who's as good as Roy Bleakie?"

"You're quitting?"

"If I can't do a good job, I have to leave. I have my professional standards, Mr. Grenoble. Can't expect me to spend my own money; if I did you wouldn't have any respect for me. Can't lose ... never have. You understand. After all, you're hiring a *better* speaker than Rabbi Gordon!"

"That I have to see."

"You will. Think – what would another lawyer do about Fertig's mentioning you, for instance? Whole business out in the open in no time..."

"You're holding me up."

"I'm protecting you."

"A fine way to protect me."

"Look. He's a bitter man. Supposing he gets the chair? Last words to the world. He'll take everyone down with him; he's that kind."

"Who'd believe what a madman said?"

"Dying words? Come off it. Sacred. Truth. Even if they don't believe him they might have a long look at you and your whole operation… for laughs."

"My business career is an open book."

"Then drop the case."

"But they'd misunderstand things. And of course there's what – well, there are discrepancies in everyone's dealings, nobody's pure. Besides, I need the money for a certain…"

"He thought everyone should be pure."

"A madman. All the world can see that."

"What you mean is that he played games with your books, don't you?"

"He tell you that?"

"I saw him a few days ago."

Grenoble was silent, thinking it over. "All right, Roy. You want in, don't you? I don't have the ready money now, you understand, but I can put your name up before the board."

"I didn't say that." He grinned. He felt the bitter taste in the corners of his mouth, under the tongue roots.

"Sure, Roy, sure. I understand."

The "Roy" irritated him. They were letting him in. Big scheme. Millions. Government support. Hockstaff had recommended … Was he in on this too?

"But Roy, that's the best I can do."

The effect of the drug was beginning to wear off; Bleakie was feeling bad; his head was swimming. He had to end it soon. Go home. Sleep. Leave in the morning. Turn everything over to his assistants, Brodney, Molnar, Bennick. He swung around in the chair and made a complete circle; his head was hot and light enough and he was sick enough to feel the breeze made by the swinging.

"You could name the new hospital Fertig General."

"That's not funny. I don't like your attitude."

"My client's influence."

"Listen, people are going to be helped by this thing – lots of people. It isn't as if we weren't giving something. We're entitled to a little profit for our risk."

"What risk? There are always the sick."

"I don't like it when a smart alec uses high-flown words and feathers his nest anyway, Roy. You're no different from anyone else and don't tell me otherwise. You I know."

"Roy Bleakie wouldn't think of it."

"What's going to happen?"

"What you want to happen. Insanity. Doesn't understand the nature. Institution for the Criminally Insane."

"I'm a businessman. I want an account of what you're using the money for, Roy; I wasn't born yesterday. I want service for this ... investment. Judge Jeffries; some of it is for him?"

"I'm surprised at you," Bleakie said and laughed. "Bribes on the mind. Old-fashioned. Can't buy a Jeffries. Not in cash. I told you, I have to salve consciences, I have to grease and smear. The whore, for instance, the bar bit..."

"I for one don't believe it. He wasn't that kind of man."

"In their hands it proves a year of careful, intelligent planning. In my hands it proves crazy logic, paranoia from the first. Of course, there's another possibility..." Bleakie grinned. His voice was going.

"What?"

"Just get him off. Look at it this way. Supposing he went mad because his kid was killed – I mean died?"

"He did."

"And then, after he killed the seven, he recovered. You see? Temporary insanity. He keeps saying he's sane."

"You're not funny, Bleakie."

"Roy Bleakie alone could do it. Biggest case, biggest coup in the history of American law. Roy Bleakie is the one. And you could rehire Fertig, Mr. G., even make him comptroller of the – what is it? – Gordon-Mercy? Act of charity. Rehabilitation."

Grenoble stood up. "I'll talk to my friends tomorrow."

"A good cause, Mr. G. Listen to this." He read from the cards; "... prosthetic devices to loving care ... stimulation of business and mercy ... open your minds, open your hearts, open your pocketbooks.' Words of the master."

Mr. Grenoble left.

Bleakie leaned back for a second and closed his eyes. He was trembling on the verge of something. He was narrowing it all down, finally finding Fertig out: The 31st of April he visited the rabbi... *And so, ladies and gentlemen of the jury, he is bereft, desperate, empty, his life blighted, alone in his tortured mind shunning even the aid of his loving, faithful,* he smirked, *abiding* (no, not abiding – too fancy) *wife, alone in the world, cut off from the future, cut off from the past* ... Pause, appear to search out the right quote... swallow a few times to clear the lump and drink down the bitterness... *'And I will make thee a great nation and a father of nations'*... *but I tell you that God did not send that Ram in place of his little Stevie. And so he was coming to the end of the line and had but a little further to go before he went off the deep end. To whom could he turn?* It was all hovering there, then, in Fertig's mind, ready to go off. Had that night done it? Long, long pause... *Now it had been many years since Fertig had gone to worship, had believed in the God of his Fathers... Indeed, he had quite forgotten God.* Come here full of hope and left... how? They were all together, somehow tied in that madman's mind by some act of mad logic and written down as simple numbers: did this, did that, meant – Bleakie struggled with it. Get home, take a few days off, recover, think it out. But then, did Sara complete it, Lucy? Did they know something was happening that night... a night like any other night after the death of her son or... was *that* the night she laughed her stagy laugh about? The night she worked for all those years... to find out too late... too late? Or Lucy, whom he called the rabbi's daughter – when? Before or after that night, or on that night? The rabbi, the secretary, Mr. Grenoble, whom he had victimized with a tithe of money and possible years in prison for probably a little embezzler's tax – better than giving his life like the Rabbi had. He swivelled two or three times and his vision revolved past the picture: it swirled white and black and burning red, looking like clouds and trees and bushes and fire and smoke and two indistinct circles, imperfect, abutting one another like worlds clashing, like cheeks pressing, like globes contending. He almost saw it all in the painting, a picture that re-dissolved into a painting, mad-action slashes on a virginal canvas, abstract expressions of God. The secretary came back.

"I don't know what more I can do for you. I've been through it so many times."

"He came. He talked to the rabbi. He left. That's all?"

"That's all."

Bleakie closed his eyes. "Look. Not trouble-making. Just want a little background. No trouble at all. Fertig spent a good part of his preparation time following the rabbi. He knew all about the rabbi. Understand. *All.* What's more, I know all he knows. All."

The secretary glared at him.

"Don't pout at me. Grow up. Would I jeopardize my case to bring out something no one wants to know or cares about? The only way I can get Fertig off is to show he was mad. It's the only way to keep him quiet, too."

"Well, my goodness, what else could a man like that have been?"

How stupid they were; how little they saw; how little they knew! "You're not understanding me."

"What would be the point in defiling the memory of a saint, Mr. Bleakie?"

"None at all. Furthest thought from my mind. Dead bury the dead, so to speak..."

"Well, he did seem agitated –"

"Yes?"

"And when he left, his foot was just outside that door and he turned to the rabbi and cried, 'But what does it mean? You have to tell me. You're the last one who can help. You of all people....' Well, a lot of people thought highly of Rabbi Gordon, a lot of people."

Bleakie tossed the index cards on the table. "So? This is what you've been concealing? Trust me."

'Well, the next thing that happened was – well, Rabbi Gordon said, 'The mantle of Belief is a heavy one; it is a leaden burden. God still works his ways and when we question, he says, where were you when I made the world? And what are we to answer? You must pray for understanding. Come back and see me in two weeks; we'll have a talk.'"

Yes, he thought, Roy Bleakie is better than Gordon.

"Then, as he turned, Fertig brushed against that little statue, the Greek athlete there." It was a naked discobolus. "It tottered on the shelf. Rabbi Gordon jumped and caught it and snapped, 'Look out, clumsy.' I suppose he shouldn't have said that."

"Who knows? I think it would have happened anyway."

"Well, we left together a few hours later. We took a walk home – I mean, through the park. It was such a beautiful night, the first night it was really springlike – what a lovely fragrance! And I thought we were being followed, but I wasn't sure. Anyway, we began to run and run and I thought I heard someone crying, as if from a long way off, 'Rabbi, Rabbi.'"

Bleakie spun around in the chair. He almost had it. What happened then? Where did he go then? ... *for it is no longer the age of miracles, ladies and gentlemen... Alone, totally mad, indeed, could anything Rabbi Gordon have said made a difference? He was mad enough to want a different world and madder to think he had a way of getting it. From that night on he began to plan.* His voice would roll out. Too bad, Roy Bleakie thought; Roy Bleakie would never get a chance to orate because it would never come to trial. Looking at the painting, he thought he saw the bare backside of a great figure lurching away through the underbrush, where, uncaring, receding feet trampled young leafage.

He stood up. He was a little shaky on his feet. His body was burning now; he was sick. He left, followed by the secretary.

Chapter 13

Was it possible to be possessed, Bleakie wondered when he came back from the rabbi's? He tried to fall asleep. He did, after a while; slept a long, long time, too; began to dream, woke up suddenly, refreshed, and thought he had slept the night, the day, and into the night. Impossible. Never happened before. The luminous dials of his night clock told him he had slept twenty minutes. He was on fire; fever illuminated the darkness with half-apprehended night-shapes. He got up, a little chilly, legs shaky, went to the toilet, and found it hard to get comfortable – when he got to the point of release his legs would give way – till he finally ended up urinating like a woman, sitting. He took his temperature afterwards, standing, leaning against the bathroom tile to cool him. Nothing: Quite normal. But chills, heat – he cross-checked with a rectal thermometer. Normal. For one second he thought, wouldn't it be funny if all the thermometers in the world were broken? What was it? A little touch of Fertigism infecting him? Now wouldn't the doctors want to treat something like that? Something they could get their biotic anti-hands on. Silly. What was eluding him? April 31; spring night; left the rabbi; got a good night's sleep… and woke, a murderer, except for the fact. Or went to Sara and… Or Lucy… He smoked a cigarette: two? three? Relax, he told himself. What did it matter? One way or the other, something, *Ladies and gentlemen of the jury*, snapped. Call-up girls especially invented for rescue of the self – nothing like flesh for a cool view of the real world. Airline hostesses – purest flesh invented – machine perfections. And he picked up the phone and was dialling for that best antibiotic of all, perfect specific against all puzzles that, in time, simply did not matter at all. But "Roy, you called," Sara said; "I've been waiting…"

He comes, her lover. It's been so long. Again, he'll stand in the doorway; the playboy's fierce, ironic smile will play about his lips, but her heart knows his heart underneath. She has quivered beneath those cruel, understanding hands. Trim as a bantam, his golden hair will be aglow under the doorlight: like a hawk for taming he'll come to her. Her arms will open even before the door shuts on the bud-heavy trees behind him and she doesn't care what the neighbours might say any more. He will dart in, swiftly close the door, and pounce on her to possess her. His look will be full of passion and her thighs quivering as if she were already exhausted. Her knees locked to steady her and she moved around the living room. She stopped: did she hear a sound from above? She sighed. No. Bell rang. He is here. She stands. Thick engorgement of the pubis, like full of a pulsing liquid sac, fat throbbing, which fluttered her hands and shook her knees… so that she had to walk splay and stiff-legged to the door.

She met him. She seemed ready to lurch forward; stopped, smiled and shook Bleakie's hand instead, meeting him with a curious and reserved formality. They moved into the house. She took his coat and hung it on a rack in the entrance hall. He waited; she led the way. As they walked into the living room, she offered him a hard drink, or coffee, or tea, or cocoa, or anything else he might want. He could imagine Fertig being greeted just this way after he had come back from tailing the rabbi and his lover-boy in the park. *He comes, ladies and gentlemen, back to the loving arms of his wife, who waits for him with a drink, liquor, coffee, tea, milk, or cocoa. They husbandwife cheekpeck or ... but could he not find surcease in those loving and compassionate wifearms?* Or ... does he tear into her for that famous once-in-a-lifetime orgasm? *That* night? After the rabbi? Determined to do it? Nowhere to turn? Save me. Blood of the coming deed, Bleakie thought and, taking the challenge, moved again towards her. She came to him. They held. She stroked his face. "Oh, Roy," she said, "you don't know what it's like; how alive I feel." She told him to take off his coat. He said they didn't have time, couldn't, didn't dare to be seen coming out at a suspicious hour. Did she know what that would lead to? The gossip – have any idea? Hang Fertig. She nodded solemnly, understanding. After all, they worked to save Harry. The sly bitch, he thought: Are you watching this, Harry? She kissed him; he stroked her, preparing to leave, content with the fact that he could have, any time, victory of permissive intents. But her hands, sliding in past his lapels, intruded to sear, feel flesh, past his jacket and shirt – one hand pulling up his undershirt to hold around his back to touch his body, her hands cool and demanding on his hot, fevered skin, the other hand sliding down past his belt to clutch his behind.

And he took her, thinking of her with contempt, on the couch, carefully watching her betraying face twisted in ecstasy – her eyes closed so that she did not have to face his inquisitorial stare. It took them longer this time. Cool, aloof, he probed now. She thrashed beneath his body while he pinned her to the couch, Fertig's couch. She, greedy to make up for every missed orgasm of her life (How many did she think would compensate her? One a week, one a night, two a night, for every day of her orgasmless marriage?), her mouth open to gobble and her ravenous hands snatching at him. Aaaaooooohohohoaoh: he giggled under the cover of a love-groan and grasped her buttock to guide and educate her whore-crude gulpings. He asked through his fingertips and cross-examined from the humid walls of her talkative vagina and sucked information from her breasts and eavesdropped to her heart's truth and requestioned her chattering thighs and took testimony into his nose. Did she confess? Did the Fertig record of her flesh tell all? Or, as a reluctant witness, fight him safe beyond the veil of an old cooled-flesh trail. She resisted. He groped and almost had it but felt the tightening, the reluctance, her hips thrust up, and he withdrew ... she retreated ... he contended with her, seeking to go beyond her, to the adversary with the tight lips, prim look. She talked suddenly, intruding: he almost made sense of her prolonged scream, parsed words out of that rungtogetherhistoryshriek, but the unbearable throb of his own penis caused him to miss the story and they both forgot the incriminations, mistaken evidence. Elusive witness; elusive without knowing it. Get her later. Tell all. *Ladies and gentlemen of the jury, she gave false testimony. Ask yourselves why? Why? All that* GLOP. *All that oil.* And, in turn, her hands like concupiscent and spastic mouths fluttered all over his body, under his clothes, furiously disarranging him.

He rested now ... content ... sleepy ... cool, the fever gone, his arms around her casually while her body, taking longer to calm, rested, jerked, quivered, rested again for longer and longer periods, disturbed now and then by spasms as from a distant storm – moans reminiscent of storm winds – all, not gone in space so much as in time.

Locked, they fell asleep – he keyed to mild maintaining tumescence and she reflexively locking him close to her. When they woke, they were trapped by the too-soon come dawn. He couldn't leave now: what if he was seen? Outside, a jealous world to which they belonged watched. She giggled. She was delighted. She got up cautiously and crept from room to room, lowering shades, blinds, till the house was twilighted and oddly timeless. He, restless, feeling dirty now, unable to leave, got up and stalked around the living room. "Do you want some breakfast?" she asked, happy to be domestic. Roy Bleakie didn't much feel like it. He had to go to the toilet. She led the way. He climbed the stairs behind her, watching the swaying, rumpled cloth on her behind. He went into the bathroom. She stood there, almost as if she expected him to leave the door open. He shut it and stood there. The smell of powders, perfumes, deodorizers hit him. No male smell. He opened the medicine cabinet. No male signs, no masculine lotions, no shaving cream, no razor. Gone forever. How sure she was! He closed the door, turned the light over the mirror on and looked in. The light gilded his hair brighter. He went to the toilet: a faint burning sensation, vaguely pleasurable, its smell being swallowed up by the chlorophyll deodorizer, absorbed into her perfumes. He washed carefully and wished he had a change of clothes. He went out. She met him with Fertig's dressing robe. She was naked under a frilled and flowered housecoat. He took off his clothes in her bedroom and put on the robe, turning his back to her while he stood there naked, not wanting to see her violating caress-stare. They went downstairs and she demonstrated the still-unlost wifely arts by making a good breakfast – eggs, sausage, kippers, pancakes – and, surprisingly, he was hungry. Always was after sex too. When they finished they strolled into the living room. She came towards him again: he turned away to walk restlessly around the living room.

What was wrong? He moved around in the crepuscular light restlessly. Did she fail to hold the famous little lawyer? How did she fail to measure up? Was she being too anxious. How long it was since she could think of herself as a woman. A difference, something just barely felt, was creeping in. She watched him jealously as he stopped to look where Harry's picture had been. Was that it? Guilt? Betrayal of his client? Dear Roy, but, she told him, explaining to his back to slow his feverish walk, a confession which clarified her position in life, life with Harry. She had been a bohemian in Greenwich Village, had an infatuation with poetry, had a few miserable and guilt-attended love affairs, taught lower-grade elementary school for a living. But when she turned thirty – the number was humiliatingly magical, devastating – she became desperate. Panic made her face certain things about herself: she was not a good poet (or was that funk too?); she was not suited to be a bohemian, because she felt miserable about casual sex – even though she tried to dignify it by calling it love – and she smiled at Roy Bleakie's attentive face to tell him *this* was different: she was freed now; she was panic stricken at not being married ... and she was miserable but helpless to think herself bound by what she had dramatically renounced to her parents ten years before. Friends had introduced her to Harry some time before. While he was not culturally involved, he was not against it. He had taken her out now and then, in manless spells, looking odd and stiff in her Village apartment, drab among the bright posters and the flaming paintings, as distorted in *her* environment as Picasso faces were in the world of the middle class. He fell in love with her and made an effort to learn about books, paintings, the important things, and, actually, he was quite perceptive, proving that all he had ever needed, all that anyone ever needed, was a chance to be exposed to the better things. Harry had been tenacious, intelligent, and purposeful, if not genuinely inspired by the arts. He had a very good job and they had, in a certain way, a good life. She smiled wanly: she had admitted to herself, she told Bleakie, that she could never really love. But that was changed: she was freed. Perhaps it had not been good of her to marry for ... convenience, call it that, but at least she faced it, and that was the basis for a mature relationship. She discussed it with Harry: he loved her enough to marry her in spite of her ... inadequacies ... in spite of her ... frigidity. And, in fairness to him, she worked hard in therapy with Dr. Anslinger. They would work it out. Every marriage had to be worked out, a view fostered by Dr. Anslinger. Many views were advanced by Dr. Anslinger, she said, bitterly. She was no longer with him – the LIFE people had found a better, more modern therapist who was working with her.

But in spite of facing up to her marriage, she couldn't help feeling that her life was being wasted. He, loving her, not wanting her to leave, fought to hold her. Frequently, in the early days, Harry felt it was a matter of persistence: work would release her love, and he would work and work and surely she must succumb, release, and then everything would be fine. Could she explain the humiliation of waiting, of even counting variant strokes, feeling colder, and then guilt-sick and disgusted for feeling that way. Then, after a year or so, their life took on its dominant pattern. They would have long periods of not having anything to do with one another, living a grey life, a mere being in the same house, sleeping in the same bed (which, thank God, was king-sized so they could sleep far apart). She kept going to Dr. Anslinger twice a week, trying to work up the courage to leave him, seeking new insights about herself and her compromise.

Of course they tried to have children, but after five years it looked as if it couldn't happen. She had suggested artificial insemination, adoption, anything. She could not face his maniacal fury – a madman: he would not have it. Had she failed him? He looked at her coldly, an inquisitor's look, and she hastened to tell him that it was funny how when she thought she had stopped having anything in common with him, thought it was Just a matter of saying, I want out, trying to leave, something reacted in her to stop her. And she was a prisoner of just having lived a long time with someone; it was a matter of fear, possibly even of not being able to sleep alone. And, because of the morality he had given her, she wasn't even able to have an affair with anyone, which, she told Bleakie, laughing her high, shrill, harsh ironic laugh, gave her the reputation of being faithful, determined to make a marriage work. It made the marriage hell.

Events followed a certain pattern. After three months, six months of this unbearable co-existence, there would come the slow working up to desperation, the crisis, the excitement of being, finally, determined to break free, the goading of the self, the daydreaming about the way it could be, the tentative plans – how she would live, little attempts to write poetry, a novel she was working on for years – the getting up in the middle of the night and sitting by the window and looking out above the gables of the house across the street, above the television antenna, at a moon tossed upon cloudy seas, pretending that Harry wasn't staring at her back. So they lived in this rise and fall, the building up – nagging, arguing – to the passionate and violent crisis. They would fight furiously, viciously. She was determined to leave. He sought to hold her. And then their mutual terror of being alone would lead to a tearful reconciliation that would start somewhere in the middle of their hate: such violence led them into sex and then, joyless, unfulfilled, drained, tired, they would agree to try it out, resolve differences, have an accounting of petty grievances, plan a series of balancing actions, and then, for a week or two, they would work hard to have children. There would be an exhausted descent to sexless tranquillity and diminished resentment, and then the apathy and ignoring of one another. But after ten years – joy in sex, she had almost none – Stevie had been almost magically conceived in one of those anger crests.

She watched to see how he had taken it. He just stared at her, hardly having seemed to hear … "Don't give me that cold lawyer's look," she said laughingly.

"Method of attention," he said; "have to, or how could I concentrate on your words and not you," he smiled, but there was a cold edge to it; and he turned to look at the shelf where Harry's picture had been, where Stevie's was still. She came close to him, behind him, against him, pressing her breasts into his back, and so they stood in the shaded, timeless gloom. "Wasn't he beautiful?" she said to her Stevie. He mumbled and she felt his back expand against her breasts. She reached around him, drawing the lapels of Harry's robe aside, pulling her own loose, turning him, pushing him, till they were against the couch and he fell down, she on top of him, straddling…

She became coquettish now and tried to make him laugh, tickling his beautiful hard naked little body. How beautiful he was, teeth so white, his head thrown back, gold hairs against the blue pillow, as she pressed the inside of her knees against his hips and jabbed her fingers triumphantly into the little muscles and bone lines along the sides of his chest. He tried to push her away, but she leaned her breasts against his thrusting hands and tickled his palms with her nipples; and he couldn't stand it and had to bring his arms down against his sides to protect his armpits and she felt, slamming up against her buttocks, his twisting hips and the sudden elevations of his imprisoned pelvis as he tried to buck her off; she loved the determined way he took a breath of air and held himself quite still – he would *not* feel tickled – till he purpled like an angry child, and her head darted down and she began to kiss, nuzzle, bite, lick his head and shoulders and he had to bring his chin down to protect himself and laughed till he was helpless as a baby, his hands up, his knees up, rolling from side to side between her legs as she pinched and grasped and clenched with her teeth the neatly incised pectoral rims, and she began to feel the stirring of his sex under her, seeking the comfort of a crevasse, and she let herself slide back and forth and down and grasped till she felt it, had it, guided it as it moved towards her inner thigh, into her, and fiercely she sucked with her muscle while she slackened her tooth-bite and ran the tips of her teeth, seeking only the skin of muscle edges, up his armpit, along his shoulder muscle, and lipped his clavicle and went again to his neck and to the jut of his chin and sucked in his tongue (would they meet inside of her?), grasping tighter, tighter, slipping down along him, swallowing, deeper and deeper, wishing there were no end to it, no narrowness to it. His laugh froze. His eyes glazed. She cradled his head. They were still like that for a long while, letting the draught chills licking along their bodies excite them, not moving at all yet, just feeling one another till it became no feel at all. He said, murmuring like a spoilt little boy, "Insatiable."

"Yes," she told him and moved her hips a little and felt the first flutter around the steady rigidity.

"You'll eat me up alive. I'm a working man."

"Yes," she said; "The famous lawyer."

"Let me go."

No, the muscles of her vagina said and with little shivery tightenings gripped stubbornly. "The client-debauching lawyer," she said daringly. And brushed his face as she moved from side to side with her hanging hair curls and moved harder. It thrust off to the side, to the top, and slid out... she gripped tighter, the great trembling starting from the muscles along the insides of her knees and shooting up to where flesh and flesh were one. "Possession is nine points of the law," she panted.

He made himself grin. Silly romantic endearments. Bad novel stuff. Very sexy. Movie love. They always twittered dirty words, he told himself, but his flesh questioned in her and did not relax. Reflex. No more. Only flesh. No information. And he began to move against her and to educate her in the finer things of life: hook her and then, wanting it, wanting in that certain famous Bleakie-way, she would barter golden admissions for love – and he knew: a thousand girl whores had taught him. And seeking for the pleasures of a come, she was becoming an athletic and passable lay and he had to work to keep himself excite-them cool under the mask of passion so he could give her her little fix and control her. Keep cool. Keep cool. Relax. Enjoy. Forget it. Give it up. She's right: Fertig's dead. And fight the lassitude that made you give up all for a moment's pleasure, that made you just as soon let her cram you, gobble you, guzzle you, love. No. No. No. Detach the functions of the flesh from feeling and feel only the skin enjoying her informative skin and – just as her face was about to freeze and the trembling radiating out of that one centre made her voice tremulo shrilly, he stopped moving suddenly. She increased her movements wildly. He pitched his rhythm another way, for another kind of kick entirely, and her body-joy had to break and re-rhythm her movements and start again from almost the beginning. He moved himself away so that she would get the least pleasure from it, not too deep, not shallow enough to excite the most excitable mound perched almost against his pubic bone. She followed. He moved away. They were against the armrest of the couch. Her hands clutched the pillow by the side of his head. Her feet fought for purchase, making climbing motions along the pillow crevasses, pulling. ... She stopped, panting. She waited.

He didn't move. "What is it?" Her voice was hoarse, almost bass. Is it me? What did I do? What's happening? What is it? Do I stink? She recalled old fears; the smell of exudations, disgusting flows, cloth-stiffening juices laved over and past her urinary opening and down and she tried boldly, brazenly, to think: Did the stink of sex offend the great, fastidious man? Or had her period begun? Did blood drench his organ? What is it, her unasked questions screamed louder than the perfectly modulated sex-pant. His cynical look regarded her unbelievingly: raised eyebrow: I know you. D.A.'s look. Oh, why can't they enjoy it for what it is, she thought, and pretended, quickly, to come and rested for a second before she uncoupled herself and went upstairs to have a bath.

Can't let her go like that, he thought; she would be angry and give the case to another lawyer. He got up and fastened the belt of Harry Fertig's gown around and followed her. He followed her from room to room, seeking information. It was early afternoon yet, but the quality of light was still twilighty. Time yet, much time. Ask everywhere, lay her in room after room, give up your story, release me Fertig, free him. He lit a cigarette. He climbed the stairs feeling the titillation of carpet and gold parquet on the soles of his feet, marching through the nubby gloom. She was in the bathroom. The shower was going. He put out his cigarette in the washbasin and heard the hiss of cooling coal louder than the shower sound. She stood there naked, one foot on the edge of the bathtub, ready to go in. Clinically, he watched the inside of her thigh. Thinner – he was sure they were slimming her down – the fashionable Bereaved and stylish Tragic. Good flesh; no scatters of blue veining, skin like a child's. She looked coldly at him, stepped into the shower, and drew the curtain around. He listened to the spray hiss against the tile and the drumming of the water on the rubber curtain, and taking his bathrobe off he pulled aside the curtain. "Let me alone," she said, but stood still while his hand slipped along her soapy flanks.

After, in the long dusk and long evening, he made love to her, possessing her in every room, searching her out, beating Fertig, beating him, chasing her, moving her from room to room against her wishes, buying information with caresses, rewarding her now and then with a long, expert coupling while she strove violently for her now-lost orgasm, not able to do it again, not able to achieve it.

When? When? he asked in the nursery. They lay in the half-darkness under faintly luminous decals, line drawings, benevolent fantasy-animals, children with enormous eyes full of tragedy and wonder, brilliantly coloured, cute giraffes, terror smiles of school days, book and golden-rule days, human-faced bears. It is too late, she moaned; he saw the mean Delia Robbia face of their lost child standing on a chest of drawers, smiling, regarding their striving bodies. She, trying to rise past him ... not here ... not here! And he, probing, inquiring, asking questions openly now. When? May I? Or was it on the night of the last day of April? When? She didn't know (sly! sly!) what he was talking about.

"No. Let me alone. Can't you accept it? He's gone. Let me alone." His hand is a question that inserts itself between my thighs. His fingers touch, coldly, twist, stroke the evocative and calculated knobs of flesh knowing, as he always does, where in flesh and hair I keep them hidden. Concealed them deeper till he tells me he loves me. His calculating tongue elicits nothing but a faint feeling now, putting another layer to the shield of chill, and though my body appears to react in old, old ways, it, again, holds within it the sphincter-clenched truth tucked deep and iced away. And his face is so eager, so terribly eager, and strained with wanting, staring over my shoulder as if he sees someone there. Who? Harry's gone.

And quickly, violently, he pulled out. Startled, caught in the middle of her slow and now hopeless mount to ecstasy, she looks at him, startled. He squatted over her, his hands by the side of her face, looking down, sardonically.

"What is it?"

"Are you wearing protection?"

She didn't answer.

"Are you wearing a diaphragm, anything?"

She didn't answer.

"Are you crazy!?" he shouted at her and reared back, standing over her; her hips shot after, her hands grabbed. He turned and hopped off and stood by the side of the nursery bed, turned away so that she shouldn't see his revengeful grin. He heard her sobbing softly now. "Oh, fine," he said sarcastically. "Can't you see it now? A baby. You want a baby. Oh, boy, LIFE would love that. Are you insane?" He sat down on the bed again and watched her. Her face was agonized. Her doubled-over body thrashed from side to side, her feet thumping against the wall. Her hands clutched her stomach, slid down between her legs and grabbed there. Her mouth was open, sucking in air. The contortions wiped away the look of girlish innocence; they put on ... old cracks in the make-up of her will, as she said, "No, no, no, don't, oh, don't, please ..."

He grabbed her wrists. "You'll hurt yourself. I'm sorry." He held her till, after a long while, she was calm. Her hand touched his shoulder. He shrugged it off. The hand fell down and lay still.

"I want your baby," she sobbed.

"Isn't it romantic?" he said and got up and left, going upstairs to the bedroom.

After a long while she got up and, naked, wandered downstairs, walking through the empty house till she got to the living room. She sat in the darkness looking towards the stairway.

She turned on the lights and got the photographs they were taking of her for the LIFE story. She looked through a thousand of herself, the usable ones checked off in red pencil; some very good ones, almost cheesecake that they wouldn't use, inappropriate to the vision of the suffering wife. She held them up like hand mirrors, posturing first before one, then another, and then still another, touched a hair-fluffing hand to her head, cupped her breast upward, looking intently at herself as if seeing herself, wondering if she shouldn't have posed nude, or in her underwear the way the photographer had wanted her to. And she began to feel better. She moved the coffee table out of the way and spread the pictures all over the carpet and began to dance over them, moving among the shiny glosspools with interpretive, balletic steps, swinging her arms freely, humming, feeling the heavier swing of her breasts centrifuging to the wilder and wilder dance till she was giddy, exhilarated, panting, feeling the sweat coat her sides from under her arms and breasts, and she laughed and reeled, this time stepping on the pictures themselves, slipping on the glossiness, laughing more and more till, after a while, she was exhausted. She went upstairs to the bathroom, where she humiliated herself and cooled herself as effectively as a cold shower could, by putting in the greasy rubber bowbend, and washed her hands free of that stinkless glop, taking a long, thorough time to do it. When she went to the bedroom, he was sitting up in bed, reading a notebook. She didn't say anything to him but got into the bed and, old position, old memory, turned on her side, away from him.

He turned the light out. They lay there in the darkness. The air was cool, quite clear, and he could hear the insulting evenness of her breathing as she slept. *And so, ladies and gentlemen of the jury, we narrow it down to one night: One night when the sanity he has held on to so painfully cracks, when he is pushed over into the realms of psychosis ... Why? Why?* He smiled. He felt tired. He would sleep for a while and get up and leave while it was still dark. He didn't set the alarm, didn't have to. He just told himself to wake up in three hours. He settled down to sleep but found the bed oddly lumpy, the mattress crested in strange troughs and deeps shaped by someone else's body: *his*. He moved around, half-dozing, waking, dozing again, dreaming strange dreams in which he had a lawyer's debate with a prosecuting Rabbi Gordon, who was all for freeing Fertig, who would then come and find him in bed with Sara. He smiled up at the darkness, at Fertig's prim face hovering over, and slept again feeling the bunched mattress push into his back, into his side, into his chest, and moved again and slept and dreamed about his debate with the rabbi, who thundered love at a jury pointing an invoking finger with an apostolic ring and he sat up again. She slept or pretended to. He touched her shoulder. She didn't move. He turned her. She seemed to sleep. He began to make love to her. Her harsh voice said (her eyes still closed).

"Harry, don't." And he felt it all going out of him, the strength, the joy, the ability, and it began to shrivel inside of her. He stabbed her again and again. She politely made moaning sounds, thrashing around as expected. And she seeing he wasn't going to be satisfied and was going to work her until her end, she pretended that her pleasure was increasing, screaming, her throat dry and hurting. The bed creaked mechanically beneath the studied violence of their bodies, dry, unoiled, predictable. The feel of flesh in flesh was painful, abrasive... And she screamed in climax, as expected. He pretended to have his orgasm. She patted his behind and he rolled off. She turned away.

He got up and walked to the window and looked out. He felt alert; the outside air seeped in, invigorating on his skin, for once free of any smoke or chemical smell. He felt healthy for the first time in weeks. He went back to bed ...

... and moved around till he found the position to fit into, the position Fertig had grooved by sleeping the same way for years and years. Comfortable now, his knees drawn high, his back curled inward, facing towards her back, he fell asleep instantly and dreamed no more.

Chapter 14

"That old fart," thought three men as they stood on the steps of the Criminal Courts Building and watched Judge Jeffries walk stiffly up the stairs. However they smiled deferentially, almost reverently: Who knew when you would have to plead before him? Judge Jeffries, turning his face neither to the right nor to the left, but keeping his near-sighted eyes staring ahead only, saw them peripherally. "Let us for once," he murmured, rehearsing what he would say to Mr. Bleakie, "plead a case with dignity and circumspection, paying attention to the case only as a case." He prepared to tell MacGruder, the D.A., "Let us for once, forget public spectacle, bombast, the body thrown to the ravening and insatiate mob." "Let us for once," he told both of them, "forget Law as Combat between gladiators." Since the conclusion was foregone, since the script called for the commitment of Fertig – so it had been suggested... "Be careful" – it was the least he could do. He was too old, too tired to withstand their pressures. He would bow out, beloved by all.

He walked between enormous marble balustrades that had enduring words about justice chiselled into them, touched up with everlasting gold-leaf, running like a frieze along the stone's edge. He walked through doors slowly, not having to open them; someone always materialized to hold the heavy glass-and-bronze door open and say "Good morning, Your Honour." Better than an electric eye.

"That old fart," thought clumps of men having their pre-hearing conferences in the hallway as he made his progress down long and marble-lined corridors. "That old fart," thought the fast-moving lawyers, the police, the court attendants, social workers, court reporters. But all still paid court to (he had heard them say it) That Ornament of, That Grand Old Man of, That Institution within an Institution, Mr. Law himself. He was, he thought, a just man; he tried to deserve their praise. He noted their deportment; they all made themselves slow down to the dignified comportment they knew he thought proper not only in the courtroom but as he passed in the hall – always turning towards him even though they were *not* in court and need not be concerned with the sin of turning one's back on the judge.

But the unregenerate criminal did not defer; they did not bow. They pretended not to notice that he, tall, white-haired, hale-bodied, granite-profiled, sparkle-eyed under the still-black and bushy eyebrows, was passing by with stately step: still a fine figure of a man, capable of dealing out a terrible justice. The depraved nowadays did not care... or fear. And no wonder... He felt as he did every morning when he saw them the futile anger at the red and rising tide of crime that lapped at the country's very security. But *they* were secure; their cunning eyes blinked; they smiled sly smiles; they hid behind their lawyer's defences: unfortunately he could not get every case. "That crusy old, that senile,..." they said, murmuring it between snickering lips as they walked on and made obscene gestures behind his back: he knew. But incantation did not save them from the cleansing and white magic of the law.

The world was coming to a terrible judgment and he was happy he would soon be out of it, retired, liberated. Criminals were not what they had been when he was young; they would not care, or notice, that each movement cost him an agony of pain, an eternity of burning, because on those marble-plated floors he made himself walk slowly and bring the full weight of his body on to his almost cripped feet. He refused canes or, worse, crutches, insisting on walking with his toes pointing uncompromisingly forward, while to relieve themselves of the intense throbbing, they wanted to deviate clownishly out of true. The only concession he would make to his ailment was to wear rubber ripple-soled shoes, which made an annoying squelch-sound as he strode.

He proceeded through the halls of the Criminal Courts Building and heard behind him the undignified clicks of heels resounding, the echoes flickering, multiplying as they sounded urgently off the marble halls; he heard the conniving whispers of lawyers sunborning perjury; he was surrounded by an aura of conspiratorial hisses and mutterings. Pride alone was barely enough to sustain him; rather it had been the insolent faces of the light-footed felons; the sinister strides of a corrupt police, the lawless skippings of the lawyers who went maddeningly true unimpaired by malefaction, balanced in spite of unregeneracy: *these* infuriated and sustained him.

Nevertheless, he went to his chambers as though he were part of the procession and pageant of the Law, which went on at all times. All forms of justice were preserved, not only in his court, but practised in all their solemnity and all their majestic pomp through his life. Indeed, as time had gone on, he became statelier in his approach. Yet he could, in spite of old forms attended to carefully, rituals gone through thoroughly, undiminished by the press of events, finish more business (he had once disposed of forty-two cases in two days) than any other judge. And due process, which extended to life itself, was denied nothing.

Whereas he had grown older, he would walk more erectly. He was almost at the end of his last term (he was sixty-seven) and a commemorative dinner was in sight. He no longer had to think in terms of political allegiance, in terms of looking forward to the next election (though years away), in terms of advancements and appointments to more honourable and superior positions (which had never come), in terms of appeasing vociferous, self-appointed guardian groups, in terms of catering, because of other obligations, to a system that emphasized expediency. He had reconsidered his position in life and permitted himself to be sweetly relieved from striving; he abandoned himself to a sense of justice and probity that brought sleep at night and permitted his sick body to rejuvenate itself so that he looked fresh and whole each morning. Still, he would hate to do anything that would force him to quarrel with old cronies...

No, he thought, he had done it wrong. They would sit there, Mr. Bleakie on his left, Mr. MacGruder on his right, and look at him as though he had gone mad. They would nod politely and continue to sit tensely, waiting only for the moment when they could fly at one another. He heard a woman's hard heel-beat. He saw Judge Mable Crossland. She was coming his way; her moist lips forming pleas and kisses. He didn't approve of her but her good-morning smile and the sight of her magnificent figure could almost melt him almost (if his feet didn't hurt so) stir his loins. She reminded him, in form, if not in face or personality, of his dead wife. She was representative of the modern kind of judge; motherly, forgiving, sentimental. That was, in fact, what law was becoming. He tipped his hat. She smiled and nodded her head. He turned away, overruling pleas for Fertig. She was carried away by her entourage of social workers. He looked after her and admired her magnificent behind. She did not belong here; no woman did.

Judge Jeffries' chambers consisted of a functional room partitioned by a frosted-glass window into a room for himself and an office for his secretary. The old Criminal Courts Building, now torn down, had large, old-fashioned majestic wooden desks in each judge's chamber. He missed those warm, redwood-panelled walls. Now, everything was made of grey aluminium, cold and utilitarian to the touch. He sighed and permitted himself to be helped off with his double-breasted winter coat. The dead and blank faces of eminent jurors hung on his walls. Would he hang on someone's wall? He transferred the small, dignified red flower from his coat lapel to the buttonhole in the lapel of his jacket. He adjusted his stiff and starched white collar and shifted his thin-knotted black silk tie. He gave his black Homburg to be brushed neatly on both sides of the crown by the deferential sleeve of his secretary and hung up. He walked over to the window and looked out. The statue on top of the Municipal Building across Foley Square, above him, was balanced on a globe that disappeared in the blaze of sunlight so that Civic Spirit danced on haze. Judge Jeffries thought they should have some sort of statue on the Criminal Courts Building – Justice, Truth, something like that. But the architects, involved in the new, the cold, the pragmatic, would never have permitted it: they designed and built like this because it was the fastest way to do things. Besides, no one had consulted him. "Hang it," he thought to Mr. Bleakie and MacGruder; "for once let us cut out the trickery, the nonsense, the chicanery, the fighting, the clownishness. Don't you see how important it is? By oratory you give them food for extravaganza."

When his secretary, grown old in his service, to be remembered in his will, went back to the outer room, he permitted himself to sit, relieving the unrelenting ache of his feet. He started to sip the coffee his secretary brewed every morning for him and had waiting on his desk, but he noted that coffee had spilled into the saucer. He called his secretary back: "Change it, you idiot." He couldn't stand the sight of slops swilling at the bottom of the saucer. He sipped at the next cup, drinking it black, uncompromised by sugar or cream.

His feet would not, this morning, stop their burning. Usually, the coffee activated his blood each morning and so, stimulating a night-stagnant circulation, eased the pain of contracting arteries. If he let it, if he gave into it, the pain would not stop but would keep on spreading. His body would dissolve into the criminality of sickness and then, in time, into the anarchy of death. He fought it. He anticipated when it would rise next, braced himself, and overcame it by a fiat act of will.

He took care reading Fertig's record as though he had given it no previous thought, as though it were clean and unspotted by all the demented furore of newspaper, magazine, and television activity; took care not to remember the slightest soiling by wild demands from civic groups, municipal and private, that Fertig be given the business, be executed in the worst way it was possible for the law to do him in. True, he had followed the reports on the rise of Fertigism: not one day went by without some new incident being reported. It went beyond the criminal; it became anarchy. An eye-shaped coffee stain marred the lower left-hand corner of the top sheet. But he had always been a clean man: when had it happened? But what punishment could they ask for? Garrotting? Poisoning? Guillotining? Law did not provide for these.

He remembered the classic execution: they hung the criminal till he was almost dead; they cut him down and revived him; they cut his testicles off; they burned his testicles in a fire while the criminal was alive, making sure he looked; they cut open his stomach; they drew his intestines out with a hook; they waited for him to die; they cut him in four and hung his parts in chains. It could no longer be done that way. But it must, those publicity sensitive jackals implied, be somehow drawn out, correspond to a satisfying equivalent-retribution so that an unrepentant Fertig would suffer commensurately.

On the other hand, the *real*, the vote-oriented, the pragmatic powers insinuated that he might "temper justice with mercy." After years of neglect they were coming around to him. Irving Hockstaff, their despicable and invaluable spokesman telephoned him. They didn't say, don't give in to the hysteria, which is going to reverse anyway. They merely said, "This is an important case: move carefully." He understood. They pointed out there was a tremendous agitation; never before had the public been so aroused; never had there been such a spectacular crime: he must be careful. Careful in what way? They were clever: they didn't say Fertig is a committable madman. How much, after all, was in his hands? All the processes were duly filtered through certain ceremonies: What happens in the courtroom itself must give him his cue for action, and a limited one at that. And, ultimately, what could he do if, to be sure, Fertig was finally found guilty?

"Hang it," he said aloud. The thing was to conduct his court with dignity, with swiftness, with justice; not to permit himself to act, to cater, to over-orate, to appear bored, to appear too interested, to feel sympathy, hate, to be perfunctory, dilatory, or to be lenient. He sighed and caught himself sighing; he noticed his hand was trembling; he stopped himself. His posture had relaxed so that his body slumped into an old man's comfortable and accepting curve: he straightened himself. They would be coming any moment. How could he appeal to them? He finished his coffee; his secretary brought in the hot glass pot without having to be called and poured more coffee into the cup.

But hadn't he, he asked himself, been waiting, waiting perhaps all his life for a case like this? He had. What wouldn't it have led to when he was young? What would it have meant when he first became a judge? It was ironic. Now he scorned and abominated what he would have done when he was young. Hungry for success, tired of having been first a brilliant lawyer just a little too long, he became a promising youngish judge who unwillingly evolved into a kind of institution that thundered at the petty, ranted in the courtroom, having to outdo the wildest lawyers in the pursuit of judgment brought to bear on the recidivists. In those days he would have thrown them Fertig; he would have offered them the hide of Mr. Bleakie; he would have served up MacGruder; they would have forgotten the legal antagonists, forgotten even the defendant; they would have remembered nothing but his stern visage like the face of a god himself presiding over the whole event. He admitted it. God, but that would have got him ahead. He admitted it. But now ... He had an impulse to drip a little coffee on the other side of the sheet, but he didn't know whether the stain would come out shaped the same way. He would have his secretary type up a new face sheet before they went into court. His still muscular jaw fastened tightly on to his false teeth till he could feel the plastic edges of the bridge biting into his gum and palate; it made him forget, for a second, the burning of his feet and the sharp, starched collar edges biting into his neck.

But now ... He had learned, living with those faces too long. He came, at last, to understand those hungry looks they wore when they came to sit every day in his court and leer, nudge one another, watch, always watch, satisfying hunger. In these tame times a stiff sentence was like the neck stretching slowly, the face turning blue. 'This is a court of law, not an arena," he said angrily a thousand times. But his very anger had been a part of the show. Years given to a criminal was like a cutting off of the testicles while the culprit watched, stricken, not quite understanding it yet: those years were his virility. Audiences smirked. "There is nothing funny in this," he barked at an invisible audience. Oh, the orgiastic satisfaction they got in watching the condemned's slow realization of the sentence imposed, the condemned horrified, like seeing the seminal sac crackling in the flame. Oh, he had thrown them out of court for that shameless, breathless hunger, they loved that show, too! He finally understood that it was the hunger of the spectators that made the defence, prosecution, and judge act that way. He would not have it now because there was nothing left of the poisonous dross of ambition in his system: he was purged.

They would be out there this morning in force: noisy, crowding up to the very bar, choking the aisles, shattering the solemn stillness with their flashing lights, deafening one with their questions, panting. Students of law would be there; representatives of papers from all over the world; radio; television. His poor regulars would not stand a chance. That terrible, that eager murmur would swell to a constant and undignified shout. Then, after he would have his attendant pound, furiously, with the gavel, after he would warn them, tell them, they would, quietly, learn their lesson.

He had to admit the case was special. He made himself, nevertheless, go through what usual business he had as he did every morning. He would not, in his preoccupation with the Great Case, slight the attention due more minor criminals. Due process was, after all, a rendering of little as well as great services. Due process worked, even a terrible case like this one, into the fabric of things so that it became a graspable event, an understood malefaction, in spite of what Bleakie and MacGruder wanted to do to continue the tumultuous circus atmosphere generated by the news media. If everything was settled, if he would be careful, they must grant him this: *his* way of running this case.

Therefore he arranged that Fertig's case follow three minor cases up for pleading. He didn't do so out of a sense of the theatric, not out of the need to pave the way to a denouement with events of increasing importance; rather, the arrangement was a moral lesson: due process. The first defendant was a thief: the plea would be not guilty. The second was a rapist: the plea would be guilty, throwing himself on the mercy of the court. The third man allegedly had killed his wife in a drunken brawl. It was important, and he always tried, that the proceeding move with a certain dignity, logic, and speed. All cases were equal. These men, too, were, like Fertig, destroyers of the fabric of society. He worked for another fifteen minutes, reading cases pending judgment, familiarizing himself with what was to come. His secretary told him that the D.A. was waiting.

MacGruder was shown in and waved to a seat. MacGruder talked banalities about the weather, about golf; his face was round, he was bearlike with thick, powerful legs and curved arms and he rolled when he walked. They made the mistake of treating MacGruder as if he had been tamed to dance. MacGruder's eyes sparkled eagerly; his voice whined now on a high, ingratiating note. But Judge Jeffries knew that MacGruder's voice could descend the scale as he warmed to his case and so,' later that day, it would growl, argue, rumble, plead, rant, exhort in beautiful roaring bass tones. For now, MacGruder made sure he was circumspect; Judge Jeffries' temper was well known. Judge Jeffries paid attention to the long briefs, turning page after page, but watched the D.A. out of the corner of his eye. Mr. Bleakie arrived a few minutes later, came in, politely said hello and, standing small, but always erect, always poised (didn't he come from a good family? the son of a colleague?), waited for the judge's hand to wave him to a chair. He was wearing one of his famous vests: an iridescent chartreuse – it was annoying. Sitting, Bleakie was almost as tall as anyone else, Judge Jeffries thought.

He put the papers down, clearing the desk of all the cases except for Fertig's, which, on its top page, showed the pale-brown coffee stain. He noticed, too, that MacGruder had managed to sit on his left, really more to the side of the desk, so Mr. Bleakie had to sit on his right, at the exact corner of the desk. He arranged a pen neatly in its well. Were they tense, he wondered? The D.A.'s face was composed, except for a slight smile that was supposed to be friendly but was really fawning, Judge Jeffries decided. Mr. Bleakie, quite handsome, sat still; he waited and didn't try to make the usual remarks they all imagined were ingratiating.

"I've called you here," he told them, swivelling his chair back and forth because his collar didn't permit his neck to twist without cutting into his skin, "to see if you won't agree to dispense with the usual bear-pit tactics for once. Because of the stink they're making of this case, the audience will be hungry, slavering for a rending of flesh. I am, in principle, against the Roman Holiday method of running the courts. We should be … careful." The D.A.'s eyes became a little glazed as if he were looking inside trying to see what it meant; his face, however, began to set for combat even before he knew what Judge Jeffries was going to say, hardening into the Mask of Determination. Judge Jeffries knew that look; he had seen MacGruder too many times. In a moment the stare would become complete, almost as though he looked across twenty or so feet of courtroom at the defendant's attorney. He leaned forward and spoke more loudly, "I want to see if we can't conduct the whole thing with a little dignity. I run a neat court. I want to keep it that way. I don't want emotional bones thrown to that mob to chew on.

"So I thought we could, this morning, before the hearing, discuss the salient points of the arraignment. We should come to agreement as to how we should handle everything and, for once, do it with a despatch. I think it's in the public interest."

"But, Your Honour," MacGruder started to say. Judge Jeffries could see he was beginning a plea. "There's so much at stake here."

"There is, MacGruder. Truth. Dignity. I know what you're going to say," he said as MacGruder leaned forward, so MacGruder decided to say nothing. Mr. Bleakie sat still; apparently he would accept it. "What's your position, Mr. Bleakie?"

"No plea, Your Honour. Sanity hearing."

"On the grounds, of course, that your client is unable to understand the nature of the charges being brought against him?" He had foreseen that.

"Sir." Bleakie sitting straight in his chair managed to look at ease. Judge Jeffries still couldn't see the signs of conflict tension that must be in both of them.

"And you, Mr. MacGruder, how do you feel?"

"Never have we heard of a more depraved crime. Because of the horror of this act, and its implications, Your Honour, the people of this state could do no less than demand –"

"Save it, MacGruder; in fact, forget it. State your position simply."

"We want to try Fertig for murder in the first degree, Your Honour. The people would contest a move to appoint a sanity hearing. It is out of the question to believe –"

"And can you leave it at that? Can we dispense with the speeches?"

"Your Honour, I *really* feel deeply about this case. It really isn't just another case." MacGruder's voice was high; he was sincere – or was it, as was rumoured, that Hockstaff favoured Bleakie for D.A.?

"Then a dignified handling should be to your advantage."

MacGruder shrugged his shoulders. Of course, Judge Jeffries thought, he didn't want to, didn't dare to see it. "All right, then it's up to Mr. Bleakie, whom, we all know!" MacGruder said, sneering.

"Mr. MacGruder, *this* is what we are trying to avoid. Forget all your past animosities." Judge Jeffries took one of the pens from its holder and placed it neatly on a diagonal across the brief. Unless he reversed the diagonal the spot would remain uncovered.

"But, Your Honour –" the D.A. began again. Judge Jeffries waved him to silence.

"And on what will you base this request?" he asked Mr. Bleakie.

"Dr. Heisenberg's report. In your hands."

"It is."

"I'll call Dr. H. to the stand."

He found Mr. Bleakie's clipped dialogue, his use of sentence fractions, amusing. Of course, in court, Mr. Bleakie spoke beautifully. How could a man who did not speak magnificently get as far as Mr. Bleakie in such a short time? "Needless to say, I know Dr. Heisenberg's views. He belongs to that modern school which states that there are no criminals, only the sick; there is no evil, only disturbance; there are no malefactors, only the hapless pawns of environment." He remembered Dr.

Heisenberg's face; it was pale, ineffectual, with that near-sighted scholar's look that showed he knew nothing of the world, nothing of people, Heisenberg had lived too long with the mad; he thought the whole world mad. Judge Jeffries had long struggled with these concepts. Law was always changing, evolving, and he sought to change with it; he had fought his inner feeling and had striven to understand, but after due consideration, he could only come to the judgment that psychiatric interpretation was merely another kind of legal loophole. He stopped, some years ago, giving lip service to psychiatry: he knew it was inexpedient; he knew it made him unpopular. But now Dr. Bridgeman's findings indicated he had been right ... He shifted his feet again and in this position his knee trembled violently, threatening to communicate the shaking to his whole body. He stopped it. Mr. Bleakie was looking at him. Had he seen, Judge Jeffries wondered, had Mr. Bleakie seen him being old?

"Dr. H.'s view one thing. Relevance to Fertig another, Y'Honour."

Judge Jeffries turned to the D.A., who was smiling slyly. Didn't the fool, he wondered, know enough not to waste his time in those silly actions? That sly, ironic smile was for the jury, for the grandstand, not for him. It betokened the sudden surprise (and he could count on MacGruder's having provided for the certain contingency of Mr. Bleakie's attempt to stop the proceeding before it even got to trial), which didn't mean a thing here.

"I've read the report," he told Mr. Bleakie. "Not one of Heisenberg's stronger efforts. I don't know if I can make much of that psychological jabber." He looked to see if Mr. Bleakie was annoyed. Mr. Bleakie seemed accepting. MacGruder was smirking. "What, in essence, does Dr. Heisenberg have to say about Fertig?"

"Client's a paranoid schizophrenic complicated by martyr complex. Suffering from disease. Mental disease. Lives in a fantasy world. Mind warped. May sound reasonable; is not. Basic promises twisted. Disease colours everything, world view. Sickness led to a feeling of personal persecution when his kid died. Acted. Killer. Unrepentant. No remorse. Martyr aspect makes need for further satisfaction. Eye for eye, tooth ... Needs retribution. Wants chair, plead guilty. Can't, of course. Suicide."

"Did he know what he was doing at the time?"

"Knows the killing wrong, but an appeal to what he considers society's true conscience. Makes for justification of the crime. Doesn't know right from wrong. Substantial incapacity. Hang on gallows, burn at stake, crucifixion. Act and expiation. Make for a better world. Excessive calm, you see; doesn't understand the seriousness, reconciliation to a deserved end. But after all, we are not living in primitive times, Your Honour."

Mr. Bleakie's vest shone out, gleaming wavy striations; the flamboyance annoyed Judge Jeffries. "We're not, as you point out, living in primitive times; I need hardly be reminded. But I trust you don't consider civilization to be an abandonment of moral principles?" After all – though he couldn't use the word without disqualifying himself – what about Fertigism? Was Fertigism, anarchy, to be the concomitant disease product of ameliorative civilization?

"No, sir."

In court, Judge Jeffries thought, Mr. Bleakie would call Dr. Heisenberg to the stand and let him tell it, giving it that aura of psychiatric respectability; then he would augment it emotionally, pulling out the stops wherever necessary, pleading for justice tempered with mercy and scientific wisdom. Mr. Bleakie would dart and swoop and hover in front of the bench, a little hero fighting giants. Mr. Bleakie always worked size to his advantage.

"But if this is so. Mr. Bleakie, I am surprised that Fertig had the good sense to retain counsel even though, allegedly, he is in no condition to make sense of the charges and, in fact, he wishes to satisfy what you, pardon, I mean Dr. Heisenberg, refer to as his *martyr complex.*"

"Yes, how about that?" The D.A. said, leaning forward.

Mr. Bleakie smiled with the faintest touch of contempt, which indicated he would not fight where the judge was pleading the D.A.'s case. Judge Jeffries saw it and was infuriated.

"Offered my services. His wife accepted in Mr. F.'s name. His wife." He managed to say it without sounding righteous.

"And without charge, of course," the D.A. sneered.

Mr. Bleakie didn't bother to be insulted. The little signs of tension, if Mr. Bleakie felt them, were still not apparent. The D.A. was breathing just a trifle faster and his eyes were glittering; his voice had descended a little down the scale and the whining, nagging note was gone. Mr. Bleakie, Judge Jeffries saw, was still quite young, but ageless in his poise. Where would he go from D.A.? Apparently he considered a judgeship a dead end. How many lawyers fought bitterly to come safely to rest in that crown of a lawyer's career, the judgeship? In public, of course, Bleakie would leap to his feet and defend himself violently against such imputations; here it served no purpose to waste high-flown words about underdogs and justice. Judge Jeffries shifted his feet; they stopped burning for a second. "Without charge," Bleakie told them.

The D.A. laughed. "We're not on stage now, Mr. Bleakie."

Bleakie refused to be baited. "No."

Judge Jeffries tried again: "How do you know that Fertig doesn't understand the charges?"

"Dr. H's report."

"Says that all criminals are sick. What does Fertig say?"

"Doesn't matter."

"*That's* a little high-handed, isn't it?"

"Report. Leave it to the experts. That's why he's in psychiatric."

"Clemente was just following standard procedure," MacGruder snapped.

"Judge Clemente," Judge Jeffries corrected.

"Your magistrate," Bleakie said and permitted himself the slightest smile.

"And am *I* Mr. MacGruder's judge, Mr. Bleakie?" His voice was raised and he could feel the painful tautness of his neck tendons raised and chaffing against the sharp edges of his starched collar.

"No offence, Your Honour," Bleakie told him.

But it wasn't enough.

So, of course, Judge Jeffries thought, he could see the way it would go. At some telling point Fertig would leap to his feet wildly and state he didn't want a lawyer, he was guilty, he should be executed. He had done it before. And he would have to tell Fertig that he could do no such thing; that in this state, because of the extreme penalty, no one was permitted to plead guilty to murder; it was tantamount to committing suicide, which the law did not allow. And, of course, this would establish the feeling in the court (who could miss it?) that Fertig was insane: who coveted suicide? They would have planned that much between them; they always did. He would be forced to tell Fertig to sit down and not make further disturbance. Fertig would refuse. He, Jeffries, would have to threaten to restrain Fertig. And Bleakie would have made his point. Unless, of course, he engaged in a little degrading discussion with Fertig and explained to him, placatingly, the way you did it with all madmen ... which, of course, would indicate that Fertig couldn't understand the nature of the charges which, presumably, his lawyer would have tried to explain to him. No one would understand Fertig's making a fuss in court: people who made a fuss always looked a little mad.

Bleakie refused to shift around like the D.A., who pulled up his chair till he was almost on a level with the front end of the desk, waiting only to stalk, to ambush, pounce, surprise, fight. Did Bleakie know too that he was infuriating Judge Jeffries with his attitude? He had determined to come in here and be fair to Fertig, and Bleakie wasn't letting him. "I hold you responsible for keeping your client under control," he snapped. Bleakie, he saw, permitted his smile to widen. Jeffries thought: of course; if Fertig was rational, a cunning murderer, then Bleakie could control him. But if not, ... to penalize Fertig was to appear a crusty, wilful, old, senile ... He sought to control himself, to be calm, to actually try and see defence's point of view. The sudden stinging pains that betokened a coming rain made him lift his feet, one after the other, as though he were marching. He looked again for the tension of a body that told him Bleakie was fighting: he saw nothing. He switched suddenly, "And what about you, Mr. MacGruder, what will you have to say?"

"I had Dr. Bridgeman, whom I suspect you know of, Your Honour –"

"Yes. Yes. I know Dr. Bridgeman's qualifications."

"Dr. Bridgeman states, in effect, that Fertig is rational; he is sane according to the principles established by the McNaughten rules: he knew right from wrong; he knew the nature and quality of his act; he is not suffering from any delusional system such as schizophrenia, paranoia –"

"Bridgeman's a hack. Used to be a *Reader's Digest* psychiatrist. Popular fare; be glad you're ..." Bleakie said. "He's for hire. Sees what he's supposed to see. Has white hair. Noble face. Irresponsible. Making a name for himself with his Ulysses syndrome. Fools the hang-hungry jury."

"You've used him yourself, Bleakie," Judge Jeffries told him, and wondered what did having white hair have to do with it.

"Before I knew."

"With all due respect, Your Honour, this is neither here nor there," the D.A. said. "Dr. Bridgeman's credentials are unimpeachable."

Little Bleakie shrugged and let it stand. In court Dr. Heisenberg would, earnestly, always ready to advance polemics for his position as Social Thinker (and finding in Fertig prime matter for his theories) state that the killings could only indicate vast imbalances, disturbances, delusions, sicknesses of an uncomprehending mind. He would, no doubt, sum up the progress of his profession in the courts. It would be a case of McNaughten modified by the liberal Bartlett bill ready to sprout, no doubt, a Fertig amendment. But calling crime disease changed the outlook. In time, if the trend kept up (abolition of capital punishment) no man would suffer the consequences of his crime and fear no more. Where was the deterrent? Didn't they say Fertig was unrepentant? Was there to be law or Fertigism? Didn't any of them see that? Or were they just playing games? Dr. Heisenberg would sit there looking noble and learned and refer to learned articles he had published in the learned journals.

Dr. Bridgeman, looking equally scholarly, would counter with, in essence – accepting the game because it was by now pervasive, irrevocable and universal thinking – his now-famous Ulysses complex, or syndrome (whatever it was); that Dr. Heisenberg was perhaps correct in his basic diagnosis of such a case *in vacuo*, so to speak, but had mistaken the symptoms Fertig manifested as indicative of ailment.

Shifting papers quickly, Judge Jeffries spilt them into two neat piles, one to his left, where Mr. MacGruder was silting now, and the other to his right, in front of Mr. Bleakie. Dr. Heisenberg was a fool; Dr. Bridgeman another. For Mr. Bleakie would counter most effectively by asking how long Bridgeman had examined Fertig: merely that. And Bleakie, Judge Jeffries thought, will catch Bridgeman when he is looking ridiculous, perhaps when Dr. Bridgeman is leaving the witness stand, half-standing, half-sitting. Dr. Bridgeman would probably exaggerate and say a few hours even though – from what he knew about the man – it had probably been a few minutes: a dangerously challengeable and foolish fiction. And Mr. Bleakie, sitting there, looking as calm and cool, almost as tall as any other man while seated, infuriating, refusing to get excited, was not a fool at all.

What joy could Bleakie get from defending such a man? Was it the same joy his father, Judge Bleakie got from defending his lost causes? Perhaps it sprung from an inheritable perversity: stubborn probity in the father became … what in the son? Perhaps the Bleakies, being rich, detached from contact with reality, with evil, had no idea of what they did. Didn't Roy Bleakie have every advantage? Gone to the best schools? Was it no longer the fashion to teach that crime was a part of human nature and hidden more deeply in it than the doctors might admit: but little Bleakie knew that.

"Dr. Bridgeman's point is this," Mr. MacGruder said; "if the killings are commensurate to the stimulus, it is not insanity: rather it is simply revenge. From Dr. Bridgeman's interpretation – the Amok reflex, he calls it –" and Mr. MacGruder grinned and spread his hands wide in apology; "you know the way they are – he states that the history of such cases, where they run amok, indicates insanity and –"

"*Insanity* is mere legal terminology," Bleakie interrupted.

"And what are we concerned with, then, but legality, but right and wrong, but morality?" Judge Jeffries asked.

"Perhaps with something greater. New precedents," Little Bleakie told them.

"At any rate, the point is that where there is paranoid disturbance, the crime does not bear relation to the stimulus. The insane – all right, *disturbed* – man feels injury, gets a random, logically insignificant stimulus, goes out and kills. Someone cheats a fellow. Broods for years. Builds up to fantastic proportions. All the world's against him. Sees someone – picking his nose, say. Construes it as a final insult; that straw. Goes on a rampage. Goes, as Dr. Bridgeman puts it, into the Amok reflex. Whom he kills has nothing to do with the injury, imagined or real. It's a total thing. Fertig didn't rim amok."

"The 'mad dog' rule is outmoded. Even granting sense of injury: emergency doctor, nurse, even, in the wildest way, receptionist. All related to injury. But what, in heaven's name, could the directors, two highly respected doctors, the hospital administrator, and an eminent rabbi – a beloved community leader – have to do with Fertig's injury?" Bleakie asked. "To say nothing of the way he killed the receptionist. All points to substantial incapacity."

"Fertig went there to kill Miss Malabar the same way. He panicked and bungled it. As for the others, there's relevance there, Bleakie, relevance and logical connection. In addition, Dr. Bridgeman says Fertig is calm, not demented in any way," Mr. MacGruder stated, looking earnestly, not at Bleakie, but at Judge Jeffries.

"Of course. Passion's now satisfied. What was he *then*?"

"We're not concerned at this time with that, Mr. Bleakie," Judge Jeffries said; "I'm only bound to be interested in one point today. You contend he cannot understand the nature of the charges. But if the hearing shows he is calm, rational, then a plea of not guilty by reason of insanity is indicated. The trial will determine what he was on that day."

"A man isn't bits. He's whole. Proof's in the fact that there's no repentance, no remorse, no sense of horror – means an inability to feel, therefore understand, what he did – flatness of affect, they call it. Sure sign." Bleakie said, and Judge Jeffries could see he was hardened to the fight. 'But sanity hearing ... Experts. They could decide. We aren't experts."

But, Judge Jeffries thought, put it into their hands and months would pass; the horror of what Fertig had done would be forgotten; the sympathetic reversal would set in; they would send Fertig off to the Institution for the Criminally Insane upstate. He would be forgotten there, but Bleakie would have bested them all and the precedent for Fertigism as a recourse would stand. Then what redress would there be? Madmen walked the earth; criminals lounged in the hallways; they slouched into his courtroom. He balanced the pen from the red inkwell against the black pen. The Bleakies protected them. If, Dr. Heisenberg, in his magnanimity wanted to *treat*, not punish criminals, that was one thing: the man was deluded. Bleakie, however, was something else. Bleakie was the son of a judge. Bleakie had been to the best schools – Harvard Law. Bleakie *knew*. But little Bleakie, he saw, had abandoned the argument for now; he saw they weren't going to get very far. And from the point of view of one who appreciated tactics, it was a good move too. Then why did Bleakie, who was a superb tactician, spoil his strategy with that loud vest? Judge Jeffries felt old; he was old. They had really begun it here; they had begun working on one another; they had begun working on him; they never waited for the proper moments; they began where they could. Mr. MacGruder, tenacious, steady, refusing ever to relent, slashed away with his oratory; already his voice had sunk still lower and he hunched over; he would not relent now, not for a moment; and perhaps that was good too. And Bleakie in appearing to decline combat was only putting it off. Jeffries' feet kept hurting. He kept shifting them to the right, to the left, trying to start a little flow of blood into them: they kept burning. Why was he bothering? The outcome was foregone. "Stop it," he said.

They looked at him. Mr. MacGruder was politely deferential; he seemed to understand. Judge Jeffries combined the brief, shifted it till it lay on the desk, equidistant from the three of them but no longer in the centre. Bleakie kept smirking. What was Bleakie thinking? Why was he so rude? And what had he accomplished? What had he wanted to get at? Jeffries was confused and befuddled; what was different here than it would be in the courtroom? He should have known: they would have their furore and it would be over. "Is Fertig really insane, Mr. Bleakie?"

Bleakie's eyes widened, his hands clawed on the chair arms, his mouth parted and his teeth glistened, and suddenly Judge Jeffries saw that expression he had seen so many times on Bleakie's face ... seeing opportunity, prey. What had he done? Why had he shown this weakness? What did Bleakie want. MacGruder saw nothing. "Dr. H.'s report," Bleakie said contemptuously and grinned.

And he couldn't stop himself from being stupid. "I know what Dr. Heisenberg thinks; I don't have to look at the report to know. I'm asking *you*. What do you really think?"

"Fertig is insane. Doesn't know the nature," Bleakie said as if explaining it to a child. He had taken out a slender, golden cigarette case and was offering Judge Jeffries one. Judge Jeffries shook his head impatiently; everyone knew he smoked cigars. Why was Bleakie working to infuriate him? He strove to be calm. Bleakie offered a cigarette to Mr. MacGruder. Mr. MacGruder refused and virtuously took out his half-crumpled pack and asked Judge Jeffries, "May I?"

"Yes. Do. And you, Mr. MacGruder, what do you feel? What do you really feel?"

Mr. MacGruder took a deep breath and the flow of oratory began; "Honestly, Your Honour, Fertig is a depraved, cunning, vicious murderer MacGruder stopped himself and took another deep breath and continued talking in a quiet, conversational way. "Fertig is quite sane. He is unrepentant. He is, after all, capable of having planned this crime for six months. He is capable enough and sound of mind enough to have carried out those murders according to his plan. Seven in one day; not one slip-up; and when you think of the planning, the split-second timing, the car... An insane man couldn't have done it. And to have with malice aforethought – the monstrousness of that man. And while he planned those murders he was depraved enough to have consorted constantly and continually with a known prostitute... other criminal elements, dregs of society ..." MacGruder looked at Bleakie triumphantly; he was springing a surprise, a surprise everyone knew.

Bleakie looked back calmly, infuriatingly. "Don't like the word *consorted*. Denials on both their parts. They talked."

"Oh sure, talked. I'll bet. When you think... You know the words: we use them a thousand times in court, but they're not enough in this case. You almost wish you never used them so much, so that when a Fertig comes along they'd have some meaning, some punch." MacGruder caught himself and stopped.

Judge Jeffries saw that Mr. MacGruder, perhaps for the first time in years, was genuinely moved, shocked. It wasn't only a question of protecting his job. Bleakie remained calm. "And doesn't that seem to indicate something about the nature of the case, Bleakie?" Judge Jeffries asked.

"Only Fertig's mad. Mad when he did it. Mad before. Sick before son's death; set it all off." Bleakie muttered it, looking past Judge Jeffries's head at the window, but he couldn't conceal the feverish glitter of his eyes.

"And Fertig had no idea of what he was doing? I mean when he pointed that pistol, pressed that trigger, what did he think was going to happen, Bleakie?"

"Not a question of *immediate* understanding. Total incapacity doesn't signify," Bleakie explained law to him. "Dr. H. says the core, madness. Delusional system. Distorts his every move, every thought."

"And you believe this?"

"Do, sir. Example, god-like detachment. Lack of fear. High efficiency. All indicate symbolic nature of killings. No passion. Makes for simple, biblical justice. Voices. No sense of realities. Cardboard evils he shot."

"Cardboard! Those were real people. They had families, backgrounds; they felt, they bled, they died," Judge Jeffries shouted at him. Did Bleakie think because it was all arranged he could be insulted... in his own chambers? He tried to stop himself and felt led further. "And hang it, Mr. Bleakie, can't you speak in sentences?"

"Try, Your Honour."

Bleakie sat silently, mockingly, not getting excited. The D.A. was nodding eagerly. He shifted the brief nearer to himself and saw, neatly printed, marred only by the coffee stain, *The People vs* (a death for a death; seven slow and agonizing deaths for) *Fertig* (it should have read *Fertigism*)... brought to the proper place of execution. "Don't you believe in viciousness, in crime, in evil?"

He thought again of execution: hung. How could such a man be mad? Evil, after all, was *real*; not a matter of nerves or stomach. And had Fertig on that day worn such a mask of calmness when he went out and killed those people as Bleakie now wore? What did Fertig really look like, Judge Jeffries wondered? He had only seen his picture in the papers: he would face the man soon. He imagined a slight man, expressionless, unemotional, with a big gun in his hands, going through the day, shooting, unconcerned and unrepentant, checking off, after he killed them, the name of each victim, writing a finish to those months and months of practice. Malice aforethought? Yes. Here was evil. Why? he wondered, and then put the question out of his mind altogether; it was the sort of question Heisenberg and the do-gooders asked. It was the sort of sacrilegious question they asked more and more these days, losing sight of what was happening to the world. No, it wasn't that he merely wanted the hearing conducted with decorum; he wanted to mete out justice, truth, right. His feet burned incessantly now; no shifting would ease the ache. The subtle malevolence pleading itself as Innocence in the grip of Compulsion, as Madness, if you will, was visibly warping Bleakie's little face, contaminating him, and he, in turn, reinfected his clients ... and Jeffries began to understand how a Bleakie could defend a Fertig. The calmness was no calmness but a sort of smirk – the triumphant and evil sense of being able to bring it off. The calmness that head wore concealed a shaking within, an unbearable tension and glee, a painful condonement of what had been done; so long as it glorified him, Bleakie would defend Fertig, or, for that matter, communism, or any other -ism. It infuriated him.

"I believe in evil, sir," Bleakie answered blandly and had the gall to look candidly into his face, masquerading as an upright man. "But Fertig is mad."

"Bleakie, we are tired of this," he said. "More and more we let them, literally, get away with murder. More and more we let our standards decline, drop till we will call *every* act against society aberration some day. The old home truths are dying. Unless we do something about it where shall it stop? There is crime. There is evil, I tell you. There is malefaction. There is wrong. There is the seed of evil in people. These are palpable things. They go about and kill at will because they know that they will not be held to account, not be made to pay. And where is the greater evil? Is it in the simple ones who rob and beat and kill, or in the ones who pass it off as aberration? Where is the evil? Is it in the ones who should know better but defend, for one reason or another, those evils? Where is the most evil? I think it is in the ones who change their beliefs for price and defend the worst excesses.

"No, I shall not grant your point.

"Fertig is a murderer. Fertig knew what he was doing. He planned it and carried it out perfectly; there's your indication. I will appoint no commission to look into his sanity. You will have to plead."

"But you don't know the man, Your Honour. Condemning –"

"I don't have to know *him*. I know these people," Judge Jeffries answered, looking at Bleakie. "I know them as I know you, Mr. Bleakie."

"But Dr. Heisenberg's report, Your Honour."

"I can accept it or reject it, as the court sees fit. After all, psychiatric reports are aids to the court, to be used or not used at the court's discretion. You will have to plead."

"I cannot enter a plea, Your Honour."

"Then Bleakie, I shall enter your plea for you. If you cannot do your job properly, I must show you how it is done."

"Isn't that a little high-handed, Your Honour. Isn't this a little like star-chamber proceedings, Your Honour?"

Judge Jeffries noticed that Bleakie was speaking in sentences now, but he was smiling. Why was Bleakie goading him? What was happening here? Was it his anger? Was he losing control? He fought to control himself. He trembled on the brink of an act of prejudice that would martyr Bleakie. The furious words were on his lips and he fought to keep from saying them, fought to continue being fair. "I don't think so, if you're not going to abide by the bench's decisions, Bleakie. You will plead not guilty by reason of insanity." How many men had Bleakie got off? How many murderers saved and set free roamed the city? How many guns did he point, by proxy, and use to kill? He would not save this one. "And Bleakie, I will remand to the City Prison. This is a dangerous man; he belongs behind bars, not out on psychiatric vacations."

"If I may say, Your Honour, isn't that being punitive? He's not a common criminal." But Bleakie was gleeful.

"No, Bleakie, he's not a common criminal."

"I don't think a sick man belongs with those others, Your Honour."

"And where *does* he belong, Bleakie? Back home on probation while we wait for the trial to come up? What if he takes it into his head to hate lawyers? After all, presumably you're defending him against his will; he might hate your selfish nobility, Bleakie," Judge Jeffries said, and he wondered if he detected the faintest reddening of face.

The secretary came in to tell them it was time to go to court. Mr. MacGruder and Bleakie rose. They shook hands. They nodded, smiled politely; they both shook hands with Judge Jeffries and left.

As he stood on crumbling feet, he was helped in taking off his jacket and helped in putting on his black robes. He settled them around his body, and tired, somehow tired too soon, he managed to stride on his crippled feet with dignity down the narrow passageway that ran along the side of the courtrooms. Ahead of him and behind him walked other figures in black, some solemnly, some without any dignity, turning off as they went, when they reached their courtrooms. Faintly, as he passed each courtroom, he could hear the chants of the attendants rising and falling as they went through the ritual of calling the court to order. At the end of the passageway, where he had the biggest courtroom, prescribed to him by seniority, he could hear *his* attendant intoning the ritual. There was a continual hubbub of excitement

coming from the courtroom; they were there. And he noticed his attendant wasn't doing it as he ordered it must be done: with slowness and
succinctness, enunciating each word; instead, that barbarous Brooklyn
accent had returned. He would have to repurge the attendant.

They were all standing as he came through the door, but he could
see by their attitudes that their postures were mere travesties of the act
of respect for the law; they heard as little of the majesty and solemnity
of the call of the court to session as they did in the other courtrooms
where everything was fused into a meaningless hum that accompanied the judge as he bounded up the stairs to his seat, clapped his gavel,
and permitted the assemblage to sit as quickly as possible. How could
wisdom and deliberation thrive in such an air? Here, in his courtroom,
each consonant, vowel, syllable, word, sentence, paragraph, the whole
grand statement of the purpose and nature of the court was reinvested,
each day, with significance; the words, spoken by the resonant voice of
the attendant, standing stiffly at attention, rose till they came up high
above the bench to the words "In God We Trust" riveted in brass letters
to the wall; and went out over the heads of the assemblage, who were,
in spite of themselves, impressed as he arrived to act it out.

But not today, he promised himself; not today.

Chapter 15

Bleakie acted dignified, set upon, the little man poised in the arena
before the bench, a warrior standing protectively between Fertig and
the ravening judge – how much better it would have been if Fertig was
on the floor and he straddled the body! Jeffries worked hard – he had
to give the old man credit – to keep himself under wraps, not to give
Bleakie the satisfaction ... but the habits of a lifetime ... Roy Bleakie
stood there, coat-skirt thrown back, flaunting the chartreuse vest. Sara
Fertig sat behind them, watching, bent forward eagerly, moist mouth
open, darting anxious side glances at her unmoving husband. On his
flank, the forces of a Vindictive Law, as played by MacGruder,. threatened. Behind the lawyers' tables, that whole packed murmuring rout,
slavering, slavering – how could Judge Jeffries have helped himself?

Bleakie turned. He saw Max Grinzing in the audience. Max winked
at him.

Fertig stood up and interrupted. A little to the side and behind him,
Sara bent forward and made a pleading, restraining motion involun-
tarily. Good. Fertig said he was being represented against his will;

claimed he hadn't even talked to his lawyer. That didn't worry Bleakie; they would interpret it as an obviously demented statement – what counsellor never briefed his client? Judge Jeffries asked him whom he wanted to handle the case. No one. Judge Jeffries read the law to him and told Fertig to sit down. Fertig said he wanted to plead his own case and started to explain his guilt. Judge Jeffries headed him off. Fertig took a step forward. Sara stood up. Perfect: unexpected but perfect. She was simply dressed: simple suit, black sweater, single strand of pearls, eyes subtly shaded to look sunken, suffering, without being garish; her hands were folded: she was being martyred by the court and her husband; shadows were worked into the skin under her cheek-bones accentuating her torture as she stared intently, longingly, at her husband. *LIFE* had done a good job, Bleakie thought.

But what surprised Bleakie, and must have goaded Jeffries even more, was Fertig's behaviour. At first it seemed as if there was a kind of demented, pedantic reasonableness to it: his didactic and disciplined voice, flat, dry, steady, kept explaining it, cutting through the judge's rising fury. Judge Jeffries tried to stop himself. For a second it even looked like Fertig's calm voice would prevail: Judge Jeffries listened to two or three sentences. Bleakie was alarmed. The court murmur was dying. Someone said "Louder!" Bleakie moved; his vest flashed. Jeffries started talking, trying to outmatch Fertig's calmness with a superior reason, explaining law as if talking to a child, or to a madman. Fertig heard him out with the air of a man who has to suffer fools. When the judge was finished, Fertig simply started talking again from the point at which he had so politely stopped. Bleakie had not expected it, this ability to withstand, this ability to go ahead! Fertig must be afraid, confused ... Bleakie looked quickly at Heisenberg's anxious face and at Bridgeman's smug one and set himself for Jeffries' ravening blast.

Jeffries shouted he would hold Bleakie responsible for his client: quiet him or be held in contempt. Bleakie tried to go to Fertig to restrain him, to calm him, making his gestures broad, child-placating. Fertig merely shook Bleakie's hand off and kept talking. Judge Jeffries threatened to have him silenced by force, gagged, if necessary. Then Sara stepped forward and put her hand on Fertig's shoulder. Fertig shook it off and raised his voice. She said, "Harry, please." There was a shrill quality to it. Fertig didn't lose discipline but raised his voice. Sara put her other hand on Fertig's arm. Fertig stepped forward. She held on. Fertig began to shout, and stopped himself, calmed himself and continued, his voice completely lost because the whole court was roaring, the gavel was pounding, Judge Jeffries' face was purple. The bailiff seated Fertig by force; Bleakie took Sara back to her seat. She did right; no briefing could have brought up that reaction: the gasp, the surprise, the quick bending of the head, and the long, sorrowful line of the down-curved neck. They were a team. Bleakie thought. The Fearless Lawyer defending an unpopular cause and The Brave Little Woman whom Tragedy struck twice – and will it perhaps hit a third time? Max Grinzing stood up and applauded. Bleakie winked at him. Max Grinzing was thrown out of court.

Fertig confused, not understanding what Judge Jeffries was getting at, tried to object again, and Bleakie permitted himself a little smile meant for Judge Jeffries who saw. Even MacGruder was appalled by the utter fury with which Jeffries in remanding Fertig to the City Prison to await trial brushed aside those trappings of reason: Heisenberg's report, which he should have at least appeared to consider thoughtfully, Fertig's obvious madness, Sara's wan face.

After the arraignment, Sara and her relatives were led out the back way to Judge Jeffries' chambers for a quick conference with Bleakie. Bleakie went to get rid of the reporters. "Jesus, that is a tough bitch, Counsellor," one told him. "Tough luck, Counsellor. That old fart …" They all interpreted it as a defeat. He almost blurted out the truth … Roy Bleakie was surprised how it hurt even to *appear* to lose. He could see Heisenberg battling to push through to him. They fired questions at him fast – what now? what was going to happen? wasn't Fertig really mad? Hold still, hold it, hold it, while he told them, boys, boys, boys, give me a break and we'll have a big conference tomorrow. Heisenberg plunged ahead; from the right and the left, Morgan and Grinzing worked their way closer to him. Morgan shouted, his glee open, "A hard one to lose, Counsellor. How is Fertig taking it? Big disappointment to him?"

Bleakie broke free: Heisenberg close behind him, caught him, and held him, whispering fiercely into his ear, "I saw you in court. I saw what you were doing. You were working to get Fertig into jail."

"Don't be silly. Reading into it, aren't you, Dr. H.?" And the reporters were backing them both into a corner Foolishly, he was glad someone had seen what he was doing.

"… manipulative personality, infantilism, ego-vampirism, sadistic…" came to his ear before Heisenberg's voice was lost in the hubbub.

"What a brutal display," Max Grinzing said. "Justice in America."

"How is Mrs. Fertig feeling?" a reporter barked.

A calm resignation, Bleakie thought; a secret and betraying glee, Bleakie thought. "Sara Fertig is appalled. She is prepared to fight it even up to the Supreme … She will stand by her husband's side," he said.

"This way, Roy. Give us a we-have-just-begun-to-fight-back look."

"Give me a break, boys. I have to go to her side. A conference…"

"I have to talk to him, Roy. If I was ever your father's friend – I just have to talk to him," Grinzing shouted. "You don't know what this man is..."

Bleakie started to move out, shouldering past Heisenberg, who said, "I must talk to you."

"Haven't the time now. Some time next week."

"I must! You don't know what's at stake –"

"Too busy."

"I'll explain to Mrs. Fertig just what it is you're doing –"

"What do you think I'm doing?"

"You know just what –"

"Occupational fatigue, Dr. H. See sickness underlying everybody's every act. Monomania. Obsession. Have to run."

"If you don't talk to me I'll talk to the reporters. I'll tell them just what I saw you do today... right now!"

"Why wreck a superb reputation with –"

"I'm warning you!"

In the light of the exploding flashlights, Bleakie could see Heisenberg's face; the mouth was tightly held, the features rimmed with perspiration studs. "All right," he told the man on the verge, "an hour from now. Canal and Lafayette. Southeast corner. Pick you up." And he was through and past and moving fast. Some reporters, Max Grinzing and Marvin Morgan among them, followed. The pursuing photoflashes threw quick long shadows on the marble flooring.

"Fertig doesn't look like a pleasant man," Grinzing said.

"He isn't."

"But neither was Dreyfus a pleasant man. It's the principle. You know, Fertig even looks a little like Dreyfus. What a man! Do you comprehend what he has done? The New Criminal..."

"He's not so much," Morgan said. "Anyone could do it. All you have to do is go nuts." They turned the corner.

"... disregards the fiction of corporate non-responsibility ... above the law, yet for the law ... I'm glad you're defending him," Grinzing said.

"Sure, like Al Capone was a great man," Morgan said. "Like Lee Oswald was a great man."

Bleakie was irritated. Would Grinzing keep on praising Fertig if there were any chance of really getting Fertig free?

"How much longer do you think you can continue to defend this kind of depraved man, Bleakie?" Morgan asked.

"You have to get me to him, Roy," Grinzing said.

"Might not swing it."

"Why not?"

"Man of your position. Liberal. Know what you'll say."

"Roy, Jeffries and the judges are afraid I'll expose them for what they are. Worse than Germany, or Alabama..."

They turned into a stairwell and began to climb; some of the reporters dropped off; a few still clattered behind. Fast, light, Morgan was ahead of Bleakie, trotting up half-backwards; Grinzing followed, puffing up. "They finally stopped Roy Bleakie," Marvin Morgan said.

"Marv. Act your age." He was annoyed.

Max Grinzing said, "You remember how Max Weber put it? *'Equality before the law and the demands for legal guarantees against arbitrariness'* (not so fast) *'demand a formal and rational objectivity of administration as opposed to the personally free discretion'* (I have a stitch in my side) *'flowing from the grace of old, patriarchal domination. If...'* (where are we climbing to?)"

"What's this I hear about Commie tie-ins?"

"Oh, Marv. Just a simple garden variety nut."

"'... however, an ethos – not to speak of instincts – takes hold of the masses on some individual questions' (let's rest for a second)." They stopped on a landing, Grinzing halfway down below. The other reporters had dropped off. Grinzing was panting out each word, *"'it postulates substantive justice oriented towards some concrete instance and person'* (Fertig) *'and on such an ethos...'"*

"Max, I have to go." Bleakie started up again. He went out on the next floor and rushed along; on the flat Grinzing caught up. Bleakie ducked into Judge Costos' office. Max and Marvin followed. Judge Costos' clerk looked up and waved to Bleakie.

"You expect me to believe that a man who didn't even handle a gun in the army, a medic..."

"'... will unavoidably collide with the formalism and rule-bound and cool matter of factness of bureaucratic administration. For this reason...'"

The telephone started to ring. Bleakie had an odd feeling that Irving Hockstaff was telephoning him, knowing he was here. How? He began to leave. The air felt oddly cooler in the hallway, making him feel chilled: was his fever returning? Bleakie clattered down another staircase followed by Grinzing and Morgan. "Max, please, not now."

"'... the ethos must emotionally reject what reason demands.' The newspapers spew their filth, the populace is prompted to lynch-law reactions, Judge Jeffries hears the maddened and mountebank antics of the yahoos against this man who has toppled the medical idols of our time."

"Now what do you call that?" Morgan asked.

"He's right, Marv."

"How about the whore?" Morgan smirked.

"Just good friends."

"Come on, Bleakie. Give."

"Nothing."

"What does the wife say about this?"

"Disturbed, of course, broken up at this display of punitive ..."

"The elite forces are alarmed because Fertig has struck a blow against the economic hierarchy, against the rich, corrupt doctors, and against the dispensers of that other opium ... It isn't so much the men who were killed, but that the symbols –"

"Those symbols lived and died," Morgan said.

"True," Bleakie said.

"Our reading public is interested in how Roy Bleakie met his first beating..."

They were back on the first floor, moving along a back corridor. "Push off, Marv," Roy Bleakie said, and jumping into the room where Sara and her relatives were waiting, shut out Grinzing and Morgan. The furious argument the family was having was choked off: silent, they all turned his way. She started to come to him; he could see she was reluctant. Angry, confused, the voices broke out again: they wanted another lawyer. He took Sara into another room, Judge Jeffries' chamber, away from the hysteria, to explain what had happened, what it meant, what would happen ... It would come out all right; the newspapers would now be sympathetic. He knew, he said, what she was going through – did she still have faith? She said she did. She didn't look at him. She was quite attractive: did he dare kiss her? Wait. Still cold to him. She might want to get another lawyer: would she dare? Watch it, he thought. He looked at his watch; he still had about three-quarters of an hour before he was to meet Heisenberg. Have to keep from her – who knew what damage that hysterical fool could do? He took her hand, squeezed it: it lay limp: he pulled her closer and started to kiss her.

"I don't think we should, here ..." She was cold.

"I failed you, Sara," he said, his cheek against her lip, looking towards the door behind which the relativeS were, trying to listen, no doubt.

"Poor Harry," she said and started to move her lips; he still had control.

"But what could we do? You saw the judge," he said and turned his head and brushed her lips, beginning to feel excited in spite of himself. Slut, he thought, whore. And his arm went around her, his hand slipping down to hold her buttock. She was beginning to breathe hard. Her eyes were closing. He had a vision. The faithful and tear-stained wife of the unjustly imprisoned, waiting outside the prison gate. He comes out. They fall into one another's arms – he, Fertig, a free man now – with tears in their eyes; battalions of callous cameramen turn away and are seen to blink, and television audiences all over the world and the *LIFE* readers write a finis to this better-than-real-life, truer-than-real-life story. And hand in hand down the twilight path of life they go, while he, the lover who has given her up for... standing to the side, unnoticed, turns away and wipes a tear from his eye... Roy giggled against her lips, when the telephone rang. He jumped. Hockstaff, he thought, and pulled her towards the door whispering, "Just as soon as I can..."

She touched his cheek, looked longingly into his eyes. "Will he be all right?" she love-said to him.

"Don't worry. Roy Bleakie's hands. Just begun to fight." He opened the door and pushed her into the angry arms of her relatives and left just as the phone was ringing the fifth time. Why run? Who said it had to be Hockstaff?

He went back to his office. His secretary gave him a sad look: what was she being sad about? Molnar, his assistant, came out of his office and started to tell him how sorry he was that Roy Bleakie had lost his case... He didn't look at Molnar. What was the fool gawking at? He went into his office. He took off his vest and thought, a trophy, should hang it up. He changed his shirt, sat down to clear up work for a few minutes... and was worried if he'd meet Heisenberg on time. Would he really...?

Why rush? he thought. Keep him waiting a while. In fact, why go at all? Heisenberg would dare. He heard the telephone ringing outside and jumped up and went to the door between the offices, opened it and signalled his secretary that he wasn't in. He left before his secretary could explain to – was it Hockstaff? Mr. Bleakie was not available at the moment.

He got his car and roared up the street fast. In fact he was a little early: Heisenberg was waiting, looking a little chilled in the spring air. Heisenberg opened the door and got into the small sports car with difficulty. Roy Bleakie was speeding off before the door was properly closed and Heisenberg sputtered to say what he wanted to say and fastened his safety belt for two blocks.

"Where can I drop you, D. H.? Back to the bin?"

"I don't approve..."

Bleakie took off, snapping Dr. Heisenberg's head back, making him gasp.

"You are involved in moving this man from an already difficult position to one that is almost impossible. Why?"

"Who said that? Why worry? We'll get him off."

"How, Mr. Bleakie."

"Ways. Trust Roy Bleakie."

"Get him into prison and then get him out again, manipulate him and events at will, is that it? Milk it for publicity and aggrandize Roy Bleakie... These are infantile and dangerous games, Mr. Bleakie. You can't play with lives. This isn't a game to that sick man, nor is it a game to me. This matter has far-reaching implications for the cause of psychiatry. You deliberately provoked Judge Jeffries. I demand to know why?"

"Getting the old fart angry was part of it. Have to see the whole picture."

"But you drove him too far. He became unreasonable."

"He's always unreasonable. Brought it to the surface. Necessary. He was determined to jail Fertig anyway. Angry, he was more likely to disqualify himself. Prejudice. Reversible error. Reversible public opinion. Very standard. Work for the underdog reaction. Took a chance. Didn't work out."

"I can't bring myself to believe that."

"You don't know *law* – practical law, day-to-day encounters with other lawyers and judges."

"I think you prefer the sense of power to get in manipulating."

"Don't use dirty words. Does motivation matter?"

"If it's irresponsible."

"But if Fertig's finally committed?"

"I'll admit you have the ability to manipulate threads –"

"That word again …" Bleakie smiled. "Relax."

"… to ends I cannot myself see, but –"

"Relax. Trust."

Heisenberg stopped. He sighed and took out a cigar and lit it. The smell bothered Bleakie. His eyes were tearing, his ears ringing. Suddenly he screeched, stopped at the kerb, got out, and went into a corner phone booth and dialled.

Irving Hockstaff answered, as if he were waiting for the phone call. "You see, Royboy. I told you –

"You heard?"

"Word gets around. You see, Roy. I told you. You don't know everything yet. You had to take this case on? I warned you and so you not only have an unpopular case, but you take a beating."

"Only a hearing, Irv. Wait till the trial. As a matter of fact –

"Or are you beginning to do foolish things like your father used to do?"

"Irv –"

"A simple, quiet hearing, commitment – was it so hard, Roy? I set it up. I'm in trouble with my good friend Jack Grenoble –"

"Have you heard from him?"

"I don't have to. He'll think you're letting him down. And me. He's a valuable friend, Roy; I can't tell you how valuable."

Was Hockstaff in on the hospital deal? "Don't worry about Grenoble." Roy Bleakie would take care of him.

"Look at the position you put me in with the committee. I go and recommend you and –"

"Sure, Irving. I lost the hearing on purpose." He grinned at his reflection on the phone-booth glass, grinned at the buildings reflected on his car's windscreen and at Heisenberg's dim, fretful face in the car.

"What do you need it? If you lose you are a bum. If you win this trial, you are a highly unpopular character. I shouldn't have to spell it out for you. I mean, as a private lawyer, fine; horn-blowing, publicity, fine; but as a potential vote-getter, well, you know what I mean... you saw what happened to your father. Sure, in time they'll forget, but it's *now* we're interested in. Unless you want to hang around till the next election – after all, you're a young man..."

"No."

"All right, listen to your uncle Irving. We'll get rid of the case quietly."

"I can't resign. A defeat –"

"Sure, you are your father's boy, all right – tenacious in a good cause."

He heard the mocking voice...

"A sanity hearing, Royboy. A nice quiet hearing..."

"A sanity hearing doesn't finalize anything, Irving. Committed. Years pass. Sane again. Comes out. Has to stand trial again. Could end up in the chair."

"That's his worry. Besides, who'd believe it... ever? Don't worry."

"Move stones, Irving. The lawyer's oratory. Not a dry eye ..." Comeback of the put-down lawyer. Justice triumphs and is compassionate, too.

"Who wants it? The longer this case is around, the messier it gets."

"... and what better gold-tongue orator could you have DA-ing it?"

"Listen, you have to learn when to cut your losses, Roy. I'll work towards it..."

"But –"

But Hockstaff had hung up. He got out of the phone booth and into the car. The car smelled close, hot, thick with cigar smoke. He started, driving fast from a standing start.

"What's going to happen, Mr. Bleakie? I demand to know. He's a sick man. He doesn't belong in prison." Heisenberg's voice was mean, nagging.

"You're sure?" Bleakie said. His voice was sharp, taut, probing, but it hurt him, not Heisenberg...

"No man belongs in a medieval remnant of..."

Heisenberg hadn't understood what he meant. "Is it possible that Fertig was *right*? Isn't it possible that he's not mad?" Again Bleakie could hear his own voice, as if it were someone else's, angry: the angriness of a shout under control: it made his throat hurt terribly. Reflected in the glass, his mouth grinned.

"Right ? I don't understand what you mean," puzzled Heisenberg. Bleakie detected the disturbed note.

"You know. Supposing he's not insane. Supposing he found out what he'd never imagined, that everything was corrupt."

"Ridiculous. He's a psychotic."

"Supposing not." Bleakie touched the notebook in his breast pocket.

Heisenberg started to explain Fertig's personality again.

They were driving down a one-way street with a staggered-light system; Bleakie was driving faster than the rate of through-speed and had to brake sharply at every corner. "Listen. Volpe, the emergency-room doctor, was a careless kid who was only going through the motions to complete his training. He didn't care. I checked him out. You know, sometimes he didn't even put in an appearance: Emergency patients were left dying around sometimes during his whole tour waiting for the next crew.

"The nurse was an easy lay chasing for a doctor husband.

"The receptionist was one of those bitter, frustrated bureaucrats – you know the type. Unless you gave her the respect she thought she was entitled to, you could die there in the waiting room." His voice was getting louder; it pained them both.

"The administrator was one of those efficient money-savers; it led to inferior service, inferior staff.

"Dr. Cartwright was a compulsive philanderer, a satyr."

"How do you know that?"

"I've followed in Fertig's footsteps, done Fertig's researches." Bleakie touched the notebook.

"I wish you'd drive with both hands. Of course Fertig would see it that way, that narrow, fanatic moralistic way, to justify –"

"No. It's true. I checked."

"But Dr. Cartwright was a superb doctor."

"Potentially the best; but while he was tearing off a piece, the patient had to wait: It might lead to mistaken diagnoses ... it led to him rubber-stamping everything that went on in the hospital."

"The lights are staggered here, you know? if you'd drive at thirty-five..."

Bleakie passed a red light. "The Rabbi was a hypocrite, a fag, a debaucher."

"That's a terrible thing to say. Fertig's statement too?" Heisenberg smiled.

"Fertig only found what half of New York knew anyway. It shocked him. He was an innocent, you see."

"In some cases innocence may be equivalent to psychosis, Mr. Bleakie."

"And the old doctor was dead anyway, and if he had the slightest amount of life left in him, he would never have let them use his name.

"There's your physiological symbolization, your paranoid rationality," he jeered.

"But to kill... These people weren't totally evil. They were men and many-sided. They did good as well as bad. These statements – if true – are not reasons for killing."

"But it led to a dead child. Fertig's son. Maybe his last chance in life – to say nothing of another scheme... they were involved in – well, put it together and maybe it leads to the kid's death.

"Admit it, the closer you get the less you know. Let's say then that these were not evil men, but the system they supported was responsible for the kid's death, and it was the system he was after – the New Criminal – it's a valid point of view. If you grant it, you begin to see he was bigger –" Bleakie said.

"Why are you hostile, Mr. Bleakie?" Heisenberg's panicky voice asked. "There are other ways than killing. As a lawyer you know that due process... You cannot apply dictatorial and intransigent methods to life. You cannot allow yourself psychotic, murderous expediencies unless you are, in fact, mad."

"You're pretty sure? Are they equivalent, Dr. H., murder and psychosis?"

Heisenberg didn't answer.

"Not all murderers are psychotic? Are they?"

Heisenberg didn't answer.

"Where do we draw the line, Dr. H.?"

"The ways of society are ingrained in us. To work to change them is the healthy act. To kill is diseased."

"Is that the rule you use, Heisenberg?"

"To be out of touch with the ways of society, that is sickness, aberration, Bleakie."

"But you can't be sure, Heisenberg; it's not so simple. Rules? What do you know about them, Heisenberg. There are surface rules and there are the hidden rules, which co-exist. But this much is true; killing is as basic to man as love. You, you and your ridiculous Christian liberal social-worker humanism: *love*; yet you people make it a golden rule that *killing is an aberration*. You believe in conscience and, unlike that poor biblical fart, Jeffries, you try to shore it up with a complicated *scientific mechanism* ... evolutionary dysfunction, psychic energy, or tragedy brought up to date. Really though, there is no such thing as conscience and to kill is the easiest thing of all. Do you know how many clients I have who have killed ... and will kill? Who don't have a guilty thought? Listen: men kill every day, every hour, every minute, even when they don't have a purpose – for fun. Look at the Germans. Look at the Russians. Look at the Chinese. Us. Them. History. Millions.

Billions. So you see, what Fertig did was easy. You could do it –"

"I couldn't."

"I could do it."

"You couldn't!"

"Life … Listen, when the killers of the world write *their* psychology books, then the answers will be in. Until now we have only your side. Life, Heisenberg, is an over-manufactured commodity. And you won't even understand that Fertig is on *your* side. A giant, Heisenberg – the New Criminal." He mocked Heisenberg and watched the shaking leg and heard the panicky note. He mocked himself and he saw Fertig … alone; they would bring him down … unless he, only Roy Bleakie … "He killed to sweep aside the fabric of a corrupt and murderous society."

"Life is sacred, Mr. Bleakie. To kill is sick. Insane. Nothing justifies it."

"And if you carry that theory to the fullest, we shouldn't condemn a Hitler; after all, Heisenberg, a Hitler is only a sick man. And those Jews, all those millions, those dead and dying people, they're the product of a sick man's dream, the result of an irresponsible inability to help himself. Right?"

"Hitler was sick."

"Sick. And if we capture a Hitler we shouldn't execute?"

"We should study him and learn what made him so that we could prevent other people from becoming like that, so that we could stop them before they kill."

"You mean that? Understand our little sick Hitler? And if we rehabilitate him, cure him, let him out into the world then … ?"

"There's not really a comparison here, Bleakie. Fertig is not Hitler."

"Treat. Analysis. Understanding. Right, Dr. Heisenberg?"

"Treatment, Mr. Bleakie."

"And for the incurables?"

"Restraint and observation."

"Imprisonment!"

"No, restraint. Compassionate restraint to protect the rest of society, to protect the aberrant from himself. The expiation of the disturbed person is worked out in that he serves as an experimental ground for the rest of humanity and so may, in the long run, save; because we gain vital information that will save –"

"What nonsense. Do you know what the Institution for the Criminally Insane is like? Prison is a heaven compared to it."

"It's a hospital."

"You know better than that. So we should call it crucifixion by compassion. I think Fertig is sane."

"That's ridiculous, Bleakie."

"If I got him back for you – supposing he tested sane?"

"Impossible."

"Is that scientific, Dr. H.? Suppose."

"It is impossible to suppose –"

"Or, look at it this way. Suppose he was insane just for the killings. What then?"

"I don't know why you persist in –"

"Then we'd be honour bound to get him off, wouldn't we?"

"I –"

"You won't face it, will you? You just won't face the implications. *I should have to plead not guilty by reason of* temporary *insanity!* Shouldn't I? Get him off! ! !"

"Mr. Bleakie –"

"Personally," he tapped the notebook in his pocket, "I don't think he was insane at all. Ever. He is, sane now. Not sick. Not psychotic. And because of that, what he stands for is bigger than any of you, and therefore you have to bring my client down, don't you. And do you know what the very sign of that bigness is? The fact that he could continue to carry out his plan after having to kill that old woman in that messy way. You don't want to face it." Neither did he. "He is a giant. You don't want the real world, but the soft world. He's sane."

"Then why are you defending Fertig, Bleakie?"

"… and that implies, does it not, that there is a possible relationship between his act and the world he acted on – a sort of justification …"

"You don't answer, Mr. Bleakie. You can't beat the fact that he has a bigger name than yours. You're envious of him, sadistic. You will make a bigger reputation than Fertig on this case, won't you, Mr. Bleakie? You think no one can finish it for Fertig the way Roy Bleakie can?"

"What an embarrassment to your psychologizing he is, to your struggle with the *psychiatric right wing*. That's all you care about? Isn't it?"

"You don't intend to persist, do you? How monstrous –"

"It's just my duty, Heisenberg."

"*Your* duty!"

"OUR duty!"

"You're –"

"Lying? My father, of whom I'm sure you know, of whom everyone knows, always followed a course right to the end, no matter how bitter. It's what made him a great lawyer and judge. I learned from him."

"You're drunk with power. You're using this all as a monstrous rationalization for publicity or – why, you're out to destroy Fertig. You're jealous. I shall warn Mrs. Fertig."

"Warn her. It won't help you."

"There are other ways."

"What can you do?"

"I can't believe that you are as cynical as that, Mr. Bleakie." He could see Heisenberg reconstituting his faith, restoring his smile, inhaling and exhaling the cigar smoke in complacent clouds. Heisenberg looked at him, and Bleakie could see, as they turned a corner, that terrible, compassionate smile that told him he was being pitied for being short, almost deformed, was compensating, was maliciously manipulating; he knew the cant. He turned another corner and roared as close to another car as he could. Heisenberg held on and did not pause pitying Bleakie and commiserating more damningly.

"No. I'm not cynical. I'm getting paid for it," he said wearily.

"But I've heard –"

"I'll get money from the court for one, his old employer for another." Bleakie laughed. "And Mrs. Fertig will pay me." Had, had, he thought. "*LIFE* will pay me. *Look* will buy my story. *Playboy*... There will be a biography. There'll be a movie, a play, a TV production, a novel deal. I get a percentage of all Mrs. Fertig's publicity involvements, and now I am involved in a very large multimillion-dollar hospital deal – Mercy Memorial Hospital ... to be called Gordon-Mercy Memorial, I believe. Listen, Heisenberg, play our cards right and I'll get you head of Psychiatric there – much bigger than City; pay twice as much as City." His fingers controlled the car. It wouldn't matter what any of them thought in the long run. *He* could get Fertig off; *he* could save Fertig; *he* could screw 'em all.

Heisenberg's lips protested; his slack eyes stared helplessly. Bleakie's greedy hand clutched at the notebook, but he didn't remove it from his pocket.

"I think you're –"

Bleakie said, "Megalomaniac? But you don't *know*, do you? Suppose he's sane? You don't *know*. You don't *know*," he told Heisenberg.

"You're not serious. You wouldn't dare."

He couldn't leave Heisenberg with that idea, so Bleakie laughed long and theatrically. "Of course I wouldn't, Heisenberg. I'm joking."

"I know what you're going to say. I can see it in your eyes. You think I should go into therapy." And he laughed again.

Chapter 16

The clanging was incessant; the clashing wouldn't stop. John Giant heard the restless sing and roar start low down on the floor, soar to the lower tiers. He felt the senseless excitement begin to itch the slobs and come, by the time they were at the gate with Fertig, to a rage of acclaim. The men yelled "Fertig! Fertig!" like he was some kind of hero. It raged around John: he didn't care, he could bend bars and walk out.

The flat voice of the loudspeakers kept saying "Kwy-ett. Kwy-ett," over and over again. It spoke into every corner; it sounded into every cell; it rolled along the catwalks that were suspended over the central abyss; it commanded into the hidden corners; it floated urgently over the cots in the aisles where the prisoners raged; it fractured against the bars; it permeated the ubiquitous urine smell; it circled up and down the brick archways, along the ramps and walks; it chiselled into and loosened the rotting mortar; it vibrated everything. The prisoners cheered, stomped, formed into endless lines in the corridors, and ran up and down in a mock lock step, yelling for about four or five minutes. The jug-backs, charging out from their quarters, kept asking the prisoners to be, please, quiet; they whined requests, asking, telling them to be good fellows, or slapped away with their clubs. And when it was going to die out, Snake Mike at the other end of the Detention House kept screaming one meaningless protest-word "FERTIG!" syncopating it with each static-fringed sound that came from the loudspeakers. The television spy-eyes rotated fast; the hidden bug-mikes vibrated faster. Snake Mike's voice got louder, annoying, "FURRIK!" penetrating the wild shrieking, exciting them all. All except John Giant, who, like some enormous nucleus of quiet and timeless power, sat on the toilet at the rear of his cell.

He looked with contempt at the terror of the man, Grombach, they stuck here because he didn't have enough ready cash to pay his traffic violations. And then, as if that wasn't enough, they compounded sly insults and brought in the *third* man, Fertig. The continued to riot; they were all penned double and triple in every cranny; and they were bored and dying with the Wait; no movement made the minutes crawl, the minutes made them itch. Fertig, wide-eyed, startled, safe in the pen, sank into his own problems. Most insulting of all to John Giant was when that slob from the other side of existence, Grombach, taking one look and seeing the Celebrity, grovelled away from Fertig. He looked with disgust at that big deal, little Fertig. Who was that little man going to hurt *now*, John wanted to know. He waited to suck something in and crush; he waited to hit out and smash. He grunted and shifted his position.

Someone screamed, "We got to have air-conditioned cells."

"...and TV."

"... and jazz."

"FUHRRRK!"

"... and women."

"... or we go on strike."

"FUHHHH!"

"Yeah," a calm voice said in a lull, "or no more muggings, no more stickups, no more rapes."

"No more work for the screws."

"Tech-no-logi-cal un-em-ploy-ment man."

"FUHFUHFUHFUH!"

Three guards double-timed along a rail-less brick way, disappearing from view of the cell, appeared again with a foot-ringing clatter, going across a metal ramp that hung suspended over the pit, winked out of sight again, ran for a second, climbing higher and higher, and were half-seen trotting, far across the void, barely visible because the light filtering down from the frost-glass dome above was like a curtain that almost obscured them. The Bird House grew quiet suddenly. There was a clash. Metal slashed along the floor, sliding and screeching along steel grooves that were not true. The annoying voice, bouncing off every projection, was gathered and refocused – amplified in that old Bastille – and was heard to say, clearly mocking, "But Mr. Correction Officer Man, that wasn't me. Do I look like a troublemaker?" The voice would not whine; it was arrogant, insistent. There was a mumbling, a whisper that no softness of distance, in that place, could disguise or obscure. The voice, triumphant now, yelled out, "They sent three this time. My rating's up."

"Three," the high voice of John said. He remembered he had once been worked over by hateful hacks for three days. They heard the sound of something banging on something: a soft sound, frightening because of its softness; wood on skin, iron on bone. With every beat the birds in all the cages and in the aisles went a little wild, and wilder with each blow as they took up the count and sang "Thud," keeping in time to the pounding. After the tenth blow the voice shouted in pain but was still arrogant, still irritating, so they kept hacking away. "Ten," John said, folding his arms and leaning back against the damp wall behind him; Snake Mike was nothing. Fertig's face looked pained. John thought, some killer – what did he expect? Each blow drove the voice a little higher up the scale, sending it into, inhumanity. They all stopped counting. The voice broke and trailed off into a long wail. And then there was only the sound of the fists on flesh. And then there were no sounds but the hissing of breaths and the voiceless static sounding out of the loudspeakers. Only John didn't care.

"Ten," a soft voice said; "he held out to thirteen yesterday."

"That's what did it; twelve, fourteen – it wouldn't have been so bad. But thirteen!"

"Well, they just don't make them like they used to. Everything is cheap these days, you know what I mean?" an old, unregenerate voice persisted.

A gate crashed. All the human voices were swallowed in that sound reverberating through all the aisles, tiers, ramps, and down to the waiting pen in the central well, and up again.

Giant John looked at the man whose presence had started it all: Fertig. Not so much. Fertig sat there and stared at the wall across the way from him, cool to it all – John had to admit – chilled away from care because he was a Big Man. Fertig. Or he didn't hear, or he didn't care, or it didn't really matter to him, or crafty, or crazy, so crazy and gone; you couldn't tell about someone like that. Not like that other, the Grombach scofflaw cringing against the wall. Now why did they, John wondered, put a man like that in with someone like him? It demeaned him. Unless, John thought, someone was trying to put him down. "You're not so much," a guard told John when he first came in; he knew. Every screw he passed took one look at him standing there, six-foot-six, wide like a chunky stump-muscled man, but huge; they had to tell him, just had to, "You're not so much." And one of them stiffed him with the club. Jab, jab. They always did that to him. They did that to him whenever they caught sight of him. They did that to him in half the pounds all over the country. To see if he was really size-tough. The little men couldn't keep their hands off him. So they put him into a little cell. It had once been twice as large but, because every city prison was turning them away at the gates, they halved the cube with floor to ceiling bars. But he knew that six syndicate men, picked up on suspicion, took up six luxurious maximum-security cells up a quiet ramp; their gates were unlocked so they could stroll around, be cosy, socialize. Four wined-up American Park apes stewed away in the other cell-half, but they were quiet; John had growled them down.

It was very good as far as jails went; he had been in real cities of hate. The screws, or the guests, those made it bad. But it was insulting: a small cell. In the other places, because the warden sold the fixings they made you sleep on the floor, where the rats, John thought, might nibble you. Two concrete slabs cantilevered out from the wall – they couldn't hock those – and were covered with two grey blankets. There was a cot without a mattress, only a blanket covering the springs. There were no roaches here, but rats; there were always fleas, or lice, or bedbugs.

The petty offender wanted to stand. There was no room. There were two feet between the bottom sleeping slab and the cot; ten feet to the back where the toilet was. The four wine tramps crowded to the cage lines and were cackling at the newest man. The newest man was going to stand because he was an amateur, wouldn't let his little white hands and white body touch anything. "Down," he growled. The scofflaw sat.

Now, after the boys who slept on the cots in the aisles had done their wild welcome dance, they crowded to the cell door and looked on like drop-mouth sightseers. John couldn't stand the undeserved curiosity. They pressed against the cell door; the bars and cross-bars partitioned them as they peered in. Floating eyes stared, brown, blue, and grey at them; lips hung, red, detached, wet, twisted into knowing sneers, flanked by fists that curled around the bars; pressed foreheads were creased into narrow bulges of flesh by the square uprights; locks of hair hung around the metal; parts of clothing fluttered loose. They praised. "Fertig," a joker said, "your roomie's a doctor." They all laughed. "Fertig, it's Rabbi John."

The razzing didn't seem to annoy Fertig at all; he just sat there and looked around him slowly and then, as if he didn't hear what they were saying, stared at the wall. Grombach fidgeted; the seconds were beginning to crawl over him; his fat, outsider's face gleamed with fright-sweat. The crowd annoyed Giant John. Noise bothered him. He needed his quiet so he could think, so the time-poison wouldn't start flowing in him.

"Fertig," the joker continued. John couldn't see who it was: he pretended to stare ahead, his face held in his fists, but he was looking for the laughing man. "Fertig, the big one on the crapper is the big rabbi. And the other one, he is a little doctor," the clown said and cackled.

"I'm not a doctor," Grombach bleated and they all laughed.

"Out," Giant John told them.

"Yes, your majesty," someone said; he couldn't see who it was. He growled and they started to break up. The bandbox boys in blue, late as usual, came running up, pleading, "All right, fellows, all right," while stabbing with their clubs in hard little digs that hurt badly. They all drifted apart slowly, grumbling; entertainment was hard to come by here.

The parking-ticket joker sat baby-curled on his cot, wishing he dared to stand so the bugs wouldn't get at him; afraid to stand because it brought him nearer to Fertig. John had drifted twenty years and he was nothing – who had heard of him? But an amateur, a little man with a big gun, a man like that Fertig laugher, sat there and smiled smug and drank it in – John could see that – drank it in. Unfair. John Giant decided, who was he but some amok punk who turned the burning tool on. Now four turnkeys trotted for Fertig, and then escorted him with respect; just two screws for John Giant. And the lonely little stiffs they stuck away here, they came up running to bow down to Fertig:

the Big Man. But John, seated on the toilet, *he* was the big man, but he couldn't tell anyone about it – was he crazy? Would he put himself in the hands of the hangman?

The hours passed neither fast nor slow for John; he had been in prisons all over the country, one or two in Canada and one in Mexico (never again). The thing was not to fidget like the parking-ticket punk and weep, "my wife, my children, that judge, my lawyer, where is he?, my home, my money, when am I going to get out?" – never and soon: that was the answer. And stop, John thought, flipping that silly fat wrist over to look at the watch the screws had taken away (bad, for John Giant would have taken it himself). The slow flow of light shift told John, who knew how to judge it, the time to the hours, to the minutes, to the forty and one-half days he was waiting for them to bring him up on simple assault so he could do his time and get it over with – those little natural shifts he had learned about when he was a backbreak plough-kid grooving a rock plain. The great, central flood of light that seeped down through the big dome turned a little white and drifted down like a mist, so the other side across the pit was scrimmed off and unnoticed except for when someone moved there. The senseless ramps arched high over the pen beneath, suspended in the milky nothing. Down there the guests waited afternoons and nights to be assigned to a bed in the aisles or in a cell, depending on the magnitude of their courage and the admirability of their crime or, for that matter, the degree of dislike their looks engendered in the registering turnkey's whims.

Dangling rope chains went from nowhere to nowhere. Brick walk and catwalk shook and clattered to a daydreaming guard's tread. The man in the central gondola turned slowly like food on a spit, his gun pointing in all directions, spun by a creaking mechanism. The animals in the aisles were betting cards on a bed for valuables; the clicks of crap games were heard from the corners: they played for cigarettes, favours, money, whatnots translatable into prestige, an extra slice of bread at mealtimes, sex precedents. The guards pretending not to notice looked the other way or ignored the evidence of the spy-eye even though one should do nothing but serve time and sense sinfulness seeping out. He discarded hours for forty days; he could shuck off two years standing on one foot if no screw had it in for him. Nothing disturbed his tranquillity till Fertig. Now, all of a sudden, he was aware that time moved too slowly, clung to him after all; the minutes were poisonous ticks that tunnelled into his flesh. Somewhere inside of him the caustic burn itched him. He recognized the feeling. John's scalp twitched. It always led to trouble. "Stop," he told Grombach. He meant that Grombach should stop sweating.

But Grombach barely paid attention to him; Fertig-fear made him John-brave.

Somewhere across the void a gate crashed. Grombach jumped. A prisoner, to start a little action, beat for a while on his cage but, since no one paid attention, he soon stopped. The sun, partitioned by little barred squares set into the window, shifted slowly from left to evening. The light streamed in from behind the John-mass so that the shadow of his head fell across Fertig's face. Some smirky little hard-rocks, picked up for knocking an old man over for a little whisky, pot, or fix money, started to whine in rock-and-roll rhythms; their wailing and moaning harmonies annoyed John because they were noisy, snotty kids whom he could take, singly or together, apart. They wore straw boaters, blue paisley-print shirts, white ice-cream pants, white shoes, and all had hearing aids and wore fake mean looks. When they came into the pen they clumped together. They rolled their sleeves and wore their collars high. John didn't have to do that to look hard-rock hot. They saw him, they knew him.

John saw the Man They Had All Read About was knotted up with some trouble he couldn't work out. Had they raked him in the court-room? Had the guards pushed at the Big One? Had they all flocked around while Fertig stood naked-shrunk there? Did the twitch-prison doctor look at him and say, "See, he's not so much," and say, like he always did when he wanted to ride a prisoner, "And I always thought that the size of a man's genitalia was the best index to a man's criminality! So how do you account for someone like this?" And then, did he hold up his thumb and forefinger with just a small space between them and wink to all around? But for John Giant he said, "Aha! Classic Lombroso with slow wit, thick skull, great strength, small forehead, bull – almost none – neck, pig's eyes close set, and huge genitalia – that wicked whang –" and hefted it casually and then flicked a fore-finger into his balls to see him jump it: he didn't; "animallike homo throwback neanderthalis type criminal you couldn't if you saw him in choir practice with white robes miss this gorilla – look up the anal, man I knew once had a knife there." Or did they shove Fertig around with cold wood clubs behind the knees, or slap their fat hands on his feeble flabby buttocks as they forced him through the icy stinging of the delousing, degerming, decontaminating sulfa shower with the others? Well, what did he expect? You accepted or busted out; John had learned. Fertig was tense. He was smoking his cigarettes up too fast. An amateur.

The awe, the sheep-faced terror with which Grombach stared at Fertig bothered him. "You. Cigarettes." And Grombach, not really afraid or noticing, went through the nail-gnaw again, gave John the cigarettes and watched that little man brooding all the time.

That Fertig was a little man worried John. You always had to watch the small ones. The small ones packed in twice as much venom as any big man. He knew. He met the small ones all over the country. In Alabama, on a chain gang, a small screw who swung his club no so much hard, but knowing just where, just how to hit and tongue-lash – Giant John picked him up one day and held him high in the bright sunshine and enjoyed for one second, the sweet, high scream before he skull-first threw the waspy hack down on a rock, and, snapping his chain, took off for the woods. He was seventeen. A jealous little man stabbed him in the back in Memphis. He turned around to kill the little man; he just reached out: his hand opened and took him by the throat and shut. He killed sixteen men all over the country. Could Fertig claim the same?

But look at them, he thought. Fertig was dying to talk. Fertig knew that Grombach was from the outside with his moans of my God and how could that judge and they locked me up and why and forever and they forgot they forgot they forgot me and alike. Grombach was scared to the point of fainting but was beginning to look like he might come out of it; he had all the questions on the tip of his tongue, and the questions were stronger than the fright. The, Face from the newspapers had come close and, yet, had not killed him. How did you do it, sir? What did you do then, sir? And when he got out, it would be, you'll never imagine what happened to me in prison. Well, look at them – Grombach and Fertig; one was fat, the other skinny, but you couldn't really tell one from the other; both were small, soft, pale-skinned, men you took things away from. The air was becoming full of afternoon talk-slowed.

Well, what if I told them I killed sixteen men? Would that Grombach give *him* the adoring look? How? By shrinking away. He could see the parking-ticket joker going mad trying to watch two directions for the most dangerous. But, John Giant knew, inside, the tensions and the year's frustrations told him, that it would be Fertig who would be the most feared, he would never admit... he wasn't crazy. Fertig was down to his last cigarette now. In the aisles they were starting to drift back. They never left a man alone. John growled.

"Fertig," the jester, dying with the afternoon's boredom said, "I tell you that man's a doctor. Look at that fink shrink. Don't that tell you he's a doctor?"

Grombach babbled, "It isn't true. I'm not a doctor. Why don't you leave me alone?"

"Why don't you leave me alone?" someone mimicked in a high, quavering voice. "Hey, doc," someone else called, "I have this ache in my left ball" ... and tried to cram his testicles between the bars. "Oh, doctor," a feminized voice shrilled, "I think I have caught the clap. Will I need a hysterectomy –" and flapped his lips and made spit-bubbles at Grombach. "Doctor... Doctor..."

Grombach whimpered. Fertig told Grombach it was all right; he didn't care if Grombach was a doctor or not; don't worry, don't worry. The din of it was working slowly on John; he could feel that prickly sensation spreading all over his body; he could feel the vein in the side of his head begin to throb, and the tremendous ridges of trapezius muscles on the sides of his neck and along the top of his shoulders were raising slowly and if they tightened, it would be a long time before they untensed, a long, aching time. The thick cigarette smoke was blowing into the cage; someone out there had a bottle and he could almost smell the liquor with his out-flared nostrils. He wanted some, but he wouldn't ask because he couldn't pay. But if the tippler came close, John would take. He growled again, a little louder this time, and the sound reached them. Fertig looked a cool, cocky bantam's look at him.

"Are you going to do something about this doctor, Fertig, or do you need a gun? Are you funking?" Someone kept pushing. But after a while they saw Fertig wasn't going to do anything at all but keep sitting there, tight and taut and staring at the wall with his slit eyes and thinking out what they had done to him. They started to drift away. Somewhere to the side, a gate clashed. They all cheered automatically, but without much spirit.

The light deepened a little more and the afternoon's haze was dissipating; the ineffectual electric lights became a little stronger. Grombach kept twitching annoyingly, still asking himself little questions like "Where are they? When are they going to come for me? What kind of a place is this?" and jumping at every sound: a shout floating up, the shriek of two men having sex somewhere, the clinking of chains. Fertig was stirring again, beginning to come out of that shock that hits them all when the judge says "Take him away." Soon, he and Grombach would move together to jaw it out. John was content to play the waiting game. He sat on the toilet waiting for them to need it, knowing that they had to come to him.

And, after a while, Grombach couldn't keep from asking questions. The curiosity was eating him up, stronger than his scare. He hemmed a little in Fertig's direction and finally asked if he wanted a cigarette. Fertig smiled and said yes. But Grombach forgot that John took the cigarettes and they both looked his way. He just stared past them and they had to ask him. He didn't even look at them. They asked again and he thought, go get your lawyers, go ask the screws, go ask the reporters, go ask the folks at home – hungering for their presence – to send some smokes; he would take them away. He killed sixteen men in his time and never asked; he would kill more if they roused him, but he would never be able to say anything about it and he would never get the big lawyers who would give him cigarettes. They stopped asking. "No," he told them.

He was alone. No one gave him. He took what he wanted. He always had. No work nurtured his muscles. He took. He took a drink. He took a woman. He took clothes. He took some money. He moved. All the grifters, all the hoods, all the punks and pimps, they had no use for him. When they picked John Giant up for drunk or disorderly, no one sprang to help him. He sweated it out. He once did two years. Sixteen. Sixteen men lay dead. A tired Legal Aid man for John, or court-assigned hacks, who haggled fee over him; little hustlers who hardly knew law. He got those. And most of the time, when they got their fees, they didn't care what happened to him. Newspapers would not debate. They put John in. He sweated it out. Or did hard labour. He would stand, not alone, like Fertig, but with ten or twenty others in front of the bored judge who made a bored speech about "unregenerate" and "example to your kind" and "antisocial", a tired lecture about wild criminals prowling and preying while John would stand stock still and clench both fists at his sides, where no one saw, and would put his thumbs between his first and second fingers. And, unless he was small-town mean, the judge gave them thirty or sixty or ninety in the workhouse, not counting how long they had rotted waiting to come up before the bench. No one would know what he did. Sixteen. And no Grombach would suck up to him. He took money; he took a woman. But he was entitled, John thought, entitled.

They got lovey, John saw. Grombach was asking questions, eyes all buggy, lips all loose and slobber-hungry about the Real Thing. But Fertig was explaining why instead of how, and how they didn't understand, and that his lawyer lied and the D.A. distorted and the Lynch, Judge Jeffries, yelled at him and wouldn't listen and jugged him and the newspapers rode him, and what kind of mad place was this. What had he expected? Alone? Aloof, dignified, like in the movies? Alone was inside and who cared for the rest, John thought. And Grombach was saying "I saw two obviously criminal types (John didn't miss Grombach's head nod a little towards him) get their charges reduced from felony to misdemeanour because they had no room in prison. They had no room!" his voice shrieked. "But they had room for me! As if I had been a –" He stopped. "An example," the fat mark moaned. "That crazy judge said *'talk up'*, and when I did, he said, *'louder, I can't hear you,'* and when I did he said, *'raise your voice in this courtroom once more and it's contempt.'* And they wouldn't take my cheque," he snivelled. "And now the guards looked the wild-animal look at *him*. In the moan and wail he wept. I tore off a man's arm in Philadelphia, John thought. They kept talking, talking.

"Is it always like this?" they asked one another cosily. "Do they always behave like this? Isn't it filthy? What made you do it? Why did the judge yell at me? I confessed." And they answered one another snugly, "I wouldn't know. I haven't been here before," and moved a little closer because they were outside men huddling.

"Talk," John said. They were all the time talking. Talking men edged him out of the good things of life; talking men weaseled their way in and conned John into doing things: a talking man took him along to strong-arm a robbery and left him holding nothing at all, running fast to get away with the take into another state, left him with nothing, nothing, nothing but the clothes on his back and an unwanted score in the shape of a slaughtered sheep, and fleeing all the way. They looked at him, mildly surprised, and went back to their talk. "Talk," John Giant said a little louder because the steady drone of their explanations ate into him and his stomach muscles knotted into big ridges and his leg muscles were starting to tauten and to fraction him up from the toilet's greasy porcelain film. Someone set up a suicide howl. The hacks were running in a funny flock towards the cell, where they were going to bang and bang on that buffoon's head.

The last outside light winked out for the evening and Grombach set up a little howl; he was going to be here for the night; they had forgotten him. Fertig tried to suck up to grace and comfort him. That Fertig, he said, "Well, think. You must have done *something* to merit a day's jail." But the fat man purpled and his eyes bulged and he dared, forgetting he had the Very Important One-Man Crime Syndicate in front of him, to tell Fertig that it might be all right for *him*, but he, Grombach, had a wife, children, father, mother, in-laws, masonic brothers, business associates, knew a judge, knew a district leader, belonged to clubs, gave to charity, and had a house; it was no joke. "But so do I – did I …" said Fertig, and John could see he was beginning to see the difference between himself and the Grombach. Well, the poor sucker, he had never been away from home, had he, John Giant sneered.

The cold discs of Fertig's glasses blazed. Grombach caught the tight cool stare Fertig gave him; his purple paled as his heat fear-cooled. And now he wouldn't listen to what Fertig had to say about the way they were treating him, what they were doing to him, but sat very scared, gnashing his teeth, forgotten, and little dribbly tears ran down his face. Fertig, having shown Grombach a piece of Truth, was trying to comfort Grombach and tell him it was all right; they would come for him in the morning; they would; they hadn't abandoned him. But there was no one at all to remember John Giant in all the prisons of the country: there was no one to care about John as he wandered the lonely streets or sat in the saloons and drank and got angry about this or that thing, and even the women, when he was through with them, they looked "animal" at him. Well, he thought sadly – the last light from the skylight turned a little misty-blue like back-country mists as he remembered them from twenty years back – he might have had these things, but he would have had to break his back for ten, twelve hours a day: the price was too high.

The two knots of muscle running down his back were stiffened and valleyed his spine; sweat washed down along the groove. The never-off electric lights shone impartially on them all and the bugs on the beds and the bugs on the men were clearly seen, feeding, feeding, ageing them all; the rats in the wall and the rats in the well below began to stir; the hours nibbled holes in the plaster. All the peeping television eyes looked on all the time, seeing the guilty and innocent alike. The gondola was drawn up to a ramp to change the guard. Most of the men were, except for the violent cases, brought away to eat … and came rioting back, singing and shouting and yelling and giving the club-swinging screws a hard time because the food always left them hungry and disgusted.

Trays were brought for the three of them. Grombach asked the guard if they had heard from his lawyer, or relatives, and the hack hit him for talking without permission. Fertig didn't say anything but sat with the tray on his lap and stared ahead. Giant John ate quickly. The guards stood and watched. When John was through he took Grombach's trembly tray and ate what was there, too. You never knew when you might not eat again.

Later, Fertig tried to talk to Grombach again, but his killer-cold look had set them apart forever now. That Grombach, he shrank away. That Fertig, he kept babbling while the spy-eyes saw and the bugs picked up that talky fool's words: it exasperated him.

John Giant reached into his pocket and pulled out a piece of mirror and pushing past Grombach, pinning Grombach's legs against the cot, pinching them, shoving him back against the greasy wall, stuck the mirror under Fertig's face. "Here," he told Fertig. Here, he thought, look at yourself. You're not so much, little man, he thought, not enough to raise one little old shout about. Look at yourself, king; look at your-self, killer king. Fertig, not understanding, didn't look into the mirror but at the big hulking man – the great head set on the thick short neck, his shoulders looking like they went from one wall on the left to the bars dividing the cube on the right – looked into his eyes, and didn't see that he could bend bars. The four winy wet-wits had got their secret ration for the night and were making themselves slobber-drunk again. Look, John thought again, because Fertig was not king, not king at all. He, John Giant, from wall to wall of the country, and between each jailing, had killed "Sixteen," his little voice said. Fertig just smiled at him. What did that smile mean? Giant John wondered. It was the little man's cunning smile and it meant much. He backed away, stepping on Grombach's foot, and sat down on the toilet seat again. He could sit there all night if he had to.

Grombach shrivelled up on his bed like a little fat ball. And then it was late at night. There were no shadows; only the barred lights were thrown back into the indigo night; the feeling, that old feeling of dark was there, and. it was as bad as if everything were black. The television eyes, trained on every part, even on the emptiness of the central pit, in which only magicians could float, half-slept. The activities intensified. The guards collected take for little favours; the boys began to push fix; the punks and their lovers coupled, and scrape-shaven nancy boys, powdered, marcel-haired, with paint-rimmed eyes, wiggled their behinds. Men howled. Men screamed at casual beatings; someone sang a prison-blues; the dandy boys in their paisley shirts harmonized a little louder because they were eighteen years old in a forty-year-world; thieves stole and restole; pickpockets dipped; goons solicited tribute. The poker game never stopped; someone offered to debag a debtor. Candy bars were sold to those who could afford the three-times price.

Fertig sat there for a long time, staring, all talked out. His eyes were narrow and his lips white and thin. John wondered what he plotted and watched him without seeming to stare. Grombach's night-frightened stare was only for Fertig, the blown-up killer. Fertig smiled once at him, but it made no difference because he terror-clung to the wall, crumpled in his soiled suit, his jaw going steadily, wearing down his teeth with the noisy grinding, burrowing away from Fertig. Fertig picked up the piece of mirror glass and looked into it. He looked back at Grombach gibbering away from him. Fertig saw.

"You see," John told Fertig. Fertig didn't pay any attention to him. "You see," he said again, but Fertig was lost in his own thoughts... or at least he seemed to be. Or was Fertig, John Giant wondered, watching him, for the moment to put the mirror silver deep into him because John had showed Fertig what he was?

So he waited.

He waited a long time.

Every muscle in his body was erect and the tense vein in his head pulsed painfully, standing out, tumescent with the blood in it. He hated that little man. His eye muscles were bunched unrelentingly and his eyes were glaring at Fertig, who was too big to even notice John. He waited.

The glitter in Fertig's eye almost stopped him; the cool, slit eyes, the hunched shoulders, the pushed-out jaw, the faint glint that came from his cruel canines through the thin, parted lips almost stopped him.

So, when the hacks, who marched in threes at night, came by he rushed past Grombach and picked up Fertig and began to hit him again and again, saying, "You're nothing, You're nothing." Grombach screamed. John kept pounding Fertig till the guards came and pulled the two of them out into the aisle and, surrounded by cheering prisoners, beat them apart. They took Fertig away and continued to beat John casually. They hit him sixteen, seventeen, eighteen times and he didn't say anything, but he had enough sense to lie there as if he were hurt: besides, the joy of his victory over Fertig anaesthetized him.

They dragged John into the cell again and left him there and went. He waited till their footsteps were gone and got up and went back to sit on the toilet seat. Grombach was sitting on the edge of the cot, near the door. The four apes next door were too gone to do anything but goggle and mumble meaninglessly. All his muscles felt relaxed and sweet now. Only Grombach there disturbed the night by moaning, so John said, "I didn't hit you." And he saw, with satisfaction, that Grombach stared at *him* now, stared at him the way he should, scared and tributefull, frightened of John the Giant the way he had been terrified of Fertig.

Chapter 17

Fertig had been in the City Prison for a week when Bleakie went to visit him. At first he was going to interview Fertig in the prison commissioner's office, but then he decided to talk to Fertig in his cell: to see how the environment was treating him, if he was holding up – was he overcoming? Fertig was in maximum security. Opposite Fertig's cell, beyond the ramp, dim forms hung in the great central pit of the prison. Sounds drifted slowly up. From above, light floated down dimly through frosted wireglass skylights. The other sounds of the prison surged up faintly, rising and falling like some endlessly beating surf. When Bleakie was let in, Fertig was sitting on his bed-slab staring at the opposite wall, from which another bed was swung. The gate clashed behind Bleakie; the guard turned his back but didn't leave: Fertig didn't look at Bleakie.

Somebody had been beating Fertig. He had a black eye under his wire-rimmed right glass; a blue bruise thickened his cheek; a patch of plaster ran along the rim of his jaw, the end of which was not properly stuck on – it hung loosely and Bleakie wanted to press it down. Ridiculous, he thought, and felt again, that inexplicable anger at Fertig. I slept with your wife, he thought spitefully, and then smiled, remembering something Sara had said: No, he thought, I don't sleep with all my clients. Be careful, he thought, don't show it; win Fertig. They might be working on Sara to get rid of me and get a new lawyer ... From somewhere far away metal clanged. Did Fertig jump?

Why didn't he turn? Bleakie was in a hurry: he had had a relapse, and the anti-histamine dose was wearing off, the familiar buzzing and dizziness was setting in. Rush. Rush. He was a busy man. You're not my only case, you know.

Fertig's hands were on his thighs, fingers together, thumbs tight along the forefinger's lengths. Typical. Reluctant still. He knew Fertig so well. And realized suddenly that this was the first time they had really been alone. Historic meeting. He thought of the thick case-folder in his office – three inches – librarian at the country medical library remembers, Abercrombie and Fitch gunman recalls with perfect fidelity, depositions; friends – Sam and Bea, you could have knocked me over with a …; relatives – he was always a good boy; police reports; passersby; neighbours; expert and non-expert testimony hearsay; newspaper speculations; a log of his discoveries made following in his steps. Who knew him better? Not even Sara. Actually, Roy Bleakie thought, they had been alone many times. He touched his coat pocket – Fertig's notebook, late-at-night reading … to encounter the mind of the author, his spirit, as it were. Take it out: show him. What would he do? Try to grab it. There! That ought to prove to his tormentors that he was sane. Silliness. Say something, he thought. Silliness. Why? Because he knew Fertig so well, did he feel Fertig should know him? Common error – hadn't made it in a long, long time. Sickness was distorting his judgment … Vacation …

Bleakie moved in. Through his stuffed nose he faintly smelled urine – vague acridity dabbed in the stone-bones of prison – and fart smell. How was Fertig doing after that good hospital diet? It was hard to be strong with weak bowels. He sat down facing Fertig; their knees almost touched. He hoped there were no bugs. Having time to take a good look at Fertig, he watched carefully, to see what effect prison had on him. He noted again the glasses, the small, ineffectual toothbrush (had there been grey in before?), the pale, prim lips, the still demanding stare as Fertig looked at him now through his one good eye. Fertig shifted stiffly; so did Bleakie – the cold, the virus … icy … feverish … made him restless … He had to move … try to concentrate… He should have taken another dose, but he hated that drowsy feeling. Had prison pallor, that curious whiteness that indicated depreciation, set in? Too soon; a week. Only a week? The drugs disturbed his sense of time.

He wasn't much, Bleakie told himself – this calm centre from which their tales all radiated. Fertig the innocent. Lucy, her cool stare still scored him … Fertig the lover – a lie at that. "Little man." The accountant with that moustache – impossible. Fertig the sexual failure. I slept with your wife, Bleakie thought. Why feel bitter? Payment for sins now; chills, virus, mild recurrent fever, enervation, won't go away, everybody has it this season; the beating heat radiated up from his aching and sweaty hands against the prison chill. Feel triumphant. Who were you to set yourself up,... but you lost, didn't you, he thought-asked Fertig. They'll cut him down here, he thought. A few more weeks, be reasonable, I'll get you off.

A shout clanged: dim, it floated a long time in that well mist. He could see fear in the face of the Man We All Know and Love. It would help, that fear, he thought, and he felt better. Fertig was down, down, defeated; Bleakie comforted himself. Well, you wanted to be here, didn't you? Won through to the place he thought he belonged. Was this a winning? And he knew it was. Turn victory into defeat – his mission. "Who's been beating you?" Bleakie asked softly, sympathetically. How much could be made of prison brutality? "Have the guards... ?"

But the correction officer heard; he turned and explained what happened to Fertig. Probably waiting for just that question.

"Why wasn't he in a cell by himself?" Bleakie snapped. The guard started to explain, but Bleakie waved him off; he didn't want any explanations that might rob him of ammunition later. "Questions?" he asked Fertig.

"I don't understand what's happening. What kind of a place is this?"

"Prison. Detention house."

"I know, but –"

"What did you expect?"

Fertig couldn't begin to explain it properly. Bleakie didn't bother to listen to the torrent that poured out; it started as a droning account of wrongs, delivered one by one in a high, precise, nagging voice, calmly, as if toting up mere debits: the lack of consideration, filth, brutality, bestiality, bad food, crowding – rising to an angry cry of outrage – a madhouse. It was a confused little speech in which the words *dignity, a little decency, humanity*, detached themselves. He had heard it all before. Was he like so many other clients?

"Don't exercise. You're not entitled," he stopped Fertig. "You're a killer. You're guilty. You confessed." That shut him up. Yes, Bleakie could see fear; that was the big change. "You're afraid, aren't you?" he asked, taking care to be friendly, confidential. "You want out, back to the wards?"

Fertig didn't answer. Bleakie was annoyed. His body ached. His hands throbbed. He was in a hurry. "Gives you the idea, doesn't it? Nobody cares here. Beat you. What are you here? Like any other killer. Like any other common hood. They won't care. Is it better here than in Psychiatric? Act a little gone. We're all a little gone. I'll get you off. Take you back to the –"

"Why are you defending me? I don't want a lawyer."

"Wife wants," Bleakie lied.

"She doesn't care."

"Of course she cares. Loves you. By your side."

"She hasn't been to see me."

"Keeping her away."

"Why?"

"The D.A. wants to break your spirit ... Loves you, Harry. With you all the way, Harry. She understands why you did it, she *sees* –"

"She cares?" Fertig asked. The lips relaxed a little; the swellings made his face look foolish. "She never told me."

"Of course she cares," Bleakie told him. "It's been very hard for her. Terrible strain."

"She had no money to pay you."

"Why worry about money? I'm doing it for nothing."

"Why?"

"I believe," he said and watched.

Fertig spoke a little less coldly, less righteously. "I don't want a lawyer. Tell her to forget."

She wants to, he thought; she will – should I let her? Is it fair? Fair? He laughed at himself. "Law demands a lawyer. If not me, then someone else. She cares," Bleakie said.

"I'm guilty."

"No one denies –" He wasn't prepared to go into it; time was running against him; the beat in his body was racing; his hands were tapping on his knees. The little motions made him feel better, but he had to get out. Why had he bothered to come? To see the lover and husband with his martyred, bruised face? He ticked off points for Fertig. "Can't plead guilty to homicide. Law forbids. A plea of guilty, first degree, is against the law. Capital punishment in this state. Like suicide. And suicide is against the law. Goes back to ecclesiastical law ..."

"But I'm not a Christian!"

Bleakie smiled and touched the knot in his tie. "It's really all in your hands. Considering everything, the best, the safest way is Institution for the Criminally Insane. That or condemnation; execution. But what if you got life? Put you in a place like this for life." Not that the State bin was any better, Bleakie thought.

Fertig seemed to be thinking it over. "Execution; that's what I want."

It was said firmly; still strong. "Be logical, Fertig, you've made your point. They're dead. Your son's revenged. You don't have to burn for it, too. I can help you."

Fertig's stubborn hands remained flat on his thighs, letting the minutes parsimoniously seep out from under the pressed-down fingers, slowing Bleakie up. "I'm guilty. I don't want to evade the consequences. That wasn't the point of what I did."

"Doesn't matter, Fertig. The range of legal possibility is narrow. The law permits little, understand?" Fertig shook his head. "One: you are guilty or not guilty. But two: where murder is concerned, murder in the first degree, you can plead only, only, *only* not guilty. *A*: If you didn't do it – which doesn't apply in this case – though we could always reverse and state that the confession was obtained by force – good time for that –"

"No."

"All right. *B*: You were insane –"

"I wasn't."

"I have to protect you."

"I don't want protection."

"You need. The law permits no other way."

Fertig was thinking about it. "You said in court that I was unable to understand the nature of the charges –"

"Manoeuvering. Listen. Act a little odd. Moment of aberration at the time of killing. Heisenberg is on our side –"

Fertig's hands stiffened; the ridge of knuckles rose a little. "He thinks I'm insane."

"Legal term." Bleakie was running out of patience. He needed Fertig. "Only a legal term; no insult. No validity in psychiatric reality. Disturbance, aberration, sickness, dysfunction – you were disturbed, weren't you? But disturbance', 'sickness', have little legal meaning: but they'll come around in time. Old laws; out of date. 'Insanity', the word, the concept, is a hangover, just a legal hangover – vestigial.

"You're all missing the point –"

"Which is this: no one cares." Fertig was stubborn and exasperating. Having been worked over, Fertig should take the opportunity. Bleakie could see the thin tendons string up on the slender wrists. "Face it. Do you think the public understands? Too subtle. To them you're only a cold-blooded mad killer … crazy but with malice aforethought; to them, anything, so long as you burn. You're the man who killed the doctors. Doctors are grey-headed, lovable, stand by your bed when you're sick. They hold your hand. Healing priests. Holy. Give you pills. Sit by your bed all night, look worried. Perform appendectomies with pocket knives and save your life on the kitchen table. Touch your body. Sacrosanct. More intimate than wives. You killed them, Fertig; all they know. Un-American. Sacrilegious. Compounded it. Killed a sweet little old lonely lady. And killed a holy man, a beloved religious leader; newspaper files of adulation as long as your arm. But who is Fertig? What good did he ever do?" Fertig started to say something. "I know what you're going to tell me about the rabbi, or the rest of them, for that matter. I know what you found out. The answer is *so what*? What's your point? Mad revenge as far as everyone's concerned. Irrational. Kill the mad dog, they say. Think you made a big discovery? If you'd tell them and prove it, they'd hate you more."

Fertig's narrow shoulders were slumped over.

"You want to die?" Bleakie asked him.

Fertig looked at him and raised his hands a little. No, Bleakie thought; no. A little more. They were almost there.

"Act a little crazy. Roy Bleakie will get you back to the ward."

"I won't go back there." His fingers were tighter, the skin on the ridge of knuckles was white.

"Where then?" Bleakie snapped his fingers at Fertig: "Home?"

"It's not that. I – going back invalidates what I did."

"Fertig, those who can understand, understand; act a little crazy."

"They miss the point."

"The medical profession got the point … and will ignore it. Who runs Mercy Memorial now? Board of ten. It will be bigger than ever; huge construction, additions, government funds, too, immense plant, probably the biggest in the world, latest equipment, computer diagnosis, many more thousands helped than before, high-speed processing of patients. They're going to call it Gordon-Mercy Memorial Hospital. Give up. Act a little mad."

Fertig didn't answer.

"Or do you want to kill off the new board? Or burn down the hospital? Leave thousands without a place to be treated? For what? To save the next person who gets a wrong diagnosis? Who understands? A few moralists? Some French philosophers. Are you an existentialist hero, Fertig? You don't even know what an existentialist is, do you? They make a fuss about you in the French cafes and talk about you like you were Mike Hammer, the Resistance, and Alyosha Karamazov rolled into one, but here, in this country, you're a doomed nut unless Roy Bleakie says no."

Bleakie leaned closer and spoke gently now, "Listen, those who care, those who are concerned still cure bodies or souls with love. The other's can't get the point anyhow. Act a little crazy, Fertig. Some of the reporters understand; couldn't write it. Or if they wrote it, their editors wouldn't print it. I mean there's Grinzing. There are always the Grinzing's. But who listens? Commie crank, they say. We won't act too mad, Fertig, nothing too wild. Man lost his case by eating a human turd in court. We'll act just a little crazier and Roy Bleakie will get you out of here."

Fertig shook his head wearily and began to scratch the inside of his thigh. His other hand scratched his back, over his kidney. For a second Fertig seemed to go a little wild, scratching all over, his knees, legs, ankles, arms, neck, head; and then he took a deep breath, held it, sat still, and looked at Bleakie again. "No." Bleakie hated Fertig for still being strong, in spite of all of it; the psychiatric ward, the prison, the beating, the fact that he had slept with Sara – no, Fertig didn't know that. He sat there, strong still, fit enough to screw that slut, after all: a big man, they had not reduced him yet. A few more months in prison – a few more months of this – felicity. He grinned. "Maybe I can do better than that. I can get you off."

"What do you mean?"

"Just that. Possibilities: you were sane –"

"I was –"

"Don't interrupt, Fertig: legally … Second, you were always and are, now, insane.

Fertig shook his head.

"*Or* you became insane at or some time after the death of your child, and are still, now, insane."

Fertig shook his head.

"Either way, it will save your life. Aren't you afraid to die?"

"Yes."

"Don't you want to live?"

"But I'm not insane."

Bleakie's irritation grew. Stubbornness, megalomania irritated his tired and chilled body, chilled his fevery hands. "Or you were insane when you did it –"

"No."

"I know. Theorizing. Planning means sanity. See what we fight? Premeditation. Rule of thumb: the mad, they do not pre-meditate."

Fertig relaxed.

"But supposing you were insane from the time of that terrible shock, the death of your child, till you killed them, which released you from your psychotic state? I can get you *free*, Harry, off: wouldn't you like that? You never considered that, did you,. Harry? No one did. Think about it. Back to your wife, home, a new life …" Roy Bleakie could just see it now; here was a dream coup to bring off. He sat back to watch the effect. Was he responding? Was he breathing faster? Never thought of it as possible. Secret dreams? Deep and hidden freedom fantasies?

"No. It's just not true."

With a pleader's reasonable mask, he continued to torment Fertig. He leaned forward and touched Fertig's hand and said, "Truth – bunkum. Save your life. Give you freedom. Move out. You and the little woman. Start all over again. California. Wonderful climate. Grow old together. To live, Harry, like a human being… Possibly even another child …"

"No!"

"Haven't you been through enough punishment to make up for what you did? Isn't the balance complete?" He grinned. He could see the idea taking hold of Fertig, Fertig fighting it, squirming, trying to shuck it off like an infection, beginning to surmise wildly, even permitting himself comfort with the sickening hope of it, whether he wanted to or not.

"No."

"Isn't it truly crazy to ask for more punishment? To ask for death? Isn't it mad? What sane man wants to commit suicide?"

"No."

The "no" wasn't strong enough, not strong enough ... he was rising to it ... his whole *body*, his whole *being* was succumbing. Bleakie could feel it coming through Fertig's hand. It was medicine to Bleakie. Terror was robbing Fertig of resistance-strength.

"I won't."

"Be realistic. The law is; you can't evade it, only use it. You'll only have to say you *were* mad. Still have your dignity. The loss of a son through negligence is grounds for a revenge-madness. We might even sue."

Fertig pulled away: his hands were flat together, the thumbs lying side by side, pressed together. "I'm not mad. I've never been mad."

Bleakie was exasperated. "That has nothing to do with it."

"Then you won't help me?"

"But I am helping you." One hand made short, sweeping motions to the side. He leaned back. His image diminished and almost disappeared in Fertig's lenses; distorted reflections of all the bars set in the windows, light filtering in, and the vast emptiness were all rendered circular and whirling there. "You're unreasonable," Bleakie said. "Look, *she* cares," Bleakie tried again. Fertig didn't answer. Did he dare mention the night of the famous orgasm?

"I won't let you do it."

"But if I do it and you make a fuss, they'll say you were mad then, and still are, won't they. And if you accept it, act rationally, they'll say you're sane now, won't they? I can do it." The whole world, he thought – never anything like it; and he laughed to see Fertig so angry, so torn about it. He almost had Fertig. A little more time in prison, a few more months – do him a world of good. He stood.

"NO!" Fertig yelled at him. One hand turned over and lay there, cupped, as if holding something. Bleakie shrugged his shoulders and stood up.

Fertig looked up at him suddenly; Bleakie could see his image doubled in Fertig's glasses, far away and small, distorted and dancing around the rings in Fertig's lenses: "*You* understand, don't you?" Fertig's fingertips had curled around; his hands were fisted, the thumbs caught inside the curl of the fingers: a baby's fist.

Bleakie's fingers drummed, his pulse beat, his heart fluttered insistently. Get out, he thought, get going. Stop in the drugstore, fight virus tension the eightfold way, he thought. Pay attention: fever, head, ringing, dizziness. But didn't Roy Bleakie have the constitution of an ox? Virus – nothing; won a case with pneumonia once. Calm face, slight anything-you-have-to-say smile; wouldn't give his opponent the satisfaction. Bleakie's satisfaction was that he laid Fertig's treacherous wife. He looked at his watch: a gesture to disconcert. The hands stabbed 12.50. Nevertheless, Bleakie admitted, "I understand." Fertig was not mad. He had never been mad.

Fertig leaned forward; his face tilted up, his neck craned. Looking down into the narrow lens-rings, Bleakie's reflection seemed to float up conspiratorially. "Help me," Fertig asked.

"Just what I'm doing."

"Help me." One finger shot out of the bunch and pointed at him.

"Leave everything to Roy Bleakie."

"Help me. I want to be brought to trial. I want to get the case to court and…"

Does he actually think I will help him? He raged inside. That innocent, that terrible innocent – blow everything – let me alone. He fought the shock of that need. He started to interrupt; Fertig wouldn't let him. He leaned a little closer, sliding to the edge of the bed, and reached to touch and hold Bleakie's lapel before he could jump back. Bleakie's image filled the eyeglasses; he could see only part of himself crammed unwillingly into the glass: swollen eye flesh stuffed him to the right; a pulse beat in the other lid, slower than his own thumb pulse's flutter, as the eye imposed itself throughout his whole left reflection. "I want you to bring me to the stand. I want you to get me executed."

A quick posture-picture shot through his mind. Not the rabbi; not Roy Bleakie, but *Fertig* gesticulating before Judge Jeffries…. "Ahhhhh," Bleakie said. "That's it, isn't it? You have this vision. The big courtroom scene. Cast of thousands. Fertig to the stand. Hush falls over. Fertig speaks. The TRUTH. Not a dry eye. Lawmakers rush out to make new laws.

"Too many novels. Too many movies. Not like that at all, Harry-boy. You've been up before judges – doesn't that tell you something?

"Expect a grand revision of ethics? Overdose of TV."

Fertig looked up; the fingers re-stiffened, tense, pulling him, refusing to believe him. "*You* can do it. You can help me explain it all at the trial. We could work on it. You can call me to the stand and let me tell what happened, how I came to see that it was the only thing left for me, for any man, to do." Fertig was pulling himself close to Bleakie, whispering at him, staring at him with the good eye; excitement lifted the swollen lid and a piece of blood-shot eye shone out with visionary fervour. Bleakie could feel himself, unwilling, being infected by Fertig. The guard, half-turned, was staring open-mouthed at the two of them. Could use him later, too. Exhilarated: fever left: head clear: eyes steady: hot combat throb – oh, he thought, how much better than a Gordon he could do it: cleared nose to sniff the acrid, invigorating prison odours as he was tempted for a second. Who could do it better for Fertig than Roy Bleakie? Cast of millions: the world itself would be there; the whole world. *Ah, ladies and gentlemen of the jury… I ask you, who do we have before us? Fertig, the malevolent, cold-blooded murderer. Fertig, the helpless madman in the grip of extreme compulsion. Or is it a third person, neither madman or murderer? Perhaps I present to you a victim who has risen up against corruption and man's inhumanity to man.*

The mayor's committee on hospitals investigating emergency procedures in the hospitals has shown us that no one is to blame for little Stevie Fertig's death, only that his death notice was dictated by the conditions of the society we live in; further, the committee would have us believe that a certain percentage of unavoidable victims must be offered up. It is this that Harry Fertig contested by his act, and contests further by offering his life up so that it may no longer be, so the Stevie Fertig's can grow up to be useful citizens of this society. But then, afterwards what? No. Childish. Fertigism. Innocence. After the furore, Roy Bleakie'd be through. Finished. No D.A.ship. Not even fit for a judge. No share of the new Mercy. He shook his hands, rejecting it. " I won't."

"Why not?"

"It can't be done. Stop me in the middle. Say Roy Bleakie's gone mad. Get you a new lawyer."

"But *you* understand. *You* can do it. *You* could work it out so we could get it all said."

Somewhere in the prison a mad laugh rang out and shrilled slowly upward, echoing again and again till it became like some wild zoo bird's scream. A brutal shout sounded. Metal bonged and a few men sang. Bleakie looked around quickly and saw Fertig jumping too. *What was he to accept then, of this life, ladies and gentlemen of the jury? That the day of the individual is fast drawing to a close and is being replaced by statistic clusters. Are we to be satisfied that what happened to Fertig – and can happen to us – should be assigned to the category of foreseeable and allowable error, an inevitable portion of the bell-shaped, or normal-distribution, curve that governs all events, both great and small? Was he to accept the loss of his son for that reason? because a random chance placed him on a deadly section of a graph? Or will compassionate prophylaxis, as the mayor's committee on hospitals proposes, insure us from entering that realm of the normal-distribution curve from whose bourne no traveller returns? Is there a place on the curve for Fertig's recourse? It is to be acceptance and adjustment? Or… And shall we bury him as we have buried his child, according to his place as measured against the utilitarian mass need. Or shall we ask why the statistics did not provide a sacrificial ram? Or are such questions hopelessly dated, quaint? Naïve? Once, after all, man had face-to-face encounters with his God. Abraham, for instance… But we all know that story.*

Is it unreasonable that a man who as been avoidably mauled by society revolt against it? And is it unreasonable that we listen to this plea? So that perhaps one night, when your loved one becomes ill suddenly … Shall we avoid the issue by calling it all madness, or shall we at least dare ask how a man like Harry Fertig, a man like you, or I, dare to rise to do what he did? Let us go back … Ahh, Bleakie thought, the bastard has infected me, the son of a bitch has possessed me. No, he thought. "No," he said suddenly and turned to go. And stopped. To hell with them all, he thought. He would. He would screw, them all. He would get Fertig off. He would get Fertig freed; after all, wasn't he sane? He almost grinned and stopped himself. "Is this really what you want, Harry?" he asked it slowly, he asked it sadly. "Have you thought it through? You want to die?"

Fertig looked up at him and slowly nodded his head.

Screw him. Screw him. Screw him, Bleakie thought. He would fix them all, Fertig, Sara, Grenoble, Heisenberg, the whole lousy blood-made public, all of them. He would get Fertig off. Biggest thing ever. Did that madman actually think Roy Bleakie would do what he wanted? How pure. How innocent. And ruin his chance for D.A.? The rest of it? They'd love him, love him. Biggest coup. Bleakie's victory. Wild-striped vest for the occasion; double-breasted; gemstone buttons…

So, pretending to be persuaded by Fertig, reluctantly pretending to be sold, he counterfeited growing conviction, as he had done so many times by acting more and more convinced. The guard was looking at them, moved, not a dry eye – change of rules. He laughed – he permitted himself – and Fertig was getting excited too. Bleakie sat down again and began to brief Fertig on what was to be done. First of all, it was going to take a few months. Fertig would have to sweat it out here. Fertig said he would; after all, it was where he belonged.

"Trust Roy Bleakie. They'll tell you all sorts of things … that I'm against you, I'm this, I'm that, to shake your confidence, but… if Roy Bleakie can't get his client what he wants, who can? Try to talk you into another lawyer… who'll get you into the bin…"

"They won't."

"I can see it now. We'll work it through, Harry. You'll get to tell your story…"

From somewhere below, a voice shouted, another joined, and soon there was a howl of rioting prisoners rioting, mounting to where the blue light hovered and the suspended guard-gondola spun. Fertig jumped, and recovered himself. His hand was shaking. "I'll get you what you want," Bleakie said. Fertig smiled; his teeth chattered. Was he scared?

Chapter 18

Bleakie went on vacation. He came back in April. He was sun-tanned, healthy, cured of his virus, feeling better than he had in years. He had gone all over the world, arriving first in Miami, where he spent two days.

Bleakie slept on the beach in the day and in his room at night. Took antibiotics and, feverish, thumbed through Fertig's notebook. Here, far away, it seemed innocuous, almost. What had he been so excited about? Even if Fertig was sane … all the time. … Did it represent a logical process or, through a series of entries, appraisal increments, adjustments, accruals, an inventory of insight and conversion, a revelation in tabular form? Here, far away, it didn't matter. He would be able to get Fertig off: the one year's madness.

Sara Fertig's long-expected life story came out in *LIFE*. Bleakie didn't buy the magazine but looked at the row of covers at the hotel newsstand. She had changed since he had seen her – how wonderful they were with their star actors! – what was it? Thinner face, plucked eyebrows, or a confident look? Would she be confident when Harry was freed? He tried to spend a quiet evening curled up with a good book – the notebook: its leaves were becoming edge-frayed – but too tired, too weak, he had grappled with it half the night before succumbing to his weariness, half-asleep, promising himself to reason it out the next morning. Half-dreaming and tossing, he made incredible speeches to a wet-eyed jury and swam in the arena of justice and back to the arena of his bed and awoke with a bad sick-taste. He was fighting against his relapse by promising himself revenge on all of them, by cursing them all out, with the act that could please no one but himself – Fertig freed. The next morning he decided to leave suddenly. Whatever insight he had was lost in the flight down to Rio, staring with dim lechery at the stewardess's trim behind.

In Rio de Janeiro he spent a week on the beaches, sunning and resting; got stronger; spent evenings in the nightclubs with girls, meeting people. Everybody wanted to talk about Fertig, but he just wanted to rest. Tired of the case. No, he'd tell them, you haven't got it right. Crazy, wasn't he, mad? Took it for granted. Well, he'd grin and say, for laughs, oh, no, not at all. Sane as you and I. Or, completely mad. Or, an agent of malevolent forces. But what about Mrs. Fertig – that poor woman, how she has suffered! – and what has she to say in her *LIFE* story? Well – and he'd just smile mysteriously. His fever was almost down to normal, but he was too weary to get laid actively, so he'd have girls up to work his tired body over, trying to conjure out virus fever with sex fever but, the girls, too, once they found out he was

Fertig's lawyer, would, even as they serviced his passive body, ask questions about the grand *hombre*, and that poor woman. Grand indeed. Get themselves all excited thinking about Fertig, that big, murderous punk. Well, they should have seen him in the life, that thin face, little moustache, bulgy, petulant forehead, those innocent eyes looking up at Roy Bleakie as he asked him to do such silly things. Did Fertig really believe that Roy Bleakie would? *Consider then, ladies and gentlemen of the jury ...* NO! Screw them all! *I ask you to free... for who has not suffered a loss...*

He got bored with Rio and flew to Casablanca, found it dull and flew across the Mediterranean to the Riviera and, having got some strength back, had a hot three-day session with some standard *gamine* who had never, thank god, heard of anything aside from her fame-striving body and didn't much live beyond the in-service she offered. And spent his days on the beach arguing with anti-American existentialists and other bohemians: The *LIFE* article was *not* a whitewash: Fertig was *not* the victim of a plot: Fertig did *not* have help: things simply did not work that way in America – never mind Coca Cola and the CIA. The man was simply mad. No, the Jewish question did not enter into it. Why assume only Jews had cornered the market on morality? The last-of-the-just nonsense – don't make me laugh, Fertig?

Went to London for a day and gave an impromptu talk that grew out of an intimate discussion about the progress of the McNaughten sanity rules in America and ended, as always, denying their anti-American talk by trying to explain a Fertig: "Why are you Europeans drawn to this man, drawn to write Kafkaesque plays, drawn to speculate, European-fashion, on secret plots, whispered conferences, hidden ties to subversive, James-Bondish, organizations? It is simply that Fertig's way is the way of the American Innocent – the individual taking the law into his own hands and acting to right wrongs. Traditionally, in our country, when there seems to be no means of redress of injustice, when the law stands helplessly by, the champion, a man who acts out of a greater moral precept, comes on the scene. Cowboy justice: the encounter of good and evil on a street. Singlehandedly he tumbles the forces of evil. The corrupt law gapes as he rights wrongs with a smoking gun. In America we don't look to Kafka or to secret political ties for explanations." And got cheered. "His age is past; we not longer need such champions; they embarrass us. Perhaps we should say that this man is ill: this may be an evasion. Perhaps we should say he is guilty, but free him, put him on a reservation as the last of his kind, the Innocent – what greater punishment can there be for the Innocent? Or perhaps we should give him what he asked for? What greater punishment can there be for an Innocent?"

When he got back to his hotel room, he had a little relapse – the excitement – and spent the afternoon sleeping, dreaming in his room. He made up his mind and left for Rome. As he was leaving, a friend gave him the copy of LIFE, but he was too drug-drunk to read it; he spent the sleepy seat-time half-dozing, looking down at the cover picture of her. She was looking out at the world with grave eyes; her face is mature, yet still young. She was wearing a black, sleeveless blouse – and he hardly recognized her arms, those arms that had held him – wearing a single strand of pearls. He looked through the pictures: Sara Fertig in her bohemian days. Harry Fertig as a college graduate. The Fertigs in happier days ... with friends on vacation, his arm stiffly around her as they stand, forced together, ... holding their newborn baby, ... him, holding Stevie as he first walked. Then, a picture of the emergency room of the Mercy Memorial Hospital, of the victims.

It had been an essentially happy marriage, she said. Probably. Who could be sure? Of course there were problems: What marriage did not have its difficulties? But they worked on them and the working-out brought them closer together. But then, as the years passed, there was no child to fulfil the marriage and they began to become a little desperate. She told of that terrible sense of inferiority that afflicts all childless women, of not being a complete woman. Strange: thin face, hollows under the cheekbones: hairshine – quite exciting, really. And she spoke frankly of the castration feelings that beset the non-father husband. Touched himself. Still there. Still signs that he was a man. Wait. Bleakie will bring him out of this. An erection, again, to think of what they will do – odd thing, to get an erection about – the big speech ... But trips to the doctor showed that the difficulties were not physical. They considered adopting a child but decided not to. Harry Fertig pleaded for artificial insemination – anything. She told her husband that if she couldn't have his baby, she didn't want one.

She told of the grim irony: being surrounded by children, as a teacher, loving them, never being able to have one of her own. They strove to comfort one another but instead they began to grate. She underwent psychoanalysis to try to remove her psychic blocks, for hysteria had closed her womb. Alienated, Harry Fertig worked longer hours. Marriage was a sacrament and they laboured to recover their former happiness, to adjust to their condition. And love won out. He remembered breasts, thighs, not so much hers, this woman whose picture was on the cover ... He laughed. Was Fertig, if he was reading this, laughing too?

And then it happened. The miracle. Somehow. She didn't know how she knew, but she *knew* the night she got with child. What told her, what secret her body whispered to her, she could not say. Her Harry, he laughed at her, and comforted her, and tried to keep her from getting too excited, too joyous, but she *knew*. For there were more things ...

… Drug-tipsy, Bleakie spent the first night in his Rome hotel bed looking from the notebook to the LIFE article. Couldn't muster the force to straighten the issues out and considered sending for his New York file. Went downstairs, drank, got a little tipsy (drugs and drink – the worst, he thought), wore a brilliant, gold-threaded vest, and went out nightclubbing; met, got taken by some producer's starlet, woke up hung over for the first time in his life with this amorphous and bright-skinned beauty beside him, her hair pink-silver, like a bubble-froth from the mouth of a man with stainless-steel teeth. He was feeling weakened, groin-achy, but better, definitely better, though it was the thunderous nineteenth-century door knock of the cuckold-ragey producer which woke him up, while she mock-quivered under the electric blanket. The producer charged in, accompanied by some hood, threatened the worst, saw who it was, recognized him – for who did not know Roy Bleakie – and Bleakie, in turn, recognized an old con game when he saw it, so sat down to talk to him about the Case. Fondling the breast of the producer's calling card, Bleakie answered such questions as what's he like? How did he do it? He's mad, isn't he?

What a story, the producer said, tapping Bleakie's side with the clubbed copy of LIFE. Yes, it is, Bleakie said, tapping the notebook on the nightstand. Movie in this. Certainly is. People are tired of these new-wavesick… Rape, hate, perversion, need a good cry – entertainment. They do. They do. Why – the producer cried, turning excitedly, moist fingers unslicking the paper while the girl fondled Bleakie under the covers – Can't you see it? Look at this:

That night… Sara Fertig Just *knew*. It was a fulfilment. But how did she know, the producer wanted to know. An angel told her; Roy Bleakie told the producer: what do you have writers for? And now, not a dry eye, they were drawn together again and of all the new little fears they had to face now, she wrote. They vacillated from foolish pride back to fear. They made plans far into adulthood for their child (he wanted a daughter, she a son). That poor bastard, the producer snivelled. Her head was under the covers and she nuzzled his side and began to take little price-lowering nips: he bargained by palping the exercise-firmed flesh of her buttocks. The Fertigs stopped themselves from wishing; they mustn't tempt fate. Fulfilment hysteria. They became superstitious and made little magical rituals of protection, did foolish things – domestic and work habits – repeated in certain liturgical patterns… and would catch one another at it and laugh hysterically, and worry again. Was she too old to have a child? Could it turn out to be Mongoloid? It was a possibility. Could anything else go wrong? Would she be able to breastfeed her child? Harry stood by her constantly, and by his strength, his fortitude, his common sense, was able to sustain her and allay her terrors. Even though she had none of the traditional, silly, food cravings, he used to pretend she did, and would go out in the middle of the night to get her uneatable concoctions, sometimes even driving all the way to Manhattan. He would rush back, acting as though she wanted it badly: they would laugh and throw the mess out. It was a waste of money, but her mind was taken off her fears. Should she have the child with twilight sleep? Should she have Natural Childbirth? She decided on Natural Childbirth: it was a never-to-be-missed experience. The day came...

... a novel, a play based on Fertig's life, book-club rights, screen rights, the whole package – I know just the man to play him.

But what about the *exclusive* rights? Don't *they* ... the producer wanted to know, shaking the magazine ... look at her, just look at her.

She could play it herself, couldn't she? Bleakie asked. Still, what would it be worth to you to get the Fertig story? You have it? I have it? Her furious face bartered excitedly deep beneath the rim of the cover: he lit a cigarette to show that he still had his hand in: one foot beat against his face: he blew smoke among the toes. One hundred G's. Send you an exclusive copy, only one in the world, Bleakie said. They shook hands on it. The producer left without taking the girl with him. Bleakie dozed, woke, copulated again, drank some more, dozed, preparatory to eating a huge meal, as the girl did push-ups and deep knee bends to keep her arguments in shape. He woke: she was gone: he left. He sent a neatly wrapped copy of *LIFE* to the producer. Was given another copy of *LIFE* on the outward flight.

Stevie was perfect, healthy; the pain of childbirth was too much; Sara had to be put under. How could they forget that night, the madness of it, the excitement? Could she describe the joy of breast feeding her own child? Her face would glow as she looked down on Stevie's face and felt that glorious twinge as those lips were at her breast; every mother would know what she meant: there were no words for it. How was he today? Did he eat well? Harry, you're worse than a mother. Perhaps they fussed more than other first parents because they were much older, almost past the child-bearing days, jumpy. He made plans for his son. They would buy a house in the suburbs; he would go to a good school; he would be a scientist, a lawyer, a doctor – never too soon, these days, to plan which college to go to. What kind of girl would he marry? What kind of grandchildren would they have? Was she being too Oedipal in her twinges of anticipatory jealousy? She knew enough to prevent it. But then ... tragedy struck ...

Bleakie flew to Australia and spent five more days there before he became irritated with Fertig-talk. Fled north to Tokyo, stayed a day, was interviewed, and flew across the ocean to Hawaii, found he had forgotten the notebook, flew back to Tokyo, found the notebook, but lost his copy of *LIFE* on the way back to Hawaii, where, feeling good, he tried to keep swimming all day, getting laid every night, no more, but kept running into people who wanted to know all about HIM. So, finally, he fled to St. Conegunde in the Caribbean, where no news media were permitted and everything was allowed, where he could really be mindless about things, have privacy; and if it cost him two hundred dollars a day, a share in the Gordon-Mercy Memorial project was going to more than pay for it.

He was tanned, rested; his head was clear at last; he was cured, once and for all. In St. Conegonde, where everything was allowed, you got a clear view of things and were able to put them into perspective.

He came back to New York on a rainy April morning. The fog and smog persisted in spite of the rain. Everything was warm and wet, sulpher-dioxide and gas fumes burned his nose, but corrupted early buds persisted. Invigorated, a new man, Roy Bleakie taxied from the ship to his office. He was in the office early, before his secretary and the rest of the staff. Telephoned his mother to let her know he was home, better, cured. He went through correspondence, looked through a list of phone messages. Heisenberg had been trying to get him. Hockstaff had called. Grenoble wanted him. Sara pined. But there had been no more phone calls, nothing, for at least a week and a half. Why? The Fertig file had grown. For about a week after Sara's story had appeared there was news-media silence. He recognized that silence: pivotal: beginning of the sappy and sob-sister sympathy flow. *Now* was the time to get Fertig to trial.

His secretary came in. The office began to come to life. Typists, chattering as if there were never a Fertig case, came in. He came out of his office. Wild greetings: kisses from all the girls – he ran an informal office – Roy Bleakie had been missed. And now that they knew he was here, he noticed a new tempo to the morning's business. Molnar, always early, came; then Brodney, and Bennick. He conferred with them; they brought him up to date. Nothing new had happened on the case at all. At first Jeffries wanted to bring the case to trial right away, furious at Bleakie for running away, furious as only that old fart could be threatening contempt, to assign a new lawyer. But a plea of illness seemed to have turned away a harsh answer. Maybe Judge J. wasn't pushing because the weight of a compassionate opinion might bury him at the twilight of an honourable career. Now, Roy Bleakie said: Now. Get it to trial. Bleakie heard their reports; Molnar told him that Dr. Heisenberg had been visiting Fertig. Bleakie was aware of a twinge of jealousy: He's mine. Hadn't they had their chance? Why torture? He telephoned Dr. Heisenberg.

Heisenberg unable to subdue the note of triumph, told Bleakie that Fertig had consented to take tests and permission had been got to administer them in prison. Of course, the conditions were not ideal... Rorschachs in the smell of urine? Anomie in a maximum-security cell? Bleakie grinned ... and was upset. What was Fertig thinking when he consented – the arrogance! Did he imagine, Roy Bleakie wondered, that he could beat Heisenberg at that rigged game? Was he weakening? Further, Dr. Heisenberg's voice rose close to the point of cracking, trying to conceal that malicious triumph, for not only were the tests proving Dr. Heisenberg right in every way, but Fertig had himself brought forth and demonstrated the core symbol of his delusion: he spoke of a certain notebook he had compiled while he was planning the crime. This notebook contained data which indicated Fertig's sanity, showed purpose, planning, care, sustained thinking.

"Was it a diary?"

"No. I spoke to Mrs. Fertig about it. We went through the house together, looking for it. Obviously it didn't exist. He seems to pin everything on the fact that his notebook, by its consistency, logic, premeditation, would demonstrate his sanity. Of course it would demonstrate precisely the opposite: the all-pervasiveness of his psychotic compulsion."

"What did he say when you told him you didn't find the notebook?"

"I didn't tell him."

"Why not?"

"Why anger him? I've led him to believe that I've found it."

"But don't you discuss it?"

"We talk about it. One of the techniques is to indicate that his recollection of the contents of the notebook constitutes a check of his memory, and thus his sanity. We cue him; he fills us in on what was supposed to be in the notebook. Of course the whole thing is symbolic rationalization-construct, a delusion, a guilt-presentation."

"But what if such a notebook exists?" Bleakie asked and thought of the producer in Rome.

"Then surely it would have turned up."

"Would it?"

"What do you mean?"

He detected the alarmed note. Have to work fast now. Get him to trial before Heisenberg had too strong a case ... the kind of case that might, with the reversal of public opinion, put enough pressure on Judge Jeffries to make him reverse himself or, worse, disqualify himself as prejudiced. How far had Mable Crossland got in her pressure on Jeffries: or Hockstaff? "What if she destroyed it?" he asked Heisenberg. "Let's say because, among other things, she might have driven him to it and didn't want that little fact out..." "That's nonsense. Why she's said in *LIFE* – anyway, a sane man isn't driven..."

"Or because a possible mention of the whore…"

"But he doesn't indicate that she exists in this notebook; we questioned him about her again and again. So, theoretically, he had nothing to hide from Mrs. Fertig."

"Perhaps she thought it would be incriminating. After all, Heisenberg, you're the People's minion, not the Defence's."

"But she should realize I'm on her side."

"Supposing she really has it. Think about that. I have to run now. Busy man; can't wait; have to catch up; the vacation left me in a hole. Think about it, Dr. H." And he hung up. Time was running out; it was happening; they were working to get it away from him. Whole, united campaign. He could tell. Instinct. Feel. He telephoned Sara.

Sara was cold; noncommittal. No, she couldn't see him. She was exhausted: the publicity from the article; he could understand how she felt, he said softly. No, she hadn't been to see Harry much: he was in good hands. People had been wonderful: they were actually sending money to her to pay for the defence. Bleakie could sense the iciness – what had he done? He knew what he did to her, he reminded himself. Was she working to get another lawyer? Who knew what they were doing to Harry Fertig to change his mind! Move fast. Move fast. Get to trial.

It was still early: he telephoned Judge Jeffries' clerk … and announced that he was ready to go to court. Not guilty by reason of temporary insanity. The clerk hemmed and hawed and evaded and told Bleakie nothing. The case was far down on the docket. His sense of being out of things was growing. If he couldn't get it to court soon, Fertig would be mad. They were manoeuvering behind his back. All of them. Conspiracy. Things were happening without Roy Bleakie. He reached for enmeshment, groped for a place to grab into the whirl of events inexorably turning without Roy Bleakie for the first time in his career … and he encountered nothing – a curious sense of isolation, like he was not there. Everyone was polite; no one said anything and Molnar, Brodney, and Bennick couldn't do it for him either.

The next morning he waited in the Criminal Courts Building, where he would encounter Judge Jeffries; he alerted the press too. The judge tried to look away from him as, using a cane, he limped down the hallway to the elevator. Bleakie followed; the press, ready to blow the whole thing into a dramatic little fight, followed Roy Bleakie. He engaged the judge in mocking conversation, nothing directly disrespectful, but… It would make the old man furious and he would bring Fertig to court so he could get at Bleakie, he thought. Goad! He got on the elevator with the judge, and with his back to the door – the reporters crowding them together he stood looking up at the judge, who was staring over Bleakie's head at the doors and ignoring his cool mocking face and tones. But on the second floor the D.A. got on and worked his way over to the judge's side. "And how's the little counsellor today?" he jeered. No answer for MacGruder. It would appear to the world that the Bleakie-Fertig underdog was taking on the forces of injustice. Jeffries wouldn't look him in the eye, but the stern face remained red, hurt, impotent; his hard old lip trembled. And Roy Bleakie felt sorry and forced himself to be hard on the poor old fart. That should start things going.

But nothing happened. The silence persisted. He couldn't get anything out of anyone. What were they doing? Making Judge Jeffries relinquish the case? He had to work harder to infuriate the judge. What? He had a twofold plan. He would get Fertig back to City Psychiatric in spite of Judge Jeffries. That would do it; throw the judge into a frenzy it would also show the world he was working for his client; and it would get the case back into his own hands again and end the isolation, mesh with the event-flow, turn it, bend it to his direction ... and get Fertig off! Two days after his encounter with Judge Jeffries, he telephoned Max Grinzing from Judge Swenson's chambers. The judge wasn't in his office. Max had been asleep: Max slept late. Bleakie told Grinzing that it was important that they meet. "What's it about, Roy?" Grinzing asked, petulant at being woken.

"I'm calling from Judge Swenson's office."

"So? Is that any reason to wake me so early, Roy? You have something for me?"

"I can't talk now, Max, but if you meet me about three o'clock in the office of the Commissioner of Prisons, I might have something interesting for you."

"What?"

"Try to understand, Max. I'm in Judge Swenson's office."

"You can't talk?"

"Right."

"Can you hint?"

"Don't be a baby, Max."

"Something about Fertig?"

"There are other criminals beside Fertig, Max. Coming?"

"Can you stop me?"

"Would I want to Max? On time for once?"

"Early even."

Bleakie telephoned the commissioner of prisons and requested a meeting at three-thirty: it would be to everyone's advantage. The commissioner, an old party hack, understood perfect what the statement "to everyone's advantage" meant; something important was happening.

Roy Bleakie was getting the feel now; action; action – that was the cure. He looked at his watch: time was running with him. He considered seeing Fertig to explain. No. What was the point?

The commissioner relinquished his office for the three o'clock meeting with bad grace. They were working against him – the little signs. For once Max was on time. His hair was wild; his collar unruly; one soiled point curled upward over his lapel. His shirt, as always, was about to come up loose over his belt. They shook hands, Bleakie had the feeling that Grinzing's hands were dirty.

"What is it, Roy? What do you have for me? An interview with … *him?*"

"I've been trying, Max. Still plugging. Maybe…"

"If you knew what this means to me. I'm planning a book, Roy, an utterly new concept of crime, and I need him, Roy, Fertig is the *new criminal*, perhaps the first of his breed…"

"Not easy, Max."

"But why?"

"Hizzoner, the fart."

"When I was in court that day… A disgrace." Grinzing's harsh, ponderous tone grated. "That judge is a madman, Roy. *He's* the one who should be on trial. A Torquemada – terrified, of course. He senses the threat to the old order. The new criminal disregards the fiction of non-responsibility of the board members, … *assigns* accountability to corporate representatives. Don't you see what that means, Roy?… how this bypasses the old, now-obsolete revolutionary systems?"

"You see what I'm up against? The hardest men to deal with are the ones who owe the fewest political favours. Judge Jeffries is soon to retire…"

"The hue and cry of the corrupt press, the mad gallop to the electric chair, and, a few years later, a reflective article *Did Justice Triumph?* What can we expect in such times, Roy? What can we expect but to condone corruption, stifle the voices of dissent, mad though they be, and permit the Russians to overhaul us and finally doom our civilization. This country is a madhouse, Roy; we can only be thankful that the Communist press hasn't decided to make Fertig their martyr. How is he taking it?"

"We've got to get him out. Back to Psychiatric. Much longer, Max, and they'll convince him he's a common criminal. Can't imagine what happens to a man here."

"Roy, I intend to write articles that will wrench their complacencies. We all know the money-mad AMA and the corrupt ethics it promulgates. We know the white sepulchres, smug rabbis, Rotarian ministers, fattened clerics, all with their passionate sermons calculated not to offend the bourgeois…"

Bleakie was becoming impatient. No one's complacency had been wrenched enough to help Roy Bleakie yet. Grinzing was running away with himself. He talked about a crusade for justice; he yammered about creating a Fair Play for Fertig Committee, a *responsible* committee, no beatniks, composed of mature, liberal, civic-minded...

But Bleakie didn't have much time. The commissioner would be waiting. "I've got to get Fertig out. An article ... a series, all helpful beyond belief. But you see my position?"

Grinzing nodded. "You're making a good fight, Roy. I can see you're tired out. I've disagreed with you about a lot of people you've defended in the past, about your methods, but now you're doing a good thing, the kind of thing your father would have done.

"Roy, you know, I've got fat, tired, foolish, and people laugh at me. You ... No, don't deny it. Windy Max, the flatulent liberal. I know what you think. But *this* time ... The fact of the matter is that what Fertig did was right. I know it in my heart. It's *all* corrupt. You know, I never used to agree with your father about his approach. But he was one of the people who redeemed this system, because if someone as pure as him could function –"

"Max –"

"No, let me finish, Roy. If America can produce a Judge Bleakie... Well, when I was younger I was handsome and strong as a horse and was outraged against everything and I *believed*, and everything had to be put down, destroyed – *Everything you have learned is wrong!* – but I never had it to do what a Fertig did – something very pure. His actions point the way. The power to act resides in everyone. A thousand Fertigs protesting injury will overthrow the system. Harry Fertig must not die. If they'd had Fertigs when I was young, we wouldn't have had all these young people, beatniks, turning their backs on this country. I never had the guts to follow through because as soon as I thought about it – Well, is violence right?" he shrugged.

"I don't think you understand Fertig, Max."

"Don't give me that insane crap, Roy. It's this world that's insane, not his. Tell me, is that patriarch, that *cadi*, Jeffries sane? Harry Fertig must not die!"

"Max, to get Fertig out, to get him back to the ward, you have to spell it out for the public. Fertig is mad."

"To be sure. I'll write –"

"Then the pressure is off the judges. New feeling planted. They think, maybe he is crazy, maybe he *couldn't* help himself."

"To be sure. And we should ask, Roy, doesn't this society offer any other way out other than a man having to resort to such a horrible crime? The Underground man acts..."

It was a matter of pruning aside Grinzing's sociological speculations. He had to connect with the commissioner of prisons. "Drove him mad. He was unbalanced. They tipped him over."

"Well then, society must look to its conscience, Roy."

"But I've got to get him out *now*."

"I'll do anything I can. I feel this very much. I'll write like I never –"

"Max, there isn't time. Something has to be done quickly. It has to be dramatic. You can help."

Max Grinzing looked at him, a little bewildered, confronted with the possibility of direct action.

"Max, if I appealed for a change of venue, I'd be denied. Jeffries wants the case."

"What can you expect from *hetmani* justice?"

"And I couldn't get the chairman of the Board of Justices, or the higher courts, to remand Fertig back to the ward. Even if I could, it would take time; and, unless the circumstances were proper, loaded, so to speak, we couldn't take the case from Jeffries. It would drag. There'd be the trial. No jury would find not guilty by reason of insanity, not with the powers so heavy against him. And Jeffries won't listen to the professionals. Jury would hang him. Simple as that. Max, every minute the case is in Judge Jeffries' hands it becomes harder to remove it. You can fulminate from today till tomorrow, Max –"

"It's more than fulmination, Roy. My articles –

"… are valuable. You can form committees …" Bleakie smiled. "Reasonable, mature men *are* capable of action, Roy."

"In how long a time?"

"I could do it in a week."

"A week? Be realistic, Max."

"Two weeks."

"I need action *today*."

Grinzing was watching, waiting for Bleakie to say what he was getting to, apprehensive, unable to make excuses because he didn't know what was going to be asked of him. His hand, pushing at soiled papers in his pocket, clenched and unclenched.

"That leaves the commissioner of prisons. *He* could remand Fertig. Direct slap at Jeffries. Commissioner's an old party hack, so he wouldn't move without good reason: orders, pressure, what's the trend, who's to offend. Makes it look as if the party organization is against Jeffries."

"Then we go to him and ask –"

"Max, isn't that foolish? In the face of opinion? What are the odds?"

"We appeal to –"

Bleakie grinned and held up his hand. "Max, reason won't corrupt him. He's not interested in existentialism. To him the *new* criminal is the same as the old. Belongs in prison. He'd laugh."

"Expose him," Grinzing proposed, angry at the commissioner's would-be laughter.

"Yes?"

"The sordid conditions of his prisons, the brutality of the guards –"

"They beat Fertig up. Doesn't belong with the criminals. Psychotic, possibly. A rebel, Max. But among rats and roaches –"

"… the state of the prison food, the unconcern for the dignity of the prisoners, the dirt –"

"… and the overcrowding, the riots."

"Yes, the riots. Yes. And a comparison of ideal penal institutions where they treat a man like a human being, where an institution is morally corrective and rehabilitative, not an Old Bailey, a Queen of Heaven, a Lubianka …" Grinzing's eyes glowed and his hair seemed more dishevelled. His collar curled and wilted upward even more till both edges were clear of his jacket and touching his fat chin. Bleakie knew that if he didn't stop him he would go off again and forget Fertig. "And a special place, the right place for the right prisoner; the disturbed treated with humanity, the political prisoner –"

"MAX!" Bleakie's sharp voice rang through the office as suddenly as when he thrust a piece of surprise information into any smug opposition's legal structure; his finger pointed accusingly.

"We go to the commissioner. We tell him to send Fertig back to Psychiatric. He refuses. We tell him you have an expose coming out, starting next week, which will blow the lid off his prisons – let me do the talking, I know exactly where to hit him – and we will not relent – I'll give you any proofs you want – until he has been removed from his post and reforms are instituted. He'll listen then. We'll tell him we'll hold up the exposé for a few weeks, possibly quash the whole thing – giving him time to correct the situation – if he will remand Fertig."

Grinzing looked at him, blinking, bewildered. "Isn't there any other way?"

"What's more, he'll release a statement to the effect that after much soul-searching, he has come to the conclusion that prison is not the proper place for a sick man. Inhumane. A *sick* man, Max."

"But Bleakie, that's blackmail," Grinzing's rough voice broke and squealed.

He heard the high and mimicking voice, "But Bleakie, that's blackmail" in his head and sneered at that high doll-like voice coming from that great, gross, liberal's body. The years had changed nothing; Max Grinding was still pure. But softly he spoke, soothingly, taking care to keep the conspiratorial tones absent, "Max, they've beaten up Fertig. That's one thing. And another, this is the only way to do it. And, in passing you must think of the others."

"What others?"

"If you threaten an exposure of conditions, the commissioner will have to do something about it, alleviate the conditions, something, Max."

"But… I don't like doing things this way."

"Who does? Time's against Fertig. Speak their language."

"There is an appeal to reason: always."

"Max, I'm surprised at you. Remember with whom you're dealing. Party hacks in office. Corrupt officials. They won't listen. Be realistic, Max. Present the club, get the results. *And get the interview, Max.* I told you, they might not even let you see him. *But Morgan has got in to see Fertig.*"

"How did that jackal do that?"

Roy Bleakie smiled. "You know."

The possibility of not getting the interview was torturing Grinzing, but he couldn't move. "I don't know. I can't do it, Roy. It's against everything I stand for. Your father –

"Goddamn it, Max! My father's dead, and this is *now*. What makes you think he could have done it better than me? Or wouldn't have done the same thing?"

"Not your father, Roy."

Bleakie shrugged and turned to go. He walked across the room. He didn't hear Grinzing move. He turned, reached into his pocket, and pulled out Fertig's notebook. "You know, Max, what do we really know about Fertig? Everyone has their ideas, but what was really in his mind as he came to his decision, actually began to plan? Sure, I have a foot thick, literally, of articles, conjectures, statements, testaments, depositions, testaments, expert reports, evidence... but..."

"If I could only get to him. I could draw him out."

"Possible. But, even so, Max, it's a funny thing: even the man pleading for himself doesn't know the true story any more: because it was *then*, and *now* he has a special case to plead. Memory plays tricks. Different answers are given to different questions posed by *interested* people. That's the tragedy of it; we can never know. But what if there was some sort of record? *Fertig's own record.*" He held up the notebook.

Max Grinzing was across the room, moving heavily, but very fast, and took the notebook. He leafed through the book getting more and more excited. His breathing was loud, asthmatic, forced through moist lips. Bleakie kept his fingers on it. "Fertig's?" Grinzing asked. Bleakie nodded. "It's Fertig's? The whole thing?" Bleakie nodded. "God, it's Fertig's – an itinerary of Death. Roy! Do you realize what this is?" Bleakie nodded.

Bleakie started to take the notebook from Grinzing's hands. Grinzing's fingers clawed and clutched but then let go. "Well?" Bleakie asked.

"I'll do it, Roy."

"You can't use it yet. Surprise at the trial. But you, only you shall get it, Max," Bleakie told him and they went into the commissioner's office.

But two days later, Roy Bleakie was passing the Criminal Court's press-room when two reporters joined him. "Well, Counsellor, congratula-tions are in order: you've done it again. Any statement for the press?"

Done what? he wondered. "Thanks," he said; "a hard fight."

"Man," the other reporter said, "that is the bluest blue I ever did see."

Roy Bleakie touched the pearl buttons of his vest. "Celebration colour," he said.

"Will reporters be allowed at the hearing?"

"Judge's discretion," Roy Bleakie said.

"Come on, Counsellor. Any prehearing words for the press?"

"Might prejudice the case."

"With Judge Mable Crossland? There isn't a prejudice in any one of her boobs and that covers territory. Ho. Ho. I make the joke." And he elaborately took out a pair of sunglasses and put them on. "It's a shame that the photosnaps don't have colour. How's Fertig taking it?"

That was it. Bypassed him. Out of his hands. No trial. Cut and dried. "Make it sound like he pulled a fast one."

"No, sir, Counsellor. Fertig can only pull his weenie. It is the policy of our paper to give credit where credit is due. I hear Marvin Morgan is calling for impeachment of the Board of Justices. Commie infiltration."

"Marv. Old Marv. We all know Marv."

"Seriously, anything to say?"

"Only that I think of this case as a cause, not just a case. Conference after."

"I like that, sir," the reporter said. "May I quote you, sir?"

"No."

Roy Bleakie went to Judge Vannifucci's chambers and telephoned Irving Hockstaff. The clerk was eating a ham sandwich; there were thin strips of limp ham fat over the judge's green blotter.

"You're a hard man to get hold of."

"I have to take a vacation once in a while, Roy. I was in Key West."

"How was Florida?"

"A pleasure, Roy. I hear congratulations are in order. By the way, you'll never guess who I ran into in Key West."

"The mayor."

"Him, too. But better, Mable Crossland."

"Oh, Mable."

"Mable. You know, she still cuts a fine figure in a bathing suit – better than girls half her age." And then Irving was silent. "Are you alone?"

"No. Not really." He looked at the clerk, and the clerk, under-standing, nodded, brushed the crumbs and ham strips into the waxed sandwich wrapper, and went to finish eating on his own desk. "All right, Irving. I'm alone."

"Congratulations, Roy. You did a good job. Now clean up this mess once and for all. I can't begin to tell you how damaging a case like this can be. You should have finished it long ago. I'm surprised at you, Royboy, and a little disappointed, too, I might add."

"Almost done. I've got him out of the pen and into the bin, Irving. The hearing... and it's all finished. Then we'll have time, you and I, for a real get-together. How're the grandchildren?"

"Couldn't be better. They were with me in Key West. I took some new movies of them. You should get married, Roy; have some children. Not only are they wonderful, but an asset to your career."

"I'm dying to see the movies."

"I'll bet. Well, I'll be talking to you."

"When, Irving?"

"Soon."

"We should get together very soon and plan a little strategy, Irving."

Hockstaff was silent for a moment. Sorrowfully, he said, "Roy, I just don't understand you sometimes. I warned you this case was poison. You had to play games, didn't you?"

"Games, Irving?"

"Don't be cute, Roy. I've met the cutest in my time and I never could stand it. I've had complaints about you."

"Who?"

"Grenoble for one, ... others. Listen, Roy, I won't lie to you. The situation has changed somewhat – about the D.A.'s slot – I can't offer it to you any more."

"Why not?"

"I told you. Who needed Fertig... ?"

"Irving, I believed in –"

"C'mon, Roy, don't give me that baloney. I'm not a senile old fart yet. I never took it from anyone and I'm too old to begin now. And Roy, the worst crap is the hypocritical, high-flown crap. Your father, God rest his soul, *believed* in that garbage; you had to respect him for that. But you, Roy, I know better."

Did he? Bleakie wondered; Roy Bleakie knew Roy Bleakie best. He said nothing.

"Games – it's your one weakness, Roy. Take a little advice. You're never too old to learn a lesson. Most of the time you get away with it, but when they catch wise, Royboy – no one likes to be conned, moved around for any reason. More than that, when people decide to fight for something, no matter why, they believe in it."

"Which means –"

"Which means MacGruder for one."

"That dummy?"

"That dummy! You think he plays games like you? You don't want to believe that it's an act of faith – you hear – an act of *faith* with him that Fertig is a cold-blooded murderer. He's serious. MacGruder never went to Columbia and to Harvard Law like you, never had near the education you did, but he believes, dummy or not, this he believes."

"Wonderful. I grant him that. Noble. And I'm here to oppose that belief."

"There's such a thing as the wrong method of opposition. MacGruder wants to be a judge badly, but more badly he wants to keep you out of D.A. So the condition for giving up that post is that *you* don't get it."

They were silent. "Roy ... are you still there?"

"So what's MacGruder in my life?"

"If it was only MacGruder."

"All right, give, Irving."

"Well, my friend, Grenoble, for certain reasons we will forbear from mentioning, could hardly like to see you in a sensitive position like the D.A."

"Games, Irving,... fun –"

"Grenoble is a man without humour – a failing, but there it is, Roy. Here's a rule for you: learn about the man who laughs and the man who can't. You also hurt the prison commissioner's feelings with your little power play."

"Since when does that hack have feelings?"

"That's what I mean, Roy; you're too cold about it, too intellectual. He never went to Harvard Law, but he knows when he's being pushed around. Here's another rule for you: hurt a man's personal feelings and he has a political pain."

"So?"

"So he's a party hack, like you say, but he carries a little weight."

"MacGruder and the commissioner together hardly –"

"There's Mable Crossland –"

"Ahh..." That slut, he thought, that lousy slut.

"Mable has this bug up her ... behind. She has decided to be New York City's first lady D.A."

"For Christ's sake, Irving."

"She has a good chance."

"I'll fight it."

"But, Roy, that means there'll be *two* judgeships open. You could be a judge."

"I hardly have the dispassionate judicial temperament so necessary to ... Irving."

"Roy, ... it's like going into your father's business."

"Maybe I want to go into business for myself, Irving. I'll fight it."

"Alone? I thought you had more sense than that, Roy."

It was foolish; he didn't pursue it. Was it the hospital? Were they offering Mable Crossland a piece of that action? Would he still get his 'fee'? Suddenly he felt like telling Hockstaff to go screw himself, to shove his political plums. And he had a quick moment of panic, as if Irving could *know* what he thought, and he felt like saying, all right, I'll be good, I won't do it again. What was the matter with him?

"As a matter of fact it is Mable who is your staunchest advocate for the judgeship."

"And since when is what Mable wants so important?"

"She really got something going for herself, Roy. Working to get Jeffries out, she worked up a considerable following: social workers, psychiatric workers, probation and parole people, the social-work unions, other judges, reform kooks ... and all of a sudden, out of nowhere, she has this grass roots strength, Roy."

"Are you crazy, Irving? Social workers?"

"It's a trend, Roy; why, it's the kind of thing your father fought for, too. They swing a lot of weight these days."

"Oh, for God's sake, Irving ... Reformers? She'd have them giving therapy to Al Capone. ..."

"It's a trend, Roy; you should know; you've used them yourself enough times."

"She'll pack the courts with thick-ankled, flat-shoed social workers and we'll be up to our fannies in do-gooders..."

"Listen, so long as do-gooders put it on the line ... Listen, Roy, why go on?"

And how many times did she screw you in Key West, he should have asked.

"Do you want the judgeship?" Hockstaff was asking.

"I don't know, Irving. It can be a dead end."

"One way or the other, end it, Roy. As long as this case hangs fire it is dynamite. I have to sell you to people who have no use for a Fertig."

He felt like saying, Don't you know how it's going to end? "Roy Bleakie will expedite."

"Move soon. I have to know. Others are around. Frankly, I'm letting you have this judgeship out of line, ... but any son of Judge Roy Bleakie's..."

"Don't think Judge Roy Bleakie's son doesn't appreciate it, Irving."

They hung up.

He was furious. Expose the whole thing. But it was pointless, Bleakie decided, to even attend the sanity hearing; cut and dried; pre-planned; packaged little show; withdraw; mend fences; forget. Still, he thought wistfully, he could leap up at some crucial point and say – what? Suicide. Defeat. Cut losses. Judge Roy Bleakie? It was all over. Poor Fertig.

Chapter 19

Bleakie sent Brodney in his place to the hearing.

The sanity hearing was held in the City Hospital in a room ordinarily used as an inter-denominational chapel. Two guards brought Fertig to a small anteroom. Brodney was curious and excited about Fertig. Bleakie always kept the good cases for himself. He was getting a chance – even though there really wasn't much to do – to come in contact with an important client. Bleakie had instructed to observe Fertig carefully. Brodney told Fertig he was Bleakie's representative. Fertig didn't seem surprised. He nodded, looked carefully at Brodney, and smiled slightly.

Brodney explained, carefully, to Fertig that the court was convening here, in the hospital. A sanity hearing was being held. He observed Fertig carefully, as Bleakie told him to, but Fertig merely nodded again. Brodney counselled Fertig to answer all questions, to feel completely free to talk, that the court was here to listen to anything – he stressed "anything" again – Fertig wanted to say. Brodney asked Fertig if he had any questions. Fertig said no, he understood. Obviously, Brodney thought, Bleakie had expected more of a reaction. Following instructions, Brodney said, again, that Fertig *could say anything* he wanted to. Fertig looked fine; no signs of madness. What if the hearing *didn't* go the way Bleakie expected it to? He would be in trouble. He knew all the arguments but – and he began to get excited – it was a chance.

In the hearing room, the flag of the State of New York and the American flag were crossed on the walls. On the opposite wall ten pictures of past directors of City Hospital were hung in a row. There was a neatly framed NO SMOKING sign on a third wall. A packing crate covered with a black-velvet throw was placed on a little one-step dais; it ordinarily served as an, altar.

They were riveting outside, adding a new extension on the City Hospital. They had rearranged the twelve short rows of chairs that faced the altar into two rows, at right angles, along one side of the long room. In front of the chairs there was room only for a narrow aisle. A table had been put in the centre of the room for the judge to sit.

When the judge came in Fertig turned to Brodney and said excitedly, "But it's a woman."

Brodney nudged him. "Stand up."

"I didn't expect a woman."

"What difference does it make?" Brodney asked.

"None," Fertig said, and was calm again.

To the judge's right and to her left were smaller tables for her two women court clerks, a court stenographer, and a court officer to sit.

Between the judge's table and one of her clerk's tables, pushed a little forward, the witness chair had been placed.

On the judge's right were defence witnesses: the senior psychiatrist, Dr. Heisenberg, and an assistant who had, from time to time, among others, interviewed Fertig. Sara Fertig was there with her mother. One of the arresting detectives, Martin, sat there. Brodney and Fertig sat on the extreme left, towards the centre, of the defence witnesses. A space, two chairs wide, separated them from the other side. Dr. Bridgemen, the psychiatrist advisor to the D.A.'s office, Mr. MacGruder, and the other arresting detective, Donnell, sat there. To the side, a chair was placed in front of the altar where, as a witness to the proceedings, the assistant corporation counsel sat.

At first the corporation counsel was interested, as everyone was, in Fertig, but later, when he saw that Fertig looked quite dull, a slight man touching tissues to his nose, very ordinary, the corporation counsel became bored. He absent-mindedly lit a cigar. Now and then girders, being raised past the window, darkened the room. The hearing was interrupted by the intermittent sound of riveting; they could hardly hear what was being said. The recording clerk frequently had to ask people to repeat themselves.

The judge, Mable Crossland, smiled upon them impartially. She was wearing a tight, black suit, with a green scarf, on which was clipped a gold, ruby-centred pin; she wore a fur hat that looked like black hair; two white curls of hair came out from under the sides of her wig-like hat and lay along underneath her Florida-bronzed cheekbones. Her heavy perfume filled the room. She ran her court in a warm, motherly way; she had small use for pageants, formalities, or rituals – this was a hearing to determine the mental competence of Harry Fertig – was he here? He was. Fertig's case folder lay on the judge's desk, in front of her.

"But where is Mr. Bleakie, the counsel of record?" Judge Crossland asked. "Why is he not here to represent Mr. Fertig?"

Mr. Brodney explained that he was Mr. Bleakie's assistant and that due to the press of business, Mr. Bleakie was unable to attend, but that he was empowered to conduct Mr. Fertig's case. Judge Crossland interrupted to tell Mr. Brodney that she was directing Mr. Bleakie to appear before her in chambers tomorrow at 10 a.m. sharp: she would consider failure to appear contempt of court. Mr. MacGruder attempted to protest: he was overruled. She dismissed court and said it would be reconvened at the earliest possible time.

The next morning Roy Bleakie appeared before Judge Crossland. She had not yet put on her robes of office: she wore a wool sack-dress with a rich, orange paisley print; curves opulently bulged the paramecia shapes as she moved. She wore a shiny green-felt *conquistadore* hat. She smiled at Bleakie's brilliant purple vest. "Roy, where were you yesterday?"

"Sent my substitute, Your Honour."

"But you should be there yourself, Roy. The people demand you to complete the brilliant job you've done up to now."

"The people, Your Honour? The newspapers? They won't be there."

"Roy, darling, why this 'Your Honour' business?" And she smiled at him and leaned forward. He was so handsome, she thought, so fierce. "You're not angry, are you? You're not going to be mad at me?"

He didn't answer. He only smiled and waited.

"Roy, I'm going to leave this up to you to judge. I'm an old woman, Roy…" and she waited for him to object. He didn't say anything… yes, an old woman, Roy, you mustn't deny it. Oh yes, I admit that nature has been kind to me, cruelly kind because one imagines … well, all sorts of things …" She waited. He said nothing and shifted. "Oh, for God's sake, sit down; you make me nervous with your Bleakie's famous courtroom stance." He stood. "Roy," she said sweetly and crossed her legs. The sound of stocking on stocking ripped through the room; he didn't move. "I've been a mother and a housewife as well as a lawyer and a judge. There aren't many more… adventures… political adventures, left to me. Do you begrudge me this last one? After all, Roy, you're young yet, very young… though wise beyond your years…"

He looked at her cruel smile: wait, he promised himself; wait. Cow, he thought at her.

"I leave it to you, Roy. If you really think I shouldn't try for D.A., Roy…" and she waited for his plea.

He grinned at her but wouldn't answer.

She looked back and shrugged. "I think you should be at the hearing, Roy. Fertig needs your spirited defence."

What could he tell her? He squeezed a flap of skin on the inside of his cheek through his teeth; it was a little swollen, but not painful – even pleasurable. He could say, this man is being rail-roaded and you know it. But wasn't this what you've been working for, she'd say? He couldn't say they've offered you a cut of the hospital scheme. She might say, but we'll be partners. Roy. Perhaps if he said he now saw the case in a new light? Then it would all be out in the open. Finish. Foolish. Or if he could say he was bored with having to go through these predetermined postures. So he told her, "Your Honour, I have not the kind of energy or time or interest necessary for this man's case. I don't think I can give him a fair representation. My heart is no longer in this case. I don't believe in his case."

"Roy, are you trying to sell me on the idea that you never represented anybody except a man in whose defence you were not passionately involved? Roy. Really?" She smiled.

He smiled back.

"Really, you *owe* it to *yourself* to finish off what you've begun so well…"

What did that mean? Be there or lose – what? The 'fee'? "But –"

"… and I won't let you cheat yourself out of the glory, Roy. Your father – how he helped me when I was a young lawyer; I'll never forget – would never let a case go unfinished."

Which meant they ordered him to be there if he wanted his judge-ship. Still…

And as though reading him, she said; "You *will* represent him, Roy. I will countenance no private agreements between yourself and the family to substitute someone else. I will consider it contempt."

"Isn't this a little high-handed, Your Honour? Star Chamber kind of thing…"

"Of course, Roy, darling. I'll see you in court, my love." She stood up.

He started to leave.

"And Roy…" She had come around the side of the desk.

He turned.

"Really. Those vests. I ask you, is it proper in a court of law?"

"And am I ordered, Your Honour, to make no private agreements with the client's family about the colour of my vest?"

"ROY!" Her voice rang out, strident, angry, and then she laughed and stepped towards him. "What a little devil you are. I just meant that there's a chance of it clashing with my clothes."

Go naked, he thought.

"Aren't you even going to give me a little kiss?" she asked, coming towards him. He braced to meet her…

But it was almost two months before the pageant of the law could be remounted, before the schedules of all the witnesses could be made to jive together and they reassembled.

Bleakie was there this time: he wore a grey suit with a black vest. He smiled at Fertig. Fertig looked calm, composed. Had he survived them then? Was it possible? It excited him. He bit down on the flap of skin in his cheek. "You know," he told Fertig, testing him, "you can say any-thing you want here."

Fertig nodded.

Bleakie saw that Fertig was strong, controlled, neat, quiet ordinary with a box of tissues in his lap. And it seemed to Bleakie that, if not heroic, Fertig was conducting himself well, holding his position. He had survived them; they would break him unless – unless what? Roy Bleakie leaped up and said, "This man is sane, was always sane; you are railroading him." They would have to listen to Roy Bleakie. Fertig blew his nose; he coughed; his eyes watered. Bleakie told Fertig again that he could say whatever he wanted to and again he observed Fertig carefully. Did he get the hint? Fertig merely nodded, accepting it, smiling slightly. Did Fertig still think Roy Bleakie would help him? Did he trust Bleakie? He didn't ask.

They waited. One of the court clerks came in after a while and told them everything was ready. They walked, the four of them, two guards, Fertig and Bleakie, into the hearing room.

The witnesses were called by the other clerk; it was done in almost courtroom style. They all had to squeeze out of the second row, moving chairs, shoving past knees, making noise, coming to sit on the witness chair.

Defence contended that the accused was unable to understand the nature of the charges. Bleakie glanced at Fertig: Fertig's face was impassive. Prosecution alleged that Fertig was sane, had been sane all along, that he was not only guilty, but a malingerer.

Detective Donnell maintained that Fertig was in full possession of his senses at the time of the arrest and subsequently. He had given his confession without coercion, without any signs of disturbance; further investigation of Fertig's pre-murder movements indicated that, in his opinion, he was sane, quite able. When Donnell was finished, he waited.

"No questions," Bleakie said. He was going to let this go uncontested, but Judge Crossland asked Detective Donnell if he was a psychiatrist. Detective Donnell said no, but that he had dealt with madmen in the past. Judge Crossland nodded brusquely and told Donnell he could go. As he passed Bleakie, his back to Judge Crossland, Donnell's mouth formed the soundless word, "bitch." Bleakie bit harder on the flesh flap and glanced at Fertig: no change – slight, controlled, closed-lip, prim smile. No more.

Dr. Bridgeman testified about his interview with Fertig. In Dr. Bridgeman's considered professional opinion, Fertig was sane. He showed how the defendant had demonstrated he was rational at the time of the killings; according to the McNaughton rules, he knew right from wrong; Fertig had murdered with malice aforethought. At the time of his interview, Fertig had known right from wrong and still understood the nature and quality of his act. In Dr. Bridgeman's opinion there was no substantial incapacity either. Mr. Bleakie didn't bother to cross-examine. Again Judge Crossland intervened; she asked for a review of Dr. Bridgeman's qualifications, though the court knew them well. While Dr. Bridgeman was huffily giving his degrees and experience in court, she looked at Mr. Bleakie. He stood up at the end of Dr. Bridgeman's recital and dryly, as perfunctory as a catechism, asked, or rather stated that, as was expected of him, Dr. Bridgeman had only spent a short time with the defendant, how could that compare to a full-dress, scientific investigation such as Dr. Heisenberg and his staff had mounted? Judge Mable Crossland smiled at him rewardingly; her white teeth were brilliant in her sun-stained face.

The assistant D.A. who was representing Mr. MacGruder and the people called Mr. Fertig to the stand. Bleakie leaned forward. Judge Crossland smiled at Fertig. Fertig had stopped smiling. Her close-fitting, black wool-knit dress constricted around her soft arms and was weave-stretched by her warm bosom, which pushed far far out because her waist was tightly pinched by a wide, tight belt. She leaned forward to make sure Mr. Fertig saw her smile so that he would not fear; her lips were almost orange, and green shadows were on her eyelids. An emerald ornament twinkled as it rose and fell on her right breast; a long, yellow scarf expanded and contracted on the black wool. The assistant D.A., by his questions, attempted to show that Mr. Fertig had a complete grasp of reality. He knew where he was: he knew what was happening: he answered questions of public fact and universal background, both personal and abstract. Fertig answered slowly, not elaborating, in a flat voice. Judge Mable Crossland nodded encouragingly; her blue-tinged orange lips kept saying soundless Yesses. The assistant D.A. asked if Mr. Fertig had planned his murders. Fertig said he had. The assistant D.A. asked if Mr. Fertig knew what he was doing at the time of the murders. Mr. Fertig said he did. Did Mr. Fertig repent of what he did? He said he did not. When Fertig finished he returned to his seat.

It was Bleakie's cue to demolish the prosecution's intention: he stated he had no questions. She looked warningly at him. Fertig saw the look; he began to smile slightly again. Bleakie looked away from Mable Crossland's crossed legs under the table.

Bleakie had to call Dr. Heisenberg to the stand for the defence first. Heisenberg's full report was in the judge's hands; he summed up his staff's and his findings. He answered Bleakie's questions with a sure and saintly smile. As a friend of the court, Heisenberg was given permission to question Fertig later. Was he so sure of himself, Bleakie wondered? Say nothing. See.

Sara Fertig was called to the stand. She was able to testify calmly, surely; everyone could see that she looked at her husband anxiously, lovingly. She testified – being questioned routinely by Bleakie. Bleakie tried to lead her to state that she found her husband at all times sane, but, by her replies, she pointed out that of course he *seemed* rational to her – as he always had – but ... Fertig's smile widened slightly, though he did not open his mouth; it gave his face a strained look. Bleakie tried to keep his questions almost disconnected to elicit confused answers, but she organized her replies and ended up leading Bleakie to conclusions he was trying to avoid. To the best of her belief her husband had been ... neurotic for a long time before the event of the child's death: disturbed, for that matter, since Sara had known him, ... but who knew, she hastily added, that that disturbance would lead to – and aren't we all disturbed? She described his behaviour at Mercy Memorial Hospital on the night their child died. She described his gradual withdrawal, the alienation from herself and life.

Bleakie hoped that the assistant D.A. would bring in, as contradictory evidence, the LIFE story, but the people's contention was limited to saying that Sara Fertig wasn't a psychiatrist, hardly able to judge in the matter? Prejudicial hearsay.

The arresting detective Martin said that he felt that Fertig at the time of the arrest had something wrong with him. It was nothing he could put his finger on, but there was something about the smile, something too unemotional and, of course, Fertig had not tried to avoid the arrest in any way and what about the peculiar way Fertig had acted, first confessing to the killing of a policeman? And he seemed to *welcome* the arrest. But the assistant D.A. pointed out that Detective Martin was hardly qualified to be a judge of who was or who was not mad, no matter how many madmen he might have apprehended in his time.

Fertig was recalled to the stand to be questioned by Dr. Heisenberg. He sat there, his smile wider, his eyes a little unseeing, in fact, not even looking in Heisenberg's direction. Heisenberg began his questioning. Heisenberg asked his name. Fertig didn't answer. Fertig was resisting. Bleakie leaned forward, suddenly hoping – for what, he asked himself; be careful, he thought to Fertig, don't act crazy, not the slightest bit; Bleakie bit harder and thought, grow up, to himself.

Fertig said, "Hasn't this gone far enough?"

"How do you mean?" Dr. Heisenberg asked softly, subtly.

Judge Mable Crossland leaned towards Fertig. Her black-clothed bosom brushed his case-folder, moving it slightly. She told Mr. Fertig that he had nothing to be afraid of here. Her voice was throaty. They could hear the seductive rustle of her body shifting. Her tone was soothing, encouraging. Careful, Bleakie thought. They were all trying to find out the truth, she said. If Mr. Fertig had anything to say, he should consider himself free to say it. She smiled at him. Her voice was low and warm. She encouraged him. With that stubborn expression he looked a little like a boy who wouldn't unless she handled it right, do what was wanted of him. Fertig blew his nose and took a deep breath.

Dr. Heisenberg asked his questions again, but Fertig didn't answer.

Judge Crossland saw that if you took away those glasses, if you took away that moustache, if he weren't wearing those slightly sagging clothes, he would be just like any little boy: surprisingly young looking. "What do you mean by acting like that?" she crossly asked, scolding him. "Don't you understand what we're trying to do here?

You're not stupid. Why are you behaving so childishly?" But though she said it sternly, she also said it humorously. Her perfume emanated strongly and suffused the room. Her silver-tipped, large hand tapped his case-folder on her desk.

Bleakie stood up, interrupting in that cleverly savage, provocative tone, forcing his anger through clenched teeth, as if trying to prejudice his own case. She felt a little twinge as though he had bitten her: he still hadn't forgiven her. What was the matter with him? She smiled at Fertig. Bleakie was trying to say it was pointless to continue, that it was obvious that Fertig was sick: that his client was not able to go on. Why cause him any more suffering? It would be merciful of the court to spare him this anguish. Fertig's smile widened; it was almost a grimace now, drawing his cheeks up, narrowing his eyes. "Mr. Fertig," she said. "You must answer Dr. Heisenberg's questions as he asks them.

"We are not punitive here.

"The court acts as a parent in the interests of the child; it is in this capacity we are here." Her luminous black eyes were on him. She felt a stirring through her body. Fertig remained stubborn, petulant. "Do you feel up to this?" she asked.

Fertig didn't answer. Bleakie asked, "May I examine my client?" Judge Crossland agreed but looked warningly at Bleakie.

"Mr. Fertig, can you tell us in your own words ..."

"Of course he can." Her voice trembled warmly as she saw Fertig's poor lost eyes.

Their moment had come and now they had to tell it well. It has been told many times. Fertig stopped, as if thinking, collecting his thoughts; he looked frightened, his eye moving up and down the length of the courtroom rapidly, his brow frown-creased; he concentrated; he was quiet a long time; his lip shook.

"Go on, Mr. Fertig," Judge Mable Crossland said.

Talk, Bleakie thought.

Bleakie felt the pain of muscle tension in his face; he fingered the buttons on his vest and relaxed his face. What would they think if they saw him looking like that? He prompted in his mind: stop, take a deep breath, think a little, do it logically, coherently. Tell them, here, tell them, it's your last chance. Inaudibly he fired rapid instructions, his teeth chattering down on the cheek skin-flap, which pained him now. Roy Bleakie could do it for him, he thought. Roy Bleakie would start it classically, simply, sitting quietly, beginning softly, starting from the very beginning. Where was Fertig's beginning? When his child died. Remember the child, Fertig; we all know the way you loved your son, your hope ... Tell about that love for your child ... Keep that child in your mind and keep that child in our minds, ... don't let us forget him, ... tell us about his innocence, his beauty, his promise – the

278

extension of yourself – your promise ... till tears are squeezed from even the slick lacquered face and tragic green-shaded eyes of Sara. Remind her how Stevie redeemed a marriage ... and tell about that newfound love. Remind. Remind. Logic or madness fall away before the fact of that dead face of the murdered child. Sara will weep; we will weep; LIFE will weep; the world will weep. Bleakie turned and looked at Sara. Would she deny, would she dare deny? If she did, he, Bleakie, would begin it again, he would ferret it out again. Stop that smiling! he thought at Fertig.

Fertig began it well enough; the deep breath helped him; seemed even to clear his nose. He spoke coherently, and had, now, that sudden sense of freedom – he remembered what it was all about – he had had it once before – no, more than once ... but when? When he killed them. When he had loved her. So he began to talk about the days before Stevie died; the days after he was born. He talked about their love, his and Sara's, and, how, after all the years of ... well, not unhappiness, yet love, ... they had always loved one another deeply. Good, Bleakie thought. How the birth of their child – well, did they understand what it meant to have new hope and love in your life, what a redirection, what a fulfilment – how it *changed* everything (had he stated it strongly enough?) – would they understand his loss completely, his and her loss? Unless they understood, perfectly, what their life had been like before – but he hastened to say, wasn't everyone's life a little like that at one time or another? And didn't it prove, after all, that if they could love, that is, love still more, fulfil the love and mutual respect they always had – though he had to say they didn't always share the same interests ... He, for instance, was an *aficionado* of detective stories ... though he did like more serious things, too, but after a hard day's work – well, you want to relax – and the logical nature of his work, his mind was more in line with – well, puzzles relaxed him (and after all, hadn't it all been a how-to puzzle: how to do it the most ... efficiently?) ... Though, with the coming of Stevie ... he had blond hair and was such a bright child – he said this even though it was his own child, but then he had always been known for his impartiality – ... which proved that he and Sara must have loved one another all the time, even from the point they were married ... How well she had stated it ...

Bleakie moved, looking at him coldly, shaking his head slightly: no. Fertig tried to look away. Bleakie moved, interposing himself.

... well, how could they have had Stevie, Fertig asked, his voice high, shaky, demonstrating an obvious truth, if there was no love, no passion? It just needed something to bring it out ... more. Stevie, he never felt tired, though they used to stay up with him a lot too ... but when you need energy, you get it from somewhere for ... all sorts of things... And he looked at Sara. His eyelid fluttered, a tremor or wink; her face quivered – it could have been a smile.

Don't ramble, Bleakie thought, get off it, get on with it; tell what happened that night, show them what they did to you, but carefully, carefully, show them that they didn't mean it, but that was the kind of people they were ... show them.

But Fertig kept on going over it so Bleakie interrupted to ask, "But what happened after the death of your child?"

And he, Bleakie, would explain how, from that time of sorrow, of emptiness (how does a now-childless house feel – it's special silences?) he had *logically, logically,* come to realize the presence of an evil in the world, an evil in the world that could – not maliciously, though – take away the child and, thus, love in your life. How do you explain a thing like that? By the power of your logic implemented with the strength of your voice, by orator's amplifications, by that soft and reasonable beginning, and by that impassioned ending, which indicated, which gave drama to the reasonableness of it all. And he saw himself saying it, bringing himself to that pitch, demonstrating, event by event, that there was no other road and Row, Bleakie realized he could have done it for him or even have prompted him, rehearsed him, because now he had all the facts, the documents, the whole edifice back there in his office, how he would have done it... His lips were still, but his larynx moved softly...

But Fertig rushed on, rushed on, avoiding Bleakie, not looking at him, talking faster as though fleeing Bleakie, beginning to wander now, trying to get himself back on the track. Well, there was the point where it was all clear to him and it was a matter of finding it again and explaining when it all fell into place and he realized *what we all know* – well, there were his talks with Lucy ... Lucy – he didn't know why, they made so much of that ... much more than there was to it ... and, of course, well, the rabbi...

Veer off, veer off the beloved religious leader. Didn't Fertig notice how they stiffened here. Tell them your wife stopped loving you when Stevie was gone. Stick to that. I'll back you up. Exhibit A... look at the hieroglyphics, truth marks scribed on it like tappings on an Edison cylinder, damaging evidence, Your Honour, the penis bearing the revelation of an abrasive and unfaithful vagina – or didn't you notice?

But Fertig was telling them, instead, that he had been misled... misled. Accept – and he had actually got a religious feeling ... and of course, he could make certain revelations (he winked) that would forever be buried in the grave with him ... a thief made honest, but why go into that? But that poor child, he wondered about her still: was she mentioned in the rabbi's will? He, who had never believed in God... events proved; after all was said and done, he was right: how could there be a

God when his child was killed? Now the truth was out once and for all. Well, the rabbi said that God didn't give a damn and couldn't send that ram ... but when he was leaving he turned to the rabbi and asked him if he remembered Fertig from that night at the hospital. ... The rabbi winked: what did that mean?

Roy Bleakie tried to interrupt and lead him back. Fertig, shrinking a little, running away, panicky, talked faster.

His child died. He accepted it for a while. When did he realize that he could not accept it? He drew a deep breath.

Now, Bleakie thought ... *And so, ladies and gentlemen of the jury, we narrow it down to one night. But how easy it is to say that the sanity he had held on to so painfully cracked and he was pushed over into strange realms of psychosis. (Diminuendo.) But is it madness to say that an inexorable logic, a dead-end born logic leads us to become aware of, not the madman, but the inner and purposive being waiting for the proper moment to emerge, for don't some of us in our lives have two births? And it is the second birth, unlike our first birth which merely brings us into the world of man, that cuts us off from all mankind. (Conversational.) It is a night when there was still hope... still a chance to accept. We have seen how he came to his wife from the rabbi's, and she (tremulo... not hammy), though she loved him, couldn't summon the right words out of that terrible grief (hint of a sob) – gone, their last chance for happiness. And, in not understanding his agitation, not even knowing what has been on his mind, she rejected him. Out he ran almost converted to the idea, not even knowing he was determined at last to do what he didn't want to do. Where?*

But it was a matter of getting a gun, wasn't it? He wrote away to all the magazines, but they knew those answers, didn't they? Not allowed without a licence. He went to Abercrombie and Fitch. He came driving down, driving like a madman, pushing his car wildly, taking desperate chances. He drove from Sara's side. Since he had come here last a vast area had been cleared away for the housing project. Only the bar and the Mercy stood. Moonlight poured down on everything, the field of levelled rubble was silver limned. Radiant plaster dust streamed upward slowly towards the skies, where it was caught by the westerly wind and dispersed. He could hear the steady distant throb of traffic, and smell the chemicals and sewage rising from the canal; detergent foamed on the oily water. Far above, staring up out of exhalate, he could see the galaxy wheel of the Milky Way. He went into Little Mike's Paradise.

They were all here. He could just imagine them coming across the field of rubble, wading through the dust, stirring dust ghosts with their feet, leaving chalky prints on the cracked-slate pavements. The lights throbbed. The sticky air rocked to their laughs; their little shrieks beat; voice and drum contended while the throbbing keen of tenors cackled out of the bright static. They all turned and looked his way, their faces pleading. He was repelled. What did they want from him? Why *him*? Leave me alone. The Abercrombie and Fitch salesman rushed madly up and down the length of the bar, driven to serve whiskies, scotches, beers, rums, wines, cocktails, vodkas, goaded by their constant cries, while madly they drank and never seemed to stop. Fertig signalled to the salesman; without asking, he brought Fertig a whisky. "Where's Lucy?" Fertig asked.

"I told you. I can't get you a pistol without a licence, but how about this beautiful wife-killing tiger rifle? Our special gun-salesman..."

Bleakie started to straighten Fertig out. Not the Abercrombie and Fitch salesman the bartender – but the look of panic on Fertig's face, the sudden quick babbling...

Bleakie relaxed. It was over. Really. Sit still. Suffer it out.

What did this have to do with his case? Judge Crossland asked.

Suddenly Fertig was angry. His voice said, coldly, he was coming to that: hadn't she said he could say what he wanted to? Hadn't she promised him? His eyes were still flat, but his smile was widened, his mouth opened now.

"Yes, but within reason," Judge Crossland said.

"Well, it is. It is. Wait. I'm coming to it."

Bleakie sat down. He tried not to listen. Forget it. Let it run its course. Address the court. But Fertig's story drew him on, drew him forward till he was leaning his elbows on his knees, staring, nodding, thinking, remembering... "You'll have to wait," Little Mike told Bleakie. "There are others. Sit. Sitting in the very chair where ..." he winked and rushed away. He was back in a little while, making his way up the length of the bar as if he were leaning into a hot, stiff wind, serving on the way, never stopping. "Put you on the list. Only six ahead of you. Be through soon."

"I'll pay more," Bleakie said, but the bartender had gone down again to the other end of the bar to begin serving all over again. He could feel the retch-hot taste of cheap liquor forcing its way up again; go home, he thought, you know it all: that night like this one. But Little Mike had taken too much money out of the change he left on the bar. Cupidity. Bleakie tried to catch his eyes. Turning, bending, swaying with glasses and ice-cubes glinting in his thick hands, the bartender made short steps to beer taps, poured out liquor from bird-necks stuck in bottles, and didn't stop or hear, in that roar, or look his way. His fat flesh bounced, he jerked, unstopping, to their drunken cries, turning and turning as Bleakie could see the sweat stain on his back spreading.

He came out of the clash, the clink, the smoke, looming out of the stink, splashed whisky into the glass and said, "Four to go." Gone again. When Bleakie came, finally, reeling to the back, through the corridor and up the stairs, past the doors, past the sinks, past the loud drip of faucets, past all the doors numbered One to Lucy, he knocked. Her raucous and laughing voice shouted something which might or might not have been the word to enter. He went in. Under the harsh light she sat, naked and white, drugged and uncaring. Bleakie felt a row of pains up his back like points pressing. A sapphire necklace twittered around her neck. "The room costs seven dollars," she said. "Hello, Harry. Come to bed."

"It's not Harry," he said. "It's me."

She cackled and held out her hand. He gave her a ten-dollar bill. She crumpled it and, tossing it lightly, she fell back, and lay sprawled and waiting.

"Sara, I have to talk to you."

"They all have their kicks," she said and sat up, crossing her legs, and waited. The harsh white light beat down on her forehead, her droop-point breasts, her puffy thighs, her belly; her pubis was like shading drawn on to a white figure, a blotty butterfly shape with a paper fold indicating womanhood, almost as a sparse reminder rather than an actuality – like a child's drawing – all a repressed amateur's draw-a-woman sketch. Her cheek, stretched tight between her cheekbone and the dropped bone of her jaw, quivered in an unstopping tic. Green bulges stared in his or any other direction.

"Let me pay you for the night.

"I have to ask you something."

"Ask. Pay. I don't mind."

"Lucy, you've got to help me."

She lay back as if basking lightly in the hot light. "With the hand, all right, with the mouth, I don't mind, but there are some things – after all, I'm not just anyone. I have the blood of killers in me ..." Her hair crawled on the pillow, flowed under the cloth creases; rills of perspiration wound down her side and snaked down from the little peaked hill her stomach made. The great heaviness of her thighs and fat knees splayed her feet outward. The white light retouched soft grossness and decay. She reached under her pillow, drew out a cigarette, and lit it. The smoke swirled upward in spirals. The smoke hovered in front of the plastic face of the Christ. The wind that swept across the empty lots around now brought in the acrid smells, of smoke from long-damped fires, brick and plaster dust, and, seeping in through every wall-crack, the old just-released cellar damps. "Lucy, did he come here that night?"

"Weird kicks. All have weird kicks."

"April 31. Night. Late. Think. Remember. Let me refresh your memory. Did he tell you you were the rabbi's daughter?"

"I showed him our stock of rifles – after all, we have the best guns in the world and what we don't have, we can have made to order. Now sir, take this rifle…"

"Princess. Stolen by…" Gypsies …" She cupped her breast, finger cocked along the side-swell, and pointed it at him. He moved. She guided the nipple, tracking him, and said, "Bang."

Bleakie said, "Fertig said

Lucy, can you get me a gun?"

"You know," she told him. "I was wrong. Like the others. Such weird kicks." She let her breast fall.

"Get me a gun."

"Come to bed."

"Lucy, I need a gun; I need it now. I can pay for it. I'll pay you, Lucy. I…"

"You want?" she sulked. "Come to bed."

"But I'm not good at this kind of thing. Really.."

"Come to bed."

"Lucy, I'm in mourning."

"Come to bed."

"Look, Lucy, later on, I'll be glad to.."

"Come to bed."

And she made him take off his clothes while coolly, contemptuously, she looked him up and down, measuring…

Let us follow in his footsteps, ladies and gentlemen of the jury, forced into a degrading act which irrevocably led him further and further into that area of loneliness from which there is no return. No return. But is there no return, you ask, no redemption? Let us think about that for one moment.

"Come away with me," the cracked voice panted, coming from inches ahead of the little of self he cased so cool to keep from melting, to keep from feeling that soft languor of body heats intruding, softening, and diminishing his purpose. Why had he said it? He didn't want it. He shook his head to scramble and re-mesh those disparate parts and said – an admonition and a notation – think of something else, of a notebook, for instance;

a black-bound notebook, not too large, flexible, but impervious like those Bibles that are always saving soldiers' lives, just large enough to fit into the breast pocket of a loosely fitting, single-breasted jacket without too much bulge; a black shield over the heart in which are kept the truth-plans.

Concentrate on that.

But out of the writhing flesh that, soft at first, enwarped him to her, held him captive, he heard a high sweet squeal that fluttered around the room off the pine-tree-and-mountain wallpaper, flowed against the knobbed chest, against the door, through the constant smell of smoke; it broke into dissonant particles against the cornucopia and round-waved against the plaster fruit, bouncing, and beat against the deaf ears and now ink-blinded eyes of the plastic Christ: high and trilling it shrilled slowly down to mezzo, contralto, and lower, lower, to a dulled pulse-beat, bass, eternal, and pleasured – subhuman in joy. And she compelled again his body, disparate and detached, to act out the shameful pay-ritual she demanded; to throb and gyrate and flutter with a pleasure that should not be succumbed to.

He kept his icy distance.

The sapphire beads clicked. He wondered how he compared with all the men, the thousands of men, those rough men, those twisted men, who had come to her and voided themselves into the never-filled receptacle. He wouldn't do it, he thought, he wouldn't let himself go. He smiled ironically. He calculated meanly: if she had two, no three, four, five a night, on the average, that would come to – if she has been doing this for, let us say, three years – not more, surely; she is so young – then … How she has suffered, he thought. But what abrasion, what wearing down has there been? Who can tell? Her flesh, unchanged, lies; and she, like a little child, lay there. He thought: if he controlled his stony self against those arms that held him first lightly and then more tightly, he must muse, in the most dispassionate way, how like a virgin she was, truly, the rabbi's daughter white under the light, white under his body: her body, undegenerated and undecomposed, lying about what her twisted face said and her strident voice shouted. Remember horrible things, he thought, so that he should not succumb to her as his body so badly wanted to: so

he thought: his son; the pillow behind her head with the smudge of hair-oil on the yellowed pillowcase; the light shining through her hairs showing her skull; the twisted smirk, when he dared to look; the half-moons of her eyes, known only by their whites; the golden hair of his lost son; and her lips, the corners drawn far up, and the fullness of the centres thinned by the strain of drawing them far far down into a pink, a smirking U tight-mouth grin of child-glee; the unsullied gold tooth that twinkled as yellow rays escaped through her lips when she lost control. And in her arms, between her thighs, she held his hip-flesh and enjoyed, as all the old pains, one by one, went away; and, woven close in that flesh – taut knees pinched his ribs, ankles locked his neck – he began to rage and roar and love came up to heat his aloofness and made him weaken.

She was young yet; how many baths would wipe away the stains of all the thrashing bodies? One for one? A cleansing for each filthying? It would be enough to absolve them. Better. They could live together, forever. Get married. Have a child. If he was almost old, she was not old. And all the emotional inventory of those unspent years would stand him in good stead, he thought, as they would love and love and make love. "Come away with me," said the voice. He thought, all is not yet lost. They could leave and take a week, two weeks, in Florida, or...

Her high, squealing voice shrieked out; she withdrew into some corner where he was not; but his flesh strove to follow and his mind was sucked after while he fought it, fought it, and said, think of something else, anything else that has nothing to do with her, think of a thousand things.

"Don't forget the gun," Fertig told her, panting; she groaned and would not stop to answer.

So Bleakie had to think of the thousand things that had nothing to do with her. How, before Fertig did it, had he gimmicked Grenoble's books so if the examiners were called in they would see that something was terribly wrong? Had he known about the All-Gordon-Mercy golden healing total complex with light-blinking illness seeker? Can't bring that up here; fearless exposer wants some of that gold too – well, omit that chain-fact. *Put it this way. A pure world demanded clean books and squared accounts, you see, an end to the disbursements for accidental deaths or taut, money-saving, doctor-skimping computerless practices indicated by the heartless account books.* But who, he asked, made you auditor? He could just hear him saying:

"There's a grand balance sheet up there, high in the sky, but the world's a better place for it." But her hands, touching his body, made him forget Grenoble's warped books ... Something was wrong with the jukebox; the drum-and-fiddle sounds were tattooing through that trembling world as the speeds went all wrong and the beats became confused. He remembered.

He would learn about them, those seven, everything they did, how they lived, everything from morning to night. In the black notebook he would roll the record of their existences and, bringing them closer and closer into one, into a fusion, he would – yes, he would. Every morning, after her night's work, she went to bed, the clerk...

But Sara clutched him; she dragged him down. And all the stinks of her little room were slowly transforming into Arabic perfumes to trap him. All the sounds were stopping. All the sights were diminishing and focusing into one bright patch of skin, soft and lovable, gently odorous, while her hoarse breath panted in his ear like keening music, a flute playing noises, strange rhythms, that he had not heard before, drawing him. No, Bleakie thought. No! Remember ... "Oh, Roy," moaned the voice, coming down to audibility and understanding for a moment, coming from somewhere beneath him. "Take me away from all this."

"Come with me. Come with me, sweetheart. Florida. The Riviera. St. Tropez. Tahiti. St. Conegonde," a voice that used to be his admitted.

But her mocking hand reached out and slid upward along the sheet, groped, fingers crabbing in the air, and scuttled under the pillow. Fumbled there and came out with a cigarette, which she triumphantly stuck into the grimace, reconstituted to receive the sudden arid shredded end. And her hand, doing that crabbed dance again, the faint muscles flickering under the paper skin of her arm, came out with a match, which, burning and bright, she held so close to his face he could feel the heat singeing away his whiskers. The smoke covered her eyes. Little puffs, moans, small hisses and pantings floated up and were sucked into God's sockets. Fertig's eyes watered and he coughed. "Please don't stop," she said. "I'll get you the gun."

It was simply not a matter of revenge, he told the court, every seat filled in the vast room, though that was a part of it, but that life was over, his son was dead, love was decayed. How many people are dying the same and pointless way? What will stop them? So it is a matter of reason, then, which sustains and buoys and translates the fantastical bang bang finger into the very real thing. And each day, so his wife didn't suspect, so the world thought – except, of course, for Mr. Grenoble and his office staff – that he was on his way to work, for he left at eight in the per-usual morning. He got into his car. He followed them. He tabulated, co-ordinated combined, pinned them spiked them shafted them held to an accounting. Much as per-usual, he did. Six months.

And when did he know?

When, ladies and gentlemen, caught in the grip of an inevitable sequence, requiring perhaps some small last logical link-event to start him off, he stood at the threshold of his home each morning and sniffed the air. He carried an attaché case in his hand; in the case was the gun, the holster, ammunition, a silencer, a sandwich, and the black notebook. His nose ran a little and the night's soft postnasal drip – he gave up smoking – made him cough. He ached and there was a kind of numbness in his left hand for having slept on it; but his right hand was strong, his practised right. Did flying birds (it was autumn then: geese winged south, but not over the city; starlings and ocean-bound gulls in certain configurations outlined against the cloudy – it was cloudy – morning on the coping stones took flight) tell him the time had come? No.

Lucy's fingers were insistent; they fluttered, curling and stiffening against him, reminding him, clawing him down. He wouldn't.

"Mother of God, what are you doing to me," she croaked. Her voice was sepulchral and her wide, dilated eyes no longer saw him; the cigarette had been consumed down to her fingers and, staining them with a terrible burn, had gone out as she made spasmodic and mystic motions, trying to thrust him off.

"Tell me," he said.

"I'll get you guns," she screamed. "I'll get you guns. Kill them. Kill them." And the sweet blood of the deed drenched her thighs and the reek of victims drove her wild.

He knew. And yelled to them, "Follow me!" Their defeat-plead eyes diamonded and their mouths all opened and they marched towards him. Out. Out. Out. Into the street. He clanked now towards the clerk's door.

Gay decorations on her door, poster, signs, symbols, announcing that out of the goodness of her heart she had given well out of a meagre salary to all the charitable organizations.

Visualize him that morning, ladies and gentlemen, standing there completely alone. Alone in a world gone mad. His finger pointed. Did he ring the bell? The bridge between his finger and the button was an inch and forever. He had held it there, every morning for six months, just like this. That distance was infinite. And to make that leap was to be converted. Consider his struggle. If he has no pity, he had spent it them. If he only came here every morning and did no more than stand before her door, acted out the fantasy, what would he be? An eccentric man with childish revenge fantasies. But when he rang that bell, he shot her.

All the months of practice had made him smooth and graceful in his little ballet – reach, pull, aim, and fire … leaving her dead on the floor after the silenced gun made a sound quite anti-climatic to its violence. How simple, how clean. Shot. Yet deafened by that chocked-off explosion. Dead. The only sign of life that hopeless and indignant glare.

The young doctor next. How hard to walk into the Mercy, go to his quarters, wake him. "My name is Harry Fertig. Do you remember me?" "No," the doctor said. Fertig shot him and, before he fell, caught him and lay him on his bed, as if to sleep. Not hard, indeed, the machinery activated demanded it. Then Fertig passed through Mercy, passed the sick as they sat on the clinic benches, apathetic, suffering, with a patience he couldn't understand any more. Would they join?

The administrator.

Dr. Cartwright.

The nurse.

The rabbi.

And further north; north to Riverdale where the old doctor lived. There, surrounded by about a hundred acres, he lived on top of a hill in a little forest. The gates hung loosely, untended, canted on rusty hinges. The road was untravelled. He sat on the portico. Did he remember his past, the days of glory? Did he remember how he killed Stevie? Blind now, and deaf, could he feel the breezes sweeping up the hill from the Hudson; those eyes like blank crystal no longer saw the sun, which set on the rim of the Palisades across the slow grand flow of the river; his ears did not hear the sound of leaves rustling to the floor, twigs crackling, or Fertig coming.

To finish it he must crash the gate.

Fertig crashed the gate and went storming up the hill.

The clouds had disappeared; all the sky seemed full of sun. The shrill pipes no longer skirl and banners do not unfurl. Where is the tapping of the drum, the brass horn to say Fertig's come? No more. All gone. Unfashionable. Yet ... under the sky, tumescent with blueness, when Fertig's filled heart and lungs were bursting, only one rush through the gate and up the hill would relieve the ache and tell Fertig he's a man. Plumes waved; thousands followed; those Fertigistic faces no longer pleaded for a saviour. Great with Grandeur was Fertig then, grown to grim proportions; a giant crashing through the brush, removing distortion from his life. Fertig's foot flailed the leaves and burst through the sheaves like a knife cutting up and through. And there he sat. On his porch. Paralyzed. Half-dead. Black-blanketed. Waiting. Old ram-sender.

"Old man, I've come for you. Do you remember me?" Fertig said.

The old man didn't answer. He knew. Swung Fertigself on to the porch and stood in front of him. Said, "You killed my child." He knew that, too, for sightless eyes wept and impotent hands kept fluttering.

And there, towering above the forest and above the far cliffs, on a level with the furious sun, shot.

It rose to a rush of words; the whole story gushed out of him; it ejaculated out of his writhing, jerking body like his nose running, his eyes watering, his bowels loosened, his throat phlegmy as he explained it. He turned more and more to Judge Crossland, leaning towards her, she to him, till their faces were close, almost touching. His pores told her; his fingers chattered; he hid nothing.

She kept saying "Yes. Yes. Of course. Yes." The riveting interrupted. He could hear her making warm, cooing sounds of encouragement. He had a little giggling fit.

And it seemed as if the earth convulsed in a great contortion. There was a sudden thunder, rolling, rolling out from the ground. And the sky blackened. And hands reached up to pluck him down. And he fell, tumbling down, down into the blackness. He groped; he embraced her fully now, lovingly, holding her while in great and rhythmic gouts he planted seed in her loving body. He kissed her lips. He held her. The hard men; the soft men; the crippled; the twisted; the dirty; the festering; he loved them. He kissed them all and felt their great answering throb come up to clutch him with love and darkness; up through the floor; up through her bed; up through her body as she pulsed and danced and grappled and loved him ...

Fertig stopped. He looked at their faces. They all looked back at him, patiently, encouraging, puzzled.

"But don't you see?" he asked triumphantly.

"But..." Judge Crossland said.

But the thrashing was pointless. Mere violence, Judge Crossland remembered: poor Roy, poor boy, for it was gone as he lay there with his limp manhood shrivelled inside her, unable. No matter. No matter. She patted his behind.

They waited; he waited. She patted the case-folder on her desk. "Yes. But now you must try and answer some of Dr. Heisenberg's questions."

The voice in Bleakie's head, the voice of his impassioned oratory, had died away. He shook his head. He knew he was beaten. First time too, in a brilliant career.

Fertig stopped. He leaned back. He looked at all of them. He was grinning now. Heisenberg asked. He didn't answer. She became exasperated. She scolded him. She reminded him they were trying to help him.

He told her, "All right then, am sick. Insane. Psychotic."

"No," she said. "No. None of that."

"All right then, not sick."

"I don't want you to say things just to please me. The people want the truth."

"You know the truth."

"Try to answer Dr. Heisenberg's questions."

Dr. Heisenberg tried again. The riveting interrupted. Her warm, approving smile was on Fertig. Her hand stroked his case-folder. She felt the great warmth welling up through her whole body. The corporation counsel doodled behind a pillar of cigar smoke. The clerks recorded. Fertig said, "Yes," and smiled. He puckered his lips and said "Yes." Judge Mable Crossland felt the hot love-pain of justice in her breasts. Fertig told her "Yes." He told all of them "Yes." He told Dr. Heisenberg "All right." He told Bleakie's angry face "Why not? Yes." He told the riveting "Of course. Yes." He began to weep.

Bleakie and Fertig were sent into the anteroom to wait for the decision. Two guards stood and watched. Bleakie sat; Fertig stood. Fertig came over and stood over Bleakie. "Want to thank you for getting a chance…"

Bleakie slumped, his arms spread on the backs of two adjoining chairs, looked up. Fertig was smiling; did he mock? It didn't seem so. And he realized that Fertig had saved him.

They were called back into the hearing room. Judge Crossland held the case-folder tightly to her bosom. Her breasts squeezed around the edges. She committed him.

Chapter 20

The Institution for the Criminally Insane lies far to the north. It is near the Canadian border. Once a month a special bus drives up. It takes three days to get there. The bus goes all over the state, driving east and west, drifting north, stopping at some cities, a town or two, a few villages, picking up passengers.

The bus leaves from the city in the evening. You are taken down the back elevator of the City Hospital and brought into a little courtyard. There, the bus sits. They help you up the steps into the bus. A little behind the driver there is a double-grated gate set in a double-thick wire fence. It keeps you in and protects the driver. They ask you if you want to sit on the right or on the left. You choose the right. They ask you if you want to sit in the back, the middle, or the front. You say it doesn't matter. They tell you that you don't have the proper attitude. You think; it will be cold outside the city so the best seat is in the back, near the engine. It doesn't matter, but you tell them the back; it satisfies them. They seat you. Underneath the thick, unbreakable, green-tinted polaroid glass, a thick beam bolted to the sides of the bus holds steel rings next to each seat. They chain you to the ring. They bring someone else after you and ask the same things. The other chooses to sit in front, on the left; he is chained. You sit and wait for an hour. The bus driver turns out the light. He starts. He drives slowly through the courtyard gate. It takes him a long time to make the turn because it is a narrow street and there are parked cars in the way.

You are driven through black streets touched with snow. Few see you pass. After an hour of careful driving, the bus passes the edge of New York. Hours later, almost in the middle of the night, the apartment houses thin out and give way to smaller houses. You know because the lights don't soar as high. The lights become more and more concealed by the branches of trees. The bus winds through the silent suburbs.

The cold doesn't reach you yet; the fumes of the engine and the steady droning sounds the motor makes lulls you. You try to see the stars, but the glass of the window is too dark; only the scattered and thinning lights of the buildings come through. The roads turn and sometimes it seems as if the bus doubles back on its track.

You doze a little and wake because the bus stops. It is parked in front of a building, which is alone in the blackness. But, peering out, you can see, far off, the few dim and clustered lights of a town. Someone is brought on. He is in a strait jacket. He is not fighting. His head lolls to one side, almost as if his neck is broken. There is a secret and eternal smile on his face. A thick belt is attached to the straight jacket. There is a ring attached to the belt. He is chained to the eyebolt and falls away. Held from falling, banging back and forth to the motion of the bus, he lolls. The bus drives on.

It takes three days to get there. They stop along the way and pick up madmen till the bus is almost full. Driving fast, the bus manages to cover the whole state. The last stop before the Institution for the Criminally Insane is at the town of Ebro. There is a sign for the town, but no buildings. It is dawn. One more man is brought on to fill the last seat. He holds one free hand over his testicles. He is chained to the middle of the bus. They give out sandwiches and coffee. They try to feed the man in the strait jacket, but food dribbles out of his mouth. The man who holds his testicles will not relinquish. The guard shrugs his shoulders and goes on.

The bus starts up again and leaves. The bus runs along a twisting road through dense second-growth. It is tangled brush and stunted pine, white-and-black-tipped. Underneath, there are patches of snow and flashes of black earth. Throughout the day there is a little sun, but that fades in the afternoon till there is a universal haze over everything. The sun is almost clouded over. You see it as a shrunken, white disc, about a quarter of its normal size. It is possible to look at it directly now, without hurting your eyes. You watch it for a while till it fades slowly and is blended into the haze itself. The others come out of their apathy; all except the man in the strait jacket and the man who holds himself. Everyone begins to talk.

You look out of the window at the bleak winter's day. The bus goes along a great arc to the left and passes a gorge. Far down the cleft you see Canada, an endless plain that seeps north to the Pole. The bus rounds and turns and goes through the white hills till it drives along the lip of a dip. They are all laughing a little, and joking. The bus's motor grinds ascending a hill. The bus breaks free of the hills and, poised for a second on the edge of a summit, you see the great slow curve of the road, black against the white hills, curving down in a grand circle slowly till it straightens out below in a shining, icy plain, green-tinged, and goes straight ahead to the Institution for the Criminally Insane.

It is built on a swamp. You see the original, old buildings, towered and turreted, brown-stoned and bar-windowed, crumpled as an old castle. It is surrounded entirely by the newer structure which gleams and shoots into the air, higher than, but contiguous with, the old part of the institution. Millions of steel plates bolted into one great face, featureless as a skin, obscure as a tesseract, reflect the land. It stands on a patch of reclaimed land, surrounded by the frozen marsh.

The bus gives a little lurch. The road curves downward. They feel it and give out a great shout. Those who are closest to the window watch; you watch; the ones on the other side strain to lean across the aisle and see, fighting with their chains and bolts, letting the manacles bite deep into their wrists. You see a few sparse Bo trees, shrunken, stripped of leaves, scattered around the edge of the swamp. A few bushes stick out of the frozen ground. The ice is tinted green by the glass; the window is chill to the touch and begins to frost over.

When the bus reaches the bottom of the hill, they all relax and begin to smile happily. Someone begins to laugh. They all join, one by one, laughing till it becomes uncontrollable. The sense of joy is infecting: you try to keep from feeling it. You fix your eyes on the black, icy hills that surround the frozen swamp. You look at the marsh, which is like fused, green glass. You feel the happiness and fight it because it is wrong, terribly wrong. The road, raised a little above the skin of the swamp, runs straight. Someone cheers. Pandemonium breaks loose. They laugh and cheer. White marsh birds rise angrily. Soft-green light suffuses everything. A white rabbit runs lightly across the swamp skin. A wolf follows. Winter reeds clatter in the perpetual wind. White-coated cats slink. Ahead, the white skin of the building gleams. There is a black hole opening for you. The bus rushes ahead. The window frosts over. All you can see is a lush jungle of ice flowers, thick and impenetrable, obscuring your world outside.